The
Female
Persuasion

ALSO BY MEG WOLITZER

The
Female
Persuasion

MEG WOLITZER

RIVERHEAD BOOKS
NEW YORK
2018

RIVERHEAD BOOKS
An imprint of Penguin Random House LLC
375 Hudson Street
New York, New York 10014

Copyright © 2018 by Meg Wolitzer
Penguin supports copyright. Copyright fuels creativity, encourages diverse
voices, promotes free speech, and creates a vibrant culture. Thank you for
buying an authorized edition of this book and for complying with copyright
laws by not reproducing, scanning, or distributing any part of it in any form
without permission. You are supporting writers and allowing Penguin to
continue to publish books for every reader.

Library of Congress Cataloging-in-Publication Data

Names: Wolitzer, Meg, author.
Title: The female persuasion / Meg Wolitzer.
Description: New York : Riverhead Books, 2018.
Identifiers: LCCN 2017031394| ISBN 9781594488405 (hardcover) |
ISBN 9780525533221 (epub)
Classification: LCC PS3573.O564 F46 2018 | DDC 813/.54—dc23
LC record available at https://lccn.loc.gov/2017031394
p.   cm.

International edition ISBN: 9780525535058

Printed in the United States of America
1   3   5   7   9   10   8   6   4   2

BOOK DESIGN BY AMANDA DEWEY

This book is dedicated to:

Rosellen Brown
Nora Ephron
Mary Gordon
Barbara Grossman
Reine Kidder
Susan Kress
Hilma Wolitzer
Ilene Young

without whom . . .

PART ONE

The
Strong
Ones

ONE

Greer Kadetsky met Faith Frank in October of 2006 at Ryland College, where Faith had come to deliver the Edmund and Wilhelmina Ryland Memorial Lecture; and though that night the chapel was full of students, some of them boiling over with loudmouthed commentary, it seemed astonishing but true that out of everyone there, Greer was the one to interest Faith. Greer, a freshman then at this undistinguished school in southern Connecticut, was selectively and furiously shy. She could give answers easily, but rarely opinions. "Which makes no sense, because I am stuffed with opinions. I am a piñata of opinions," she'd said to Cory during one of their nightly Skype sessions since college had separated them. She'd always been a tireless student and a constant reader, but she found it impossible to speak in the wild and free ways that other people did. For most of her life it hadn't mattered, but now it did.

So what was it about her that Faith Frank recognized and liked? Maybe, Greer thought, it was the possibility of boldness, lightly suggested in the streak of electric blue that zagged across one side of her otherwise ordinary furniture-brown hair. But

plenty of college girls had hair partially dipped the colors of frozen and spun treats found at county fairs. Maybe it was just that
Faith, at sixty-three a person of influence and a certain level of
fame who had been traveling the country for decades speaking
ardently about women's lives, felt sorry for eighteen-year-old
Greer, who was hot-faced and inarticulate that night. Or maybe
Faith was automatically generous and attentive around young
people who were uncomfortable in the world.

Greer didn't really know why Faith took an interest. But what
she knew for sure, eventually, was that meeting Faith Frank was
the thrilling beginning of everything. It would be a very long
time before the unspeakable end.

She had been at college for seven weeks before Faith appeared.
Much of that time, that excruciating buildup, had been spent
absorbed in her own unhappiness, practically curating it. On
Greer's first Friday night at Ryland, from along the dormitory
halls came the ambient roar of a collective social life forming, as
if there were a generator somewhere deep in the building. The
class of 2010 was starting college in a time of supposed coed
assertiveness—a time of female soccer stars and condoms zipped
confidently inside the pocket of a purse, the ring shape pressing
itself into the wrapper like a gravestone rubbing. As everyone on
the third floor of Woolley Hall got ready to go out, Greer, who
had planned on going nowhere, but instead staying in and doing
the Kafka reading for her freshman literature colloquium,
watched. She watched the girls standing with heads tilted and
elbows jutted, pushing in earrings, and the boys aerosolizing
themselves with a body spray called Stadium, which seemed to
be half pine sap, half A.1. sauce. Then, overstimulated, they all
fled the dorm and spread out across campus, heading toward

various darkish parties that vibrated with identically shattering bass.

Woolley was old and decrepit, one of the original buildings, and the walls of Greer's room, as she'd described them to Cory the day she arrived, were the disturbing color of hearing aids. The only people who remained there after the exodus that night were an assortment of lost, unclaimed souls. There was a boy from Iran who appeared very sad, his eyelashes clustered together in little wet starbursts. He sat in a chair in a corner of the first-floor lounge with his computer on his lap, gazing at it mournfully. When Greer entered the lounge—her room, a rare single, was too depressing to stay in all evening, and she'd been unable to concentrate on her book—she was startled to realize that he was merely looking at his screen saver, which was a picture of his parents and sister, all of them smiling at him from far away. The family image swept across the computer screen and gently bounced against one side, before slowly heading back.

How long would he watch his bouncing family? Greer wondered, and though she didn't miss her own parents at all—she was still angry with them for what they had done to her, which had resulted in her ending up at Ryland—she felt sorry for this boy. He was away from home on another continent, at a place that perhaps someone had mistakenly told him was a first-rate American college, a center of learning and discovery, practically a School of Athens nestled on the East Coast of the US. After managing the complicated feat of getting here, he was now alone and quickly becoming aware that this place actually wasn't so great. And besides that, he was also pining for his family. She knew what it was like to miss someone, for she missed Cory so continually and pressingly that the feeling was like its own shattering bass vibrating through her, and he was only 110 miles away at Princeton, not across the world.

Greer's sympathies kept collecting and expanding, while in the doorway of the lounge appeared a very pale girl who stood clutching her midsection and asking, "Do either of you have something for diarrhea?"

"Sorry, no," said Greer, and the boy just shook his head.

The girl accepted their responses with a grim weariness, and then for lack of anything else to do she sat down too. Curling through the porous walls came the smell of butter plus tertiary butylhydroquinone, alluring but inadequate to the task of cheering anyone up. Moments later this was followed by the source of the smell, a big plastic tub of popcorn conveyed by a girl in a robe and slippers. "I got the kind with movie theater butter," she said to them as an added inducement, holding out her bowl.

Apparently, Greer thought, these are going to be my people, tonight and perhaps every weekend night. It made no sense; she didn't belong with them, and yet she was among them, she was one of them. So she took a hand span's worth of popcorn, which was so wet that her fingers felt as if she'd draped them through soup. Greer was about to sit down and attempt a conversation; they could tell one another about themselves, how bleak they felt. She would stay in this lounge, even though Cory had encouraged her earlier not to stay in tonight, but instead to go out to a party or some sort of campus event. "There has to be something going on," he'd said. "Improv. There's always improv." It was her first weekend at college, and he thought she should just try.

But she'd said no, she didn't really want to try, she would rather get through it her own way. During the week she would be a super-student, working in a carrel in the library, her head bent over a book like a jeweler with a loupe. Books were an antidepressant, a powerful SSRI. She'd always been one of those girls with socked feet tucked under her, her mouth slightly open in stunned, almost doped-up concentration. All written words danced in a chain for her, creating corresponding images as clear as the boy from Iran's bouncing family. She had learned to read before kindergarten, when she'd first suspected that her parents weren't all that interested in her. Then she'd kept going, plowing through children's books with their predictable anthropomorphism, heading eventually into the strange and beautiful formality of the nineteenth century, and pushing both backward and forward into histories of bloody wars, into discussions of God and godlessness. What she responded to most powerfully, sometimes even physically, were novels. Once Greer read *Anna Karenina* for such a long, unbroken bout that her eyes grew strained and bloodshot, and she had to lie in bed with a washcloth over them as if she herself were a literary heroine from the past. Novels had accompanied her throughout her childhood, that period of protracted isolation, and they would probably do so during whatever lay ahead in adulthood. Regardless of how bad it got at Ryland, she knew that at least she would be able to read there, because this was college, and reading was what you did.

But tonight, books were unseductive, and so they remained untouched, ignored. Tonight college was only about partying, or sitting in a bland dormitory lounge, bookless and self-punishing. Bitterness, she knew, could give you an edge. Unlike pure unhappiness, bitterness had a *taste*. This display of bitterness would be for no one but herself. Her parents wouldn't witness it; even Cory Pinto, down at Princeton, wouldn't. She and Cory had grown up together, and had been in love and entwined since the year before; and though they'd vowed that throughout the four years of college they would Skype with each other all the time—the new video feature would even allow them to see each other—and borrow cars to visit each other at least once a month, they would be entirely separate tonight. He had gotten dressed in a good sweater in order to go out to a party. Earlier, she'd watched as the Skype version of him came close to the webcam, all pore and nostril and rock-ledge forehead.

"Try to have a good time," he'd said, his voice stuttering slightly because of a glitchy system configuration. Then he turned and held up a finger to John Steers, his off-camera roommate, as if telling him: Give me two more seconds. I just have to deal with this.

Greer had quickly ended the call, not wanting to be seen as "this"—someone to deal with, the needy one in the relationship. Now she sat in the Woolley lounge, lowering and lifting her hand into and out of the popcorn, looking around at the tacked-up posters for the Heimlich maneuver and indie band auditions and a Christian Students picnic in West Quad, come rain or shine. A girl walked by the room and stopped; later on she admitted that she had done this more out of kindness than interest. She resembled a slender, sexy boy, perfectly made, with a Joan of Arc aesthetic that immediately read as gay. She took in the sight of the bright room of lost people, frowned in deliberation, and then announced, "I'm going to check out a few parties, if anyone wants to come."

The boy shook his head and returned to the image on his screen. The girl with the popcorn just kept eating, and the girl in distress was now debating with someone on her cell phone about whether she should go to Health Services. "I know that on the plus side they could help me," she was saying. "But on the minus side I have no idea where they're located." Pause. "No, I cannot call Security and have them *escort me there*." Another pause. "And anyway, I think it might just be nerves."

Greer looked at the boyish girl and nodded, and the girl nodded back, turning up the collar of her jacket. In the dim hall, they pushed through the heavy fire doors. Only when Greer was outside in the wind, feeling it ripple along the thin material of her shirt, did she remember she was sweaterless. But she felt certain that she shouldn't break the moment by asking if she could run up to the third floor and get her sweater.

"I thought we could sample a few different things," said the girl, who introduced herself as Zee Eisenstat, from Scarsdale, New York. "It will be like a test kitchen for college life."

"Exactly," said Greer, as though this had been her plan too.

Zee led them to Spanish House, a freestanding clapboard building on the edge of campus. As they walked in, a boy in the doorway said, "*Buenas noches, señoritas*," and handed them glasses of what he called mock-sangria, though Greer got into a brief conversation with another resident of the house about whether the mock-sangria was perhaps actually not mock at all.

"*Licor secreto?*" Greer asked quietly, and the girl looked at her hard and said, "*Inteligente.*"

Inteligente. For years it had been enough to be the intelligent one. All that had meant, in the beginning, was that you could answer the kinds of questions that your teachers asked. The whole world appeared to be fact-based, and that had been a relief to Greer, who could dredge up facts with great ease, a magician pulling coins from behind any available ear. Facts appeared before her, and then she simply articulated them, and in this way she became known as the smartest one in her class.

Later on, when it wasn't just facts that were required, it got so much harder for her. To have to put yourself out there—your opinions, your essence, the particular substance that churned inside you and made you who you were—both exhausted and frightened Greer, and she thought of this as she and Zee headed for their next social destination, the Lamb Art Studio. How Zee, a freshman, knew about these parties was unclear; there had been no mention of them in the Ryland Weekly Blast.

The air in the studio was sharp with turpentine, which almost served as a sexual accelerant, for the art students, all upperclassmen, seemed highly attracted to one another. They were twinned and tripled, with skinny bodies and paint-spattered pants and drawn-on hands and ear gauges and unusually bright eyes. In the middle of the white wooden floor, a girl was being carried around on a guy's shoulders, crying, "*BENNETT, STOP IT, I'M GOING TO FALL OFF AND DIE, AND THEN MY PARENTS WILL SUE YOUR VISUAL ARTS ASS!*" He—Bennett—carried her in staggered circles while he was still sufficiently young and powerful and Atlas-like to hold her like this, and while she was still light enough to be held.

The art students were into one another and one another only. It was as if Greer and Zee had stumbled upon a subculture in the clearing of a forest. "The male gaze" kept getting mentioned, though at first Greer heard it as "the male gays," but then finally she understood. She and Zee slipped away not long after arriving, and once outside again they were almost immediately joined by another freshman who confidently and unapologetically attached herself to them. She said her name was Chloe Shanahan, and she seemed to aspire toward a certain mallish brand of hotness, with spiky heels and Hollister jeans and a Slinky-load of thin silver bracelets. She had wound up in the art studio by mistake, she told them; she was actually looking for Theta Gamma Psi.

"A frat?" Zee said. "Why? They're so disgusting."

Chloe shrugged. "They apparently have a keg and loud music. That's all I need tonight."

Zee looked at Greer. Did she want to go to an actual frat party? She wanted it less than most things; but she also didn't want to be alone, so maybe she did want it. She thought of Cory leaning against a wall at a party right this minute, laughing at something. She saw an array of people looking up at him—he was the tallest person in any room—and laughing back.

Greer, Zee, and Chloe were an unlikely trio, but she had heard this was typical of social life in the first weeks of college. People who had nothing in common were briefly and emotionally joined, like the members of a jury or the survivors of a plane crash. Chloe took them across West Quad, and then they looped around behind the fortress of the Metzger Library, which was all lit up and poignantly empty, like a 24-hour supermarket in the middle of the night.

The Ryland website showed a few nominal photos of students in goggles doing something with a torch in a laboratory, or squinting over a whiteboard jammed with calculations, but the rest of the photos were social, cornball: an afternoon of ice skating on a frozen pond, a classic "three in a tree" shot of students chatting beneath a spreading oak. In fact, the campus only had one such tree, which had been over-photographed into exhaustion. In daylight, students straggled to class along the paths of the inelegant campus, occasionally even wearing pajamas, like the members of a good-natured bear family in a children's book.

When nighttime fell, though, the college came into its own. Their destination tonight was a large, corroding frat house thundering with sound. *Greek life,* the college catalogues had called this. Greer imagined IMing Cory later, writing, "greek life: wtf? where is aristotle? where is baklava?" But suddenly their usual kind of shared, arch commentary that kept them both entertained was irrelevant, for he wasn't here, not even close, and now she was inside a wide doorway with these two randomly chosen girls, heading toward the noxious smells and the inviting ones, and, indirectly and eventually, toward Faith Frank.

The house drink that night was called the Ryland Fling, and it was the pastel pink of bug juice but immediately had a muscular, slugging effect on Greer, who weighed 110 pounds and had eaten only a few small, sad anthills of food from the salad bar at dinner. Usually she liked the pleasing snap of clarity, but now she knew clarity would just lead her back to unhappiness, so she drained her first hyper-sweet Ryland Fling from a plastic cup with a sharp nub on the bottom, then stood waiting in line for a second one. The drinks, plus what she'd already drunk at Spanish House, were effective.

Soon she and the two other girls were dancing in a circle, as if for the pleasure of a sheikh. Zee was an excellent dancer, her hips sliding and her shoulders working, yet the rest of her moving with studied minimalism. Chloe, beside her, drew shapes with her hands, her many bracelets chiming. Greer was free-form and unusually unguarded. When they were all exhausted, they plopped onto a bulbous black leather couch that smelled vaguely of fried flounder. Greer closed her eyes while an annoying hip-hop song by Pugnayshus began to swell:

"Tell me why you wanna rag on me
When I'm in a state of perpetual agony . . ."

"I love this song," Chloe said, just as Greer started to say, "I hate this song." She stopped herself, not wanting to impugn Chloe's taste. Then Chloe began to sing along: ". . . *perpetual a-go-ny . . . ,*" she enunciated, as sweet and reassuring as someone in a cherub choir.

Above them, Darren Tinzler strode down the wide, majestic stairway. He hadn't been identified as Darren Tinzler yet, hadn't been given significance, but was still just another frat brother standing in front of the amethyst stained glass on the landing, thick-chested and with an overhang of hair and wide-set eyes beneath a backward baseball cap. He surveyed the room, then after consideration he headed for the three of them and their concentration of femaleness. Chloe tried to rise to the occasion like a little mermaid lifting toward the ocean surface, but she couldn't entirely sit up. Zee, when he dubiously turned his attention to her next, closed her eyes and held up a hand, as if quietly shutting a door in his face.

Which left Greer, who of course wasn't available either. She and Cory were sealed together, and even if they hadn't been, she knew she was too mild and focused for someone like this bro, though she still looked appealing in a very specific way, small and compact and determined, like a flying squirrel. She had straight, shining dark hair; the shot of color had been added at home with a drugstore kit in eleventh grade. She'd stood over the sink in the upstairs bathroom, getting blue all over the basin and the rug and the shower curtain, until in the end the room looked like the set of a slasher film on another planet.

She had imagined that the streak in her hair would be a temporary novelty. But when she and Cory suddenly became involved senior year, he'd liked touching that unexpected swatch of color, so she'd kept it. In the beginning with him, when he sat looking at her for an extended moment, she often instinctively dipped her head down and glanced off to the side. Finally he would say, "Don't look away. Come back to me. Come back."

Now Darren Tinzler turned his cap around and tipped it to her as if it were a top hat. And because of those powerful Ryland Flings, which had seriously loosened Greer, she stood and reached her hands out on either side of her waist, as if lifting a skirt in an air-curtsy, and bobbed her head. "Such a fancy occasion," she murmured to herself.

"What's that?" Darren said. "Blue Streak, you are shit-faced."

"Actually, not true. I am only pee-faced."

He regarded her curiously, then led her into a corner, where they rested their drinks on top of a careless pile of warped and long-ignored board games—Battleship, Risk, *Star Wars* Trivial Pursuit, *Full House* Trivial Pursuit. "Were these rescued from the Great Frat House Flood of 1987?" she asked.

He looked at her. "What?" he finally said, as if he was annoyed.

"Nothing."

She told him she lived in Woolley, and he said, "You have my sympathy. It's so depressing there."

"It really is," she said. "And the walls are the color of hearing aids, am I right?" Cory, she remembered, had laughed when she'd said that, and told her, "I love you." But Darren just looked at her again in that irritated way. She thought that she even saw disgust in his expression. But then he was smiling again, so maybe she had seen nothing. The human face had too many possibilities, and they just kept coming in a fast-moving slide show, one after another.

"It's been kind of not so great," she confided. "I wasn't supposed to be here at Ryland, actually. It was all a big mistake, but it happened, and it isn't fixable."

"Is that right?" he asked. "You were supposed to be at another college?"

"Yes. Somewhere much better."

"Oh yeah? Where is that?"

"Yale."

He laughed. "That's a good one."

"I *was*," she said. Then, more indignantly, "I got in."

"Sure you did."

"I *did*. But it didn't work out, and it's too complicated to go into. So here I be."

"Here you be," Darren Tinzler said. He reached out in a proprietary way and rubbed the collar of her shirt between his fingers, and she was startled and didn't know what to do, because
this wasn't right. His other hand ran experimentally up her shirt,
and Greer stood in shocked suspension for a moment as he found
the convexity of her breast and encircled it, all the while looking
her in the eye, not blinking, just *looking*.

She jerked back from him and said, "What are you doing?"

But he held on, giving her breast a hard and painful squeeze,
twisting the flesh. When she pulled away for real he took her
wrist and yanked her close, saying, "What do you mean, what
am I doing? You're standing here coming on to me with your
bullshit about getting into Yale."

"Let *go*," she said, but he didn't.

"No one else here is going to fuck you, Blue Streak," he continued. "It would have to be a mercy fuck. You should be grateful that I was into you for two seconds. Get over yourself. You're
not that hot."

Then he let go of her wrist and pushed her away as if she had
been the one who had been aggressive. Throughout all of this
Greer's face had turned warm and her mouth had gone as dry as
a little piece of fabric. She felt herself swallowed up once again
inside the usual feeling of being unable to say what she felt. The
room was eating her up—the room and the party and the college and the night.

No one appeared to have noticed what had happened, or at
least no one was surprised by it. This tableau had taken place in
plain sight: a guy putting a hand up a girl's shirt and grabbing
her hard and then pushing her away. She was as inconspicuous as
Icarus drowning in the corner of the Bruegel painting they'd
studied on the very first day of class. This was college, and
this was a college party. Pin the Tail on the Donkey was being

played, while several people chanted, "Go Kyla, go Kyla," in monotone to a blindfolded girl who held a paper tail and took lurching baby steps forward. Elsewhere, a boy was softly puking into a porkpie hat. Greer thought about running to Health Services, where she could lie on a cot beside another cot that perhaps now held the girl from Woolley with diarrhea, the two of them having started college so inauspiciously.

But Greer didn't need to go there; she just needed to leave this building. She heard Darren's mild laughter pattering behind her as she moved quickly through the crowd, then out onto the porch with the groaning swing in which two people lay clasped, and then down onto the college green, which, she could feel through the heels of her boots, was still spongy from summer but already starting to turn brittle at the edges.

She had never been touched like this before, she thought as she began a shaky speed-walk back across campus. In the hard, dark night, alone with herself in this new place, she tried to figure out what had happened. Of course boys and men had often made rude or lurid comments to her, the way they did to everyone, everywhere. At age eleven Greer had been muttered at by the bikers who hung around the KwikStop in Macopee. One day in summer, when she'd gone there to buy her favorite ice cream bar, a Klondike Choco Taco, a man with a ZZ Top beard had come close to her, looked her up and down in her shorts and little sleeveless shirt, and made his assessment: "Sweetie, you're boobless."

Greer had had no way to defend herself against ZZ Top, no way to say anything spiky or do anything to stop him or even just call him out. She'd been silent before him, *sassless* and undefended. She wasn't one of those girls who seemed to be everywhere, hands on hips, those girls who were described in certain books and movies as being "spitfires," or, later on, "kickass."

Even now, at college, there were girls like this, fuck-you confident and assured of their place in the world. Whenever they came
upon resistance in the form of outright sexism or even more generic grossness, they either vanquished it or essentially rolled their
eyes and acted as if it was just too stupid for them to acknowledge.
They wasted no thought on people like Darren Tinzler.

On the college green now, people walked together in the
resuscitative air, having left parties that were winding down, or
heading toward other, smaller ones that were just starting up. It
was the middle of the night; the temperature had dropped, and
without a sweater Greer was cold. When she got back to Woolley the girl with the popcorn was asleep in the lounge, cradling
her big plastic tub, which now contained just a cluster of unpopped corn kernels at the bottom like a congregation of
ladybugs.

"Someone did something to me," Greer whispered to the
unconscious girl.

Over the next few days she would repeat a version of this to
several conscious people, at first because it was still so upsetting,
but then because it was so insulting. "It was like he felt he was
entitled to do whatever he wanted," Greer said on the phone to
Cory with a kind of incensed wonder. "He didn't care how I
felt. He just thought he had the right."

"I wish I could be there with you now," Cory said.

Zee told her she should report him. "The administration
should know about this. It's assault, you know."

"I was drinking," Greer said. "There's that."

"So? All the more reason that he shouldn't be messing with
you." When Greer didn't respond, Zee said, "Hello, Greer, this
is not tolerable. It's actually pretty outrageous."

"Maybe it's a Ryland thing. This wouldn't happen at Princeton,
I don't think."

"Jesus, are you kidding me? Of course that isn't true."

Zee was innately, bracingly political. She had started with animal rights when she was young; soon after, she became a vegetarian, and over time her depth of feeling for animals extended toward people too, and she added women's rights, LGBT rights, war and its inevitable flood of refugees, and then climate change, which made you imagine future animals, future people, all of them imperiled and gasping, having run out of possibilities.

But Greer hadn't yet developed much of a political inner life; she only felt sickened and reluctant as she imagined filing a report and having to sit alone in Dean Harkavy's office in Masterson Hall with a clipboard on her lap, writing out a statement about Darren Tinzler in her overly neat, good-girl handwriting. Her letters were still bubbled and fat and juvenile, creating a disconnect between the content of what she was writing and the way she wrote it. Who would even take it seriously?

Greer thought about how victims' names were kept out of sexual assault reports. The idea that *something had been done to you* seemed to implicate you, even though no one said it did, making your body—which usually lived in darkness beneath your clothing—suddenly live in light. Forever, if someone found out, you would be a person with a body that had been violated, breached. Also, forever you would be a person with a body that was vivid and imaginable. Compared with something like that, what had happened here was small potatoes. And then, once again, Greer thought of her own breasts, which could also be described that way. Small potatoes. That was the sum of what she was.

"I don't know," Greer said to Zee, aware of a kind of familiar vagueness sweeping around her. She sometimes said, "I don't know," even when she did know. What she meant was that it was more comfortable to stay in vagueness than to leave it.

As the moment with Darren Tinzler receded, it became less real, and finally it simply turned into an anecdote that Greer deconstructed more than once with a few girls in her dorm, all of them standing around the common bathroom carrying the plastic shower pails that their mothers had bought them to take to college, so that they resembled a coalition of children meeting at a sandbox. Everyone knew by now to keep their distance from the odious Darren Tinzler, and finally the topic exhausted itself, and exhausted the people thinking about it. It wasn't rape, Greer had pointed out; not even close. Already it felt much less important than what was apparently going on right now at other colleges: the rugby-playing roofie-givers, the police reports, the outrage.

But over the next couple of weeks, half a dozen other female Ryland students had their own Darren Tinzler encounters. They didn't even necessarily know his name at first; he was just described as a male wearing a baseball cap and having "eyes like a carp," as someone said. One night in the dining hall Darren sat with his friends and watched a sophomore for a long, unhurried amount of time; he gazed across the crowded space at her while she raised a spoon of fat-free something or other to her mouth. Another night he was in the reading room of the library, slouched at one of the butterscotch tables staring at a student as she forged her way through Mankiw's *Principles of Microeconomics*.

And then, when she stood up to talk to a friend or to bus her plate or to get some supposedly UTI-curative cranberry juice from the spigots with their miraculous free-flow that defined college life, or simply to stretch a little, joints going *pop-pop-pop*, he stood up, too, and strode toward her with resolve, making sure that they had cruised into a side-by-side position.

When they were together in an alcove or hidden behind a wall or otherwise away from all onlookers, he started a conversation. And then he perceived her politeness or kindness or even her vague responsiveness as interest, and maybe sometimes it was. But then he always made it physical, a hand up a shirt, or on a crotch, or even, once, a finger swiped fast across a mouth. And when she recoiled he became angry and squeezed her hard so she cried out, and then reeled her in, saying some version of, "Oh, like you're so shocked. Give me a fucking break. You're such a little whore."

In every case she jolted back from him, saying, "Get away," or simply storming off, saying, "You sick fuck," or saying nothing and later telling her roommate what had happened, or maybe telling no one, or else worriedly polling all her friends that night, asking them, "I don't look like a whore, do I?" and having them gather round her and say, "No, Emily, you look incredible. I love your look, it's so free."

But then one night in Havermeyer, which was still known as the "new" dorm, though it had been built in 1980 and had a Soviet style amid all the eclectic architectural overreach that defined the Ryland campus, a sophomore named Ariel Diski returned very late to her room to find a boy waiting in the fourth-floor hallway's defunct phone booth. There was no longer a phone in the booth, just a series of chewing-gum-plugged holes where the pay phone had been ripped out, and a wooden seat to sit on in this useless little chamber. He opened the squeaking glass accordion door and stepped toward her, detaining her, talking to her, and even saying something that amused her. But soon he had touched her rudely and was edging her into her room; she pulled away from him, at which point he got mad and reined her in by her belt loops.

But Ariel Diski had studied Krav Maga in high school with the Israeli gym teacher, and she got Darren in the center of his chest with a perfectly executed elbow strike. He brayed in pain, doors opened up and down the hall, people appeared in various states of undress and standing-up hair, and finally Security lumbered into the building with their sizzling, muttering walkie-talkies. And though Darren Tinzler was gone by that time, he was easily identified and apprehended back in Theta Gamma Psi, where he was pretending to be deep in a one-person round of *Star Wars* Trivial Pursuit.

Soon the other girls rallied and came forward, and while the college initially tried to avoid any kind of public airing, under pressure officials agreed to hold a disciplinary hearing. It took place in a biology lab in the pale, leaking light of a Friday afternoon, when everyone was already thinking about the weekend ahead. Greer, when it was her turn to speak, stood in front of a glossy black table lined with Bunsen burners, and half-whispered what Darren Tinzler had said and done to her that night at the party. She was sure she had a fever from testifying, a wild and inflamed fever. *Scarlet* fever, maybe.

Darren was without his usual baseball cap; his flat, fair hair looked like a circle of lawn that had been trapped and left to die under a kiddie pool. Finally he read a prepared statement: "I'd just like to say that I, Darren Scott Tinzler, class of 2007, a communications major from Kissimmee, Florida, am apparently kind of bad at reading signals from the opposite sex. I'm very ashamed right now, and I apologize for my own repeated misunderstanding of social cues."

A decision was handed down within an hour. The head of the disciplinary committee, a young, female assistant dean, announced that Darren would be allowed to stay on campus if he agreed to undergo three counseling sessions with a local behavioral therapist, Melanie Stapp, MSW, whose website said her specialty was impulse control. An illustration showed a man frantically puffing away at a cigarette, and an unhappy woman eating a doughnut.

There was a strong but diffuse outcry on campus. "This is

misogyny in action," said a senior when they were all sitting in the Woolley lounge late one night.

"And it's just amazing that the head of the committee apparently had no sympathy for the victims," said a sophomore.

"She's probably one of those women who hates women," said Zee. "A total cunt." Then she began to sing her own version of a song from a musical that her parents used to like: "*Women . . . women who hate women . . . are the cuntiest women . . . in the world . . .*"

Greer said, "That's terrible! You shouldn't say *cunt.*"

Zee said, "Cunt," and everyone laughed. "Oh, come on," Zee went on. "I can say what I want. That's having agency."

"You shouldn't say *agency,*" said Greer. "That's worse."

Greer and Zee were part of long conversations about Darren with other people in the dining hall; they stayed until the food service workers kicked them out. Anger was hard to sustain, and despite these conversations and a tightly reasoned op-ed by a senior in the *Ryland Clarion*, two of the girls involved said they didn't want the case to drag on any longer.

Still Greer kept thinking about him. It wasn't the actual encounter that remained—that was almost gone except for a trace memory—but instead she fixed on how unfair it was that he was tolerated there. *Unfair*: the word sounded like a child's complaint hollered bitterly to a parent.

"Sorry, I am done with thinking about him," Ariel Diski said one morning in the student union, after Greer tentatively approached her. "I'm super-busy," said Ariel, "and he's just a dick."

"I know he is," said Greer. "But maybe there's more to do. My friend Zee thinks there is."

"Look, I know you're still invested in this," said Ariel, "but no offense, I'm pre-law, and I can't get stressed. Sorry, Greer, I'm done."

That night, Zee and Greer and Chloe sat in Zee's room, painting their toenails the brownish green of army fatigues. The room gave off a fermented chemical smell that made them all feel a little sick and a little wild. "You could go to the Women's Alliance," Zee offered. "They might have some advice."

"Or not. My roommate went to one of their meetings," Chloe said. "She said all they do is bake brownies against genital mutilation."

Ryland wasn't a very political place, so you took what you could get. Every once in a while a wave of protest unexpectedly lifted up. A few years into the clanking Iraq War, Zee and two sophomores were sometimes seen out on the steps of the Metzger with a megaphone and handouts. Then there was a series of protests by the very small but well-organized Black Students Association. The climate change group had become a persistently grave presence, and Zee was part of it as well. The sky was falling, they told everyone again and again, the hot and seething sky.

"You know," said Zee, "I once made and sold T-shirts to raise money to stop animal cruelty back in Scarsdale when I was a kid. I'm thinking we could make T-shirts with Darren Tinzler's face on them and give them away. And beneath it could be the word 'Unwanted.'"

Money was pooled, and fifty cheap T-shirts were quickly purchased from an online closeout wholesaler, and Greer, Zee, and Chloe stayed up late in the basement of Woolley among the stored bikes and chugging laundry machines and the sluice of toilet water through overhead pipes, ironing transfers of Darren Tinzler's face onto synthetic fabric because it was cheaper than having them printed. By four a.m. Greer's arm was still strong as she ran the hot, pointy anvil over and over the image of Darren's bland paleness—the baseball cap worn low, the unusually wide-set eyes. He had a stupid face, she thought, but buried in it was a brutish, cunning instinct.

Soon afterward, Chloe gave up, standing and reaching out her arms, saying, "Must. Have. Bed," so a few hours later it was just Greer and Zee who sat yawning in the bright entrance to the dining hall, trying to get people to take their T-shirts. "Free T-shirts!" they told everyone, but in the end they gave away only five. It was a disappointment, a sad failure. Still, Greer and Zee wore theirs as often as they could, though the fabric shrank a little in the wash and Darren Tinzler's face was stretched and slightly distorted, as if he'd put his head in a copy machine.

They were both wearing the T-shirts the night Faith Frank came to speak.

Zee had seen the announcement for the lecture in the Weekly Blast and was very excited. "I've always loved her," she said to Greer. They had become friends in an accelerated way because of the night they'd spent with the T-shirts, scheming, talking, free-associating. "I know she represents this kind of outdated idea of feminism," said Zee, "that focuses on issues that mostly affect privileged women. I totally see that. But you know what? She's done a lot of good, and I think she's amazing. Also, the thing about Faith Frank," she went on, "is that while she's this famous, iconic person, she also seems so approachable. We have to go see her, Greer. You have to talk to her, tell her what's hap-pened. Tell her. She'll know what to do."

Greer knew shamefully little about Faith Frank, though the night before the lecture she fortified herself with some intensive Googling. Looking facts up online comforted her; the world could be out of control, but still there were answers that could easily be found. Yet while Google provided timeline and con-text, it gave her no real sense of how a person like Faith actually became her whole self.

In the early 1970s, Greer saw, Faith Frank had been one of the founders of *Bloomer* magazine, named for Amelia Bloomer, the feminist and social reformer who published the first newspaper for women. *Bloomer* was known as the scrappier, less famous little sister to *Ms.* magazine. The magazine had been very good in the beginning, not as polished or sophisticated as *Ms.*, never particularly well-designed but often filled with columns and articles that were absorbing and charged. Over the decades, readership had gone way down, and finally the magazine, once seen as a bulletin from the front, became as thin as a manual that came with a small appliance.

But Faith, who had been described as "a couple of steps down from Gloria Steinem in fame," remained visible. In the late 1970s she began writing books for a popular audience that sold well, with their feisty, encouraging messages of empowerment. Then in 1984 she had an enormous hit with her manifesto *The Female Persuasion*, which essentially implored women to see that there was a great deal more to being female than padded shoulders and acting tough. Corporate America had tried to get women to behave as badly as men, Faith Frank said, but women did not have to capitulate. They could be strong and powerful, all the while keeping their integrity and decency.

People really seemed to want to hear this message, including every woman who had gone to Wall Street and ended up miserable. Women could get out, Faith said; they could start cooperatives, or at least they could challenge the prevailing culture at their firms. And men, she added, could use some persuading to balance their long-established toughness with a new gentleness. Balance, she told them, was everything. The book had never gone out of print, though each new edition needed to be severely updated.

Because Faith was poised and articulate and effective when

interviewed, she had been given her own short segment on PBS's nighttime magazine-format TV show *Recap*, where she interviewed other people; sometimes she chose sexist men as her subjects, and in their vanity they seemed to have no idea of why they had been selected. They appeared on-screen, occasionally preening and making objectionable remarks, and she calmly and wittily corrected them—and sometimes just easily took them down.

But though Faith's interviews were popular, by the mid-nineties the whole show was canceled. Faith was still writing books by then, but they had stopped selling well. Over the years she had continued publishing more modest sequels to *The Female Persuasion*. (The most recent one, in the late nineties, about women and technology, was *The Email Persuasion*.) Finally she stopped writing books entirely.

In the earliest photographs Greer found, Faith Frank, a tall, slender woman with long, dark curls, looked tenderly youthful, open. In one shot she was seen marching in DC. In another, she was gesticulating intensely on the set of one of those cultural-roundtable talk shows that used to be on late at night, with the guests on white swivel chairs in bell-bottoms, chain-smoking and yelling. Faith had gotten into a notorious debate on-air with the proudly male chauvinist novelist Holt Rayburn. He'd tried to shout her down that night, but she'd kept speaking in her calm and logical way, and in the end she'd won. It made the papers, and ultimately ended up being the reason she was offered her interview segment on *Recap*. Another photo showed her wearing her infant son in a sling while squinting at a magazine layout over his loosely screwed-on head. The photos kept moving forward through time, with Faith Frank still retaining a version of her elegant, lustrous self into her forties, fifties, sixties.

In most of the photos she was wearing a pair of tall, sexy suede boots, her signature look. There were interviews and profiles; one made reference to her "surprising impatience." Faith could apparently get angry quickly, and not just at chauvinistic male novelists. She was depicted as kind but human, sometimes difficult, always generous and wonderful. But by the time she came to speak at Ryland College, she was seen as someone from the past, who was often spoken of with admiration, and with a special tone of voice reserved for very few people. She was like a pilot light that burned continuously, comfortingly.

The chapel, when Greer and Zee arrived that night, was only two-thirds filled. The weather was unusually bad for fall, flurries spiraling widely, and the place had the smell and feel of a children's coatroom, with slick, streaked floors, and people trying to find a place to stow their damp outerwear, only to end up bunching it up and holding it awkwardly against their bodies. Many of the students had come because their professors had made the lecture mandatory. "She's been very important to a lot of people, myself included. Be there," one sociology professor had said in a mildly threatening tone.

The event was supposed to start at seven, but apparently Faith's driver had gotten lost. The sign at the entrance of Ryland was so modest that it might have advertised a small-town pediatric practice. At 7:25 there came a squall of activity from over on the other side of the chapel, and then a raw front of incoming damp night air as the double doors were pushed open and several people powered in. First came the college president, and then the dean, followed by a couple of others, all excited in their coats and unflattering hats. Then, hatless and shockingly recognizable, Faith Frank entered with a few people, including the provost, and stood unspooling a blood-colored scarf from her throat.

Greer watched as the scarf unwound and unwound, a trick scarf as long as a river. Faith's cheeks were so bright they looked freshly slapped. Her hair was the same dark brown mass of curls it had always been in pictures, and when she shook it out, snowflakes sprang off it as delicately as atoms scattering.

As in the photos of her from over the decades, she had a striking and sympathetic face with a very strong, elegant nose. The effect was one of glamour and importance and gravitas and friendly curiosity as she looked around at the medium-sized crowd, and Greer supposed that she might have perceived the chapel as half-empty or half-full, depending on her perspective.

The incoming party quickly got seated up front, and then the college president, stuffed thickly into the upholstery of a flowered dress, stood at the podium and gave a worshipful introduction, her hand on her heart. Finally Faith Frank rose. She was sixty-three years old and a forceful presence in a dark wool dress that hewed to her long, rangy middle; of course, she wore her suede boots. These particular ones were smoke gray, though she still owned a whole color spectrum of boots, which let everyone know she had once been a knockout, a sexual powerhouse, and maybe still was. She wore several rings on the fingers of both hands: chunky, arty bursts of gemstone and silver. She looked completely composed, not at all rattled, though she had been late to her own speech.

The first thing she did up there was to smile down at everyone and say, "Thanks for braving the snow. Extra credit for that." Her speaking voice was specific, appealingly throaty. Then she went quiet for a few seconds, and it seemed as if she was only just now coming up with what she might tell them. She held no notes. Apparently she was going to *wing* it, which was unimaginable to Greer, whose intense academic life up until now had been spent making full, reassuring use of binders and color-coded dividers and highlighter pens that lent her reading material the colors of two different kinds of lemonade—a wash of yellow or pink.

Greer had never known anyone in Macopee who was at all like Faith Frank. Certainly not her ragged and ineffectual parents. Cory, even in his short time at Princeton, was surrounded by people who had traveled widely and lived lives in which they had often been in the presence of worldly, formidable figures. But Greer hadn't been exposed to anyone like that. In truth, she didn't even realize it was a possibility. "My head was cracking open," she told Cory the next day.

At the podium Faith said, "Whenever I give a talk at colleges I meet young women who say, 'I'm *not* a feminist, but . . .' By which they mean, 'I don't call myself a feminist, but I want equal pay, and I want to have equal relationships with men, and of course I want to have an equal right to sexual pleasure. I want to have a fair and good life. I don't want to be held back because I'm a woman.'"

Later, Greer understood that what Faith had actually said in her speech was only one part of the whole effect; really, it was about more than her words. What also mattered was that it was *her* speaking them, meaning them, conveying them with such feeling to everyone in this room. "And I always want to reply," said Faith, "'What do you think feminism is, other than that? How do you think you're going to get those things if you deny the political movement that is all about obtaining that life that you want?'" She stopped for a moment, and they all thought about this, some of them surely thinking about themselves. They watched her take a slow and deliberate drink of water, which was somehow, Greer realized, highly interesting.

"To me," Faith continued, "there are two aspects to feminism. The first is individualism, which is that *I* get to shape my own life. That I don't have to fit into a stereotype, doing what my mother tells me, conforming to someone else's idea of what a woman is. But there's a second aspect too, and here I want to use the old-fashioned word 'sisterhood,' which may make you groan a little and head for the exits in a stampede, but I'll just have to take that chance." There was laughter; they were all listening, they were all with her now, and they wanted her to know it. "Sisterhood," she said, "is about being together with other women in a cause that allows all women to make the individual choices they want. Because as long as women are separate from one another, organized around competition—like in a children's game where only one person gets to be the princess— then it will be the rare woman who is not in the end narrowed and limited by our society's idea of what a woman should be.

"I'm here to tell you," said Faith, "that while college is the most formative experience you will ever have as an individual— a moment when you can read and explore and make friends and make mistakes—it's also a moment when you can think about how you can play a social and political role in the great cause of women's equality. Now, when you graduate, you probably don't want to do what I did, which is to go off to Las Vegas to be a cocktail waitress in order to get away from my parents, Sylvia and Martin Frank. You wouldn't like the little ruffled uniform I had to wear. Or maybe you would."

There was more laughter, indulgent, approving. "Me in Las Vegas—this is a true story. I was desperate to get away because my parents had made me live at home during college. They wanted to make sure I would stay a virgin. God, that was no fun." More laughter. "And I'm happy to say things have changed since then. It's so wonderful that all of you have so much more freedom than I did. But along with that freedom can sometimes come a sense that you don't need other women. And that isn't true."

She stopped again and looked out over the whole room, sweeping her gaze across them. "So the next time you say, 'I'm not a feminist,' remember all of this. And do what you can to join the fight, which is ongoing." She paused. "Oh, and here's a final thought. Along the way, as you're fighting for what matters, you will definitely come up against resistance, and that can sometimes be upsetting and even throw you off course. The truth is that not everyone is going to agree with you. Not everyone is going to like you. Or love you. That's right, some people will be really mad at you, and maybe even *hate* you, and that is going to be hard to accept. But my feeling is that if you're out there doing what matters—if it's any consolation at all, *I* love you."

She smiled a brief, encouraging smile at them, and that was it; Greer folded, she was taken in completely, taken up, wanting more of this forever. Faith had made her little joke about loving them, but as Greer listened to Faith, what she herself felt seemed closely related to falling in love. Greer knew all about falling in love—the way discovering Cory had shaken her around, messed with her cells. This was like that, but without the physical desire. The sensation wasn't sexual, but the word *love* still seemed relevant here; love, which pollinated the air around Faith Frank.

Surely other people here felt it too, didn't they? And even if they'd been in a teenage stupor for years, staring at themselves in every reflective surface, frowning at their image as they popped a pimple with a little *splat* of greenish milk against glass, and railing to friends about their dumbass parents, or being forced to come to the chapel on this night despite being the kind of people Faith had described, who blithely went around saying they weren't feminists, now a revelatory gong had been struck inside them. It vibrated and vibrated, and seemed like it would never stop, for here was this new, formidable person, speaking in such an exciting way about their place in the looming, disturbing world. Making them want to be more than they were.

Faith said, "Okay, well, I think I've just about run out of things to tell you. I'm going to be quiet now and give the rest of you a chance to talk. Thank you so much for listening."

The room erupted with appreciative clapping, as loud as if an object had been dropped into a pan of hot oil from a great height. Greer immediately began clapping "like a maniac," as she would say to Cory. She wanted to clap as loud as anyone in that room.

Someone in the back called out, "FAITH, YOU ROCK!" and someone else shouted, "EFFING AWESOME BOOTS!" which made Faith Frank laugh. Of course she had a great laugh. The head went back and the mouth opened, the gullet exposed as if she were a sleek and elegant seal about to swallow a fish.

The chapel was warmed a few degrees by human heat and excitement, and it smelled even more strongly of people and their wet jackets. The whole place was ripening. Faith looked out over the crowd, and hands went up.

There was a dull, boilerplate question: "Do you have a message for the young people of today?" and then a hokey question that required Faith to assemble her dream dinner party: "You can invite anyone," said the questioner. "No restrictions on what country they're from, or what century. So who would you choose?" Greer remembered later that Faith had chosen Amelia Bloomer, the namesake of her magazine; and the hot young singer Opus, who had recently played the Super Bowl halftime show; also, the Italian Baroque painter Artemisia Gentileschi; the aviatrix Bessie Coleman, who was the first African-American woman to hold a pilot's license; Dorothy Parker; both Hepburns,

Audrey and Katharine, "Because I like their style," she said; and all four Beatles. And finally, "To liven things up, let's throw in a couple of ardent anti-feminists," said Faith. "Although I might be tempted to spit in their food."

It all blew by quickly because Greer had been distracted at the time, thinking that if she herself threw a dinner party, the main person she would want to invite was Faith Frank. She suddenly imagined Faith sitting comfortably in the Woolley first-floor lounge in her cool, tall boots, eating a bowl of instant ramen that Greer and Zee would have prepared for her in the microwave.

A decrepit professor in the history department with skin like crumpled tracing paper asked such a narrow question ("Ms. Frank, I'm reminded of a little-known statute from the bad old days . . .") that it could be of interest only to him. The audience grew restive and bored; people hunched down over their phones, or poked each other and whispered, or actually began chatting openly.

The dean cut his question short, saying, "Perhaps you can ask Ms. Frank about this afterward. But I think we should move along now, in the interest of time. Let's have one more question, people, and please make it a good one."

Greer's hand flew right up, her whole arm shaking slightly, but still she kept it in the air, perilously. She wasn't going to ask a question, exactly—only the vaguest approximation of one. She felt as though she had to establish contact with Faith Frank before it was too late. She'd thought it would be enough just to come here tonight and hear a lecture given by this admired and determined woman, and maybe feel cheered up by it after the whole rotten Darren Tinzler experience, but she couldn't let the night end yet, couldn't let Faith Frank get back into her town car and be driven back through the gates and away from here.

Then, beside her in the pew, Zee's arm went up too. Of course she had a real question, a political one; she probably even had follow-ups. Faith nodded her head in their direction. At first it was unclear which of them she was calling on. Greer tried to read Faith's gaze—the female gaze, she thought with giddiness. But then she saw Faith seem to zero in on her, specifically *her*, Greer; and Greer looked quizzically at Zee, making sure she was reading this right. Zee gave her a quick, affirmative nod, as if to say: Yes. This is yours. Zee even smiled, wanting Greer to have it.

So Greer stood. It was sickening to be the only one standing, but what could she do? "Ms. Frank?" she said, her voice coming out like a tiny lamb-bleat in this sacred space. "Hello."

"Hello."

"There's something I want to ask you."

"*Duh*," she heard a nearby girl quietly mutter. "That's why you raised your hand."

Greer took a breath, ignoring this. "What are we supposed to do?" she asked. Then she stopped right there, unsure of what to say next. Faith Frank patiently waited.

When it was apparent that Greer wasn't going to say anything else, Faith said, gently, "Do about what, exactly?"

"About the way it is," Greer pushed on. "The way it feels. Things like *misogyny*, which seems to be everywhere, kind of wallpapering the world, you know what I mean? It's still acceptable in the twenty-first century, and why is that?"

"I'm sorry. Can you speak up?" asked Faith, and this request further mortified Greer, who could not really speak up, even now. She thought it was possible she would faint; Zee watched her, concerned.

Greer held on to the lip of curved wood on the pew in front

of her. *"Misogyny?"* she said again, a little louder, but her intonation lifted the word uncertainly at the last syllable. She despised it when her voice did this. She had recently read about the phenomenon of girls lifting the ends of their sentences, as if unsure whether what they were saying was a statement or a question. Uptalking, it was called. I don't want to be an uptalker! she thought. That kind of talking makes me sound foolish. But it was always so much easier to turn a statement into a question, because in the end you could backpedal and say you were only *asking*, and then you wouldn't have to endure the shame of being wrong. Greer remembered lifting the edges of an imaginary skirt and curtsying at Darren Tinzler, because he'd been looming over her, tipping his cap, and she hadn't known what else to do. If you were female and insecure, apparently you sometimes lifted words at the ends of sentences, and you even occasionally lifted nonexistent garments.

She was careful now, knowing that if she rattled on for too long about misogyny, people's heads would drop down to their chests and they would all go *zzzzz*. You needed to jazz things up when talking about a topic like this; you needed to be a dynamic, electric messenger, the way Faith Frank was.

Because, she knew, everything wasn't hopeless. It was true that the women's movement of Faith Frank's day hadn't taken away contempt for women or injustice once and for all, like a mother's hand passing a cool cloth over the hot head of the world. But despite the churn of rape and sexism; despite the wrist-slap Darren Tinzler had been given; despite unequal pay, even now, and the pathetically low number of women running anything powerful, whether corporation or country; and despite how densely packed the Internet was with blocks of male solidarity and fury—"Bros before hoes!" came the musketeers' cry, as well as trolls' starkly articulated descriptions of cutting off the body parts of female journalists and celebrities—in many ways the world was so much more hospitable for women now.

Opus, that gorgeous singer with the knockout voice—and one of Faith's dream dinner-party guests—had had a recent hit with an anthem called "The Strong Ones," which could frequently be heard across campus, through speakers propped in open windows.

And that funny, sad, affectionate, sometimes slightly disturbing play *Ragtimes*, essentially a series of skits about getting your period, or not getting it, which took the characters from age twelve through adolescence and then adulthood, through pregnancies both wanted and unwanted, and wound up in a hot-flash-and-hormone stew of later life, had had a robust off-Broadway run and was now being performed inexpensively all over the country in local playhouses and community theaters. All that was needed were four folding chairs and four female actors. Celebrities liked taking part in the New York and LA productions; it had become a status symbol to be in this show, which had made a great deal of money for its playwrights, who had been best friends since sixth grade. "Sharon got her period first," according to a profile of them in the *New York Times*. "Maddy got hers a week later."

Then there were the feminist blogs that had sprung up, though *Fem Fatale* was the best and most well-known of them by far; out of Seattle, it was personal-essay heavy, often sarcastic, talking openly about sex acts and bodily functions, and described itself as "sex-positive, snark-friendly, and in-your-face, but also just a damn good read." The blog was seemingly fearless and able to address any subject, regardless of blowback.

Greer had been reading *Fem Fatale* all fall, even as the women writing for it—a bodybuilder, a porn star, and various funny and searing young cultural critics—could intimidate her with their bold confidence. They weren't much older than she was, and already they had a voice. She wondered how they'd gotten it.

Greer took a shuddery breath and said to Faith, "Maybe you can see my T-shirt? And my friend's too," she added with magnanimity. "We're wearing them because there was this assault and harassment case on campus this fall." She pronounced it like *harris*-ment. God, why? It was bad enough to be an uptalker, but now she was a pretentious uptalker. This was nothing like the natural, confident way that Faith Frank spoke. "They just held a bogus hearing," Greer added. "The decision they reached was a travesty."

She could hear the first stirrings of response in the pews—someone hesitantly clapping, and someone else saying, "That's *your* opinion," followed by mild hissing from another part of the chapel. "The person in question was told to get a little therapy," Greer said, "and now he's allowed to stay here, despite assaulting various women, including me." She needed to pause. "So that's the face on our T-shirts. Not that the T-shirts worked either. No one wanted them. So I guess I'm asking you what we can do next. How we can proceed."

Greer quickly sat back down, and Zee gave her a little hug. There was a tense, collecting moment, during which the whole chapel seemed to try to figure out whether it was worth it to get worked up all over again about this issue, which had already been decided and was officially over. Most people immediately seemed to decide it wasn't worth it; it was a school night, a shitty, wet, windy night, and it was already getting late. Three-to-five-page response papers to Machiavelli's *The Prince* still had to be written for one of the freshman colloquia. Moms and dads still had to be called. "I need more money in my account," sons and daughters would flatly announce in place of hello.

Faith Frank seemed to grow briefly taller behind the podium, and then she leaned forward onto it, resting her folded arms there, and quietly said, "Thank you for your question, which I know was heartfelt."

Greer didn't move or breathe; beside her, Zee was equally still.

"What amazes me again and again is how alarmingly improvised the legal process is on campuses," said Faith. "So what should you do? I don't know the circumstances here, but I know that you and your friends should definitely keep the conversation going."

She tipped her head up, about to say something more, but then the provost stood and said, "I'm afraid we're out of time. Let's thank our guest for this magical evening."

There was more applause, and Faith Frank receded, and that was the end of it. Greer watched as people surrounded Faith, planting themselves in her line of vision in order to have individual encounters with her. Even the ones who had been unimpressed before seemed to have been changed now. Students and professors and administrators and locals ringed her like the townspeople in an opera, though Greer hung back, with Zee right beside her. Greer had already had her public exchange with Faith Frank, and it had been nearly overwhelming and then in the end unfinished and disappointing. But there was nothing to do about it now; the crowd had thickened fast around Faith.

"God, I would love to meet her, even for a second," said Zee. "I mean, she's right here. But there are too many people, and it would just be another fangirl moment. I don't want that."

"I don't either."

"Are you heading back to Woolley?"

"Yeah. I have to work," said Greer.

"You always have to work."

"That's true."

"At least we heard her speak, and you got to talk to her," said Zee. "You did good. Want to get a pizza? Graziano's delivers late."

"Oh, sure," Greer said. Pizza would be their consolation prize: two girls alone late at night with the soft solace of warm dough.

They pushed their arms into coat holes, and Zee put her watch cap on her head and inched into a pair of big oatmeal-colored mittens. She could wear boys' clothes, girls' clothes, and it all seemed like a casually shrewd fashion choice. Together they began to walk toward the exit. People who had been surrounding Faith were now splintering off into separate, smaller groups, or wandering away individually. Greer felt oddly hollow and even a little tragic. It was as if she'd been carried for a moment, squealing, on Faith Frank's shoulders, and had then taken a tumble onto the hard, cold floor.

Now, out in the vestibule, she saw a flash of maroon, a blood-colored thing. A scarf, she realized, *Faith's* scarf, floating slightly as it was ferried by its wearer into the ladies' room; as it was ferried there by Faith Frank herself. The irony of this, she thought: Faith Frank having to use a ladies' room, submitting to the word *ladies* even now, into the twenty-first century.

"Look," Greer said quietly.

"Let's do it," said Zee. "You can finish up what you started. And we can each try to have a moment with her."

Inside the warm ladies' room, with its milky gray, acoustically sensitive tile, only one stall was in use. Zee and Greer took the ones on either side of it, trying to look like normal people availing themselves of a public bathroom. Greer sat down and dipped her head, seeing the edge of a woman's gray suede boot beneath the divider. She held very still and didn't make a sound.

From the other side of the graffitied wall, with a disturbing message scratched onto it in a very small hand—*please can anyone help me i like to cut myself*—there was a pause, and then the predictable release. The single strand, the straight line from body-opening to waiting water, the ordinariness of Faith Frank, famous feminist, peeing.

The vulnerability and realness of women were on display right here, and Faith flushed and emerged. Greer stood. Through the space between door and frame she watched Faith go over to the mirror. Zee hadn't come out of her own stall yet. She was obviously waiting, kindly allowing Greer to approach first. But Greer noticed then that Faith was leaning on the sink for a moment, closing her eyes; and then Faith sighed. Greer knew that Faith was taking a second for herself, which she probably really needed. Tonight everyone had wanted something from her, and it had all had a cumulative effect. No one was a bottomless well of giving; not even Faith Frank. Greer had been all set to burst forth and try to finish her conversation with Faith, but now she hesitated. She didn't want to add to Faith's burden. But she couldn't keep staying in here forever, so she unlatched the door and walked to the sink, smiling tentatively at Faith, attempting a state that would appear the opposite of demanding.

Faith looked at Greer in the mirror and said, "Oh, hello. You were asking me a question in there, right? And then the evening was suddenly cut off. I'm sorry about that."

Greer just looked at her. Faith was apologizing for not finishing her exchange with Greer, a stranger, in the chapel. How are you *like* this? Greer thought, she who could barely manage her own needs, and to some extent Cory's. But it all came naturally to Faith; she had been doing this for a very long time.

"That's so nice of you," Greer said. "It's just that . . . when you told me to speak up in there, it was hard for me? Listen to that. My voice just goes *up*. I don't really know how to be," she admitted, and then she stopped talking.

Faith considered her. "Tell me your name."

"Greer Kadetsky."

"All right, Greer. No one said there was one way to be. There isn't."

"But it would be nice to be able to say what I think, what I believe, without feeling like I'm about to have a stroke."

"Well, that is certainly true."

"I had a teacher who used to tell the boys to use their inside voices. I'm thinking, maybe I should use my outside voice."

"Maybe. But don't be hard on yourself; don't beat yourself up. Just try to accomplish what you can, and what you care about, while being yourself."

Greer quickly licked her dry lips. Zee was still in the stall, giving Greer this time with Faith. Any moment now she would appear, and Greer would have to cede the floor to her. "I cared about this thing that happened here," Greer said. "This entitled guy who said things and grabbed us. We testified, but it went nowhere. I feel like I don't belong at this school," she added. "It's the wrong place for me. I knew it would be wrong."

"So why did you come here?"

"My parents screwed up when it came to my financial aid," Greer said hotly. "They acted really badly."

Faith kept looking at her. "I see. So you're quiet but you're also furious," she said. "It seems like it's very hard for you to keep asserting yourself. But you're doing it anyway, because you want to find meaning, is that right?" Greer hadn't thought of it that way, exactly. But as soon as Faith said it, she understood it to be true. She wanted to find meaning. That had been the missing piece, or one of them. "I admire that," said Faith. "I admire you."

Before Greer could even think about what had just been said,

Faith reached out and took Greer's hands, as though they were about to sing a children's song. Greer could feel Faith's rings, which came together like brass knuckles. Faith stood holding Greer's hands and attentively studying her, seeing her.

"I don't want to seem ungrateful," Greer said. "I have a full scholarship, which I know is huge." She began to worry about how long they would keep holding hands; was she supposed to be the one to let go?

Faith said, "Look, you're allowed to be angry if you feel you weren't treated fairly. I know that, believe me. But yes, a full scholarship is definitely huge. Most women graduate from college with mountains of debt, and since women earn far less than men, they end up paying it back far longer, and it's absolutely crippling to them. You won't have that problem. Don't forget that, Greer."

"I won't," Greer said, and as if this were the correct answer, Faith released her hands. "But this place," Greer added, "and the way it's run, it's so unfair. After the hearing, the administration was like, 'Okay, Tinzler family of Kissimmee, Florida, we're happy to keep taking your tuition money. And we're happy to give your son a diploma at the end just like you were expecting. No worries!'"

"So, unfairness is your theme?" asked Faith.

"Isn't it yours too?"

Faith seemed to consider this, and she was about to answer when the stall door opened. Zee came out, smiling, and went to the sink, where she washed her hands with a surgeon's vigor. Greer felt disappointed that her time alone with Faith Frank had now ended, but she gallantly stepped back as Zee dried her hands and then positioned herself in the middle of the bathroom.

"Ms. Frank," said Zee. "I thought you were magnificent up there."

"Oh, thank you. That's very kind of you to say."

Probably Faith Frank had some faculty reception to go to. Maybe faculty members were gathering in President Beckerling's living room right this minute, milling around awkwardly as they waited for the guest of honor to arrive. But Faith appeared in no hurry to leave here. She turned back to her own image, scrutinizing it again briefly, without the female self-hatred that she had once warned about in an op-ed in the *New York Times* during Fashion Week.

"No, thank *you*," Zee persisted. "You gave me so much to think about. I've been your super-fan always. I know that sounds semi-stalkerish, and I don't mean it that way. When I was growing up we had to do a project for school called Women Who Made a Difference. I really wanted to pick you. But Rachel Cardozo got there first, alphabetically, and that was that."

"Ah. Sorry. So who did you end up choosing?" asked Faith.

"The Spice Girls," Zee said. "They were great too, in their own way."

"They certainly were," said Faith, amused.

"I've always related to you," Zee went on easily, "because I think being an activist is just part of me. I'm gay, which is also just part of me, and hearing you speak tonight about all the work you've done with women, and how inspiring they've been to you," Zee said, "I had a new thought, which is: Well, no wonder I like women. They're wonderful." She thrust out her hand for a shake, and Faith shook it.

"Good luck to you," Faith said. Then she looked at Greer. "Actually, I don't have only one theme," Faith said to her, returning to the exact place she and Greer had left off in their conversation. "And neither should you," Faith continued. "The thing that happened with your parents—whatever it was, Greer, it wasn't fatal. You should use that experience and find a way to be bigger than it. And the thing that happened here, the sexual assault case—"

"You think we should be bigger than that too?" Greer asked, surprised. She thought about what Faith had said in the chapel about how they might play a role in the great cause of women's equality. Because of that, she'd expected Faith to say to her now: Keep going, Greer Kadetsky. Never stop fighting. Punch your way through this. You can do it.

"No," Faith said. "It sounds like you already did what you could. You made your point. If you seem to be hounding this person, then sympathy will redound to him. It's too much of a risk to take." She took a second. "And also, what about the other women who are involved? Do they want this revisited?"

"Two of them said they definitely don't," Greer admitted. She hadn't thought about this much, but now she remembered what Ariel Diski had said. "They just want to forget about it and move on."

"Well, they get a say, don't they? Look, there's a whole world out there. Lots to see, lots to be angry about and cry about and do something about, well beyond the bounds of this campus. Other cities and communities. Go have a look." Faith appeared to be about to say something else, but then someone entered the bathroom—the provost, maddeningly interrupting for a second time, calling out, "Whenever you're ready, they're waiting for us at the reception."

"One sec, Suki," said Faith, and the provost withdrew.

Greer remembered how Faith had sighed at the mirror. Now, without thinking it through, Greer said to her, "I bet you wish you could go back to your hotel right now instead of to a faculty reception."

Faith said to Greer, "Is it obvious?" Greer thought: No, it's not obvious, but I saw it. "When you give lectures," Faith went on, "the receptions are part of it. Do you know how many turkey pinwheel sandwiches I've eaten in recent years?"

"How many?" Greer asked, then immediately felt like an idiot. It hadn't been a question.

"Too many," Faith said. "Too many damp little sandwiches in mid-decomposition, and too much sherry served in cut-glass goblets like something from a Renaissance Faire. But when you're on the academic lecture circuit it comes with the territory. Anyway," she added, "this'll be fine. Your provost is a friend of mine from the early days. So it'll be good to catch up."

"She's your friend? Oh, I see. I wondered why you came to Ryland," said Greer, but it had begun to feel as if Faith had come here just so Greer could meet her.

"And as for *this* young man," said Faith, and for a horrified moment Greer thought she meant Zee, and that all this time tonight Faith had somehow thought that androgynous Zee was *male*, an interloper in the bathroom. But Faith did not mean Zee. She was pointing at Darren Tinzler's face on Greer's T-shirt, and she said, "Just forget him. There's plenty more for you to do."

"I agree," put in Zee.

"Throw yourself into new experiences," Faith went on. "Why *not* try to use your 'outside voice'? You know, I sometimes think that the most effective people in the world are introverts who taught themselves how to be extroverts."

Then, as if remembering something, Faith reached into her large, soft shoulder bag and took out a brick of a wallet, from which she withdrew a business card. In raised letters on heavy, cream-colored stock it read:

Faith Frank

Below it was the title "Editor," and then all her contact information at *Bloomer*. Greer took the card from her and held it as though it were a winning lottery ticket. What could it be redeemed for? Probably nothing. But just having been given the card was a reward unto itself, and a kind of small shock. Faith had taken an interest in her. She had even said she *admired* her. And now Faith was giving her permission. But permission to do what? The answer wasn't at all obvious.

Twelve years later, when Greer Kadetsky herself became famous, the first chapter of the book she wrote would describe this long-ago ladies' room scene. She would playfully tease her very immature younger self for having gotten so worked up during the moment she'd had with Faith Frank, and for feeling so excited when Faith had given her the card.

In itself, that card was a kind of abstract prize, a reminder not to stay hot-faced and tiny-voiced. Faith, who a little while earlier had stood and held Greer's hands, was offering her nothing but permission and kindness and advice and an expensive-looking business card. She hadn't come out and said, "Be in touch, Greer," but it felt like more than anyone had ever given her except for Cory.

Probably, Greer thought, Faith was now going to give a business card to Zee as well, which would have made sense, since Zee was the authentically political one, the picketer and leafleter and longtime fan, at which point the two friends would be even. They could walk back to Woolley together and eat their pizza from Graziano's and sit talking about the evening and admiring the matching business cards they'd been handed.

But instead of giving Zee a card, Faith closed her wallet and returned it to her bag. Greer suddenly wished that she could peer inside. Some childlike instinct made her wonder what was in there. Thunderbolts? Gold leaf? Cinnamon? The tears of a thousand women, collected in a small blue bottle?

Faith said, "Well, the provost awaits. And you know the old saying: 'One must never keep the provost waiting.'"

"Lao-Tzu," said Zee.

Faith Frank didn't appear to hear. She opened the door and gestured toward the stenciled letters of the sign. "Good night, ladies," she said.

TWO

The Eisenstat family car was a genteel, boxy Volvo, scented lightly with machine oil. As if to further fortify that this was a car belonging to someone's parents, on the backseat was a splayed-open, wavy, crisp old copy of *Scientific American* and a chunky purple folding umbrella still in its sleeve. Zee's mother and father, both judges in the ninth judicial district in Westchester County, New York, had apparently told their daughter that the Volvo was absolutely not to be driven by her friends. "No one else is on our insurance," they had said. "The only driver can be you." Yet Zee had ignored this warning, lending the car to Greer, who had become her closest friend at college, and who was now driving it southward this Friday afternoon in February, as she had driven it twice before, both times to see Cory at Princeton.

Soon Greer was walking purposefully across the hand-polished campus. She carried a backpack with schoolwork in it, and as a result she looked like someone who went to Princeton, a thought that struck her with a complicated charge. Moments later there was Cory, leaning out the window and waving as if he were a trapped prince. He clattered down the stairs and opened the front door, and Greer pressed herself into the middle of his overly tall, thin tree of a body.

When they reached his room, the door opened upon a mess even more extravagantly chaotic than usual. Clothes, books, DVDs, empty beer bottles, hockey sticks, audio equipment, all of it massed in piles, indefensibly. "Were you guys burglarized?" she asked.

"If we were, the burglar missed a lot of Steers's expensive shit." He gestured to the Klipsch speakers, one of which was a surface for a few beer bottles. Nearby lay a lone Air Jordan 4 Thunder, too small to be Cory's. They lay together on his bed, on top of some unfolded laundry from this morning's load, which strangely still held a little vestigial warmth from the industrial dryer all these hours later. "Steers is always lending me things to wear to parties," Cory said. "Of course nothing fits. I'm way too tall for anything."

"You still feel self-conscious?" Greer asked.

"About being tall?"

"No. At Princeton."

"Well, I'm always going to be the kid with the housecleaner mom and the upholsterer dad."

"There have to be other people here like that," she said.

"Yeah. There's a girl from Harlem who lived in a shelter. Another kid grew up on a houseboat in China, and now he's TA'ing multivariable calculus. But it still gets awkward sometimes. My Secret Santa, Clove Wilberson?"

"Who is named that?"

"Well, she is. She couldn't believe I'd never worn tails. It's tricky here. Everyone's nice, but it's always possible to seem socially ignorant. In that way, you're pretty lucky being at Ryland."

She looked at him. "You're really saying that to me?"

It was still a sensitive topic, his being at Princeton and her being at Ryland. And she was still so angry with her parents, who had caused this to happen. But lately the environment felt different—both at school and inside her, that little province you carried around throughout your life, and which you were unable to leave, so you had to make the best of it. Greer had noticed, when she was very young, how, looking straight ahead, you could sort of always see the side of your own nose. Once she realized this it began to trouble her. Nothing was wrong with her nose, but she knew it would always be part of her view of the world. Greer had understood it was hard to escape yourself, and to escape the way it felt being *you*.

At the beginning of college, she had felt lonely and furious and aimless. But lately the Ryland campus was brighter and more welcoming. Sometimes conversations and events and classes and even just walks to town with a friend were exciting to her. Greer wondered what she was missing being here at Princeton this weekend; she was sure she was missing something. She didn't seethe and stew anymore. No more sitting in the Woolley lounge in despair. Even the boy from Iran had found his way by joining the Model Rocketry Club; the other members, a cheerful, eclectic group, often stopped by Woolley with their motors and their plywood, and yanked him from his room. He spent less time mourning his faraway family, and more time in this dynamic world.

You needed to find a way to make your world dynamic, Greer knew. Sometimes you couldn't do it yourself. Someone had to see something in you and speak to you in a way that no one else ever had. Faith Frank had swept in and had that effect on Greer, though of course Faith had no idea that she had done anything like that. It seemed unfair now that she didn't know. It seemed wrong not to tell her.

Greer often thought about how Faith had paid attention and been patient and kind and interested and inspiring that night. She had a frequent, grandiose fantasy of writing to Faith and saying:

I want you to know that after you came here, things changed for me. I can't really explain it, but it's true. I'm different. I'm involved. I'm more open, less resentful. I'm actually (to use the technical term) happy.

"Why not write her?" Zee had asked recently. "She gave you her business card. It has her email on it. Just send her a little note saying whatever."

"Oh yes, that's what Faith Frank really wants and needs. To be pen pals with a freshman at a shitty college that she has no memory of visiting."

"She might like to hear that things are good with you."

"No, I can't write her," said Greer. "She wouldn't remember me, and anyway it would be abusing the privilege of having her email."

"'The privilege of having her email,'" said Zee. "Listen to you. It's not a privilege, Greer. She gave you the card, and I think that's great. You should use it."

But Greer never wrote. Occasionally, professors paid attention to her, but it wasn't the same. One of them, Donald Malick, taught her freshman English colloquium, and he put a "See me" note on the last page of the paper she wrote about Becky Sharp in Thackeray's *Vanity Fair* as anti-heroine. The syllabus had taken the class headlong through very different kinds of novels, but Greer had particularly loved this one. Becky Sharp was awful in her naked ambition, and yet you also had to give her credit for being single-minded. So many people seemed muddled in their desires. They didn't know what they wanted. Becky Sharp knew. After the paper was returned to her, Greer went to Professor Malick's office, which was a ruckus of slanting books.

"You did a fine job with this," he said. "The concept of the anti-hero, or in your case anti-heroine, isn't something that everyone intuitively understands."

"I think what's interesting is that we like reading about her. Despite the fact that she's unlikable," said Greer. "Likability has become an issue for women lately," she added self-importantly. She had read an article about this in *Bloomer*, to which she now subscribed. She wished the magazine were more consistently interesting to her; she wanted to love it, because of Faith.

"You know, I've written a whole book on the anti-hero," Professor Malick explained, "and I'd like to lend it to you." He reached out and ran a finger along the spines; it made a clickety sound like a quiet xylophone. "Where are you, anti-hero?" he asked. "Come out and show your anti-heroic face. Ah! There you are." Then he yanked out the book and pressed it on Greer, saying, "I can see from your papers, which apparently you actually write yourself—will wonders never cease—that you have a good mind. So I thought you might want a little extra reading."

But he was a sour man with breath like scallions, his teaching and writing style difficult and self-referential, and no, never really likable. And though sometimes in class she let images from novels carry her away, soon she had been carried too far away, out of literature entirely and into something unrelated. Being with Cory in bed, or whatever she, Chloe, and Zee were doing on campus that night.

Later, Greer read her professor's book, because she was the kind of person who felt she had to read it because he had given it to her. Unfortunately it was resistantly academic, and, flipping through to the page of acknowledgments, she saw with some irritation that he had thanked his wife, Melanie, "for being willing to type my long manuscript for her hopelessly 'butterfingers' husband, never once complaining." He added, "Melanie, you are a saint, and I am humbled by the gift of your love." Greer thundered through the book as she'd said she would, bored by the maddening text that refused to yield. She didn't know what to say to him about it, so she said nothing, and in any case it wasn't a problem because he never asked for it back.

Greer had been spending a lot of time lately with Zee and Chloe, and also with Kelvin Yang, a Korean-American drummer who lived upstairs, and his roommate Dog—named affectionately by his family because *dog* was the first word he'd spoken. Dog was a big, handsome, and effusive person in a parka who often said, "I love you guys so much," and embraced his female friends with a sudden seizing-up of emotion. They all went to parties together, though never again at any of the frats. They traveled in one group, like children inside a camel costume. They went on snowy hikes, and took a Chinatown bus down to a climate change rally in DC, and they sent one another links to articles about the environment, or US involvement in endless wars, or violence against women, or the whittling away of reproductive rights.

That semester, Greer and Zee had been volunteering at the Talk 2 Us women's hotline in downtown Ryland. They spent long evenings in the storefront sitting around playing Boggle as they waited for the phone to ring. When it did ring every once in a while, they would listen to stories of nebulous sadness and self-hatred, or sometimes more focused despair. They would speak soothingly, as they had been trained, and stay on the line as long as necessary, finally connecting the caller with the appropriate social-service agency. Once, Zee had to dial 911 because of a girl on the phone who said she had swallowed an entire bottle of generic Tylenol after a breakup with her boyfriend.

Greer became a vegetarian like Zee. This was easy to do in college, where tofu and tempeh grew on trees. She and Zee sat in the dining hall with their plates of beige protein. Late at night they sat together in one of their dorm rooms, having long, searching conversations, which in the moments they took place seemed notable for their candor and feeling, though much later on would seem notable for how young and untried and guileless they had been.

"Tell me what it is that interests you about men sexually," Zee had said once after midnight in her room. Her roommate was off elsewhere with her hockey player boyfriend, and they had the place to themselves. The roommate's side of the room was covered with posters of the men of hockey, fierce and strong, mouths stuffed with rubber. Zee's side was an ode to equality and justice and in particular anything having to do with animals or women.

The words *men* and *women*, deposited into conversation casually, were recent additions to their vocabulary. After a few usages, they became less strange, though throughout their lives *girl* would always be in play, a useful, durable word, signaling a confident state that you would never entirely want to leave.

"Because I don't understand why people are so different from one another," Zee went on. "Why they want entirely different things."

"Well, that's genetics, right?"

"I don't mean why am I gay. I mean on a feeling level. Is it just visual, what we like or don't like about other people?"

"No, not just visual. There's the emotional part too. There's that line that Faulkner said, about how you don't love *because.* You love *despite.*"

"Yeah, I love that line. Just kidding! I never heard that line, obviously. I've never read Faulkner and probably never will. But the feeling, what makes it sexual?" asked Zee. "I mean, do you actually like the penis, objectively? 'The penis.' That sounds so official. And like it's the one penis in the world. Am I allowed to ask you that, or is it too private and I'm freaking you out right now?"

"I like Cory," Greer replied, and the answer seemed a little too easy and prissy and terse. How could you possibly explain to someone else why you liked what you liked? It was all so strange. Sexual taste. Even *regular* taste—loving caramel, hating mint. To be a heterosexual woman did not mean that you would be attracted to, let alone in love with, Cory Pinto, but Greer was. So maybe it was a good enough answer. Everyone on campus kept hooking up every weekend; it was a relentless activity, like IM-ing, but she didn't know what it would feel like to sleep with someone she barely knew, someone she hadn't grown up with.

Here she was with him now, in his college bed, which looked exactly like hers. Both beds had extra-long sheets, a weird detail of college life. After college, sheets would immediately shorten to their normal length.

They came in close for a long kiss, and as he began to lift her shirt and touch her they could hear a key crunching in the lock, and they sprang apart. Steers, his roommate, came in, the earbuds in his ears emitting a thin and distant stream of rhythmic rage. He nodded to Greer without removing them, then sat down at his desk under a spill of light from his perpetually lit gooseneck lamp ("He never shuts it off," Cory had said. "I think he's KGB and he's trying to break me") and proceeded to master a chapter of his engineering textbook. In response, Greer and Cory took out their own books from their backpacks, and soon the room was like a study hall. Cory was reading a bulky book for his econometrics class; Greer was reading *Tess of the*

D'Urbervilles, and underlining so often that some pages were entirely marked up.

"What are you marking up?" he asked, curious.

"Things that stir me," she said without self-consciousness.

Later, when Steers left the room again, she knew they would return to the bookmarked kiss, and to another kind of being stirred, or maybe a related kind. Love ran through everything Greer read—love of language, love of character, love of the act of reading—just as it ran through everything that had to do with Cory. Books had saved Greer as a child, and then Cory had saved her again later on. Of course books and Cory had something to do with each other.

With Steers gone, Greer's Abercrombie jeans would be unsnapped and unpopped and her shirt and bra removed, all by Cory, who never got tired of stripping her. He would work everything off and would then sigh and lean back on his elbows on the narrow bed and have a good look at her, and she would love this moment so much that she couldn't speak.

She hadn't been able to explain any of it to Zee. All people, male or female, were helpless in the specifics of their own bodies. Cory's penis sometimes angled to the left. "If this was an object you'd bought in a store," he'd said to her once, "you'd probably return it. You'd tell them, 'It's crooked. It looks like . . . a shepherd's crook. I want a better one.'" "I would not," Greer had said. She would not have returned it, because it was his. Because it was him. She was touched that they were discussing something that no doubt he would rather die than discuss with another person. Which meant that she wasn't another person, really; that they were tangled together and indivisible.

Before they had become that way during their last year of high school, Greer had prowled the days in what had felt like isolation. Throughout her childhood she'd carried a soft aqua vinyl pencil case with a picture of a Smurf on it, as if to prove that she was like everyone else at school, though if anyone had asked her to name a single fact about the Smurfs, she would have had to admit she knew nothing. Smurfs weren't interesting to her in any way, except as social currency, which was something she understood she partly lacked.

Her parents had never cared much about fitting into the community in their small western Massachusetts town. They sold ComSell Nutricle protein bars, setting up a display of their thin collection of wares in people's living rooms. Greer's father, Rob, also painted houses around the Pioneer Valley, but he was sloppy, sometimes leaving cans of paint on people's porches; months later, a crusted roller might be found in the azaleas. Greer's mother, Laurel, worked as a so-called library clown, performing in the children's rooms of public libraries all around the valley, though she had never invited Greer to come watch her show, and Greer had never pushed. It was just as well that she didn't see the act, she'd thought as she got older, for it would have been painful to witness her mother trying too hard, in clown makeup and a red wig.

Her parents had met back in the early 1980s when they'd both joined a community of people living on a refitted school bus in the Pacific Northwest. Everyone on that bus wanted to live differently from how they had always thought they would have to live. None of them could bear to go off separately and lead conventional, regimented lives. Rob Kadetsky had "climbed aboard," as they all called it, after graduating from the Rochester Institute of Technology with an engineering degree, and then having no luck with a few solar-related inventions that had initially seemed so promising. Laurel Blanken had climbed aboard after dropping out of Barnard and being afraid to tell her parents, to whom she dutifully sent bogus postcards each week, hoping they wouldn't notice the postmarks:

Dear Mother and Father,
My classes are amazing. My roommate got a gecko!
Luv,
Laurel

Rob and Laurel quickly fell in love on the moving bus. They stayed on board as long as they could, taking brief, seasonal jobs, showering at local YMCAs, and sometimes eating cold food out of cans. At first their life felt unconstrained, but after a while they couldn't ignore the limitations of a bus existence, and they came to hate waking up in the morning with a corrugated cheek from sleeping against the emergency lever on a window, or a rash on a leg from a night's adhesion to a vinyl seat. They wanted to have privacy, and love and sex, and a bathroom.

Life on the bus became unbearable, but regular life still seemed unbearable, too. Caught between a conventional life and an alternative one, Rob and Laurel came east and split the difference. The house in working-class Macopee, Massachusetts, bought with a little family money on Laurel's side, became not dissimilar to a school bus. It remained underdecorated and slightly uncomfortable, and it seemed almost in motion, never fully grounded. There were bathrooms, though, and running water, and no parking tickets clustered on the window.

Rob unsuccessfully tried to get companies interested in his inventions again, and he did his painting jobs, and he and Laurel sold protein bars, and they had Greer, and eventually Laurel became an occasional library clown. Over the years, they struggled financially and in other ways, never getting a grip on the world, smoking much too much pot and letting the smell of the smoke wind through the house, though Greer kept her knowledge of all this a hazy, inchoate thing, the way children both perceive and don't perceive their parents' sex lives.

But it was more than that. She had the sense, itself as strong as a trail of smoke, that the life she had with her parents wasn't normal, wasn't right. But if she told anyone about it, if anyone really knew, that would have been worse. It wasn't that she would be taken away by Child Protective Services; it wasn't like that. But families were supposed to eat together, weren't they? Parents were supposed to dole out food and ask questions like "How was your day?"

The Kadetskys had a kitchen table, though it was often spread with cases of protein bars and stacks of order sheets. Her parents weren't "social," they said, when she asked why they didn't eat meals as a family very often. "Plus, you like to read while you eat," her mother had said. Greer definitely remembered her saying it, but she wasn't sure which had come first: that comment or the actual fact. In any case, from then on she did think she liked to read while she ate. The two acts became inextricable. Greer usually made dinner for everyone: nothing elaborate, usually chili or soup or chicken parts breaded with cornflakes. Her parents would wander in at some point, grab plates of food, and take them upstairs. Sometimes she could hear giggling. Primly she stood at the oven, her face heated from the blast. Finally she made a plate for herself and sat alone at the table, or cross-legged in her bed upstairs, a book propped up behind her plate.

All that reading *took*. It became as basic as any other need. To be lost in a novel meant you were not lost in your own life, the drafty, disorganized, lumbering bus of a house, the uninterested parents.

At night she stayed up in bed reading by a flashlight, its beam quickly dwindling. But even as the light bailed, Greer read until the very last minute, consuming a yellowing circle of stories and concepts that comforted and compelled her in her aloneness, which went on year after year.

It was the middle of fourth grade when the new boy showed up in school. She realized that she had seen him on her block over the weekend. Cory Pinto, a tall, skinny, lightly olive-skinned kid, had moved into the house diagonally across the street. Within a few days after he appeared in school, Greer understood that he was as intelligent as she was, though unlike her not at all afraid to speak up. The two of them outpaced all the other students in their class, who often seemed as though they had been blindfolded and spun around each day and then told to make their way through the curriculum.

In the past, whenever the class had been broken up into reading groups, Miss Berger could do little for Greer besides let her go off by herself into the top group, the Pumas. Or, more exactly, the *Puma*. But suddenly Cory was with her in the corner, and there were two Pumas now, a pair of them. A few yards away, they could hear Kristin Vells, a member of the lowly Koalas—an odd-looking animal weighed down by its thick pelt and chunky legs—sounding out a line in her red reader, *Paths of Wonder*. "Billy wan-ted to go to the ro . . . to the ro . . . ," she tried.

"To the *rodeo*," Nick Fuchs finally cut in with impatience. "Jeez, can't you go any faster?"

There in the corner where Greer sat with the intense, too-tall new boy, they both had goldenrod-colored readers called *Paths of Imagination* open on their laps. "Book 5," it read at the top in discreet Garamond font. The plots of the stories in *Paths of Imagination* were extraordinarily dull, and in this dullness Greer trained herself the way a soldier preps through deprivation, knowing that one day it might all be useful. Apparently Cory Pinto felt the same way, for he too tolerated and absorbed the true story of Taryn the Recycling Girl from Toledo, who by third grade had collected more bottles than any child ever had, getting into *The Guinness Book of World Records* and potentially saving the world.

Cory Pinto was still a novelty, being new, but he was more than that. His voice was strong, though not obnoxious, making itself known among the other boys' voices, some of which were both strong and obnoxious, prompting Miss Berger to stand up at the front of the classroom a number of times and stare down at all the boys, sternly reminding them, "Use your inside voices!"

Greer only possessed an inside voice, no other. During breaks she sat on the floor under the whiteboard eating Pringles from a can with the other incredibly quiet girl in the class, Elise Bostwick, who had a dark, slightly troubling personality. "Do you ever think about poisoning our teacher?" Elise casually asked her one day.

"No," Greer said.

"Yeah, neither do I," said Elise.

But Cory, as skinny as anything, spoke up easily, and was popular and confident. What made it worse was that he barely ever seemed to be paying attention, and instead had a dreamy carelessness about him. Greer could see it when he stood at the bus stop on Woburn Road each morning. At age nine he resembled a thin, easygoing, quietly handsome scarecrow. She could even see it when he used the water fountain, the way he closed his eyes and articulated his mouth to anticipate the shape of the flowing water before he pressed the metal button.

Greer, in her little acrylic pressed shirts and with her Smurf pencil case, felt mowed down by him. He wasn't only smart, he was also somehow joyous and independent. Again and again, because of their intelligence and their test scores, they were thrown together, but they never discussed anything at all unless they had to. She didn't want to know him, and she didn't want him to know her either. Or her family. Greer felt hotly ashamed of her parents, as well as their house. The Pinto house, however, was spare and clean, and their refrigerator door was a vertical leaf bed of Cory's report cards and certificates and papers with gold stars, all of which Greer had seen because once, the month he'd moved in, she'd been assigned to work on an after-school project with him on Navajo customs.

She had entered his house that first time and taken note of how neat it was, and, more unhappily, the refrigerator shrine to Cory. "You're like God around here," she said to him.

"Don't say that. My mom will get mad. She's very religious."

This was another way in which the families were different. The Kadetskys were atheists—"lowercase a," her father always said, afraid that deification could slip into a nuance of typography.

Cory's very small, busy mother, Benedita, came into the kitchen, where they were working that day on their project, and she proceeded to serve them small blue bowls of *aletria*, a warm Portuguese dessert that weirdly had noodles in it. The image of a mother at the stove, fussing over food that she would make for her child and his classmate—staying there long enough to cook it, and even to watch them both eat it—was painful. Sometimes from across the street Greer had noticed the Pinto family getting ready for dinner. Then, when they sat at the table, she could see the tops of their heads going in and out of frame as they bent to eat, and it all upset her. The discrepancy. The difference. The normalcy of this family across the street, compared with the uneasy oddness of her own family. Beyond that, now, the taste of the *aletria* was shocking in its deliciousness, showing her that when a mother cooked, she could make magic. Mrs. Pinto approvingly watched them eat the dessert, proud of her own skill and enjoying the fact that they were enjoying it. Or at least that Cory was.

It was easy to tell how much she loved her son. At nine, seeing a mother's unhidden love, Greer was naked in her own lack of love. Naked and, she was sure, pathetic. Mrs. Pinto probably looked at her with sadness and sympathy: the carelessly raised little girl who lived across the street. Maybe that was why she was giving her this dish of ambrosia; it was the least she could do. As soon as Greer thought this, she pushed the dish away. There were still a few spoonfuls left, but she didn't want to eat them. The Navajo project was quickly finished, and then Greer went home, pretending indifference to this boy and his family. But something new had happened. She had seen how loved he was; she had seen that being loved that way in real life, not just in a novel, was possible.

It was eight years before she would return to the Pintos', and then, when she did, there was no *aletria*; she no longer desired it, or even consciously longed to be "parented," as people said these days. Because finally she was a full-strength teenager, and feeling separate from one's parents was, as she would say to Cory, part of the job description. It didn't often matter to her that she had been ignored and left to come of age mostly alone in the house. She had long since gotten used to it and had come to accept it as her life. But now at the Pinto house there was Cory himself—different Cory, teenage, emotionally and sexually attractive Cory, who was not only as bright as she was, but was interesting as well, with a serious face and long hands and a hair-free chest, and a way of being with her that soon seemed unrelated to the way anyone else was with her.

By then, at age seventeen, both of them were deeply involved in the furthering of their own individual brands. He was a basketball player, having been drafted onto the Macopee Magpies, where the coach didn't pressure him to be particularly good, just tall. When he wasn't on the basketball court or laboring over the grindstone of his studies, Greer had seen him standing over the ancient Ms. Pac-Man machine at Pie Land Pizza. Quarter after quarter was slipped into the slot, and as the grimy, curving display fluttered to life, Cory became the master of this world too, his name appearing at the top of the players list that the management of Pie Land had posted on the wall. People wrote in their own scores, and at the end of the week a champion was declared. PINTO had been written in green Sharpie.

It seemed unfair that he should dominate in this realm too, Ms. Pac-Man being, after all, female. Though really, Ms. Pac-Man with her sunlike orb of a head, and legs in red bootlets, lacked the parts that would separate her from her male counterpart. She was breastless, and there was no lower body to hold the sexual mysteries that would excite Pac-Man himself, he who required no "Mr." before his name.

In high school Greer had sometimes sat at Pie Land on weekends with two or three friends, all of them on the obedient, good-girl track but with a slight offbeat aesthetic, as if to compensate. The blue streak that Greer put in her hair was like a neon sign lighting up the set of delicate facial features below. Maybe Cory Pinto noticed her; maybe he didn't. But Greer and the others noticed him, and more than that they watched him from the side or back as he played the game. His wing bones shifted, his jaw went tight; he was in a state of absolute concentration.

"What's so fascinating to him about that game?" Marisa Claypool asked.

"Maybe it helps him focus," said Greer, though the question really should have been: what's so fascinating about Cory Pinto?

She watched intently as the globular Ms. Pac-Man kept eating everything in sight. Did it matter that that character was female? Greer tried not to pay too much attention to her own femaleness; the world would do that for her. But her breasts did exist now—she was no longer boobless, as she'd been called outside the KwikStop—along with a tapering waist, and a vagina that menstruated in its secret, brilliant way each month, observed only by her. No one else knew what went on inside you; no one else cared.

One day, early in the winter of their senior year of high school, Greer Kadetsky and Cory Pinto and Kristin Vells thudded off the bus onto Woburn Road, one after the other as usual, but this time after Kristin walked away Cory hitched up his huge backpack and turned around to look Greer in the face, saying, "You think that test in Vandenburg's class was fair?" Up close, she saw the pastel mustache making a soft inroad over his lip, and the small, crescent-shaped remnant of an injury scabbing on his cheekbone. She recalled his having had a small Band-Aid stuck there not too long ago, from some kind of boys-horsing-around accident.

"Fair how?" she asked, confused that he was talking to her suddenly, and with such force.

"All that material about electric potential, et cetera. None of it turned out to be on the test."

"So you learned extra," she said.

"I don't want extra," Cory said, and she realized that the unnecessary information weighed him down. It was like the way swimmers shaved their bodies, wanting nothing to get in the way of their proximity to the water.

Without any negotiation, he followed her up the path to her

house. "You want to come in," she said flatly, not a question, even though she didn't know exactly why she was inviting him, or what they would find inside now. But as soon as she opened the door she could smell a far-off scent rising up from the basement to meet them.

"Whoa," Cory said, then laughed.

"What," she said flatly.

"Superweed, parental variety," he said, and she just shrugged as if she didn't care.

Her parents' cannabis was stronger than what the stoners at Macopee High smoked. Rob and Laurel Kadetsky procured their mellow marijuana from a farmer friend and his wife up in Vermont. Sometimes in Greer's childhood she would accompany her parents on a road trip there. She'd once sat on the couch while Farmer John painstakingly plinked out "Stairway to Heaven" on the banjo, quietly singing along, *"Ooh, it makes me wonder . . ."* Beside him his wife, Claudette, showed Greer and her mother the patchwork baby dolls, made of pantyhose pulled over balled socks and bits of fabric and called Noobies, that she was trying to sell. The Noobies' faces had the vague, mashed expressions of people stoned on Farmer John's superior product.

The day that Cory came to the house, marijuana was the opening theme. It had been a while since Greer had caught a tinge of it during the day, and it upset her that on the one afternoon of her life that she had brought her longtime secret nemesis Cory Pinto home with her, this was what she'd found.

"I'm sorry, it's just funny," Cory said as he sniffed the air. "I'm going to get a contact high just being here. I'll need Cheetos and M&M's pretty soon, so get them ready."

"Shut up. And why is it funny?"

"Oh, come on. Your parents are these stoners, and you're this ambitious good girl. I think that's funny."

"I'm honored by your description of me."

"I wasn't trying to insult you. I see you all the time with college brochures. You're trying for the Ivies too, right?" She nodded. "I think we're the only ones in the grade," he said. "I think it's just us."

"Yeah," she said, softening. "I think so too." They shared a single-mindedness that you couldn't teach someone; a person had to have it as part of their neurology. No one knew how this kind of focused ambition got into someone's system; it was like a fly that's slipped into a house, and there it is: your housefly.

When Greer's mother appeared, dressed in her clown collar but not the shoes or wig, she seemed self-conscious. "Oh," Laurel said. "I didn't know you were bringing someone home. Hi, Cory. Well, I'm off to do a show." She opened the door. "Dad's down at his workbench." Rob Kadetsky sometimes puttered around in the basement, listening to cassettes of eighties bands on an old Walkman and working on something involving radio waves. Greer and Cory watched Laurel walk to her car in a modified version of the clown suit that she wore to her occasional gigs.

"What exactly does your mom do again?" Cory asked.

"Take three guesses."

"Accountant."

"Ha ha, you're hilarious."

"I mean, I've seen her outfit," he said. "Obviously I know the basic concept, but it's not like she's going under the big top, is she? Elephants and a ringmaster and a family trapeze act?"

"*Library* clown," said Greer.

"Ah." Cory paused. "I didn't know library clown was a job."

"It isn't, really, but she made it into one. It was her idea."

"Well, that's resourceful. So what does a library clown do, exactly?"

"She goes around to libraries dressed as a clown, and I guess she tells jokes to the kids and reads to them or something."

"Is she funny?"

"I don't know. I don't think so."

"But she's a *clown*," Cory said thoughtfully. "I thought being funny would be a prerequisite."

The entire time Greer and Cory were together in the house that afternoon, her father never emerged from the basement. The two of them sat tensely in the den on the old plaid couch, and Cory played with a lighter that one of her parents had left there, flicking it with his thumb and touching it to the wick of one of the small white candles that sat in little glass cups on a windowsill, furred with dust. Then he upended the lit candle and waited until a clear teardrop of wax had dripped off and landed on the back of his hand, where it immediately turned opaque.

"Amazing," he said.

"*You* sound stoned. What's amazing?"

"The way you can tolerate hot wax on your skin for a second. Why is it tolerable? If a car runs over your foot for a second, is that tolerable too?"

"I don't know, but please don't try it at home."

"And if someone else drips wax on you, does it hurt? You know the way you can't tickle yourself?" Cory said. "Is it like that?"

"I have no idea," said Greer. "I've never thought about any of this before."

In one move Cory yanked up his shirt so that his long torso was revealed. Cory and Greer were the two brains of the grade, but here he was being mostly a body, a *torso*—what a strange word. It was one of those words that if you said it aloud a few times, it disintegrated into nonsense: *Torso torso torso.*

Cory lay down on his back along the wooden coffee table, which creaked with strain, his legs hanging over the edge. "Okay, do it," he said. "The wax."

"You're going to break my parents' table."

"Come on, just do it," he said.

"You're deranged. I'm not going to drip wax on your stomach, Cory. I'm not some dominatrix on a website."

"How do you know there are dominatrices on websites? You just gave yourself away."

"How'd you know the plural was *dominatrices*?"

"Touché," he said, smirking.

"Shut up," she said, the second time today that she'd said that to him. *Shut up*, girls said to boys, and the boys were thrilled.

"Come on, I just want to see what it feels like," said Cory. "You're not going to kill me, Greer."

So she found herself tipping a lit candle onto Cory Pinto's stomach, peering down as the flame softened the wax, which formed a transparent pearl of liquid, and then the liquid met skin with a soft little *dollop* sound. He drew back the muscles of his abdomen, and exposed his teeth and said, "Shit!"

"Are you okay?" she asked. He nodded. The wax hardened into a white oval above the small depression of his navel. She thought that they were done, but he didn't get up, and then he asked her to do it again. Now she wasn't thinking about whether this would hurt him; obviously it would, but not too badly. She was thinking, instead, that the feeling of dominating Cory Pinto was new, the feeling of being in charge of him, going past him, and that it was sort of great.

The following Saturday, her parents drove up to the farm in Vermont, and Cory came over in the afternoon without even the pretense of studying or talking about school. He brought no books or notebooks or graph paper or laptop. Later, she could barely remember how they moved from school talk to what happened next. But after sitting at the kitchen table for a while, she invited him upstairs to see her room. After about thirty seconds of looking around at all her things—the snow-globe collection, the trophy for winning the spelling prize, the many, many books, from *Anne of Green Gables* to *Anne of Avonlea* to Elie Wiesel's *Night*—Cory said, "Greer," and she said, "What," and he said, "You know what." He smiled at her in a new, sly way, which both shocked her and didn't, and then he took her face between his hands, kissing her so swiftly that their teeth knocked. As soon as she felt his tongue tip she heard him groan, and the sound made her feel as if a spoon were stirring her organs around. Then Cory took her by the shoulders and maneuvered her back so she was lying down and he was lying on top of her, their hearts competing. Greer was so excited she didn't know what to do with herself.

"Is this okay?" he asked, and she couldn't think how to answer. How could it be okay? That wasn't the word for it. He touched her breasts beneath her bra, and both Greer and Cory were silent and shocked from the strength of the sensation. When he opened her bra and kissed her breasts she thought she might faint. Can you faint lying down? she wondered. In a little while, after much touching, he unsnapped her jeans with such a loud sound that it was like a log popping in a fireplace.

Then his fingers hovered tantrically inside the nanospace between jeans and underpants, and he started to get inexplicably and weirdly chatty. "I'm going to make you come," he said in a voice that was unfamiliar. "I'm going to make you want it," he went on. Then he asked, a little unsurely, "Do you want it?"

"Why are you talking like that?" she said, confused.

"I was just saying what I felt," he said, but now he looked as if he'd been caught in something.

And though, once in a while in bed after that day, he would speak to her in a similar, strange way, she was usually able to bring him around quickly to being himself. Not that being themselves was any less disorienting. The freedom of that, the idea that you could have preferences, and that they were your own and it was up to you to know what they were—you and the other person—terrified her.

The second time they were together in bed, he boldly whispered, "So where's your clit?" The word was almost alarming when spoken by Cory and actually meant to refer to a part of Greer.

"*What?*" she said, because it was all she could think to say. She was stalling.

"Where is it exactly? Show me." His voice, after this moment of bravado, faded out.

"It's over here," she said, gesturing vaguely and miserably. In fact, she didn't know. She was seventeen years old and she had been too embarrassed until now to comprehend her own anatomy. She'd had hundreds of orgasms alone in bed, but she could not draw a map to the place where they had originated.

That night, after Cory had gone home to his house across the street, and Greer was left in the quiet wonder of what had happened between them, she went online and Googled the words *clit* and *diagram*, so that now she would know, and then next time he would know too. If you ever wanted to get an accurate picture of who you are, Greer thought years later, all you had to do was look at everything you'd Googled over the past twenty-four hours. Most people would be appalled to see themselves with this kind of clarity.

Now she and Cory were constantly together. He told her about his parents, how he'd felt ashamed when he was younger that they had accents and menial jobs. She told him about being an only child, and having parents who were often indifferent to her. "I will never be indifferent to you," he said, and she realized that he was on her side, and that she wasn't alone. They were becoming seriously attached, and their sexual activity was a mix of gasping thrill and excruciating misfire. Sometimes he accidentally hurt her, and sometimes her own hands and mouth became misguided hummingbirds. They tried and tried. They had petty arguments about whether they were compatible.

"Maybe you're not the right person for me," he said once, testing out the words.

"Fine. Maybe you should go out with Kristin Vells," she said. "You can help her with reading. I bet she'll appreciate that."

"Believe me, we won't be doing any reading."

Greer turned away, upset and hugging herself, and she realized that she had seen this kind of behavior in TV shows and movies: the emotionally fragile girl with her arms crossed protectively around herself, maybe even stretching out the arms of her sweater. She didn't understand why she was so easily willing to take on this predetermined female role. But then she realized she actually sort of liked it, because it made her part of a long chain of women who had done exactly this.

Sometimes all it took was a distraction to make them both return to themselves. They would play one of his three-and-a-half-year-old brother Alby's video games for an hour or two, or send IMs filled with private jokes—it was amazing how quickly private jokes could develop—and then they would both remember they were compatible. "I don't know that I love you yet," Greer warned Cory one afternoon when they lay brazenly in her bed with her parents moving around downstairs. But she had said it only because she did know.

"That's all right," was all Cory said. But they knew that this was love, and that this was also desire, the two forces forming a substantial and circular current.

Then, a week later, Greer said, "Remember what I said about love? Is it too late to change it?"

"It's not an answer on a test."

"Well, okay. Then I love you," she said quietly, trying it out. "I do."

"I love you too," he said. "We're even."

At her house the next afternoon, now certifiably in love and even, they had what was considered actual sex. It was a little embarrassing and certainly imperfect—Cory gnawed at the condom wrapper for a long, tense moment—though occasionally, over time, it would become perfect. Her house was used for exploration; in the Pinto house they weren't even allowed into his bedroom, so instead they sat in the living room on the sofa with the plastic covers zipped onto it, and there was always fragrant food cooking, and sometimes an aunt wandered in or out.

What she particularly liked about being at Cory's house was that Alby was often with them, lolling all over them on the couch. Alby was a late addition to the Pinto family, having been born when Cory was fourteen. Alby's dented, empty juice boxes dotted the back of the Pinto family car, along with his action figures lying facedown or faceup, bent-armed or straight-armed, frozen in mid-kick or mid–karate chop, waiting for him to return to the car and reanimate them. Alby resembled a small Cory, funny and antsy and precocious, very likely brilliant; and he loved his older brother and also seemed to love Greer.

Alby often carried his box turtle with him, holding it as tenderly as if it were a newborn lamb. The turtle had wandered unobserved into the Pinto yard one day a few months earlier and had sat for a long time in the scrub grass in the sun, giving the appearance of a rock, or an antiquarian law book, dusty, brown, gold, green. But Alby had recognized it for what it was and said, "That's my turtle," claiming it immediately and naming it Slowy. "Because they are *slow*," he explained to his family.

Alby had easily determined that the turtle was male. "The boy turtles have red eyes," he said, because he had read it in a children's science book, having learned to read at age two and a half. Alby would lay the two-pound box turtle down on the couch and then he would lay his own thirty-eight pounds on top of his older brother, who fastened him in place. Alby asked Greer to play video games with him; he was an expert, with advanced hand-eye coordination. He often wanted her to look at books with him—they were both obsessed with books—and Greer found that soon they were making their way through entire series together, taking turns reading aloud. He liked the *Encyclopedia Brown* series best, books that she had once loved.

"Why did the Meany parents name their son Bugs?" Alby asked, concerned.

"That is an excellent question."

"Or, maybe it was the author, Donald J. Sobol. Bugs Meany already has a bad last name. Now he has a bad first name too. It doesn't seem fair."

"You even feel sympathy for the bully," she said. Alby burrowed in hard against her.

How resourceful people are, Greer thought now as she lay in bed with Cory in his dorm, recalling this moment. Cory's little brother had burrowed into her, ensuring that even when they were apart, she would remember him and love him. And still she kept burrowing into Cory, and also, distantly and metaphorically, into the spectral figure of Faith Frank, who had swept down upon Greer's newly adult life and made her want something. We burrow and burrow, attempting a hidden path. We are canny in our burrowing, Greer thought, though we never want to admit it. Across the dorm room, Steers kept the light on all night.

There was a moment in the middle of college, imperceptible at the time as an actual moment, when talk started to shift from classes, majors, parties, and symbolism in literature to jobs. Once it happened, jobs won out, and classes and majors and novels and academic debates took on a sweet, quaint whiff of the past. Jobs made you sit up straighter and scheme, trying to think of any connections you had ever made and could now use. Everyone was thinking and worrying a little about the long run, that abstract road that supposedly might lead to happiness, before it led to death.

The science majors, if they weren't applying to medical school, were thinking about working in a lab, while some of the liberal arts majors were planning careers in early-childhood education or sales. Or else, like a few people they knew who had already graduated, they imagined themselves working in publishing, answering phones in sprightly voices, saying, "Magda Stromberg's office, this is Becca!" dozens of times a day, when really they wanted to be Magda Stromberg, not Becca. A number of them would be taking jobs in fields that possessed a certain impressive weight simply as words: Marketing. Business. Finance.

None of them wanted to be like the occasional Ryland graduate who stayed around and haunted the campus. There was one who had graduated three years earlier, and he worked as a barista at the Main Bean downtown, and made a show of leaving whatever book he was currently reading splayed open, title facing up, beside him next to the pumps of syrup and the pitchers of steamed milk, and he'd try to catch the eye of one of the current students buying coffee. The student would take his cup and add packet after packet of raw sugar, gearing up for a paper he had to write that night, while the barista no longer had to gear up for anything except another day behind the counter. It was bewildering the way a place that had held you tightly for four years simply released you at the end, no longer responsible.

Greer had started to imagine becoming a writer; she saw herself writing essays and articles and eventually maybe books with strongly feminist themes, though probably that was the kind of work she would do late at night at first. She would have to start earning a salary to support her writing. She couldn't have a life like her parents. But if she had a real job, and didn't have to fall into poverty, then she could try to write when she could, and maybe she would have some luck.

Though Zee was definitely more of the nonprofit type than Greer was, now Greer could see working for a while in communications for someplace that was *good*. She also imagined that she might write to Faith Frank and tell her about it: "As I try to figure out what to do with my life, I have a job writing the in-house newsletter at Planet Concerns. Again, this is probably because of the conversation we had in the ladies' room. I'm trying to make meaning, as you suggested."

Soon Greer was saying to Cory, unasked, "A nonprofit. That could work at first, while I write at night, don't you think?"

"Sure," he said easily, but he didn't really know what he was talking about; neither of them did.

"Chloe Shanahan's friend works for an organization that brings art to people with disabilities. Her brother is blind," Greer added, then felt she had to put in, "Not that she wouldn't have worked there anyway."

"But probably she wouldn't," Cory said.

"True."

It seemed that you came to what you ended up doing, and who you ended up being, through any number of ways. Being a writer had a dreamy impossibility about it, but she liked to imagine it anyway. She became increasingly able to see herself writing on the side while working someplace decent and honorable. "It won't be marketing," she told Cory. "It won't be fashion. It won't be," she added gratuitously, "library clown."

Cory had become friends with two people he'd met in a class on economic development at Princeton, and after talking fiercely around the seminar table about poverty, and later continuing the conversation outside of class, the three of them talked about developing a microfinance app after college. Both Lionel and Will came from wealthy families that were considering investing in their sons' app. The three of them were now buzzed with the idea of it, swarmed with plans.

"I think this is actually going to happen," Cory said to Greer. "It's exciting, though it has to be handled right. There are people out there throwing around these terms, *microfinance, microloans*, but essentially ripping other people off. When it works it can make a huge difference to small-business owners. But the interest can be incredibly high. So we're going to do it in a way that's low-interest. We're not going to rip anyone off. Also, women apply for these kinds of loans a lot," he added, and though this remark was a self-conscious nod to feminism, a nod to her, she didn't mind.

Greer imagined Cory in shirtsleeves in a little office somewhere in Brooklyn, his phone blowing up with the sound effects of a cash register dinging as loans went through. But mostly, in this image, she saw Cory's happiness. At the end of an industrious day, he would come home from microfinance, and she would come home from nonprofit. They would talk about policy, and problems Greer was having with her writing, and drink beers on the fire escape, and once in a while from that fire escape they would watch fireworks, which appeared at intervals over the skies of New York for no good reason except a general excitement about the city—living there and being young, wanting to see color shoot across its skies. Late at night, when Cory slept, she would stay up beside him in bed with her laptop, writing fiction and essays and notes for articles that she hoped to publish. She'd already started keeping a notebook of ideas.

After college they were going to be living together in Brooklyn and hoping they could find a way to afford it; this was the plan now. They'd have a small, bare-bones apartment. Greer saw a jute rug on the floor, and imagined its unforgiving texture, and then the cold floor a few feet later as she padded to the bathroom after sex in the night, or before work in the morning.

"Neither of us is great at cooking," Greer noted. "We can't microwave everything when we live together."

"We'll learn," he said. "Though can you tolerate me cooking meat, and turning the place into a meat palace?"

"Separate pans and good ventilation," she said. "That'll help." Vegetarianism had become a fixed state for her, and she never wanted to go back.

Now, when Greer couldn't sleep sometimes, she thought of her future with Cory, each detail burnished and discrete. She imagined Cory's size-13 foot peeping out at the end of the bed, the two of them sleeping together every night, finally, and no longer in a bed meant for a child or a college student. A bed that could hold both of them easily, casually.

Whenever you saw a young couple that had recently moved in together, you knew there was something substantial going on with them. All that love, all that fucking, all that flipping through catalogues on a treasure hunt for linens and furniture and small appliances that had been designed expressly with them in mind. The prices had to be slightly out of range, and yet, upon reflection, not! We can do it, the couple said to each other. We can make it work. The prices spoke of the big step this would be, buying this table or chair or immersion blender; but unlike in the past, when men would leave home decoration and kitchen assembly entirely to women, putting together a life was now a joint activity. It could happen in bed, even, where you might study a website or a catalogue together—the new, engrossing literature of the first flush of adulthood—warm body to warm body, in a festival of imagining. To commit to actual things composed of wood and metal and fabric was to make real the vagueness and unreality of love.

For now, they were tolerating college apart well. They had full course loads, and there had been a thrilling election followed by a new president; and they made weekend trips to see each other, though sometimes Greer could perceive little incomplete flashes of the life Cory led that had nothing to do with her, and she was anxious about them. He might say, "Steers and Mackey and Clove Wilberson are forcing me to join the Frisbee team."

"They are physically forcing you?"

"Yes. They said I must surrender."

She had to wonder about Clove Wilberson, whose name came up too often. Greer Googled her, and found an entire Clove Wilberson dossier online, much of it having to do with field hockey, which Clove had played at St. Paul's School and now played at Princeton. A photo of her, mid-run, featured assertive bones beneath the skin of an oval face, and the obvious exertion that moved her blood. Her ponytail was captured mid-flight. She had enviable upper arms. She was definitely much better-looking than Greer, who sat studying the photo and silently asked: Clove Wilberson, have you been to bed with my boyfriend?

But it was a question she didn't really want answered. Greer and Cory had originally acted as though being apart for college was a natural occurrence, though all the couples they knew— even the ones at the same school—had broken up after a while, getting knocked off one by one in a kind of protracted Agatha Christie rubout.

Maybe, Greer thought, the sense of longing helped keep her and Cory together. She herself had had moments when she'd almost strayed from him. Sitting at someone's off-campus party late at night once in the fall of junior year, she felt the hand of her friend Kelvin Yang stroking her hair. They'd all been singing the song "Hallelujah" with its three million verses, while Dog accompanied them on ukulele. They were sitting on a rug in a dim room, wailing the beautiful, dirgelike song that reminded them of young love and what could so easily be lost, and there was big, built drummer Kelvin beside her. She let him stroke her hair and she even leaned against him, noting his unfamiliar smell with almost clinical distance, then deciding she liked it, then actually lying down in his lap. He leaned over and gave her a kiss, a couple of kisses, notching them here and there in a way that was like a parent but not. Greer thought about how her own father had rarely kissed her when she was growing up, and she wondered if, because of this, she had become one of those women who would always disastrously need a man front and center in her life, and who couldn't manage without one.

Was it okay that she needed Cory the way she did? What would Faith Frank have to say about this? Everyone seemed to want love, whether they admitted it or not. This Greer knew as she let herself be kissed by Kelvin, just a little. She disliked it when her friends remarked on the longevity of her relationship with Cory, as if it were such an unnatural feat. "You guys are amazing," said Zee. "I have never had a relationship that lasted even two months."

Cory was the only one she wanted to see in the morning, not a stumbling fleet of dorm-mates, and not a roommate in some tiny railroad apartment. Roommate culture was booming. People found other people to live with easily these days through websites and message boards, and they moved in together and marked their milk in the refrigerator and left each other notes when something had been done that wasn't to their liking. A friend who had graduated a year earlier described standing tensely in place when she found a note that read, "Kindly dispose of sushi containers THE NIGHT you get them. The next day it smells like a fish factory in here, FOR FUCK'S SAKE."

The *kindly* was deadly. Greer and Cory would never write *kindly*. Their own sushi containers, which would hold his tuna and eel, and her inside-out avocado roll, would be disposed of or not, and if their little phantom apartment smelled like a fish factory, so be it. Love was a fish factory—love, with all its murk and stink. You had to really love someone to live with him or her in close quarters.

"Soon," Cory said, "soon," willing time to pass in the way it did when you were young. Later, Greer knew, when they were finally living together and taking for granted the small details of a life spent close-up in a broth of shared DNA, and swirled sheets, and a havoc of days and nights, she would think, Slow down, slow down. But for now, still in college, heading toward what was theirs, they both thought, Hurry up.

THREE

Cory had been born Duarte Jr., but because his name was foreign and his parents were immigrants with accents, right before the move from Fall River when he was nine years old he'd announced that he was changing Duarte Jr. to something else. The new name he picked was as American as possible. Cory was the main character on *Boy Meets World*, which Duarte Jr. had watched obsessively for years. *Cory* was such a popular and reassuring and normalizing name. He had to beg his parents to call him that, though his father refused. "Duarte is my name too," his father said. His mother was resistant at first as well, but then she caved out of love.

"Is important to you?" she asked, and he nodded, so she said, "Okay."

Not long after his new name had become fully affixed to him, he realized it was embarrassing to have named himself after a character on a TV sitcom. But Duarte Jr. had become Cory now and forever, an American boy like all the other American boys in school. And he did fit in well in Macopee—an outgoing, quick-witted, exceptionally tall boy. In Fall River there had been a significant Portuguese population. Here it was different. When Duarte Sr. and Benedita came to the Macopee science fair, his mother stood in front of an experiment involving condensation and asked in a loud and unembarrassed voice, "What this thing do?"

The following day, Cory heard the condensation kid say to someone else, using an accent, "What this thing do?" followed by skittering laughter.

Cory burned from this; he twisted and he burned, but he fiercely ignored it, drawing attention away from his parents by continuing to be smart and strong and funny and capable and outgoing. Somehow these traits, strenuously demonstrated, were the antidote to being seen as different. Only when he got home from school at the end of the day, unlooping the straps of his backpack and dropping it onto the floor in the front hall of the house, did he feel he didn't have to prove himself. He knew he could be himself at home, and that it would be welcomed.

His mother had loved him since birth with fierce reverence, never holding back the way his father did, but instead depositing trace kisses all over Cory as if scattering rose petals. He came to assume that he had earned this kind of treatment, and over time he figured that one day a girl would love him the very same way. He was confident of this throughout childhood and then even during the hideous period in which he was so underweight and long-limbed that he looked like one of those handmade wooden folk-art marionettes. He was confident even as a vague mustache formed itself like spreading mildew above his lip, while the rest of him stayed boylike, the chest concave. Then he was no longer a marionette, but instead he was one of those mythical half-and-half animals. Except instead of being half-man, half-

horse, Cory was half-man, half-boy, forever trapped in a morti-
fying *between* state.

Still, somehow, he remained confident, having spent his entire life with his parents praising him and calling him Genius
One, or Gênio Um. His brother, Alby, was Genius Two, or
Gênio Dois. Both boys had been similarly anointed, and all they
had to do was keep being brilliant and industrious. They were
never asked to help out around the house; that was women's
work. All they needed to do was learn, and prove themselves
academically, and soon suitable rewards would come.

One day in seventh grade on a trip to the relatives' house in
Fall River for Christmas dinner, his cousin Sabio Pereira, known
as Sab, who had been his close buddy when they were very young,
beckoned Cory upstairs. From deep inside his closet Sab proudly
produced a copy of a magazine called *Beaverama*. "Where'd you
get this?" Cory asked, shocked, but Sab just shrugged and gloated
at his secret access to hard-core porn. The women in the photos
were pliant, both literally and figuratively open.

"I'm going to fuck this one's brains out," Cousin Sab cheer-
fully said, the two of them sitting cross-legged on the bed with
the magazine between them like a little warming campfire. "I'm
going to seriously come all over her face. She's going to want it
from me again and again. She's going to *need* it from me."

"You're thirteen," Cory felt he had to point out.

The boys looked at Sab's rotating carousel of porn whenever
Cory's family came for a visit, and over time the images became
less new and less shocking. They stared at the photos, studying
them hard for their future application in their own lives. One
month there was a pictorial called "She's Hot 4 U—*Sizzle!*" in
which a girl dripped candle wax all over a guy's naked torso.
Other times, Cory and Sab sat together actually reading the text

in *Beaverama* that was thinly scattered among the pictures. *Beav-erama*'s advice columnist, Hard Harry, wrote:

> *Learn how to find her clit quickly. Ask her to show you where it is—she'll like that! Guys, if you can make her come she will be sooooo grateful, she will do anything to you. And I mean anything. Seriously not exaggerating!!*

"What do you think 'anything' means?" Cory asked Sab. His cousin shrugged. Neither of them had enough imagination yet to even think of what else a girl could do to you, what powers she possessed, which you would want her to unleash upon your naked form. But eventually, going online to meet their daily porn requirements, they learned. The men in these scenes shouted out things to women, and the women shouted back. "I'm going to make you come!" the men cried. "Yes, yes!" the women cried back. "Do it now!"

The girls Cory knew at school had none of these skills. They could, though, walk the balance beam, and they could tap out IMs to one another at the speed of light. Over time he went out with a couple of them and furiously kissed them and touched them, and then later on he went further with two different girls, trying out the language that had come from all the long hours spent in the company of porn.

By senior year of high school, many of the boys in his grade played a game called Rate 'Em. Cory, fully handsome at this point and finally inhabiting his body as if he actually owned it and didn't lease it from a disreputable place, was walking down the hall when Justin Kotlin grabbed his arm and said, "Pinto, you in? Rate 'Em time."

Cory turned to see a row of boys leaning against the wall. Every time a girl approached, the boys huddled together and each of them gave her a number rating, and then Brandon Monahan added the numbers up on his Texas Instruments calculator and came up with the average, which was hastily recorded on a piece of paper and then held up for everyone to see. Kristin Vells got an 8 (she lost points for being a skank), and Jessica Robbins, who was super-religious and wore plain jumpers and black shoes with buckles on them like a Pilgrim, got a 2.

"Sure, whatever," he said. Distantly then, he saw that Greer Kadetsky was wandering their way. Though they were still in all the same accelerated-track classes, he hadn't really spoken to her in years. He had seen her over time; she had an after-school job a few days a week in the mall at Skatefest, where the employees wore horrible outfits and matching hats, but he had never really looked at her critically before. Now he did. She had an appealing but imperfect face, a spot of electric blue in her brown hair, and black jeans and an Aéropostale T-shirt that stretched across her smallish breasts. But he could see for himself now, for the first time over all these years, that quiet, fiercely hardworking Greer was also crisp and ready and serious and special, and maybe, actually, even a little bit beautiful. This realization, coming after all this time, was almost startling.

Beside him, all the boys huddled over a calculator like employees at H&R Block during tax season, and finally a number appeared, which was then scrawled with a flourish on a piece of paper.

6

Greer Kadetsky was a 6. No, no, that was all wrong, Cory thought; she wasn't a 6, that was way too low, and even if she was, that number would make her feel bad. He didn't even think before taking the piece of paper from Nick Fuchs, who was routinely called Nick Fucks, when he wasn't being called Nick Pukes.

"What are you doing, Pinto?" Fuchs said as Cory turned the notebook upside down, transforming the 6 into a 9.

Cory had rescued Greer from a moment of public humiliation, but she wasn't even looking. Turn around, Greer Kadetsky, he wanted to say. Turn around and see what I have done for you.

But she had her narrow back to the row of boys, and the bell rang and everyone started to scatter. Cory crushed up the piece of paper in his hand and walked away, and as he did that Nick casually stuck out a leg and tripped him. "You piece of shit," Nick whispered as Cory went down, his cheek scraping the sharp edge of a locker where the metal had peeled back. A little flap of skin had opened on his face, and he knew he would need to go see the nurse, and that there would be Neosporin in his immediate future. But the pain wasn't too bad, and all he could really keep thinking about was that he had rescued and praised Greer, and had now taken an injury for her, and yet she knew none of it. That same afternoon, on the bus, he sat directly behind her, with the bandaged cut on his cheekbone lightly throbbing while he studied the back of her head. It was a very well-shaped head, he noticed. It was definitely not the head of a 6.

Greer had nothing in common with the women of *Beaverama* and all those websites, except that beneath her standard-issue high school clothes she possessed a good body, apparently full of holes the way all girls' bodies were. It could make you slightly psychotic if you really focused on the idea that girls had holes under their clothes. Holes that suggested, in the absence they pointed out, that they could be filled, and that you could do the filling. He had turned a 6 into a 9; together the numbers made 69, which embarrassed him even to think about, but right away he saw two heads bobbing up and down in a bed like separate buoys in the ocean.

His deliberate, crafted sexualization of Greer Kadetsky increased day by day. It was only three weeks after Greer Kadetsky had been rated and Cory had been deliberately tripped and sliced his cheek on the locker edge that he decided it was time to establish contact with this girl he now contemplated deeply and continually. He turned to her one afternoon as they got off the bus and said something inane about Vandenburg's physics test being "unfair." Then he lightly followed Greer up the path to the Kadetsky house, and from there it began.

His cousin Sab almost immediately sensed the change in him, for each time the Pintos went to Fall River lately, Cory turned down Sab's invitation to look at porn. "Oh come on, don't be a pussy. Instead, come *look at* pussy," Sab said. But Cory didn't want this anymore, and Sab called him a faggot. Sab had been changing too, becoming mean and angry, and doing who knew what with his friends. Hard drugs. Dark things. When they saw each other, there were long, cold silences. But Cory was far away from Sab now; he was leaving him, and leaving his whole family.

"When you're both in college I'm going to visit you," Alby, now four, said one afternoon when Greer was over at the Pinto house and they were sitting in the living room. "I'll bring my superhero sleeping bag and unroll it on the floor of your room."

"Wait, which of us are you going to visit, Alby?" Cory asked, his hand in Greer's hair, lazily rubbing her head. "That is, if Greer and I aren't at the same college, which we really hope to be. Preferably at one of the Ivies," he added with casual arrogance.

"First I'll visit Greer, then you," said Alby. "And one day you can visit me at my college."

"And I can sleep in *my* superhero sleeping bag when I do," Cory said.

"No," said Alby seriously. "That makes no sense. When I go to college you'll be . . . thirty-two. You won't want a sleeping bag. You and your wife will want a bed."

"Yes, Cory," said Greer. "You and your wife will want a bed."

"Greer could be your wife," Alby said. "But she has to convert to Catholic like us."

"How do you know about converting?" asked Cory.

"I read about it."

"Where, in *The Little Golden Book of Converting*? You scare me, Alby. Slow down, brother. You don't have to know everything already."

"Yes I do. Ask me a question, and I'll tell you the answer."

"Okay," said Cory. "When did the dinosaurs go extinct?"

Alby slapped his forehead. "That's too easy," he said. "Sixty-five million years ago."

"He'll be good when he gets to *Paths of Imagination*," Greer said. "He'll whip right through it."

"Yeah, he'll kick Taryn the Recycling Girl's butt."

"By the time he's in school," said Greer, "Taryn the Recycling Girl will be sitting on her porch thinking about the highlight of her life, the time when she was a child and got into *The Guinness Book of World Records*."

"Actually, she'll probably be dead," said Cory. "The toxic chemicals in all the bottles she collected will have given her cancer and killed her."

"Who's going to be dead? Give me another one," said Alby, full of lofty excitement.

Cory thought about this. "Okay," he said, and he smiled at Greer. "Try this one. Define love."

Alby stood up on the plastic surface of the couch, which crunched beneath his feet. He wore a thin old red Power Rangers sweatshirt, handed down from Cory and already too small, the image and the lettering half rubbed off and cryptic. "Love is when you feel, like, oh, oh, my heart hurts," Alby said. "Or like when you see a dog and you feel like you have to touch its head." He looked at Greer. "Like the way Cory is touching your head now." Cory stopped the movement of his hand, just froze there in her hair.

"Whoa," said Cory softly, taking his hand away. "You're like the Dalai Lama, man. I'm afraid to let you go walking around outside. Some people might come and bring you back to their country and make you live in a gated palace."

"That would be good," said Alby. "They can do that if they want."

Greer suddenly reached over and touched Alby's small, sleek head. Cory watched his girlfriend pet the head of his brother, as if Alby were a cocker spaniel, smooth-furred and enormous of eye.

Cory and Greer would try to be together for college; that was what they agreed, and they were optimistic it would happen. On the spring day when most of their college decisions would be revealed online after five p.m., they rode home from school barely talking. The hydraulic doors of the district school bus unshuttered and released them with a vacuum pop onto the mouth of Woburn Road. Behind them, distantly, was Kristin Vells. Kristin was not on an academic track, and so they had never even had a conversation with her over all these years; they thought she was dumb, and she thought they were dumb, each in a different way. Kristin went home to her house, probably to smoke and nap, and Cory and Greer ran pounding down Woburn toward the Kadetskys'. It was only three thirty. They lingered for a while in Greer's bedroom, undisturbed.

"Whatever happens today, we're solid, right?" he asked her. "And we'll be solid next year too."

"Of course." She paused. "Why, what are you expecting to happen?"

He shrugged. "I don't know. It's just that they don't know us, these admissions committees. They don't know what we're really like. Or that we do best when we're with each other."

They had decided that they would find out their college decisions together, first at her house, and then at his. At five p.m. Greer went first, sitting at the kitchen table and logging in to the relevant websites one after another, alphabetically. Her hand shook a little as she entered her password and waited. "We received a record number of applicants . . . ," came the tumble of words. The shock of rejection was strong: Harvard, no. Princeton, no.

"Oh shit, oh shit," said Greer, and Cory gripped her hand.

"It's insanely competitive," he murmured. "But really, screw them, Greer. They're just wrong."

"This is what you meant when you said we're solid, isn't it?" Greer said, her voice rising. "You thought I wasn't going to get in, and you were trying to prepare me."

"No, of course not."

The Yale decision still hung there at the end of the alphabet, but by now Cory felt sorry for her and worried for himself, and didn't hold out too much hope for her for Yale, if she hadn't gotten into those others. Greer clicked indifferently on the Yale link and entered her password, and when the music flooded out all at once, the Yale fight song—*"Bulldog! Bulldog! Bow wow wow!"*—they both started to shout, and then Greer cried and he put his arms around her, so relieved, and said, "Nice work, Space Kadetsky."

Her parents wandered in then, her father looking for something to eat and her mother cradling her flip phone and talking into it about a new shipment of ComSell Nutricle bars, "which," she was saying, "we now have in Banana Blast."

"What's going on?" Rob asked, and then Greer told them, and he said, "Oh shit, it's already five? We lost track."

Cory wanted to say to Greer's parents: You lost track? Are you shitting me? Don't you know what you have here with this girl? Don't you know how hard she works, and how much she loves it? Why can't you be more proud of her? Why can't you appreciate her? It's so easy to do.

"Mom, Dad, I got into Yale," Greer said. "You can read the letter. I left it up on the computer."

Next he and Greer ran across the road and up the incline, and right away Cory sensed something strange going on inside his own house. Both of his parents knew that today was when decisions would be handed down. They were so invested in this whole process, and yet where were they? They were behaving almost as cavalierly as the Kadetskys. They should have been waiting for him by the door, he thought. But then his mother was upon him out of nowhere, throwing her arms around him. "Around my legs," he later insisted, hyperbolic. How such a small woman could have given birth to this tall, thin pole-child was bewildering, as even Cory's father was only of medium height and build. Their first son had gone beyond them in all ways.

"What's going on?" Cory said, and deeper in the house other voices rose up. He heard his brother shouting, "He's home!" followed by the thumping of Alby's sneakers as he raced overhead and then leaped down the stairs with Slowy in hand, arriving at the same time that Aunt Maria pushed into the room from the kitchen, carrying a large aluminum pan containing a sheet cake. His father was right behind them, carrying a second cake. Cory was confused. The first cake was spread thickly with blue-and-white frosting, with a brush fire of candles on top. The air in the room was tinged with a distinctive birthday smell.

"Look at the picture," his aunt said, and at first neither Cory nor Greer understood why the cake had been decorated with an illustration of an animal.

"A cow?" Cory asked. "But why?" It did look like a cartoon cow, though not quite, with a freckled face and an angry expression. No one answered, and Cory said, "Listen, you guys. You know the decisions are live online right this minute, right? These cakes are great, but I really have to go check."

"Cory," Alby said, gesturing in the air with the hand that held his turtle, which waved in halfhearted protest. "Don't you get it?"

"No."

"It's a bulldog."

As soon as Cory hesitantly said, "Yale?" his father presented the second sheet cake to him. This one was frosted white and orange with a big rust-colored animal in the center. Though it too resembled a farmyard animal, Cory and Greer both understood now that it was supposed to be the Princeton tiger.

"You got into both places. A full ride!" said Alby, as if he really understood the significance of this.

Cory stared at his family. "But how do you know already? I haven't even logged in."

"Forgive me," said Benedita. "I enter your log-in and then your password. I know them."

"Greer123," said Alby, and over to the side Cory could see Greer's pleased expression. He ought to have been furious with his mother for denying him his moment of reckoning, but he wasn't. Also, she was so happy right now; both of his parents were. Tonight the news would be all over Fall River, and all over Portugal. "Harvard turned you down," Alby continued breezily. "But who needs them, right?"

The crimson cake, baked alongside the others, just in case, was still in the kitchen, and would later be tossed in the trash. Benedita had spent the day baking with Aunt Maria, whose own son, Sab, wouldn't be going to college. Out of all the cousins, Cory and Alby had long ago been pegged as the most academic ones. Cory had already proven himself in this way, and Alby was certainly going to follow, and most likely exceed, his older brother. The day they had discovered Alby could read was when, still a toddler, he'd been gazing at a box of Fruity Pebbles at the breakfast table, and in the clatter of the morning kitchen had quietly begun to whisper to himself, "Red 40, Yellow 6, BHA to help protect flavor."

Now Cory would have to pick between Yale and Princeton. A bulldog or a tiger: what a decision. If he went to Yale, he and Greer would be together. So really, it wasn't a decision at all. Yale was where he would go. Greer and Cory sat at the kitchen table eating slices of different-colored cake, both of which tasted identical on the tongue. No one in the world had ever eaten sheet cake for taste, only for celebration. "Greer got into Yale too," Cory told his family, and they exclaimed politely over her success.

"Full ride?" Alby asked.

"I didn't look yet. I was so excited." Greer stood up from the table. "I have to go home and see."

"I'll come," Cory said.

Back at the Kadetsky house, they found Greer's parents staring at the computer. "Shit," her father said as they approached. "This is not going to work."

"What are you talking about?" Greer said.

"The aid package." He sighed heavily and shook his head.

Suddenly Cory understood the whole thing; it revealed itself before him, sickeningly.

"What?" Greer said, still not getting it.

"We can't swing it," said Rob. "They were extremely stingy with us, Greer."

"But how can that be?" she asked. She and Cory examined the paragraph about the "amount of award." The next paragraph said something like, "Given that you did not choose to provide the appropriate information and documentation . . . ," and then went on to apologetically say that Yale could only offer so much and no more. The amount it had offered was a token. Apparently Rob, who had volunteered to handle the financial aid forms, hadn't actually completed them. He had left out parts that had seemed too complicated, or else too intrusive. Rob explained this calmly but haltingly now.

"I'm so sorry, Greer," he said. "I didn't know it would have this effect."

"You didn't know?"

"I thought they would come back to us—the financial aid people—and say they needed more information. I filled out what I could, and then it got to be too much, and I got pissed off at how much they wanted from me, answers I didn't know, and would have to go digging around for, and I guess I did a half-assed job." He paused, shaking his head. "That's what I do," he said. "That's what I always do."

Laurel picked up a letter that was lying on the table. "There's one more thing, though. One more place. I just went and got the mail. Ryland," she said.

"What?"

"You got in! They offered you a really extraordinary package. Room, board, even spending money. I was worried you'd be upset about Yale, so I opened it. This solves the problem."

"Right, *Ryland*," Greer said with sarcasm. "My safety school.

Where my guidance counselor made me apply. A school for dummies."

"That's not true. And don't you want to see the letter? You won something called the Ryland Scholarship for Academic Excellence. It has nothing to do with finances, it's only based on merit."

"I don't actually care."

"I know you're upset," Laurel said. "Dad fucked up," she added, giving Rob a sharp, furious look, and then her face grew pinched and she began to cry.

"Laurel, I thought they would come back and ask for the information again later," Rob repeated, and he came and stood beside his wife, starting to cry too. Both of Greer's parents, these hapless, slightly unruly-looking people, were crying together and hugging each other, while Greer sat with Cory at the table with her hands in fists. Cory thought about how your parents brought you into the world, and you were supposed to stay close to them, or at least near them, until the moment when you had to swerve away. This, now, was Greer's swerve. He was witnessing it in action. He reached across and grabbed her hands and opened them. She relented, let his fingers wind together with hers. His own parents had filled out the financial aid forms perfectly, intimidated, while Cory guided them. He had bossed his parents around, telling them what to fill in on every single line. His parents were innocents, but they had done the right thing, while Greer's parents, who should have known better, hadn't.

"But look," Laurel went on. "We have to move forward now. And this Ryland scholarship is pretty amazing. You'll do fine. You and Cory both will. You're both so smart. You know how I think of you two? How I picture you? Like twin rocket ships."

Greer didn't even respond. She looked at Cory and said, "Maybe I can call Yale." So he and Greer went upstairs to her room to make the call. First Greer was put on hold, and finally a harried woman answered. All in a rush Greer started to tell her tale of anguish while Cory sat on the bed beside her. Greer's voice was soft and unclear, even in this moment of urgency. He'd never understood this about her. He himself was certainly imperfect—defensive, sometimes condescending—but at least he could speak up without anxiety, and his voice came out easily. "I . . . the forms weren't really . . . and my dad said . . . ," he heard Greer say. He wanted to tell her, Say what you mean! Speak up, girl!

"I'm sorry," the woman finally interrupted. "The financial aid decisions have already been made."

"Okay, I understand," Greer said quickly, and then she hung up. "Maybe my parents could call," she said to Cory.

"Go ask them," he said. "Tell them it's important to you. Say it in a serious voice, like you mean business."

So they went back downstairs, and she approached her parents and said, "Would either of you call the office at Yale for me?"

Her mother just looked at her anxiously. "This is your father's department," she said. "I wouldn't know what to say."

"Didn't you just call over there? What did they say to you?" Rob asked.

"They said the decisions were already made. But you could try," Greer said. "You're a parent. Maybe it would be different."

"I can't," he said. "The bureaucracy of it all; it's not for me." He looked helplessly at Greer. "It's just nothing I could do comfortably," he added. Then, for emphasis, he said again, "I can't."

They actually weren't going to try to help her, Cory saw with astonishment. He was witnessing a tableau of Greer's entire childhood being enacted before him, and it created in him an intense fury, as well as a desire to protect Greer and love her harder.

Greer accepted the full ride at Ryland, and Cory chose Princeton; if he'd gone to Yale it would've been a constant, sharp reminder to Greer. Their paths were now diverging precipitously—the swerve affected not just her and her parents but also him—so they would have to work to keep themselves as close as possible.

On their last night together at the end of the summer, up in her bedroom with a strong rain battering the windows, Greer lay in Cory's arms and cried. She hadn't cried about college before now, because her parents had cried that day in the kitchen and she had wanted to distinguish her own response from theirs; also, she had wanted to be better than they were, stronger. But she cried there in bed with Cory.

"I don't want to be this damaged person," Greer said, her voice choked, her face turned sharply away from him.

"You aren't. You're totally fine."

"You think so? I'm so quiet! I'm always the quiet one."

"I fell in love with your quiet," he said into the little blue section of her hair. "But that's not all you are."

"Are you sure of that?"

"Of course I am. And other people will start to see it too; they really will."

The rain came down and they barely moved, and then finally when it got late they rose with little groans and separated so they could finish packing up their childhood rooms, going through the task of selecting what they still cared about—what made the cut because it was still a part of them—and what was necessary to leave behind for good. Greer scooped up her collection of snow globes and her Jane Austen novels, even *Mansfield Park*, which she had never particularly liked. It was as if the books were a lineup of stuffed animals that had graced her room all these years; that was how much they comforted her. Cory, who would be leaving for Princeton in the morning, left behind his row of NBA bobblehead figurines on a shelf so Alby could have them. But after hesitating he took the boxed set of *The Lord of the Rings*. He wasn't particularly literary, but he loved those books and would never stop loving them. Pretty soon Alby would want to read them too, he knew, and when that happened he would lend them to him.

The next day, after goodbyes so ardent and extensive that they had a World War II quality to them, Cory went off in his packed family car for the trip down to New Jersey; Greer would go to Ryland two days later. At Princeton Cory was given a job in the Firestone Library, checking out books in an enormous, grand room; he ate his meals in another enormous, grand room.

He and Greer Skyped at night and made the effort to travel frequently to see each other. He spoke to her about being intimidated by Princeton but loving it there too, and about playing Ultimate Frisbee on the greenest fields on earth. He didn't tell her that he worried about staying faithful to her, and worried more broadly that what they had agreed to was going to be difficult to sustain. Girls at Princeton flirted with him all the time—WASPy blond girls who had grown up in houses with names, and a cool black flute player from LA, and a boho genius who lived in the Netherlands though she was American, and was named Chia.

Then one day in the dining hall, he heard one girl say to another, "Here's something about me that you didn't know. I made it into *The Guinness Book of World Records*."

And the other girl said, "Really? What for?"

"Oh, I collected more bottles for recycling than any other kid ever had. It was my thing. I was famous in Toledo. I was such a little dweeb."

Cory whipped around, practically spitting cobbler. "You're Taryn the Recycling Girl?" he asked, shocked. "I read about you in my fourth-grade reader!"

And the girl, who happened to be gorgeous, with wavy dark hair and dark eyes, nodded and laughed. That night on Skype, Cory made Greer guess who he had met that day. "Just *guess*," he said, but she was unable to guess, and so he told her. He left out the detail that Taryn the Recycling Girl from Toledo was really hot now, and that she had asked him if he wanted to meet for a drink sometime. "Glass, not plastic," Taryn had said, giving the words a suggestive, James Bond quality.

And then there was Cory's Secret Santa, Clove Wilberson, who had grown up in Tuxedo Park, New York, in a house called Marbridge. "Dang, Cory Pinto, you are the cutest and the wootest," Clove said to him one day, in response to nothing.

"Both?" he said mildly.

He also didn't tell Greer that one night Clove Wilberson came up to him after a party and said, "Cory Pinto, you are miles taller than I am, so I can barely do what I want to do."

"Which is what?"

She'd pulled his face down toward hers and kissed him. Their mouths touched in a meeting of soft surfaces. "So did you like that, Cory Pinto?" she asked when they pulled away; for some reason it amused her to always call him by his full name. Then she quickly said, "Don't answer that. I know you have a girl-friend. I've seen you with her. But it's okay; you don't have to look so scared."

"I'm not scared," he said, but almost immediately he felt compelled to run his hand across his mouth.

Sometimes he would see Clove's room from below, and when the light was on he would imagine going up there and not saying anything, but just pulling her onto her bed the same way he pulled Greer onto the bed when she came to Princeton or he drove up to Ryland. Everything Clove Wilberson said to him was through a scrim of teasing.

And whenever he saw Taryn the Recycling Girl, she would say, "So when are we drinking out of glass, not plastic, together?"

How would he get through four years of college not having sex with anyone but Greer? He was excited by different girls all the time, now that he wasn't with Greer every day. He wished he could say to her, Let's have one day a week when we get to hook up with someone on our own campus. Someone who means nothing to us, but who fulfills a shallow hormonal need. You can hook up with that drummer friend of yours; he is totally into you, I can tell. But Greer would've been shocked, and he couldn't hurt her.

Back home in Macopee over spring break freshman year, when they were sitting together at Pie Land studying, Greer had reached across the table and absently touched Cory's face. Her hand stroked his cheek, for a moment staying on the small, pale scar there, which was now over a year old. He had imagined that when they were older and in the next phase of their lives, living in their apartment together in Greenpoint or Red Hook—or was it Redpoint and Green Hook?—that would be the right time to confess to her his modest but valiant tale of having once saved her from the indignity of having a group of high school boys declare her a 6, and then taking an injury to the face for it.

"I always knew you were really a nine," he'd been planning to say. But he was slightly older now, and changing; and lately

Greer had begun to speak to him with a certain halting elo-
quence about the way women were treated in the world. He finally understood how arrogant his confession would have been.
His little scar, which had grown thin and white and nearly invisible, had been a badge of honor connected to a story he'd looked
forward to telling her. Now he knew he never would.

Near the end of college, Cory thought there ought to be a
book called *The Alcohol Speaking*, in which people wrote
about all the things they had done while drunk. The problem
was that they might not remember them when it came time to
write them down. Princeton was full of decisions made while
drunk. Cory had hooked up with Clove Wilberson twice sophomore year and then again once junior year. It had been the alcohol speaking, he knew, and he had been full of regret and
remorse each time it happened. He couldn't really blame it on
Clove, but there she was one night, practically doing a lap dance
for him. Cory had such long legs that they often just fell open
when he sat in chairs. Years later on the subway in New York,
women would look annoyed with him and he didn't understand
why, until once during rush hour a woman stared him down
and said, "Enough with the man-spreading." He was mortified,
and clapped his legs back together like a machine part.

But in a butterfly sling chair in an overdecorated suite at
Princeton sophomore year, after a vodka tasting given by a senior named Valentin Semenov, the son of a genuine oligarch,
Cory leaned back and let Clove pour herself over him like syrup.
"Oh my God," he said when the lights went low and she opened
his fly. A zipper being opened was like a little shock, especially
when the hand holding the zipper pull was not Greer's. Greer,

whose absence was now as strong as a presence, and the worth of whose love was unquantifiable, making Cory perhaps richer than the richest oligarch.

I'm sorry, he thought, I really am, but as he was thinking this, the alcohol wasn't just thinking but was in fact *speaking*; and beloved, invaluable Greer, with her blue streak and her sexy little body and her growing desire to be more outgoing and do something of meaning in the world, fell straight down through a trapdoor, away from him, away. Meanwhile, Clove Wilberson cleverly sidestepped that trapdoor, straddling Cory on the butterfly chair and then eventually in her bed. Finally he saw her dorm room not from below but from within. Loads of ribbons and trophies for field hockey. Loads of doodads that belonged to a rich girl. While they were in her bed, her parents called twice, and both times she took the call. She told him she had a horse named Boyfriend Material, who would be running in Saratoga that summer. "Bet on him; I'm confident he's going to win," she said sweetly into Cory's ear.

The next day he said, "Clove, listen. I can't do this again."

"I know you can't." She didn't seem upset, and he thought: Was I no good? But he knew he was good. He was unruined, and strong and energetic. Because of Greer, mostly, he knew what he was doing sexually. Clove smiled at him and said, "Don't worry, Cory Pinto."

So he didn't worry, but two more times over the course of college he returned to her, starting up the pattern of shame and absolution and cycling unhappily through it. But it was the alcohol speaking every time. Being apart from Greer allowed these changes to happen. There were other changes, too. During the fall of the presidential campaign, he and Greer skipped weekends that they were meant to see each other, and instead went separately campaigning. Greer went to Pennsylvania on a

Ryland bus; Cory went to Michigan on a Princeton bus. Clove was somewhere on that same bus, but he sat up front with Lionel, and across the aisle from Will, his two future microfinance startup partners. They were all overexcited by the campaign, and could stay up all day and night in the way you could only do without penalty when you were that age.

For weeks after the election Cory was so elated; elated and relieved and unworried about the future.

"Hey, Cory, Will and I wanted to talk to you," said Lionel one evening as the three of them walked across campus. "Looking ahead here, we can't get going on the startup right out of school. We'll need a year or two. By then we'll have more capital."

"The thing is," said Will, "because of the economy our dads are feeling less generous."

"So we should all make a pact to go out there after we graduate and earn a shitload of money ourselves first, and use it later," said Lionel. "Like saving up acorns for winter. Will and I are both going to try to get jobs in finance or consulting. You should do that too."

At first this news depressed Cory, and he refused to consider their suggestion. But much later, as graduation drew closer, he became more comfortable with the idea of consulting for a year or two, though it wasn't at all what he had planned. So many people around him were becoming consultants. Along with banking and business school it was one of the paths of least resistance. The top firms swarmed the top campuses, and many of the students went willingly.

Over a designated period during Cory's senior year, recruiters from consultancies and VC firms and banks descended upon Princeton in their good tailored suits. They distinguished themselves from the students, who carried backpacks and were dressed in rumplewear; and from the male faculty in their oatmeal tweed and low-slung corduroys that revealed their deflated, tenured asses; and from the female faculty in shaggy, earthy, academic, latter-day Stevie Nicks dress, ambling into the long, less frequently tenured (as Greer had pointed out) homestretch of the rest of their lives.

After the initial interview, a man and a woman from Armitage & Rist took Cory out to dinner in downtown Princeton, at one of those Ye Olde restaurants where parents took their sons or daughters when visiting from far-off hometowns. The consultants urged him to get an appetizer first; did they think he was hungry? he wondered. Were they thinking of him as Vaguely Ethnic Scholarship Male, Exhibit A?

"Get whatever you like," one of the two recruiters said, a man ten years older than Cory and wearing a stylish suit and narrow Beatle boots. His female colleague, with hair and skin that looked highly touchable, wore a red leather skirt and jacket that fit her tightly, futuristically.

"You know, it'll be fun to see where you go," the woman said to Cory as he ate, and as the two of them simply watched him eat, rather than actually eating much of anything themselves. Ordering was not the same as eating.

"Even if you already know you don't want to go with us," added the man. "Even if you're fielding offers, Cory, but are leaning in another direction."

"I'm not doing that," Cory said, but because there was food in his mouth, it came out like "*Uhnahdoonthah.*"

"The world is totally open now," the man went on. "It's changing before our eyes. When you look at the profile of our firm—of all the firms, really—it's a great time to be you. I envy you, actually, Cory. I'm excited for you and all your options."

But what did they mean by *you*? Did they mean because he was a millennial? Or was he being lumped into the minority category again, because of his last name? Back during freshman year someone had slipped a flyer under his door inviting him to a meeting of one of the campus Latino organizations. "We'll be serving *chalupas*," it had read.

In the candlelight of their corner table at the restaurant, the man and woman from Armitage & Rist wooed Cory Pinto like two lovers proposing a three-way. So Cory ate salty smoked salmon on crisp little rounds of black bread, and a rack of meat like something on *The Flintstones*, followed by a ramekin of crème brûlée with a hard scorched crust on top that, when you cracked it with the tip of your spoon, felt as satisfying as if you were breaking ground to build your dream home. The recruiters were so complimentary throughout dinner, even as they left out a lot of specifics. The firm had offices in New York, London, Frankfurt, and Manila, they said, but Cory stressed that he definitely needed to be in New York. "We hear you," said the woman.

Back in his dorm room after the meal, lightly burping little bursts of aerated fish and mustard, Cory had Skyped with Greer at Ryland. "Well, guess what, they sold me on it," he said.

"Is that right?"

"Yep. They threw a lot of red meat at me and that did it. You would've hated what I ate. You would've actually been grossed out by the whole evening. But I have to admit I was into it. I mean, it was so ridiculous, having strangers from a 'firm'—even that word is so weird—fawn over me like I was somebody. Having capitalism itself seek me out and think I might actually have something to offer it! It's just for a year—two, tops—but I'm telling you, Greer, if you're down with it, I really might do it."

"You say it like you're talking about some dangerous activity."

"Everything has risk."

"What do you think the risk is here?"

"Oh, just that I will become a consulting asshole, while you become someone good."

"I don't know why you say that," Greer said. "I don't even have a job yet."

"You will."

"I do actually have an idea for someplace interesting to apply," she said with surprising coyness.

"Tell me."

"No. Not yet. It probably won't become anything, and I have to find out first. But anyway," she said, directly into the camera, "even if you become an asshole, and even if I become this sanctimonious person, we'll be doing it in front of each other, for each other. Finally. And doesn't that count for something?"

He didn't answer right away. She looked at him hard, and he could swear she seemed to know everything about everything he had ever done, all that was good and all that was shameful. For a second he almost wished the Skype connection would blink out briefly, the way it sometimes did in the middle of an important moment. But it stayed strong, and Greer just smiled at him and placed a single finger on the screen, most likely in the exact place where his mouth was.

PART TWO

Twin Rocket Ships

FOUR

She had come down by bus, staying awake and sitting up straight the whole time so she didn't inadvertently fall asleep and crease her clothes and face, winding up looking the way she imagined her parents had looked back on the school bus before she was born. She needed to look uncreased and responsible now, like someone who should be hired to work at this modest feminist magazine that had survived long past its peak. Someone who should be hired to work for Faith Frank.

Greer had told very few people about the interview, but even fewer knew that she didn't really love *Bloomer*. Though it had started out in life as a tough little readable magazine, after almost forty years it was somewhat soft, and had a hard time competing with blogs such as *Fem Fatale*, which had shifted away from personal essays and was embracing a radical critique of racism, sexism, capitalism, and homophobia. Recently *Fem Fatale* had run a cartoon of Amelia Bloomer wearing the bloomers associated with her name, which had words on them that read, "*Bloomer* magazine," and in a dialogue bubble she was saying, "Time to give another pep talk to straight white middle-class women."

Fem Fatale's staff was young, and from their offices in a former candy factory in Seattle they wrote about and organized around issues like queer rights, trans rights, and reproductive justice. *Bloomer* tried, too, but while the editorial staff was pretty diverse, and diversity was among the topics frequently covered, there was a formal, slightly uneasy quality to the magazine. It hadn't made a graceful leap forward. Even its website was slightly grainy and sleepy.

Bloomer's offices were now located in a small commercial building in the far West Thirties. As Greer walked down the narrow hall she could hear the whinny of the dental drill behind the door of a Dr. L. Ragni, DDS. Across the hall she buzzed at the door of *Bloomer*, but no one answered, so she stood waiting. She coughed, as if that might help, and watched as someone approached Dr. L. Ragni's door and was buzzed in at once. It was a bright spring workday in New York City, and for whatever reason, no one was answering the door at *Bloomer*.

Greer turned the knob, but the door was locked. Then she banged, but still no one appeared. She was confused, but more than that the lack of response made her realize how much she really wanted a job there, and that if she didn't get one she would be very disappointed. Faith Frank had seemed to offer something unusual in the gray light of a ladies' room three and a half years earlier, so now Greer stood for too long knocking on a door in this hall of dental offices and actuaries and startups. She knew there were people behind the *Bloomer* door; she could hear them moving around and talking. It was like when you heard mice behind your wall but couldn't find a way to get to them.

That past Wednesday, Greer had nervously called the number on Faith Frank's business card, which had spent all of college in a slot in her wallet. During the occasional wallet purges that took place during times of great boredom, the card had always made the cut. Whenever she'd seen it, she'd remembered the night it had been given to her, and she would feel a specific excited and highly alert feeling.

In recent weeks, Greer had been sending various applications to nonprofits, but had received only one interview at an organization that disseminated a lifesaving nutritional supplement in developing countries in Africa. That interview, which took place over Skype, didn't go well. She had no background for this kind of work, and the pediatrician interviewing her kept being called away, leaving her to sit awkwardly in front of the empty screen for minutes at a time, staring at a poster on his wall of a dying child in her mother's arms.

Finally, after all the conversations in the dorm about starting out in the world and choosing a particular field, Greer thought to apply for a job at Faith Frank's magazine. It would be meaningful work where she could use her writing skills. During the day she would essentially be paid to be a feminist, and at night she could work on her own writing. Zee agreed that it was worth trying. "It would be a good fit for you. Me, I'm so bad at anything having to do with the written word," Zee added. "Which is a shame, because it would be great to work for Faith Frank."

Greer had explained to the person who answered the phone at *Bloomer* where and when she'd met Faith. Somehow the next day she had gotten a call back, and the assistant had said, "Faith remembers you." These words were so startling. Greer didn't know how it was possible that Faith Frank remembered her after three and a half years, but she actually did.

Now that no one was answering the door at *Bloomer*, it all seemed like an elaborate, sad prank. Finally, after far too long a time, the door was wrenched open by a young woman who looked at Greer and rudely said, "Yes?"

"I have a job interview with Faith Frank."

"Well, that's a shame."

"Sorry?"

The woman just turned and walked into the warren of offices, past the unoccupied reception desk. In the distance a couple of women clustered in a hallway. Greer looked for Faith, but she didn't see her. There was something so very wrong here. The unfriendly person at the door, the knot of employees, the atmosphere of loss and worry and shock. Then the cluster of women split in half, so it was like curtains parting, and between the halves Greer got a straight-shot view of a small office at the end of the short hallway, its door open. Inside two women were embracing. One of them was patting the other one on the back. The woman doing the comforting, it was now revealed, was Faith Frank. She was the one they all looked toward in this upsetting moment.

"Did someone die?" Greer asked a middle-aged woman who stood nearby.

The woman regarded her evenly. "Yes. Amelia Bloomer," she said. When Greer kept looking at her, uncomprehending, the woman explained, "We're *folding*. Cormer Publishing is pulling the plug once and for all. Happy deathday to us."

"Sorry," was all Greer could say. Her first thought, much to her shame later on, wasn't about what this meant for the mission of the magazine, or its staff, but what it meant for her.

Faith, who had been at *Bloomer* the longest, was in her middle sixties now, and the love that people felt for her, Greer knew, had to do with their feelings about the past more than anything else. *Fem Fatale* would be a far better place to work than *Bloomer*, though there was no money at the blog.

Now she had no job working for Faith Frank, and never would. But as she experienced the news through her own self-absorption, she became aware that the office was growing quiet.

Something was about to happen. Faith stood straighter and looked around, preparing to speak. "Listen, my friends," she began. Not, "Listen, people!" like an officious and exhausted teacher, and not, either, the latest iteration of the way people spoke to groups, "Listen up, guys," especially since these were mostly women here. "Oh, I'm heartbroken today," said Faith. "I know we all are. But we're heartbroken together. We've done a lot. We marched together. We celebrated together. We fought for the ERA, and reproductive rights, and against violence. And right here, in our offices, we wrote about it all. And we sat in one another's living rooms and talked about everything under the sun, and we ate sprouts together. Lots and lots of sprouts. I believe we're the ones who put sprouts on the map." There was sentimental laughter. "Look, some of what we did succeeded, and some of it failed spectacularly—ERA, I'm talking to you— but what I know and you know is that all of it mattered. And it still matters. We're part of history, the history of women's struggle for equality, though of course I don't have to tell you that. We've been doing this forever, and we'll keep on doing it." She looked up. "Oh, please don't cry, because then we'll all cry, and we'll end up dissolving in a puddle of tears like women in the eighteenth century." Some people laughed through their tears, which fractionally changed the mood. Then Faith said, "You know what, I take that back. Let's all cry! We'll get it out of our systems once and for all, and then we'll go right back out there."

Faith was as she had been when she spoke at Ryland: kind, intelligent, allowing for other people's emotions. The truth was that she wasn't a rare or particularly original thinker. But she was someone who used her appeal and her talents to inspire and sometimes comfort other women. Greer wouldn't get a job at *Bloomer*, for *Bloomer* would no longer exist in any form, and she wouldn't even get a chance to sit for an interview with Faith Frank, which would have been exciting, regardless of the outcome.

"This is over, and now we have to scatter," Faith told everyone. Then she gestured around her. "But *this*," she said, "isn't over, and we all know it never will be. We're not going away. I'll see you all out there."

The women applauded, and some cried, and several of them began to speak in overlapping voices and take group photos. Someone opened a bottle of champagne, and then music played: fittingly, Opus's old hit "The Strong Ones." Greer took that moment to leave, and as she walked out she heard the lyrics that opened the song:

> Don't ever think I'll be easily beat
> Just because I'm wearing Louboutins on my dainty feet
> We are the strong ones
> We are the lithe ones
> We are the subtle ones
> We are the wise ones . . .

Greer felt congested with disappointment, and something more substantial and different. She headed back into the hallway, where, behind other doors, the sounds of everyday life were released: the squeal of a dental drill, the throb of dubstep, the chirp and murmur of people getting business done. The world spun even as a modest but once important feminist magazine did its death rattle and then died.

Cory was in a coffee shop on the corner of West 30th Street, waiting for her as they'd arranged. She hadn't been able to tell him what time her interview would be over, so he'd said, "Don't worry, I'll just plan to be there." He was in the back booth now in an orange Princeton hoodie, an econ text open in front of him. These days a soul patch and a thin mustache served as a framing device for his mouth. Wordless, Greer slid into the booth beside him and he opened his arms to her, so she went into them. "It didn't go well?" he asked.

"They're closing."

"Oh no. Bad luck. Come here, you," he said, and she turned her face up to his so he could kiss her mouth, her cheeks, her nose. He wanted her to get what she wanted. He hadn't even met Faith Frank, though he'd listened to Greer talk on and on about her after the lecture freshman year, and she'd given him a real-time course in feminism as she herself was getting it. It was much the way Greer had learned about microfinance from Cory, or at least its outlines. Here he was now, waiting for her, sympathizing with her.

"You'll find something," he said. "And they'll be lucky to hire you."

"Who's 'they'?"

"Whoever."

"It's not just the job, exactly," she said after a moment. "It's also her and what she stands for. And how she acted when I met her. Faith Frank."

"Yes, I know. My competition."

He reached out and played with the edges of her hair, rubbing them between his fingers. He did this sometimes, she noticed, when he wasn't sure how to comfort her. She remembered the way Darren Tinzler had played with her shirt collar, not to comfort her but for his own pleasure and interest. It made Cory nervous to see her unhappy, and she knew he wanted to swoop in and do something. Of course, it was true that he also liked to touch her. She leaned even closer, and Cory palmed her entire head with his big hand. He was touching her head, her face; then his hand was on her neck, the thumb stroking the scooped hollow above her collarbone, and she kissed the side of his face. They were both slightly stale, having traveled from their colleges that day by bus and train. She would've liked to be in a bathtub with him, and she realized that they had never once taken a bath together. They would do that when they lived together, when all of this had been figured out and resolved. She pictured his long legs displacing the water in their tub.

"I realized today—it got kind of sharply defined for me— that I wanted to know her," Greer said. "And I guess I wanted her to know me too. I know that's hubristic. A word Professor Malick loves." She paused. "Maybe I'll write Faith Frank a note, kind of a condolence letter. You think that's okay?"

"I think you know what's okay."

"Zee once told me I should be Faith Frank's pen pal, but of course that was ridiculous. At least now I have something to say to her."

That night, Greer sent Faith an email:

Dear Ms. Frank,
I came in for a job interview with you this afternoon, and I was there when you said goodbye to everyone. Listening to you talk, I felt like I knew you. I think everyone must feel that way. Thank you for all you've done over the decades for women. We are so lucky to have you.
Sincerely,
Greer Kadetsky

Greer began sending her résumé out more. The plan had been that after commencement, which would take place in a couple of weeks, she and Cory would spend a month up in Macopee living at home before going down to the city to try to find an apartment in Brooklyn. But Greer still had no job waiting for her. She became worried about what would happen, even a little frightened at the uncertainty. Then one day Cory received his own disappointing news. Armitage & Rist had changed their offer, and now wanted him to come work in their Manila office. They enhanced the deal with even more money, but the news was shocking, and he had been afraid to tell her.

"Do we ever get to be together?" she asked.

"Yes."

"What if you tell them you won't go?"

"Then I have no job. All the entry-level consulting jobs have been locked down by now, and I need to be a big earner. Lionel and Will and I agreed on this. Look, I feel like crap," he said. "I wanted us to be in our place. I pictured the whole thing. Framed shit on the walls. Big spoons in the kitchen."

"Spoons?" she said. "We never discussed that. You pictured spoons?"

"Yeah," he said, a little shyly.

College ended in a fractured, frantic way, just as it had begun. Greer and Zee began to pack up their dorm rooms, and neither of them was happy about what immediately waited for them. Zee would be moving back home to her parents' house in Scarsdale, to live there while training to be a paralegal, which both her mother and father had urged her to do—"semi-forced me to do," Zee said—because she had no other plans, and no skills. She would have liked looking for a paid job as an activist, perhaps as a community organizer, she'd tentatively suggested, but they had swept it away. "Be serious, and think long-term," her mother had said. "Those jobs don't have earning potential."

On the very last night, the entire Ryland senior class took buses to a scruffy beach an hour away from campus, where a bonfire was built and Dog brought out the ukulele again, and many sad, emotional songs were sung. Greer and her cluster of friends sat together in a huddle. Zee walked on the sand in circles, saying, "Really? It's all over now? This is so depressing. It's like a final field trip for people at a hospice."

Greer went back up to the house in Macopee while she figured out what to do next. Cory flew business class to Manila on Cathay Pacific, settling in under a downy blanket, drinking a glass of Shingleback McLaren Vale Shiraz as the lights in the cabin dimmed. "All you need to know about my new life," he texted her when he landed, "is that they gave me pajamas to wear on the plane."

In Macopee Greer found a full-time job at Skatefest, the same place where she had worked part-time in high school. She spent her days now handing out skates, and her evenings sending out her résumé and eating morose dinners, often by herself in front of a novel. She was finally not as angry at her parents as she used to be, she realized—they were too marginal for that, too weak—but her connection to them seemed vague, as if she had to remember who exactly these two people were. Being here is temporary, she thought. It's just a lily pad. It's what happens to you after college. I will be able to leap off one of these days.

Cory sometimes called from Manila while Greer was sitting at the skate-rental counter in the middle of the day. It was twelve hours later where he was; their lives were opposites in all ways. "I'm lonely and I'm bored, and I miss you something sick," he said.

"I miss you too. Something sick," she added. "I like that."

"I want to be in your bed right this minute, Space Kadetsky," he said. "Why can't I make myself really small and crawl through the holes of the phone?"

"Maybe you can." She paused and sighed; he sighed too. "I had a dream last night," Greer told him, "in which we agreed to 'meet in the middle.' Which was a raft on the ocean."

"Was it nice?" he asked.

"Very. But then somehow my mother was there, dressed as a clown. Kind of spoiled the mood."

"I can imagine. You know," he said after a second, "maybe we could do something sexy over the phone."

They'd had occasional phone sex and Skype sex during college; Greer had always felt a little nervous, afraid that somehow it would be intercepted. "The NSA doesn't care about your orgasms," Cory had said. "Believe me." But then again, she tended to be on the quiet side even when they had sex in person. "A nun and a mouse had a baby, and that is me," she'd said to him once after they'd slept together in her childhood bed.

Now she said, "'Do something sexy over the phone'? I can't, Cory, I'm at work. There are people here." She felt the back of her neck prickle at the thought. In the distance, teenagers and parents with little kids were moving around the Skatefest rink. The sound was like an ocean, coming at her in scratchy waves as the skaters moved closer and then receded. She thought of Cory on top of her, his hands all over her, proprietary, welcome. Her arousal lifted her away from the smells of people's feet and the glass box of rotating, candied-looking hot dogs.

"You got something more important to do, Kadetsky?" he asked.

"Yes."

"What?"

"Rent skates to skinheads."

"Ah."

"I wish I could do it, though," she said sadly. "I really, really do."

"I know."

Sadness, excitement, then sadness again; it all rose and fell like the sounds of skaters scuffing the floor of the rink. Hold tight! she thought, conveying this to both herself and Cory, thinking of them in bed together, and the joint effort couples had to make to be a couple, and stay a couple. If one let go, then that was it, both of them fell. Hold tight! she thought, imagining his body, and her own much smaller body against it.

"You should go to sleep," Greer finally said. "It's late where you are."

"I have to look over my deck pages."

"I'm afraid I don't know what that means."

"I'm afraid I don't either, but I'm pretending I do. We're flying to Bangkok in the morning for a meeting. I miss you," he said again. "Imagine me in my douchey white shirt and tie."

"I bet you look hot," she said. "Imagine me in my orange Skatefest tunic and little cap."

And so it went, conversations with Cory on a different continent while Greer leaned across a sticky, shellacked skate-rental counter. After work in the evening she drove her parents' old Toyota home along the highway. Sometimes, on Woburn Road during that standstill summer, she would park the car and get out to talk to Cory's brother, Alby, who was now eight years old and handsome, big-headed, and could often be found outside on his Razor scooter, powering down the slant of the driveway.

"Time me, Greer, while I go around the block," he said one evening when she came home from work in her parents' car. He'd been waiting for her, she realized, riding in circles until the car pulled onto the street. So she agreed to time him with the stopwatch that he held in his hand for just this purpose. "I want to beat my personal best," Alby said. "You know what that means, right? It's the best record a person has thus far."

"I can't believe you just said 'thus far.' Well, actually I can."

"Miles Leggett told me his dad calls me an idiot savant."

"Well, then his dad has no idea what he's talking about."

"Someday he'll know. Like when I win the Nobel Prize."

She laughed. "Aim high. What field are you going to win it for?"

"Oh," said Alby. "I didn't know you needed a field. Do I have to decide now?" Even as he said this, she knew she would recount the conversation to Cory tomorrow, on Skype.

"No," Greer said. "You definitely don't have to decide now. Okay, go ahead, I'll time you."

"Keep an eye on Slowy too," said Alby, and then Greer saw that his turtle lay humped in the grass at the side of the driveway.

"Ready?" Greer asked, and Alby nodded. "Get set," she said. She paused and watched him angle himself forward. "*Go!*"

Greer lifted the start button as Alby headed down the driveway; soon he was out of view. The front door of the Pintos' house opened, and Greer turned to see Benedita on the front step, looking for her son. There was always a stiffness between her and Greer. "I'm timing him, Mrs. Pinto," Greer explained. "He's going around the block on his Razor."

"All right," Cory's mother said, coming over to her, and the two women stood in silence, neither one moving, both of them short, and as still as the turtle at their feet. They waited for Alby, the way sailors' wives used to wait for their husbands to return from the sea. The silence seemed to go on for too long, and then, as if the sound barrier had suddenly been breached, there came a scrape of wheel on road, and they both looked up at the same time and saw Alby make the turn onto Woburn and head in their direction. Watching him approach, they both shifted into a state of unaccountable, shared happiness.

Alby kicked his way back up the slanted drive and wound up at the feet of Greer and his mother. He was out of breath, his face hot, his narrow shoulders heaving. "Greer, what was my time? What was my time?" he asked her. At which point she realized that she had forgotten to stop the little silver stopwatch, which still beat on in the palm of her hand.

One night late that summer when Greer was sitting in bed at her computer, an email popped into her inbox from an address that she didn't recognize: FF@scvc.com. She clicked it absently, assuming it was spam. Later she would say to Cory, "What if I had deleted it and never wrote back? It makes me ill to even think about."

> Dear Greer Kadetsky,
> You wrote me a very kind note a couple of months ago at
> a low moment for me. I fear I didn't write back; my
> apologies. You can imagine the volume of notes I received.
> I'm reaching out personally to a small number of people as
> I put together a team for a grand new venture, and since
> you'd been interested in applying for a position at *Bloomer*,
> I wondered if you might be interested in coming in for an
> interview for this instead. It will be very different, though
> I'm afraid I must be slightly mysterious about it at the
> moment.
> Warmly,
> Faith Frank

Warmly! That was a new one to Greer. She had never seen anyone sign an email that way, and it seemed to her somehow not only adult but also more than that: rich, sophisticated, knowledgeable. She wanted to sign her own return email to Faith that way too, but felt that it would be like a little girl trying on her mother's ball gown. Greer wrote a response quickly, a pulse tapping in her eyelid:

Dear Faith Frank,
I was just sitting here checking email and suddenly you appeared. Different email address, same person. Of course I am VERY interested in your grand new venture, despite the mysteriousness—or even because of it. Please let me know how to arrange an interview. Thank you so much for thinking of me.
Sincerely,
Greer Kadetsky

Then it was even more shocking when Faith wrote back immediately.

Dear Greer,
That's wonderful! My assistant Iffat Khan will be in touch with you in the morning.
Warmly,
Faith

P.S. Why are we both still awake? As my mother used to say, we should hit ourselves over the head with a frying pan to get to sleep!

To which Greer replied:

Dear Faith,
Note to self: must buy frying pan. No chance of sleep

now. Too excited about prospect of gnv (aka grand new venture). Good night!
Greer

Three days later she was on the bus going back down to New York City. The address this time was a mirrored glass midtown skyscraper called the Strode Building. In the lobby Greer was ID'd, and a terrible photo was taken of her in which she appeared to have a snout. Worse, she had to wear the photo as a badge, and was sent through a turnstile that flung its jaws open to admit her; and then she shot up to 26, where the elevator opened onto a space so blank and white and expansive that she could not tell if it was still under construction, or if this was the way it was permanently meant to look. It was like a floating space station, an empty field with a complicated geometry of cubicles hinted at in the remote distance, everything white, and no boldface institutional name hovering above the reception desk, so she still did not know exactly where she was.

"I have an appointment with Faith Frank," she told the receptionist with pleasurable but carefully modulated self-importance. The young woman nodded and spoke into a headset, and momentarily another young woman appeared—elegant, composed, a tiny stud in her nose the size of a seed.

"I'm Iffat Khan," the second woman said. "Faith's assistant. It's great to meet you. Come on back. Faith's in with some people." Greer followed her down a white hallway that led like a tributary into a large white office. At a long white desk that was made from a repurposed door—a remnant of a building in which secret suffrage meetings had taken place long ago, she'd learn on her first day of work—sat Faith Frank, and around the room, standing and sitting, were several women of various ages, and two men.

Faith rose to greet her. Of course she had grown a few years older since the night in the Ryland Chapel, and up close the change was slight but noticeable; she wore it well. Faith still was a person of gravitas and glamour, intelligence, cheekbones, warmth, greatness, all of which was once again exciting. Faith introduced her to everyone, but Greer could barely pay attention to the names, and soon these people stood and left, so it didn't really matter who they were. If she was hired she would immediately learn their names.

"Did you get some sleep since I wrote you?" Faith asked.

"Yes, did you?"

"Not a whole hell of a lot."

"Well, then it's a good thing I brought you this," Greer said. She reached into her bag and with a flourish brought out the small frying pan she had bought at the Target near her parents' house and carried with her down to the city, just in case it seemed appropriate to give it to Faith, which, she'd figured, it probably wouldn't. But now she was taking the risk. Faith looked surprised, but then she smiled. Suddenly they had a private joke between them.

"Oh, that's a good one," said Faith. "Very funny. I'll definitely conk myself over the head with it when I can't sleep. And whenever I do that, Greer, I'll think of you." She put the pan on a side table and said, "Let's get down to business before someone comes in with another emergency." They sat together on a white sofa that looked out on the skyline, the workday. It was impossible to look out on the city from high up without thinking for a second of 9/11, even nine years later. Any overarching view of the city seemed to call for a brief, noble hush. Smokestacks steamed; lights stuttered; there was movement along the grid. The quiet moment now wasn't unpleasurable. It was just a moment of seriousness, born in something terrible, but now uncoupled from it.

Faith took a pull on the mug of tea in front of her. Nearby

were little tins of oolong and Earl Grey and jasmine. A tea ball lay on its side, with sprouts of used leaves poking through the holes like hair in old-man nostrils. "After *Bloomer* closed," Faith began, "I was in a daze, maybe even a mild depression. I went up to my weekend house just to regroup. And one day I got a call from an old friend. We go back a number of decades, and our paths have been very different, to put it mildly. He's Emmett Shrader, the venture capitalist." She paused. "You do know who I'm talking about, right?"

Greer nodded, but she wasn't completely sure; she knew who Emmett Shrader was, *roughly*, just as she had once known who Faith Frank was, a little less roughly, though she badly wished she could Google the venture capitalist and billionaire right now, as she had originally done with Faith, so she could be knowledgeable during this interview. "He said he wanted to make me an offer," Faith said. "I thought that meant he would buy *Bloomer* and it would have yet another life, straggling along. But he said no, sorry, it wasn't that; *Bloomer* was no longer viable in today's world."

"Not even the website?" asked Greer. "I mean, if you revamped it, obviously. No offense," she quickly added. "But I've wondered about that."

Faith shook her head. "No. He said he admired our mission all those years, admired our determination, but that he has bigger plans. He told me he wants to bring some of the ideals of feminism out into the world in a new way. So here's what's happening," Faith continued. "His firm is underwriting a women's foundation. What we're going to do, mainly, is connect speakers with audiences. We want to address the most urgent issues concerning women today. We'll have summits, talks, conferences. He's offering significant funding." She paused. "I know we'll get criticism, Shrader being Shrader."

"Pardon?"

"Oh," said Faith, "he is who he is. He hasn't always put his money to good use. He's funded some pretty questionable ventures. You can read up on it. I have. It doesn't make me happy, but he has also frequently been heroic with his money, and he seems genuine in his desire to make this work. It's a risk. But he's promised to really go deep. Of course that's not all of the criticism we'll get. There's also me."

Greer wanted to say, Who could criticize *you*? But she knew who could; she had seen them on blogs, and of course in the comments section of *Fem Fatale*.

"I do what I can," said Faith. "I do it for women. Not everyone agrees with the way I do it. Women in powerful positions are never safe from criticism. The kind of feminism I've practiced is one way to go about it. There are plenty of others, and that's great. There are impassioned and radical young women out there, telling multiple stories. I applaud them. We need them. We need as many women fighting as possible. I learned early on from the wonderful Gloria Steinem that the world is big enough for different kinds of feminists to coexist, people who want to emphasize different aspects of the fight for equality. God knows the injustices are endless, and I am going to use whatever resources are at my disposal to fight in the way I know how."

"As long as you keep wearing your boots," Greer impulsively put in. She remembered then that she had thought working at *Fem Fatale* would have been more exciting than working for Faith Frank, but she understood that it wasn't true.

Then Faith said, "There's another aspect to the venture that I wanted to tell you about, Greer. And this was the reason I finally accepted the position, after telling Emmett no." She leaned in a little closer. "Here's the deal. Fairly often," she said, "we'll actually be able to initiate a special emergency project that will make an immediate difference in some women's lives."

"That sounds great," said Greer, though she couldn't imagine what any of this really meant except in some blurry way that involved a line of strong women standing under a rain shower of funding. She wanted to be in that line. Despite often being so quiet and uneasy, she wanted to seem like an appropriate and inevitable choice: Greer Kadetsky, the young woman with the hot face, who works as fiercely as that hot face would suggest.

I will work so fucking hard for you, Faith Frank, she wished she could say.

"We've already started doing this. I recently got Emmett to release funds to an organization focused on improving the health and well-being of women of color living in the rural South. By the way, we're calling ourselves Loci," said Faith.

"Excuse me?" said Greer.

"I know. I had the same reaction. But it grows on you. Loci, as in the plural of locus. Because there are so many issues to focus on, concerning women, and so many places to put our energy. It's not the greatest name in the world, but we reached the deadline and didn't have anything better. People see the word on the page, spelled L-O-C-I, and they think: Oh God, how am I supposed to pronounce this? Is it Lo-kee? Lo-kye? Lo-sigh? The dictionary gives you all three options. Me, I'm firmly in the *sigh* camp."

"Then so am I!" said Greer.

"Emmett wants me to complete my team very quickly. I've already brought several people in, and they've started working. He rented this enormous space for us here. God, it's so different from what I'm used to. You saw the *Bloomer* office. I'm used to places where three people share a desk, and the elevator always breaks. That's what sisterhood means to me. But now we've hit the big time. ShraderCapital wants us close by, and they're right upstairs on twenty-seven." She glanced upward in illustration, then laced her hands and looked directly at Greer. "So what do you think?" she asked.

"I think it sounds amazing."

"It does, doesn't it? Does it fit into your master plan?" Faith asked.

"Not sure I have one."

"Really? I thought everyone did at your age. Mine was to get as far away from my parents as I could."

Greer became self-conscious. "I'd like to work here. That's my plan. And at night I'd like to do some writing. Maybe I could even become a writer someday, but for now I want a job that will kind of put me in the world, I guess, and help me . . . make meaning. That's what you said when I met you. Anyway, I think this job could be that."

Faith nodded seriously. "Okay. I'll be blunt with you, Greer. I'm not interviewing you because of your brilliant intellect. I know you're smart—your grades are great, and frankly you're a good, instinctive writer, and I think you'll have some real luck with that. But you're, what, twenty-two? When I was twenty-two I knew nothing about anything, and I went skipping off into the world."

"To be a cocktail waitress in Las Vegas," Greer said, remembering.

"Yes, exactly. No, I'm interviewing you primarily because I think you're promising. And hey, you also brought me a frying pan today, which was witty. So if you're willing, I'd like to bring you on board."

"Oh, Faith, thank you," Greer said, flushing. "I'm definitely willing."

"The job will of course be entry-level. Much of it will probably feel boring and repetitive."

"I doubt that."

"No, it's true, hear me out. You'll be one of our bookers. Eventually you'll be much more involved with a variety of things here. It's up to you how quickly that happens."

Greer could barely stay seated as Faith described the specifics of the job to her. She wanted to crouch down on the floor like a weight lifter and raise the long white length of sofa into the air with Faith Frank still on it, just to show her that she could.

Two weeks later, Zee helped Greer move into a studio apartment in Prospect Heights, Brooklyn. She could never have lived in such a place by herself if Emmett Shrader hadn't been unusually generous with all salaries at Loci. The apartment was a simple, grimy box in a small building, and it needed a deep clean that neither Greer nor Zee was willing to give it, but it also possessed original moldings and pressed tin ceilings, and the lease was hers. Through friends Greer had found a bed, which had been placed in one part of the L-shaped studio; she also bought a compact little sofa, lightly used, that could open into a place to sleep if a friend stayed over, and this she wedged tightly into a corner across the room. The walls held only a few generic prints, for now. There was a flower-slash-vagina painted by Georgia O'Keeffe. "Not the original, in case you were wondering," she'd said to Cory when she gave him a Skype home tour, carrying her laptop around the room.

While Zee assembled an IKEA chair for her, Greer continued the tour for Cory outside alone with her phone, providing audio narration, describing the farmer's market within walking distance, and Grand Army Plaza, and the park, and the Brooklyn Public Library with its big gold doors. Nearby, she said, hulked the Brooklyn Museum and also the Botanic Garden, and along Washington and Franklin were Caribbean beef patty emporiums—"Not that I will ever set foot in them, but you will, soon enough"—and check-cashing stores and taxi dispatchers.

Late that first afternoon, with the place unpacked and set up enough to be functional, Greer and Zee sat on the front stoop. "I love your street," Zee kept saying as it got chilly out there.

"Me too," Greer said. "But it feels so strange." She looked at Zee. "You okay up there in Scarsdale? Not too lonely?"

"I'll manage. One nice thing is the refrigerator with the ice maker. And the heated toilet seats and all that."

"Come stay with me as much as you want," said Greer. "Really. You can just show up. I'll give you a key."

"Thanks."

"I really appreciate everything," Greer said. "Today would've been so much harder. Just getting set up. I mean, you are the best, Zee. You always are. I just want to say that." She felt the potential for tears now, with a mixed cause. Friendship; fear.

"It's nothing," said Zee. They sat together a little longer, neither of them wanting to end the day. "Well, I should catch Metro-North back," Zee finally said. "Judge Wendy says she's making a special lasagna tonight, and my presence at the table is requested. I'm sure you want to be alone here anyway."

Greer wanted to say, Don't leave yet. She hadn't meant to live alone. She couldn't stop thinking that Cory was supposed to be there, the two of them setting up house in a sweet early-twenties way that was so hopeful. Zee took off, and later that night, lonely but also excited, Greer brought in a boxed and bagged dinner from a place several blocks away called Yum Cottage Thai. This will be my neighborhood place, she thought, and then she realized: I have a neighborhood place. Greer stood over the small kitchen sink eating vegetable pad thai with efficient, feral automaticity. She smacked her lips loudly, just because she was alone and could, and wiped orange oil and a trace of peanut dust from her face with the side of her arm.

Later, when she was getting ready for bed, thumps and clicks emanated from the apartment upstairs, and a sound of something being dragged. She had no idea what any of those sounds were, but she imagined that if Cory lived with her they would be discussing it right now. "It's like they're bowling up there," she would say to him, and together in bed they would fashion a scenario that involved the upstairs neighbors and their in-home bowling alley. "What's the name of their league?" she would ask him. Cory would come up with something quickly, like, "The Gentrifickettes." And then, of course, Greer and Cory would make their own various private sounds.

Work would start in three days. When she'd first gotten the job at Loci, he'd asked her, "Did you look into everything about ShraderCapital, and Shrader himself?"

"To a certain extent," she said.

"You should read up. It's what anyone would do."

She saw that a great deal had been published about Emmett Shrader; some of it focused on morally problematic companies he'd been involved with, and some of it focused on his philanthropy. Because Greer knew nothing about venture capital— "VC," people sometimes called it—or what the business dealings of a billionaire might be like, she couldn't make too much sense of it except to understand that he had a mixed record, which didn't seem unusual. But Faith liked Shrader and had described him as "an old friend," and that was obviously significant.

On the night before Greer's job was to begin, Zee met her for a drink in Brooklyn. She too had work in the morning, having begun a paralegal job at the law firm of Schenck, DeVillers. They sat on unsteady stools drinking beers and crunching wasabi peas in the low, honeyed light. "So it's all starting for you," said Zee. "Remember this moment. Take a snapshot of it in your brain."

"What moment is that?"

"The moment before it all begins. The moment before you start, you know, your life."

"I don't know if it'll be my life. Maybe I won't even be good at it."

"You'll learn to be good. You're good at a lot of things, Greer. Writing. Reading literature. Love."

"That is a weird skill set to mention."

"You are amazingly competent," said Zee. "You got hired by Faith fucking Frank's foundation. A peck of pickled peppers. I bow down before you."

"And I bow down before you," said Greer. "You got me to Faith Frank. You made me go to that lecture. I probably would've stayed in my dorm room with my note cards. And then none of this would be happening." She paused. "You get me to do a lot. Or at least to think about things differently."

"Awww."

"Anyway, we have Ryland College to thank for our friendship. We will leave them all our money."

"They aren't getting a cent," Zee said. "When I see the alumni magazine I'm like, really? Why would I want to read this? Stupidy Stupid, class of '81, now works in strategic planning."

"Along with his wife, Sally Stupid," said Greer.

"But they could write about you in the class notes," Zee said. "Greer Kadetsky, class of 2010, now works for Faith Frank."

"That does sound good," said Greer. Then, suddenly realizing the conversation was only about her, she said, "Things will fall into place for you too, Zee. I'm sure they will."

"Listen," Zee said, more quietly now. "I have something."

She reached into her jacket pocket, and Greer imagined that she was going to take out a small, sentimental gift, beautifully wrapped. Inside would be some sort of amulet that Greer could carry or wear around her neck as she began her first real job.

But Zee had no gift box in her hand, no charm on a chain. Instead, she had an envelope. Was it an emotional letter about how much their friendship meant to her? That would be very touching. Women were allowed to tell each other what they felt without holding back. Women could now say, "I love you," without any hesitation or discomfort or a sense that there were sexual overtones between them, even if one of them was gay.

"Oh," said Greer, reaching out to take it. "Thank you, Zee."

"It's for Faith, actually."

Now the letter was an uncertain object, something Greer wasn't sure she wanted. It was as if she'd been tricked, cleverly served a summons without knowing it. "What do you mean?"

"Well," said Zee, "last night in my bedroom in my parents' house, I stayed up really late and made one of those lists in my head that you're supposed to make so that you know what you should do with your life."

"That's what this is? A list?"

"No, no, wait. Anyway, for this list, first you're supposed to think of the things you definitely don't want your life to include. And I realized how much I don't want to be a paralegal—it doesn't excite me—and I know how much I don't want to be a lawyer, at least not the corporate kind. I see these young associates, the ones who work really late and do corporate law, and they're on call like doctors, except their work isn't in the service of humanity, unless it's the pro bono stuff they're allowed to do once in a while. I mean, they're like the opposite of Doctors Without Borders. Lawyers Without Souls, I think of them. But the firm gives them a great salary, and in the beginning, to excite them and kind of confuse them, they take them out to baseball games and dinner, and they give them tickets to see Cirque du Soleil—which in my opinion is a punishment, not a gift—all those people in tights, with diamond shapes painted on their faces. Is there anything worse than a harlequin? But it all takes too much away from you, and doesn't give you fortification. Or a good feeling. Or a sense that you're actually doing something decent during your two seconds on earth. And you know what? I don't want it."

"So what do you want instead?"

"Well, actually, I'd love to work for Faith Frank's foundation too," Zee said gently. "If she'll hire me."

Greer couldn't think of what to say, but she was shocked.

Zee traced her finger in worried little swirls on the bar. "I know you're surprised that I'm suddenly saying this. Because I've never said it before. My parents have really pushed me to do something that could be a career. But what you're doing—it actually could be a career. And I thought maybe I'd be an asset to Faith. I've been an activist, sort of. I always thought that in my fantasy I would work somewhere young and radical. This isn't that. But Faith has been this big figure in the feminist movement, and I think I could learn a lot from her. Anyway, it was just a thought."

"I see," said Greer blandly.

"I want to be able to come in and do something real, wherever I work. Something that I'm really energized about." Zee's voice was getting a little thin and choked. "My parents love being judges. They wake up in the morning and they're like, 'Rah rah, the sun is shining, let's go to our chambers, darling.' And look how excited *you* are about starting your job. I want that feeling too," said Zee. "I figure there are a lot of things to do at your foundation, and my parents would approve, because it would actually be a normal job with a paycheck. I could just run around and do whatever Faith Frank needed. I could mill her tea leaves or something; isn't that a thing? And maybe every once in a while she would impart some amazing piece of older-woman wisdom, and tell us stories from the past, and I'd happen to be in the room and get to hear it.

"And also, wouldn't it be a blast if you and I worked at the same place? Because you know how friends drift apart after college. Their lives become so different, and they don't have a lot to talk about anymore. We could keep that from happening to us."

Greer took a sip of beer and tried to keep her voice light and unalarmed as she said, "So what did you write in the letter?"

"Oh, you know, I explained to her who I am and why I want to be part of what she's doing. I did the best I could. I warned her of my minimal writing skills. I reminded her that she met me the same night she met you. In the ladies' room at our college. And then I gave her the Zee Eisenstat saga. The abridged version, don't worry."

"I'm not worried," Greer said. The feeling of the night had shifted sharply, and Zee apparently didn't even understand why. She was just sitting there in her usual, steady Zee way, looking at Greer, waiting for encouragement. Instead, Greer wanted Zee's letter to disappear, which of course it wouldn't, and she knew she would dutifully give it to Faith. Greer toyed with it now and leaned it against her beer bottle. The envelope was opaque, so she couldn't see what Zee had written. "She's your closest friend, Greer," Faith would say after she'd read it. "What do you think, should I bring her aboard?" And Greer would say, "Absolutely."

The letter, slanted against brown glass, seemed to emit its own light. Greer lifted her bottle, and the letter dropped onto the surface of the bar as if it had been felled.

"So," Zee said, "what time do you have to be at work tomorrow?"

FIVE

The light fixtures at the Loci Foundation had been outfitted with special energy-saving coils that were still in beta, and were not quite bright enough for the tasks at hand, causing everyone who worked there to strain a little too hard, as though squinting over a medieval manuscript. Greer didn't mind. The pale, nearly celery-colored light over her cubicle up on the twenty-sixth floor burned with its low, unusual hue while she stayed extravagantly and almost piously late, though it took her too long to realize that her eagerness and effort might seem a little extreme. She worked with enthusiasm, but almost immediately she figured out the parameters of the job, and she understood that what she would be doing at Loci wasn't going to be intensely interesting. Faith had warned her of this during the interview, but it had seemed impossible. And the work wasn't boring, exactly—that was too harsh a description—because Greer was still in love with the *idea* of work. The term "the work world" seemed accurate, the office environment like its own planet made up of conference rooms and spring water dispensers and paper recycling bins. But the tasks of this job were mild, repetitive, and seemed removed from the large, grand venture of helping women. She could easily have been working in corporate party-planning, she thought at some point late in her first morning there.

At her desk Greer was either on the phone or on the computer, hunting down yeses or maybes from potential speakers or their assistants or reps, and setting up travel plans, learning the abbreviations for the world's airports, some of which made no sense. Why was Newark EWR instead of, say, NWR, or even NWK? And why did Rome have to be the unmemorable FCO? Cory's brother, Alby, would probably know; this was the sort of information he liked to gather.

During lunch break on Monday, someone passed around a takeout menu and whoever wanted food circled their choice, and cash was collected. Takeout on that day was from a Middle Eastern place, so Greer looked down the vegetarian column and ordered a falafel wrap. She thought that maybe they would all sit around together with their food, talking about the foundation and their desires and aspirations, but instead everyone just took their lunch back to their own cubicles, so Greer did too, eating in self-conscious aloneness at the space that she'd outfitted like a dorm room, with photos of Cory and Zee, and a good supply of ComSell Nutricle protein bars—the half-decent Raspberry Explosion, the sand-dry Double Vanilla—that her parents had offloaded to her. Cory texted Greer during that first day, asking for photos. She sent him pictures of the elevator and the little kitchen, and a long shot taken across the entire floor, which included the backs of various people's heads. "Also, send anecdotes from your life," he said. "Remember, I work in consulting, so I'm pretty bored." But so far she felt removed from anything of significance. She had the sense that soon, much too soon, she would want to do more here. Other people at Loci were clearly already doing a great deal more. While she and the other booker, a shaved-headed gay man named Tad Lamonica, were left out of the daily meetings, she often glanced over into the glassed-in conference room. Faith could be seen sitting at the head of the table. Also in the room were the three researchers, Marcella Boxman, a sexy twenty-three-year-old polyglot; Helen Brand, stylish, thirty-five, a former union organizer and the only African-American on Faith's team; and Ben Prochnauer, good-looking, resolute-jawed, five years out of Stanford and most recently part of an antihunger startup; as well as Bonnie Dempster and Evelyn Pangborn, who were firmly old-guard second-wavers, both in their sixties. Bonnie was a lesbian who still wore what used to be called, rudely, a Jewfro, and candelabra-like earrings that she made herself out of scrap metal. Evelyn was patrician and wry and dressed in a good wool suit. Both of them had been with Faith since the start of *Bloomer*.

On the third day, in the middle of the meeting, Greer heard raised voices coming from the conference room. She looked over and could see an arm gesticulating behind the glass. It was Faith's arm, recognizable even from across the floor. And there was Faith's voice, too, though it had a strain to it. Greer heard her say, "No, actually that is *not* what I meant. Let's start again. Marcella, *go*." This was followed by Marcella Boxman's voice *going*, speaking carefully, as if to disguise fear. Then there was another remark from a still-irritated Faith, and then someone else cautiously defended Marcella, until finally the meeting was flowing the way Faith wanted it to. And Faith, mollified, could finally be heard saying, "Nailed it!" and everyone laughed a little too hard in relief.

When the greenish glass door finally slid open with its *shush* sound, they all looked merry and satisfied, even Marcella. In fact, Faith had her arm around Marcella, as if reassuring her that everything was fine, the bad moment had passed, and it didn't matter anymore.

Faith could grow impatient and angry, as she had been described, but most of the time she was easygoing and generous, particularly to her assistant Iffat and the rest of the support staff. Greer had already seen her speak kindly to the old custodian who emptied her trash, even though he had accidentally thrown away a diploma from a college in Minnesota that had given her an honorary degree.

Faith was one of those people, Greer had started to see, who was seductive to almost everyone. Seduction was a power move to Faith, and maybe even a compulsion, but it seemed to happen effortlessly, and was in the service of a greater good. She wasn't a firebrand or a visionary; her talent was different. She could sift and distill ideas and present them in a way that made other people want to hear them. She was special. But still, apparently no one knew much about Faith's private life. Even her backstory. There had been plenty of interviews, but she remained a combination of warmth and mystery—and perhaps she liked it that way. To keep people from the particulars of your life kept you from being seen as one thing or another, and so it was possible you could be thought of as anything, or even as everything.

They all wanted to know her; Greer sensed this as a secret, quietly present, all-office wish. Greer knew that Faith had been widowed long ago and had a grown son, but that was about it. Did she have a boyfriend? What a ludicrous word to use when describing her. She was far beyond boyfriends; she would tower over them, dwarf them. And she had mentioned that she had a weekend house; what did it look like? Was it gabled? And what *were* gables? And what about her apartment on Riverside Drive? Only her assistant Iffat had ever been there, and as if knowing

Faith wouldn't want her to say anything about it, Iffat hadn't ever described it to anyone.

When Faith approached Greer's cubicle the afternoon after the tense meeting and said, "Hey, stop by today, okay?" Greer became anxious, worrying that she had made a mistake and was going to be called out on it. It was awful to displease Faith, and wonderful to please her; the equation was absolute, as Professor Malick might've said. No one ever forgot the way it felt to be on the receiving end of Faith Frank's pleasure or displeasure. But Faith was smiling now. When Greer came into her office, she brought with her the letter from Zee tucked into a folder. She'd dutifully carried it to work since Monday, waiting for a good time to give it to her. At first, though, it had seemed too soon, and too nervy to assume that she could try to have a friend hired. But Zee was waiting to hear what happened, so maybe this would be an okay time to try.

In Faith's enormous office they sat on either end of the long white couch. The light was slanting in, falling on Faith's cheek and revealing the faintest, nearly invisible layer of down that could only be seen from this exact angle, not that Greer would ever tell anyone she'd seen it. Faith leaned forward with her good, distinctive smell—Cherchez was the name of the scent, Greer had overheard her say to Marcella, who was herself so stylish that she would soon no doubt be marinated in Cherchez too.

"Tell me your impressions about what we're doing here," Faith said. "Be honest. Don't worry about my ego. I'm curious how it seems to you so far. The grand new venture. Is it actually grand?"

"At this point, maybe it's a baby grand."

Faith smiled at her, and it wasn't even funny! But it was in the neighborhood of funny, and Greer followed it up immediately by offering a variety of suggestions, all very different, so that Faith couldn't hate all of them. She had a suggestion about switching the order of two of the proposed events at the first summit, which was to be in March, on the theme of power.

Without changing her tone Greer lightly moved to another idea. "And I was thinking maybe we could look at some of the newer feminist blogs and see what they're up to." As soon as she said it, she thought about how the writers there sometimes took swipes at Faith: "The author of *The Female Persuasion* tries to persuade us that being in bed with ShraderCapital is perfectly fine. Corporate feminism much, Faith Frank?"

Faith just nodded at Greer. "Sure, we can have a look," she said. "You know, though, I was brought in to do the things I know how to do."

Greer, like all the other people Faith hired, knew there was a difference between working for Faith and working for a radical organization. But they all loved being led by this strong, appealing, dignified, older feminist; and they loved what she stood for.

When the conversation was almost over, everything had gone so well that Greer didn't want to ruin it with the clumsy intrusion of Zee's letter. So she still chose not to mention it. Soon she would bring it up, she told herself; soon. But walking back down the hall, feeling almost jaunty now—jig territory—Greer understood that she really didn't want to give Zee's letter to Faith. She didn't want to share Faith with Zee. She was still trying to figure out her place here at Loci—where she fit, where she didn't. Of course, she would certainly give the letter to Faith tomorrow, but she would do it only out of obligation.

By Friday afternoon, Greer hadn't yet found the right time to give the letter to Faith. She realized now that she wasn't going to give her the letter after all. At around five thirty, still at her desk, Greer was surprised to hear voices gathering in the distance. "Get your jacket, Boxman," someone called. It was Ben. Men often seemed to call women by their last names when they were flirting.

"That's Boxwoman to you, Prochnauer," said Marcella, playing along.

"Did someone reserve a table?" asked a voice that was familiar but not quite placeable, and then Greer recognized it as belonging to Kim Russo, the COO's assistant from up on 27; they'd met briefly when Greer got the ShraderCapital tour earlier in the week.

"I did," said Bonnie Dempster, distinctly. "The back one, in case we're too loud."

"Oh, we're definitely too loud," said someone else. Evelyn, maybe. "They have the best dirty martinis. Olive juice."

"All of Jews what?" said Ben. "All of Jews are . . . circumcised?"

"No, actually they are not," said Tad. "And I happen to know."

"She said 'olive juice,'" Marcella said, and then there was unstoppered group laughter, and the elevator arrived with its pointed *ping* and the voices faded as the whole group was swept downstairs together. They were going to a bar, and Greer had not been invited. Suddenly she lost the easy pleasure of sitting there working late. She had already gotten used to the idea that she wasn't going to be invited into certain meetings, but Tad wasn't either, and Faith had made it clear it wasn't personal. Yet Tad was with the rest of them now, and no one had invited Greer to come along.

It was perfectly still in the office now. It occurred to Greer, as if it were a revelation, that she was lonely there, something she hadn't exactly noticed before. Now it seemed so obvious. Across the big space, evening began to color the windows. Greer sat unmoving and suddenly vulnerable, and soon she heard a sound in the distance. Footsteps; maybe it was a straggler heading off to the bar with the others. The steps were heavy and male. Then there was whistling. Greer sat and listened. "Strangers in the Night," she decided after a moment. The steps came close, then stopped. Greer looked up and was shocked to see Emmett Shrader peering down at her. She had met him only once, on Tuesday morning when he had come down to the twenty-sixth floor for an awkward meet-and-greet with the Loci staff. He had walked into the larger of the two conference rooms with his young assistants dancing around him like sprites, and an older assistant, homely and probably long-suffering, slightly behind him.

Shrader was seventy, lion-headed, with longish silver hair and, that morning, a dark, sleek suit and expensive tie. "Hello, hello!" he'd said to everyone with forced conviviality, and they'd introduced themselves to him one by one, including the support staff. But by the time they were halfway done, you could see he couldn't bear to be detained any longer and that he was desperate to bolt. As a result, they all began saying their names at nervous, faster and faster clips, and soon they were through with the exercise and he was gone. Tonight he was in shirtsleeves, released from his suit and tie, but there was something slightly alarming about the sight of an important man in a moment of repose. Anything could happen.

"Which one are you?" he asked, actually entering Greer's cubicle.

"Greer Kadetsky," she said.

She looked around frantically at the trappings of her own little space. Her cheap plastic Goody hairbrush was on the desk;

she'd used it earlier, and now she could see a few hairs flowing from it. She took in the scent of this very rich man and realized it was unambiguously exciting, or at least exotic, because it had nothing to do with men her own age, those hipsters or little boys who all smelled of smoke and cheese fries and Starbursts and macchiatos. Cory often smelled of the protein bars she gave him by the case, and a cheap shampoo he grabbed from the drugstore that was supposedly made with balsam, but to which he paid so little attention that he once referred to it as "my balsa wood shampoo." She'd said, "You think you're shampooing your hair with balsa wood? Like, what kites are made of?" He had shrugged and said he hadn't ever thought about it.

But someone gave a lot of thought to the way Emmett Shrader smelled and dressed and presented himself. He had a look and smell of holdings and real estate and absolute certainty. In such close proximity to him, Greer felt she desperately needed to hide her ratty hairbrush. "So what do you do here?" Emmett Shrader asked, actually seeming curious.

"Booking."

"What does that mean, you pick the speakers to tell their sob stories?"

"No, I just try to get them to come. Other people pick them."

"Sounds fascinating. Why are you here so late?"

"You're here late too," she pointed out.

"I have an excuse," he said. "I was hanging out with your boss-lady. She and I have a two-person soirée once in a while. If I didn't get a chance to sit and talk with her after hours, then I don't know what I'd do. I need that."

"She's wonderful," said Greer, spontaneously, and her voice came out sounding so reverent that Shrader laughed.

"She is," he agreed. He looked at her with a thoughtful new expression. "You're a Faith Frank groupie, is that right?" he asked.

Greer hesitated uncomfortably. "Well, I don't know about that. I admire what she does."

"Oh come on, tell me. You look up to her, right? You think she can do no wrong. You want to please her and all that craperoo."

"Okay, sure. But I really do admire what she does."

"Well, me too," Shrader said.

They were quiet and companionable for a moment. He reached down onto her desk and spun her hairbrush, probably because he just needed to do something with his hands. Greer had read that the founder of ShraderCapital was restless, often bored, with an extremely short attention span. Many years later, after Greer was well-known, someone at a dinner party in LA would ask her if she could name a quality common to successful women, and she thought about this for a second, then said, "I think a lot of them know how to talk to men who have ADD." Everyone at the table had thought this was a very funny answer, but maybe it was actually true.

"So," Shrader said. "You don't like to go out with all the other people at the end of the week? Out for potato skins and the blooming onion, or whatever they eat to absorb all the alcohol?"

"No one invited me." She heard the self-pitying sound to her words.

"No one had to invite you," Emmett said. "Come." He gestured for her to follow him, so she did, confused and cautious, walking behind him along the floor and down the hall and into Loci's communal kitchen. There, above the coffee machine, was a handwritten and prominent sign: "FRIDAY DRINKS!" it read, followed by when and where to meet. Somehow, in her absorption, she hadn't seen it.

"Friday afternoons are a thing," said Emmett. "Everyone goes out. The people from my floor and yours."

She understood that she had been doing everything wrong there, except for the work itself.

"You can still catch up with them," Shrader said.

So Greer went back to her cubicle and pulled her jacket from its hook. Then she hurried down the street to the old brown façade of the Woodshed with the leaded glass windows, and there they were in the back, most of the team from 26, as well as some young associates and administrators from 27. When Greer walked through the hot, full bar and arrived at the pushed-together tables, Helen Brand raised a hand in greeting and said, "Everyone, make room." They all rearranged themselves, opening up a space for her, and she slipped in between Ben and Kim Russo from upstairs.

"Howdy," said Kim. She raised a glass to Greer—"A Cosmo. So dated, I know," she said, "but I need something at the end of another ratfuck week"—and drank. "Let's get you something strong too," she said.

"Sure, though I'm not sure I need something strong-strong. My job isn't too stressful. I actually wish it was."

"Did you hear that?" Kim said to the table. "Her job 'isn't too stressful' but she wishes it was."

"You'll get there, Greer," said Helen from down at the other end. "I came on only two weeks before you did. It accelerated quickly."

"Well, your job is different. You have more to do."

"If you want more to do," said Kim, "then do more. That's the rule of thumb in any workplace."

"Good to know," said Greer.

"Make yourself indispensable. I somehow made the COO think I had a deeper skill set than anyone else, and he bought it. Now he calls me on weekends to do extra work, and I can't be like, 'No thank you, Doug, I'd rather not.' Anyway, I got a bonus this year."

"There are no bonuses at a women's foundation," said Helen. "But I knew that going in."

"The bonus," said Ben, "is when Faith smiles at you. Then it's like being smiled at by God."

Greer took a sip of the cold drink that had appeared before her and said, "I would like to be smiled at by God."

"If God is actually a man, maybe you'll be winked at," said Kim.

"Or murdered," said Marcella. "Seriously, why do men hate women? There are so many words in the English language that men use to describe their hatred of women. *Bitch. Whore.* The C-word. It's like the overused thing about Eskimos and snow. But we never discuss this—the actual why of it. Ben and Tad, I'm looking at you."

"Come on, Marcella, I don't hate women," said Ben, holding up his hands. "Don't look at me."

"And don't look at me either," said Tad. "Most of the time I'm like, 'Why do I have to share a gender with you, you piece of shit?' It's like when you have a bad relative who has the same last name."

"Faith said men are scared of women," said Bonnie. "And that's the key to everything."

"Right," said Evelyn. "And she said it once on TV with that asshole novelist. Back in seventy-whatever."

"Evelyn and I were both in the studio audience," said Bonnie. "And afterward, we all went out for fondue. Most of you won't know what I'm talking about, but it was the age of fondue."

"There were used skewers wherever you looked," said Evelyn. "I can't remember exactly what she said men were scared of."

"Whatever it was," Ben said, "I'm sure she was right. Men know that women have our number. Like, women can see through us—"

"Yes, you had a hamburger for lunch," said Bonnie, to laughter.

"—and they can tell that we're full of shit. But the world keeps propping us up, and women know it, and we know you know it, so maybe we hate you because you have something on us. You're basically witnesses to a crime."

Greer, listening, thought about how she wished Zee were part of this. Then she remembered why Zee wasn't, and felt a new, strange peppering of shame. She also thought about how Ben was like a young feminist's dream, so good-looking and on the side of women, not threatened by them at all. Cory could be described that way too. Ben's leg was against hers now, maybe not consciously. His other leg was probably against Marcella's leg. Marcella in her little skirt and tights and heels. Marcella Boxman looked like she worked not for Loci or for Shrader-Capital, but for *Vogue*. Distantly, Greer recognized her own envy of the way Marcella moved through the world. Marcella had Ben's interest, and she had survived Faith's criticism, and she would probably end up being a powerful figure of some kind. It was a good thing that the first summit was about power; Marcella could pick up some tips to hasten its inevitability in her own life.

The group was laughing, and the back room of the bar heated up further. Greer was overexcited being there, and the talk got loud, and louder, and then it peaked and the mood became reflective and even weary. The drinks stopped coming, and the evening started to wind down. Ben and Marcella would now have part two of the evening, Greer thought: going home to one of their beds. And the other people in the group, did they have partners waiting too? Was Greer the only one who would be alone?

"Time to tear ourselves away," said Helen.

People started to get out their wallets to throw down money, but just then someone urgently said, "*Faith,*" which didn't in and of itself mean anything, because Faith's name was always getting said, a constant, a heartbeat, a rumbling *blurp* in the water cooler. But then Greer looked up and saw Faith walking toward the table. Wallets went back into bags and pockets, for the night apparently wasn't over yet after all.

"Faith, over here!" called Bonnie. Around the back room, a few people at other tables looked up and whispered to one another. They smiled, and one person said, approvingly, "Faith FRANK!" then everyone went back to their conversations. This was New York, where famous people drank from the same trough you did, and where, in the scheme of things, Faith wasn't all that famous. The long tables, pushed together, were filled to their maximum, but everyone squeezed even closer, and Greer found herself jammed further against Ben; she could feel the key ring in his pocket. Across from Greer, Faith sat down, and almost immediately a martini appeared before her, its glass perfectly beaded, extra olives in a pyramid at the bottom.

"I'm very grateful for this," Faith said. "The world is so enormous, but if you have places where they know what you like to drink, then all is well." Everyone casually talked to her, but no one wanted to monopolize her. Greer noted the way Faith maneuvered her way along the table without actually moving, like a figure in a painting whose eyes follow you around the room. She said something to each person, sharing a sympathetic or amused expression.

Greer had been talking to Kim when Faith broke in. Kim was

telling her how women in a corporate environment were not always good to one another. "We have this woman upstairs who will go unnamed," Kim said. "She's a heavy hitter in VC, and awful to other women. I hear stories all the time. I was in the elevator with her and she just stood there staring at the door, not saying a word, not even hi, and I wanted to say to her, I know I'm just an assistant, but don't you know that we're supposed to be decent to each other? I totally get that you feel threatened, because you've been made to feel this way. The ranks of women are kept really, really thin, so everyone feels that they're the only one allowed in, and they can't afford to be nice to other women."

Cunts, Greer thought. That is what Zee called women who hated women. She remembered the song with those lyrics that Zee had once sung.

Suddenly Faith said, "So, Greer, you're making friends here? Finding your way?"

It was the drink, partly; that was what she thought later. It was the drink, and the late hour, and the coincidence that Greer had been thinking about Zee at that exact moment; of course, she'd been thinking about Zee a lot all week, because of her letter. Kim turned away, talking to Iffat and Evelyn and giving Greer a moment with Faith; Ben, on Greer's other side, was talking to someone at the next table. No one was listening to Faith and Greer. "I have a friend who wants to work here," Greer suddenly said to Faith, almost in a whisper. "She wants me to give you a letter that she wrote, telling you about herself. You met her with me back in college."

"Ah," said Faith.

"But if I'm really being honest with myself, I know that there's a reason I haven't given it to you yet."

"Okay."

"I guess I really don't want her to work here."

"She wouldn't do a good job?"

"I'm sure she'd do a terrific job. She's been an activist. She just puts herself out there. Plus, she was the one who told me about you in the beginning. She's wonderful. I just don't think I want to share this experience with anyone. I think I want it for myself." Greer was waiting now for Faith to condemn her or absolve her. Greer's purse with the letter in it, down at her feet beneath the table, felt as dangerous as a nuclear suitcase.

"I see," said Faith. "And do you know why that is?"

"I have an idea," Greer said. "But if I say it out loud, I don't know how it's going to sound."

"Try it."

"My parents never knew how to be parents," Greer said, and Faith nodded. "The house was always messy, and I felt like we were all boarders in a boardinghouse. We didn't eat together that much. They didn't really get involved in the particulars of my life: my schoolwork, my friends. None of it was very interesting to them. They had this idea about being 'alternative,' but really I think they were mostly pretty marginal. They were potheads. They still are."

"I'm very sorry," Faith said gravely. "I wish someone had recognized what was going on, and tried to help your family be more of a family. It must have been confusing. A child just wants to love her parents and be loved, and it seems like it should be simple to do that, but sometimes it's not." Hearing the words in the past tense was kind of a revelation. That must have *been* confusing, Faith was saying, but it is no longer all that relevant.

"I think they were disappointed in me," Greer said. "I was so different from them. But I wanted something more." She realized how easily she was speaking to Faith. It wasn't like the time in the ladies' room. "I was very ambitious. I studied like crazy," she said. "And I read novels day and night. I had a mission."

"Which was?" Faith speared an olive in her drink, slid it between her teeth.

"To absorb everything in the world. But also to escape."

"Makes sense."

"So I'm not saying that this excuses what I feel about my friend working here," said Greer. "But I think it's the truth. She would be shocked if she heard me saying that I didn't want her." She paused. "She's going to ask me what happened, either way, and I'll have to say something." Greer thought about it. "I could tell her I gave you the letter, but that there were no jobs. If I did that, would it make me a terrible person?"

Faith didn't answer, but just kept looking at her. "Greer, shall I read the letter and make a decision about whether your friend should come in for an interview?" she asked gently. Greer couldn't answer. "Or do you just want to let it go?"

"I don't know."

"Well, my offer to read it stands," Faith said. "You can put it on my desk Monday. Or not."

"Thank you," was all Greer could say, miserably.

There was a silence, and Greer thought Faith was going to turn away, perhaps in disapproval, and talk to someone else. But instead she said, "I like the way you try to figure things out, Greer. You're genuine and thoughtful, even about parts of yourself you're not proud of. Want to do some writing for me?"

"*Sure*," Greer said. "I'd love it."

"Good. We're going to have small events around the city in the months before the first summit. These will be media lunches and dinners. There will be maybe twenty-five guests, max. Very intimate. The speakers I have in mind are women who've experienced injustice firsthand and tried to do something. None of them are slick. None of them are used to public speaking. They're not going to be at our summits, but we want them for these small events, kind of like teasers. It's important that they really know what to say. And I think, having read your fine writing, and hearing you talk tonight, that you'd be someone who could help them shape their words into something good."

"That sounds excellent," said Greer. "Thank you, Faith."

"You're welcome. Done."

And that was it. Greer would write small speeches for Loci. In this way, she would make herself indispensable. The whole evening had been tremendous, even the difficult part when she'd confessed about the Zee letter. Greer knew that the night would stay in her mind for a long time, and she would remember sitting at that long table drinking and chatting more and more easily with other people who wanted to do good in the world. And one of those people had been Faith. Faith, who approved of Greer. The approval was as soft as velvet, and the desire for that approval was, also like velvet, a little vulgar. It didn't even matter, Greer thought, that nothing had happened tonight that would make Faith think: What a special night this was!

Faith wouldn't think: I loved talking to that young Greer Kadetsky. I know that Greer had a moral choice to make about the letter her friend gave her to give to me, and I watched her struggle with it. She is finding her way, young Greer, and I was glad to be there to watch, and to assist if I could. Tonight was a lovely night, a bracing night, a memorable night.

No, Faith wouldn't think the night had been unusual at all. But Greer would.

Just then Bonnie Dempster said, "Faith! What was that witty thing we chanted at the ERA march, remember?"

Faith turned to Bonnie and said, "Did it go, 'One, two, three, four'?"

And Bonnie said, "Yes, it did! And what came next?" to

which Faith said, "Oh, Bonnie, I have no idea whatsoever." Then, to everyone, "Senior moment." There was laughter.

The letter from Zee, still at the bottom of Greer's purse, instantly became less significant. At work again on Monday, Greer forgot about it; she literally did not think about it once, and Faith didn't mention it. Faith had a lot of demands on her time, a lot of people asking her questions, soliciting her advice, calling her up, emailing her at all hours.

A few days later, when the fact of the letter suddenly struck Greer again, she thought that it was too late now. Too much time had passed. Faith had probably forgotten all about it, and Greer should just let it drop. That was what she told herself.

That night, though, Zee called from her childhood bedroom in Scarsdale, where she was sitting beneath her old posters of the Spice Girls, and Kim Gordon of Sonic Youth, and endangered baby animals crouching in tundra or field or forest. "So did you get a chance to give the letter to Faith?" she asked.

Greer paused, sickened, madly thinking. "Sorry to say," Greer said, "there are no jobs there."

"Oh," said Zee. "That's too bad. I know it was a long shot. Did she say anything about what I wrote?"

"No, sorry."

"No worries!" said Zee, a joke between them. Then, "I appreciate it that you tried. I've got to get out of this law firm soon, somehow."

A confession to Faith, then a nonaction, then a lie. That was the sequence, and then it was done. Greer wondered, afterward, if everyone had a certain degree of awfulness inside them. There were moments when you idly glanced into the toilet or into a tissue after you'd used it, and suddenly remembered that this, *this* was what you carried around inside you all the time. This was what was always waiting to be let out. When she got off the phone, the letter went into a bottom drawer of her dresser. She wondered exactly what it said, though she would never read it, and she would never tell anyone else what she had done. Only Faith knew.

The following day when Greer arrived at work, she found a folder from Iffat on her desk containing printouts about the women who were coming to give talks at the small media lunches and dinners. Over the next couple of months these women came into the office one after another to be interviewed by Greer. They told her their stories about being harassed, or denied equal pay or the chance to play sports, and trying to do something about it. Once they started talking, and realized how carefully Greer was listening, they talked more openly.

What the stories had in common was a deep and grinding sense of unfairness. *Unfair* could burn you up. Sometimes the women seemed entirely burned up the minute they started talking, but other times they just seemed defeated, and they cried into their hands as they sat in the conference room with Greer. Their faces became congested, and they were so exposed that she wanted to shield them, knowing they were surrounded by glass, and that some greenish, blurred version of them could be seen by everyone walking past. When they cried she sometimes cried a little too, but she never stopped taking notes or running the little digital recorder. She learned she didn't need to say much; it was better if she didn't. Later on, after they left, Greer sat down and wrote the speech as if they were telling it into her ear.

The first speech Greer wrote was for Beverly Cox, who worked in a shoe factory upstate where the men were paid more, and on top of that where the women were degraded and harassed, and they all had to work together inside a hotbox roiling with fumes. The product they made there was high-end shoes for wealthy women, all pointed toe and weaponized heel. Greer sat in her cubicle playing back a tape with headphones on, listening to Beverly haltingly describe standing in a line of women making heels, while across the way a group of men made soles, and were paid more for it. After Beverly discovered the discrepancy and complained to the manager, she was harassed and threatened by male coworkers. They changed the lock on her locker so she couldn't open it; they slashed her tires; they left threatening and pornographic messages at her workstation. The smells of leather and glue became associated with degradation; they were in her head and on her clothes all the time. The lawyer she called for help put her in touch with the foundation.

"I'd get out of my car in the parking lot each morning and walk into that factory like I was walking a plank," Beverly had said, and then she burst into tears, and Greer had said, "Take as long as you need." On the tape, for a very long stretch, all that could be heard were Beverly's scared, shaky breaths, and once in a while Greer saying, "It's okay. I think it's great that you're speaking about this. I really admire you." And then Beverly had said, "Thank you," and blown her nose loudly. Then there was more silence. Greer didn't try to shorten it. A person needed to take her time when she talked about what had been so hard for her. Greer sat in her cubicle, listening to the breathing, and then, again, the talking.

When Beverly delivered the speech at lunch in an Italian restaurant in midtown to a small crowd of local media, everyone was quiet, appalled. Of course it was exciting for Greer to be the one who had shaped the speech, and to know that Faith, who was also in the room, knew it too. Faith came over to Greer afterward and lightly whispered, "Nailed it."

But what excited Greer now wasn't only Faith's praise. While it would always feel extraordinary to know she had the admiration of Faith Frank, what also excited Greer was that the speeches she was writing might give the women who delivered them a chance to be ambitious too; as ambitious as she was.

Winter dissolved, and the office hummed louder and the beta lights burned longer and perhaps even greener, and work often extended deep into the night. Pizza was often ordered late, giving work the quality of a college all-nighter. Ticket sales still needed to be ramped up, Faith told the whole office once at two a.m., a slice of pizza in hand. The in-demand disabled former governor who was supposed to come give a barn burner at the first summit about sexual assault in the disability community had just canceled. "It's crazy here," Greer said to Cory on Skype even later that night. "No one can sleep, or have a life outside work. We're all basically doing only this." But she was excited, and he could hear it.

"Lucky you," he said from his own desk in Manila, where it was afternoon and he was shuffling around papers in the service of companies he didn't really care about. Other people in his office cared, but he didn't, or at least not enough. "I think I'm supposed to like it more," he'd said once. "Like you do."

Everything, Faith said, depended on the success of the first summit. If it failed, then maybe ShraderCapital would pull out. Though the ticket sales were a problem, the advance press had been impressive, with camera crews appearing at work, and interviewers disappearing into Faith's office for a long one-on-one.

On a Monday in March, a little over a week before the summit, after night had fallen and everyone was staying at work as long as they were needed, Faith said she had an announcement.

She stood up before them and said, "I know you're all tired. I know you're worn down to the bone. And I know you have no idea how the summit is actually going to go. Neither do I. But I want to say that you are all the best people I know. And you have all been working your asses off, and there's just so long that that kind of *asslessness* can go on"—laughter—"without someone having a nervous breakdown. Probably I'm that someone. So I've decided that what we all need is to get the hell out of here."

"Right now?" someone called. "Taxi!"

"Oh, I wish. Actually, what I mean is that I'd like to invite you all to my place upstate this weekend. There will be food, and wine, and I think we'll have fun. What do you say?"

It was very late notice, and though it wasn't a command performance, of course everyone would go. It would be like entering a fortress and seeing its mysterious insides. They'd get to know a little more about Faith, who left very few clues about herself. On Saturday the group took the same train, and then they split up into different taxis, and headed for Faith's house. Apparently there was very spotty cell phone service there in the woods. "Tell your loved ones you will be out of commission," Faith had said to them.

Greer's taxi plunged off the main road and onto a small weedy one that took them past a scrambled mess of greenery, and kept plowing through until suddenly the greenery thinned and parted, revealing a pretty brown-shingled house with red trim in the middle distance, with Faith standing on its porch, waving. She was actually wearing an apron and holding a rolling pin, and her hair was blowing. She looked like a beautiful, brave pioneer woman.

Once inside, Greer couldn't even fully take in all the particulars of Faith Frank's weekend house. Objects radiated various degrees of meaning, some of it probably imagined. A maroon leather chair was positioned beside a reading lamp, the leather indented and the dye rubbed off where Faith's head had tilted against it over dozens of years. Briefly, when no one was looking, Greer sat in it, leaning her head back, but though it was no big deal she leaped up in a moment, like a dog that knew it wasn't supposed to be on the furniture.

Greer's room, which at first glance was simply a guest room, revealed itself to be something more. Across from the narrow white wrought-iron bed stood an old dresser with some knick-knacks on it, among them a small, dusty trophy, on which was engraved:

Pee Wee Summer Soccer—1984
Lincoln Frank-Landau
Most Cooperative

Faith's son had spent summers in this room. Now he materialized like a genie from the gold-plated trophy. Even in phantom form he was a mild threat, giving Greer, a perpetual only child, a sense of what it must be like to have a sibling. Or at least what it must be like to have a sibling if you were the child of Faith Frank. You would both be very lucky, except for the fact that you had to share your extraordinary mother. But maybe Lincoln had always felt he'd had to share her. Faith fought for women and girls—"When the world doesn't look out for them, we have to," she'd said—and maybe Lincoln had been in competition with them.

And maybe Lincoln had also felt he'd had to share his mother with the people at her job. For even now, Faith was intensely involved with the team at Loci. She went out of her way to call

Greer into her office sometimes, or to sit with her and a couple of others at lunch once in a while, all of them with paper plates on their laps. She asked Greer about her life, and Greer shyly told her about Cory living on the other side of the world. Faith continued to praise Greer for the speeches she had been writing. Sometimes the women who told Greer their stories stayed in touch afterward, telling her about their lives—a new job, or a setback.

"You really bring out the voices of these women," Faith had said recently. "I know we've talked about how hard it is for you to speak up sometimes. But maybe you've compensated, because I have to say you're an excellent listener. And that is just as important as speaking. Keep listening, Greer. Be like . . . a seismologist, with a stethoscope pressed against the earth. Pay attention to the vibrations."

Here at the house, Faith's voice could be heard in the distance; she shouted something, and someone laughed and shouted in response. Now there was hammering on the door, and then a slightly less loud sound of other doors down the hallway being hammered on too. Marcella called, "Faith wants us downstairs for cocktail hour and food prep!" Everyone appeared downstairs within a minute or two; there were no stragglers.

In the kitchen Faith held up a knife and said, "Who wants to be my sous-chef?" and everyone volunteered, their hands shooting up. But Greer's shot up the fastest.

"Okay, Ms. Kadetsky, the job is yours," said Faith. "Can you do the onions first?"

"Sure." Greer could do onions; they would unflower in her hands. If Faith had said, "Can you solve Fermat's Last Theorem?" Greer would have said, "Why yes I can," and then sat down at a blackboard, chalk in hand, and done it.

Faith handed her a mesh bag swelling with onions. Greer

positioned herself at the counter, hoping to look like someone who belonged here. A pinot noir was brought out, along with hand-blown tumblers of different colors. Greer's was sea-glass green, with little bubbles of imperfection trapped inside like carbonation, and she welcomed the bite of the wine and felt it charge to her head and her thighs at the same time.

"Tonight is steak night," Faith announced to the kitchen, and there were sounds of approval.

Greer was going to say, "I can just eat the side dishes," but then the subject changed, so she would remind Faith of her meatlessness later. Now everyone began talking about the summit, which would begin Tuesday.

"I still wish we'd gotten Senator McCauley," said Helen. "I can't let go of it." There was studious quiet. Whenever the senator's name came up everyone became a little depressed, almost destabilized. Senator Anne McCauley from Indiana was a powerful force, an antichoice steamroller, an alarming figure who had done a lot to chip away at women's reproductive rights, and in particular the reproductive rights of women living in poverty. Despite being in her late sixties, Anne McCauley showed no sign of stopping.

"I tried," said Tad. "I sent her office a slavish and eloquent letter. I used all my rhetorical flourishes, but they didn't work."

"It would be weird if she did agree to come," said Iffat. "She's no friend to women."

"No, it wouldn't be so weird," Helen said. "She speaks at lots of events. She likes a good debate."

"I swear, she's going to try to run for president," Evelyn said. "I know she's getting up there in years, but still."

"She scares the shit out of me," said Bonnie.

Marcella said, "I grew up in Indianapolis, and I remember when she was running for reelection. She had this whole campaign against her pro-choice opponent. I remember there were pictures of fetuses."

They talked about abortion rights, and the composition of the Senate, and about human trafficking, which was a subject Faith felt particularly strongly about, her voice sharpening whenever it came up. And then somehow there was a brief side trip into a discussion about a TV crime show from the UK with a hot female character named DCI Gemma Braithwaite, who was beleaguered by the sexism in her department and the violence in her district. Most of the people there loved Gemma Braithwaite, and the entire group, Faith included, quoted aloud a line from a recent episode, which had become sort of a catchphrase: "I shall take no shite from anyone. *Sir.*" Then they all laughed, and drank some more.

Helen started talking about women being part of an economic structure so unjust that it could only be fixed by undoing the whole thing. "Piece by fucking piece," she said, and Ben raised his glass. Faith dismissed this. "Even if that ever happened here," she said, "women would still get shafted. Look at Cuba and Venezuela. Women there still aren't equal."

"What's your perspective on that?" Greer heard herself ask. Everyone looked at her. Marcella's mouth was pulled tight, as if she was thinking: You dunce; who would ask such an ignorant question? But no one else looked at Greer like that; certainly not Faith, who was glad to try to answer.

"I think the ideas about what men are and women are, what they *essentially are*, go very deep," she said. "That women are subordinate. That women will always be thwarted. These are the ideas that have taken hold everywhere. Sure there's an economic piece, and that's always been true. But there's a psychological piece too, and we can't forget it." A few of them nodded, although they'd heard versions of this from her before. Bonnie and Evelyn, who in particular had certainly heard many versions of this, looked happy to hear it again.

"I've noted," said Faith, "that when people speak about feminism they take one tack or the other. Our foundation has to look at all of it. We need to keep thinking about the role that economics plays. Because no matter how fair a society is, it's still going to be women who have the babies. And that sets them up for housewifery and the double day." She reached up to a high shelf and pulled down an old salad spinner. Lettuce was rinsed and dumped in, and then Faith yanked hard on the string again and again, as if it were an outboard motor. She kept talking over the din. "Even in highly evolved places like Sweden and Norway, women end up doing most of the shitwork. Though they probably call it something cute—the way IKEA names all its furniture, so it sounds better. I have a chair at home named 'Leifarne.' But we still need to see things for what they really are." She let the salad spinner putter to a stop, then glanced around at them; everyone was listening, and no one had the recessive, tuned-out quality that could happen when groups of people got together and drank.

"Bonnie and Evelyn and I are so old," Faith said, "that we remember the sixties as if it were yesterday—"

"—or this morning," said Evelyn.

"And let it be a cautionary tale. The women's movement back then had to separate itself from the male-dominated left because, you know what? The left wasn't all that interested in us. My sense is that we're going to be seeing that again. We're going to come up against progressives who will say that women's problems can't be solved under the current system, but that everything will change for women more or less automatically when that system is changed. We're also going to need to show that we support anti-racist work. You know I got Emmett to pour special-project money into a reproductive justice group, and also an organization that supports young black women writers. But of course that's not enough. Anyway, I hope our first summit makes a big splash. I hope we make a difference."

They were all silent, and when she was done speaking, Tad said, "Thank you for inviting us here, Faith. It's really an honor."

"Oh, don't feel that way. I want you to feel relaxed around me." Faith smiled a peculiar smile, amused at herself, and added, "Which is why I drugged all of your drinks."

"Faith Frank embroiled in a roofie scandal," said Ben. "*That* would make the news."

"And get more attention for Loci," said Greer.

"That reminds me," Faith said. "Someone tell me about the music we've started to line up. Because if it were left to me, I'd be bringing in the feminist folk singers I met years ago at Lilith Fair. And that would be . . . well, very far from *ka-ching!*"

Everyone laughed now, and Helen said, "Oh, Faith, you know what? I just love you."

"And I love you too," said Faith.

"We got Li'l Nuzzle, by the way," Marcella said.

"No shit?" said Tad.

"Is it L apostrophe I-L? Or L-I apostrophe L?" asked Ben. "I can never remember."

"I don't know," said Greer. He smiled at her and she smiled back, then they both looked away shyly.

"I'm afraid I don't even really know who that is," Faith said.

"A hip-hop act," said Iffat. "She's awesome. You'll love her, Faith."

"I guess *Big* Nuzzle wasn't available," said Greer. She looked down at the onions and saw that somehow a pyramid of slices lay on the cutting board; how had she cut so much already? Also, she noticed with some bewilderment that the wine was gone from her green, bubbled glass.

"As I said, we've got an excellent slate," Faith said. "Our naval commander. Our activist nun."

"I love how we don't even remember their names," said Marcella.

"*I* remember their names, and you should too," said Faith. "But not tonight. Tonight, we drink wine and eat steak and kick back and chill out."

Greer refilled her glass and looked around at everyone, thinking then how lucky she was to be here with these people, this focus group of the old and the young, the heavy and the thin, the black and the brown and the white, the gay and the straight and possibly the bisexual. Though Zee would say all of this was a completely reductive way to see people, and probably it was. But tonight Greer took in the fellowship of everyone here. The famous and the unknown, the bitter, the salty, and the sweet. And even the umami. Faith was umami, in a way, Greer thought—a special and separate taste that, once you'd tried it, you wanted more of.

As they talked and laughed and drank, Greer imagined telling Cory every detail after the weekend. He liked stories from her New York life, just as Greer liked stories from Manila, where he lived a life in mirror-opposite to hers. She already had so much to tell him from this weekend.

I stayed in Faith's son's bedroom, she would say, and I imagined what it would have been like to have had Faith as my mother.

Complicated, I bet, Cory would reply.

Yes, definitely complicated.

Greer saw herself now as if through Cory's vision; she imagined herself seen by him from the doorway, the light in the room gilded. And then her hand, cutting onions with new, slightly reckless assurance, slipped, and the blade of Faith Frank's knife slid deep into her thumb.

"Oh shit, oh shit!" Greer cried, jumping back, as though she could escape her own injury.

They were all upon her, and distantly she heard Evelyn murmur, "Look at all that blood. Oh, I'm not good with blood." Everyone rushed around but no one knew where anything was except for Faith, who calmly took charge, finding a very old, yellowed tin first-aid kit in the back of the drawer beside the refrigerator.

"No one has ever left here thumbless," Faith assured Greer, who was so mortified and furious at herself for ruining the moment that her eyes streamed with real tears, not onion tears.

"Really? What about Thumbless McGee?" asked Tad, and the comment was followed by silence, and Tad quickly saying, "Sorry. I make bad jokes when I'm nervous."

Faith turned to them and calmly said, "Why don't you all go take your drinks into the next room. Greer will be absolutely fine. I will tend to her."

"Are you sure?" asked Iffat, going into assistant mode. "Isn't there anything I can do?"

"I've got it under control. Thank you, Iffat."

Faith stood beside Greer over the deep stainless-steel sink, where she ran a thudding flow of cold water down upon the bloody thumb and then dried it, keeping pressure on the wound, and then squirted on some antibacterial ointment, and wrapped Greer's thumb in a swaddling of gauze and adhesive. The light touch of this powerful woman was profound. So too was her choice to use her power in this tender way. Maybe that's what we want from women, Greer thought as her thumb pulsed and percolated with blood. Maybe that's what we imagine it would be like to have a woman lead us. When women got into positions of power, they calibrated and recalibrated tenderness and strength, modulating and correcting. Power and love didn't often live side by side. If one came in, the other might go.

Faith was saying, "Let's keep it like this for a while and see if it stops. Hold it up; keep it above your heart. I don't think you'll need a stitch."

"I can't believe I cried like that."

"What's wrong with crying? I think it's underrated," said Faith.

"But right now I feel like a little girl whose mother is fixing her boo-boo. It's so embarrassing."

"Not for the mother. I remember doing that when my son was little." Faith pushed her hair back from her face and said, "In my experience, the rewards don't necessarily come when you think they will with your kids. And sometimes they come very, very infrequently."

Greer thought again of the pee wee soccer trophy up in the bedroom, and the highly cooperative boy who had won it, now in his thirties and off somewhere else. "So when do they come?"

"Oh, let's see," said Faith. "When they're happy, isn't that what everyone says? Or when they're asleep. Sometimes I was ashamed of how much I liked it when he was asleep. He was a good kid, but it was just so much work. And at least when he was asleep I knew where he was and exactly what was happening with him."

"And what about now?" Greer asked lightly. "What's he like?"

"Now? Now I don't know all that much. His life is his life. He's a tax attorney, and he's very different from me. Not sure he needs me too much. And I never get to watch him sleep. I've decided that there should be a national holiday once a year, when grown children have to let their parents tuck them in one more time."

She was silent, and Greer didn't rush in to speak. Faith was revealing herself, opening up, becoming slightly more known. There was a glimmer of mutuality, and Greer didn't want to do anything to discourage it. They were standing together in silence at the sink, by the window that overlooked the dark yard, which was lit with a single floodlight, into which now pranced a deer, as if on cue. It stopped in the cone of light, looking around.

"Ah. My occasional visitor," said Faith.

The deer had one leg tipped up as though it had been making its way across the grass when suddenly it became lost in thought, maybe thinking about berries, or leaves, or about the curious figures of the older woman and the younger one who stood framed inside a small window. Faith moved slightly, and the deer startled, then dashed away.

A little later, after Greer had recovered and was being treated by everyone as if she were a minor heroine, the grill was lit and the question of the steaks came up again. "I assume that no one has a problem with meat?" Faith said. "If you do, speak now or forever hold your peace."

"Your piece of tempeh, you mean," said Iffat.

Greer was about to mention her vegetarianism, which every- one else knew anyway, after all those times when they'd ordered lunch, but none of them looked expectantly toward her now. Apparently people never really paid as much attention to you as you thought they did. Having so recently had that moment of intimacy with Faith at the sink, she thought about Faith's appar- ently mildly disappointing son, and somehow she felt sure that turning down Faith's meat would also be a disappointment to

Faith. Greer fervently did not want to disappoint her, so she didn't say anything.

"All right," said Faith. "Even though it's a little brisk out there, I'm still up for firing up the grill. Everyone likes it rare, I hope?"

"Yes!" came the chorus, including Greer, who surprised herself.

Through the window Greer saw Ben and Marcella mime a quick, flirty sword fight with grill implements. Tonight probably they would share a bed, and maybe their lovemaking would even be heard through the walls, to everyone's general embarrassment and awe. The grill smoked and sputtered and began to give off the smell of meals once cooked and now half-conjured.

At the table, a steak was speared up by a long fork and dropped with a thud onto Greer's plate by Faith herself. "Voilà," said Faith. "These came out well, I think. Hope they're not too bloody."

"Bloody good," said Tad.

Greer glanced with a fixed smile at the enormous slab of steak, which was already pooling in blood, as if it were the head of a person who'd just jumped off a roof. Faith deposited a lump of herb butter on top of Greer's steak, and it immediately spread its arterial death over the stingray-sized surface.

"Dig in, Greer, even with your war injury," said Faith.

"Yes, my stump," said Greer.

"And please, none of you wait for me." Faith went to tend to the next person.

Greer picked up the fork with her injured hand and clumsily held it; she sat with fork and knife at the ready, wondering how she could possibly eat this steak. It was a dark reddish blue inside, unnatural, even perverse. *Cool*, she had heard that was called.

All around her, people were eating and exclaiming. "Oh my God," Marcella moaned quietly, and Greer imagined her in bed with Ben. "This is amazing, Faith."

"Best fucking steak I've ever had," said Tad.

"You know, Faith, if the foundation doesn't work out," said Helen, "you could open a restaurant and call it Faith Frank's Feminist Steakhouse. Every steak would come with roast potatoes, creamed spinach, and the promise of equality."

Greer was the only one who hadn't praised Faith's meat; she soon became self-conscious about her silence and felt she had to contribute something. "And every steak at the feminist steakhouse also comes with access to the salad bar!" she added. Faith, recognizing this was meant to be funny, smiled at her.

Greer got busy cutting a perfect cube and then spearing it. Glancing at it in the light, she was reminded of one of those drawings of a cross-section of a piece of human tissue. To eat meat when you hated it and when you hadn't eaten it for four years was an aberration, nearly a form of cannibalism. But also, she told herself, it was an act of love. In eating this, she was being someone Faith would want to continue to confide in and listen to and rely on; someone she would want to cook meat for. Greer deposited the piece onto her tongue, hoping it would somehow dissolve there like a sugar cube, but finding instead that it obstinately retained its shape, its integrity, not ceding any muscle or fat. The inside of her mouth was like a slaughterhouse in miniature, with a hint of cedar closet. It was disgusting.

Do not be sick, she thought sternly. *Do not be sick.*

Greer tried to reframe the idea of eating meat; was it really all that different from, say, what took place in sex? In the beginning with Cory, Greer had been both excited and afraid. But soon she was less afraid. Other people, she learned, were not so bad. Cory was just another person, a soul inside a long membrane. He was an animal she deeply loved. Just as this, now, this cubic inch of lost and mournful cow, wasn't so bad either.

Goodbye, cow, she thought, picturing the distant green blur of a meadow. I hope your short life was at least sweet. She swallowed hard and forced herself not to cough it up. The steak went down and stayed down.

"Yum," Greer said.

On the train platform on Sunday morning, waiting for the 10:04 to take them back to the city and the final days before the first summit, everyone turned on their cell phones again and watched them stutter into service. The phones lit up, the apples popped in, and the Loci team peered with great interest at what they had missed in their absence. They turned away from one another and stalked the platform, listening to voicemails and reading messages.

Greer saw with confusion that she'd received thirty-four voicemails and eighteen texts since she'd arrived at Faith Frank's house. It made no sense, but there it was, an extravagant cascade of urgency, almost all of it coming from Manila.

SIX

The Ninoy Aquino International Airport at sunrise had an impossibly long line outside the entrance, leading up to the metal detectors through which every person had to pass, not just those who were flying today. Cory Pinto, crying for the past couple of hours in spasmodic waves, shuffled in along with everyone else, his eyes burned into little embers. He was trying to keep it together, as people said, but it wasn't working very well.

Once he was through the detectors, a voice on a loudspeaker whispered something about flight 102, and Cory knew he had to move fast. He pushed through the people standing in bunches ahead of him, saying to them, "Excuse me! *Makikiraan po!*" but nobody moved. People stood seven or twelve deep, clutching luggage or backpacks, or in some cases a loose congregation of boxes bound with tape.

Cory had no luggage; he'd forgotten to bring anything. All rational planning had fled from him after the news arrived in the middle of the night. He'd gotten the call, and then he'd stood in the living room of his apartment and said to McBride, his roommate, "I have to go."

McBride, whom he had known slightly at Princeton, though they were in different social groups and would never have been friends, looked up from where he'd been half conked out on the leather sofa with its rounded arms and cold slippery surface, re-playing old missions of Red Dead Redemption on the Xbox that he'd had shipped there from his parents' house when he'd first been hired by Armitage & Rist.

"What?" McBride said. "It's three in the fucking morning. Where you gonna go, man?" Music came from his butt-ugly speakers, which always reminded Cory of a housefly's eyes, each one with a round black convex circle at the center. Pugnayshus's silly rap lyrics played:

I saw you sittin' there at the Korean foot spa
I saw you sittin' there with all'a your chutzpah

Their third roommate, Loffler, fresh from a finance degree at the Wharton School, was asleep in his room, which always reeked of the cheap weed that he had purchased on a trip to Sagada and riskily brought back for all the roommates to partake of. They were all earning so much money, and while they didn't want to throw it around and expose themselves to danger, they didn't want to be miserly either. They lived in this cushy high-rise in the Makati district, away from the crowded streets, letting themselves rest in the deep, silk-lined pocket where the expats lived and worked and played and spent their money.

"Something happened," Cory said flatly.

"That's about as nonspecific as you can get," said McBride. "You want me to guess?" Cory began to cry again, his face cor-rugating in pain, and of course McBride didn't know what to do. "Help me out here," said McBride. "Somebody die back home?"

Cory nodded his miserable face.

"Like your grandma or something?"

He shook his head no.

When his cell phone had rung in the night, Cory had sat up in bed and seen his parents' number. It irritated him that they had trouble remembering the time difference between the East Coast of the US and Manila. Now his entire night's sleep had been wrecked by the ringing phone. He spoke into it in a tight, unfriendly voice, wanting to convey to his parents that he was *grown* now, that he had responsibilities and needed his sleep. But his father was crying and saying the most insane thing in Portuguese, "*Sua mãe matou seu irmão!*"

"What?" He must have translated it wrong. "What are you talking about?"

"Your mother killed your brother."

His father's voice came out in frightening anguish as he told how Cory's mother, backing out of the driveway, had accidentally run over Alby, who had been playing there, unseen. Alby's back had been crushed, a bone breaking off and entering a pulmonary artery. He'd held on for a while, but in the OR in Springfield he had died.

"What? Are you sure?" Cory asked pathetically, raking his hair in the dark, then rubbing his face, trying to find something to do with his now flapping, now flying-away hand.

"Yes. She did this," his father said. "I can't look at her."

"Where is she?"

"Sedated. They gave her a shot."

"All right. All right," Cory said, trying to think. "Maybe you need to be sedated too. I'm going to the airport now. I'll try to fly out in the morning. It's night here. It'll take me a whole day."

Even as he said this, he couldn't imagine looking at his mother again either. Cory pressed his phone between his hands and then called the airline, sitting and listening to a scratchy brass instrumental version of "The Strong Ones" that ran in a loop. After he made a reservation he called Greer, who he needed now in a new, adult way. It was as if he actually thought she could do something. But the call went straight to voicemail. "Where are you?" he said into the phone. "I need you." He had never said those words to her. *Love*, all the time, but *need*, never.

Frantically he kept calling back and speaking in a louder and louder voice to her recorded voice, then hanging up. He texted her multiple times too, saying, "Call me," but got no reply. There was no way he could leave the news about Alby in a recorded message, no way he could say the words into empty air. He needed Greer to be listening in real time as he spoke them, so that as he exhaled the facts she would inhale them in a kind of mouth-to-mouth resuscitation. "Call me, please," he whispered, as if maybe modulation would somehow get her attention. "No matter what time. Something really, really bad happened."

When there was still no answer, he remembered that she'd told him she was going away to Faith Frank's house for the weekend, and that she would be out of cell phone range. Faith Frank, who was like a superhero to her. You would think some- one as powerful as Faith Frank would be able to get a signal at her house. He paced the small room, which was a stew of his belongings, the wastebasket frothing over with papers, and empty bottles of San Mig Strong Ice standing together on the bureau. The whole place was overcome by a general sense of disorder and reek, all of which would be dispensed with by the housekeeper, Jae Matapang, who cleaned up after the three high-paid young Americans who could not take care of themselves. "*Boys*," she sometimes said, shaking her head when she showed up and looked around the apartment. "Always make such a mess." Yet she never seemed displeased.

In the darkness, his stomach cramping, Cory slipped out of the drawstring bottoms he'd bought at the Greenbelt Mall and dug into a drawer to find some boxers. Jae took their laundry to a room in the basement that none of the men had ever seen. "Hey, Jae," the three guys always said, handing her their things, and she silently accepted it all, washing their pee- and semen-dashed underclothes and ironing their shirts so they could show up looking impressive and confident at Armitage & Rist's office in the Rufino Pacific Tower, the tallest steel-framed building in the Philippines.

Cory thought it was entirely likely that he would become a mad person at age twenty-three, and would wander the streets of Manila. Jae would see him out there and would feel bad, thinking, One of the messy boys has become insane. The tall one!

Because he had no time to look for anything else, Cory slipped into a pair of black dress pants that were heaped on his desk chair, and then he jammed his passport into the front pocket of his pants and headed out the door. Riding to the airport in the back of a cab with a broken seat belt that lay uselessly across his lap like a flail arm, he watched as the sedate burble and glitter of Makati receded.

He hadn't gotten used to life here yet. From the start it had been unfamiliar. As he traveled to the Philippines on Cathay Pacific not long after college ended, the flight attendants had welcomed him like a long-lost friend. He lay down and found that he did not seem out of place, or like an impostor. Not only that, but his long self seemed not too long for that sky bed, which was like a cradle that rocked him as they crossed the ocean.

So Cory Pinto, from Macopee, Massachusetts, ate various

pieces of dim sum as well as a minute steak; he ate without worrying about how much he was eating. Life at Princeton had set him up for his new life, which had even started to seem earned, though at other moments he knew that he had earned nothing. Distantly behind him came the moans and discontents of economy class.

In Manila, an apartment had been found for him and the others. The building had an absurd name, the Continental Arches. Makati was a wealthy, cushy zone, but once he stepped outside the district he was in fast-moving Manila, which was its own trip. Most of the people Cory encountered there spoke excellent English, but still he tried to learn Tagalog, because many locals didn't speak English well, and he wanted to not be a snob when he went outside of his little hive; he wanted to make an effort. Once in a while he and his roommates would go out on the town drinking in local bars and eating cheap meals in dives in a particular area that the orientation materials from Armitage & Rist had specifically warned them to avoid.

They rode on jeepneys, those half-bus-half-jeeps painted wild, bright colors and sprayed with graffiti; sometimes they featured illustrations of devils or eagles and were accompanied by words or phrases like MONSTER-MOBILE, or JESUS LOVES ME SO HARD, or MISS ROSA AND HER BROTHERS. Inside, passengers sat on two long benches facing each other, knee to knee, and were taken on a shockless, bouncing ride wherever they wanted to go in the city. "*Bayad po*," Cory said nervously the first time he rode one, passing his money forward. Later on, it all became easy and almost natural.

Manila had impressed itself upon Cory in light and heavy ways: the wealth that was concentrated in Makati; the K-9 teams that sniffed around the cars entering the driveways of the top hotels, trunks popped so security guards could look inside with flashlights; the exotica and the twisting extravagance of the foliage; the fish stands and the fruit stands; the fragrant food at even the tiniest little joint; the beautiful children running everywhere; the shocking poverty; and the malls, God, the malls, where so much activity took place because they were air-conditioned and the air outside was air-conditioning's opposite. Manila could be a kiln, and they all baked in it together.

But now, after months of being there making money and eating adobo and crispy *pata* and staying out late partying with clients, far from Greer, who was waiting for him while she lived her own life in another city, here he was in a state of unmanageable grief, roaring in a taxi with a broken seat belt toward the Manila airport to fly home to be with his family because his brother was dead. He was glad there was no seat belt; he didn't even want one. "You can crash this car if you want," he said to the driver. "I don't give a shit."

"What do you say?" said the driver, looking in the rearview mirror to assess the situation.

"You can drive straight off the road. I want to be dead. I want to die."

"But I don't want to die," said the driver. "I think you're a crazy man," he added with a tense laugh. But his curiosity bested him, and in a milder voice he asked, "Why do you want to die?"

"My brother was run over by a car and killed. My mother was driving."

"I am sorry," said the taxi driver reflexively. "Your *brother*. A little boy or a man?"

"A little boy." Cory recalled his brother's intelligent, animated face, knowing it would de-animate and recede over time. It would have to.

"Oh, that is terrible." Then, without a word, the driver pulled onto the shoulder of the highway. The sky held a smudge of incipient sunlight. They sat together in the unmoving car and the driver pulled out a pack of Jackpot menthols and tipped out one to Cory, who took it from the slot in the plastic partition. The driver slid him a lighter, then took it back and lit one for himself too. In silent misery they smoked.

The night turned to morning, accompanied by the taste of a proffered menthol Jackpot cigarette that still stayed on his tongue as he moved through the airport terminal to travel home. This time, no business class seat was available, and the firm probably wouldn't have paid for it anyway. He would have no bed to cradle his tall and suddenly fragile self. Cory sat in the only seat he could get, in the very last row by the toilet, a middle seat where he was squeezed between a big meaty man and a big meaty woman. He was wedged there, crying and watching a Filipino movie without the subtitles, because he figured it would fill his head with words he couldn't follow, and fill his eyes with brightly moving colors and flashes of flesh.

There were no deaths of children in the movie, only drama that involved love and marriage and infidelity and sex, always sex, which interested everyone on every continent. Then the movie was over and he was back to himself, lodged unhappily in the narrow space between his seatmates. One of them—he wasn't sure which—smelled of spice and yeast and something a little disturbing and unnamable. But he had been crying so hard and had been releasing such toxic, alarming chemicals that for all he knew, it came from him.

Greer was already waiting in Macopee by the time he arrived. He had flown to LA and then on to New York, and then took a bus up to Springfield, and a taxi to town, which was snowy and cold, reminding him that he had no coat with him. Cory hadn't brushed his teeth or gotten washed in a full day; he was a stinking, soaking being with a furred face and mouth. He'd cried intermittently on the flight, feeling ill and suspecting that this kind of illness would always be with him, either an acute or a chronic expression, depending on the day. The idea of never seeing Alby again, the two of them never having one of those conversations that flew in different directions like an unstable firework, wasn't something he could exactly believe.

The taxi pulled up in front of the Pinto house. Various cars were parked out front, blocking the driveway; he recognized Aunt Maria and Uncle Joe's green Pontiac. Cory entered the house through the unlocked door and his relatives descended upon him, some of them crying, and then they parted, revealing Greer standing there alone. She'd braved the Pinto family scene even without him; she hadn't just been hiding out in her own parents' house until he arrived. His relatives left the two of them in the living room.

"Oh, Cory," she said, which were the right words. "Oh, Cory, come here. I love you. Oh, honey, I love you."

She had rarely called him honey, and he thought: This is weird. *Honey* was for a moment of extremeness. She had reached out from their usual vocabulary and into that of some other generation; the words that they usually used wouldn't do. *Honey* was weird, but it was a bridge across the terrifying open space between where they had been and where they now were. A honeyed bridge that would take them forward as best it could. They sat together, him smelling so disgusting, even to himself, and Greer so sweet and scared, her eyes a startling red.

He was a young teenager when his brother was born, and what an indignity that had been: a baby in the house, going *wah*

wah wah when you were trying to sleep, or do your homework, or think about sex. For a long time Cory had ignored the boring, explosively gassy baby, but then finally the baby began to crawl, and that was interesting, and then he began to talk, and that was super-interesting. The things he said! The things he asked! At age two, to Duarte: "Tell me about fertilizer." And at age four, to Benedita, regarding one of the macaroni spirals on his plate: "Do you think it feels tense? It's all wound up. That's what Cory says when he feels tense. 'I'm all wound up.'"

"I can't believe this," Cory said to Greer now, his head in his hands. "What can I do?" he asked, looking up at her.

"What do you mean?"

"To make it not be true."

"I see." She nodded seriously. "I'll help you."

"How will you do that?"

Greer paused, thinking it through. "I don't know," she said. "But I will."

Together they sat on the couch with its slippery plastic, and then Cory lay with his head in Greer's lap, both of them wordless and crying for so long that after a while they heard the *click-click* of a gas burner being turned on. Apparently someone had the idea that eating dinner would be appropriate.

"You got off work to come here?" he thought to ask.

"Oh, it wasn't a big deal. Forget about it."

"But wait," he said. He tried to focus, a tremendous task, and then he remembered something. "Wasn't your thing now? Your Loci thing? With all those people speaking at a conference center? Do I have the dates wrong?"

Greer shrugged, which gave the truth away. The first summit—"Women and Power," she'd once explained, slightly embarrassed and excited by the sound of it—which she had been working toward since starting at Loci, would start tomorrow morning, and she was needed there. Except she wasn't there; she would miss it.

"You're sure it's okay that you're not there?" he persisted.

"Of course it is." She paused. "When are you going to go upstairs and see your mother?"

"I don't know."

"Cory, you have to. I'm going to go see her too at some point, if you think she'd want that. But you definitely have to go to her now."

Somehow he found the ability to go up there. His father was out at a bar with one of the uncles, and had been out for most of the day. His parents' bedroom was dark, the shades pulled, and he walked right in without knocking and just stood there at the bedside, his hands behind his back like a sentry. His mother lay on her side under the chenille bedspread that Cory and Alby used to sit on and pick at, all the little nubs and knobs offering interest and engagement to their always-moving hands.

She was a mess, of course, able to lift her head only a little. "Why couldn't you see that he was in the driveway?" he finally burst out cruelly.

She craned her head up at him. "Cory, you're here."

"Yes, I'm here."

"He wasn't in rearview mirror," she said.

"Were you actually *looking*?"

"Yes, I swear! I don't know what happened," she said, and she turned away again.

He felt ashamed at the ease of his own cruelty, and said, more calmly, "Well, okay. Okay. Anyway, I'm here." Then he left the room quickly.

Cory's father didn't return all day, and the aunts took care of Benedita, so Cory went to stay with Greer across the street at the Kadetsky house. Both of Greer's parents hugged him and spoke kindly to him, and then left them alone. He showered for a long time in the upstairs bathroom, and then he and Greer lay in her bed and had effortful but strong sex. It had been months since he'd touched her, and he was as responsive as ever, almost as if, through sex, he could work out the insurmountable problem of death. He bumped up against her with his hipbones in a familiar way, though he noticed that her body seemed sleeker now. This was the New York City version of Greer. The version that lived and breathed a life that wasn't his.

You would've really liked sex, bro, he thought as Greer touched his penis. You would've loved it. A girl actually touching you down there, and you touching her! Doing it openly, mutually. On *purpose*, bro. Alby had been interested in everything; he'd liked to explore. He would have been all over some girl someday, a brilliant girl who would have been his equal.

There was a wake with an open casket—it was just unspeakable to spend the day in the presence of his brother's small body—and then a funeral mass at the Catholic church. His mother fainted at the grave and his father helped her up, though grudgingly. They were barely speaking, so maybe it wasn't surprising when, two days after the funeral, Cory's father appeared on the doorstep of the Kadetsky house, politely asked to see his son, who had set up camp there, and then, alone with him in the kitchen, told Cory that he was going back to Lisbon for a while.

"*Now?*"

"Yes. I need to get away a little."

So he left, and there was no word from him for a few days, which was surprising to Cory, who just assumed he would be in touch every day. His mother, in all her distress, now had an additional refrain. "Where is Duarte?" she asked from her bed.

"He went for a short visit to Lisbon," the aunts and uncles and Cory told her several times.

But there was no word on when he would be back, so using the phone card in the kitchen drawer, Cory called his father to confront him. "What's the deal?" he said.

"I will stay here for a while longer."

"What's 'a while'?"

"I don't know."

"Okay, be straight with me. You're not coming back, are you?" Cory said, and there was some deflection, and then a sigh, and then the admission that no, he was staying there for the foreseeable future.

"But Mom can't manage," Cory said. "She just lies in bed."

"She has her sisters. And I'll give her money. Plus, I will leave her the car. Now she can go around killing anyone she wants."

"But this is a crisis."

"I'll miss you, but I can't live with her anymore. My cousin offered me a job here. You are a great son," Duarte added, breaking down.

When Cory told Greer, she said, "How can he just *do* that?"

"You'll have to ask him yourself, if you happen to see him again."

"You can stay here with me as long as you want, you know," she said. "My parents barely notice that you're in the house. Or that I am."

"Don't you have to go back down to New York soon? Your job?" he asked her.

"It'll keep."

"Greer, you blew off your summit. I can't believe that you did that. That I made you do that."

"You didn't make me. I wanted to."

"But they needed you there, right?" She didn't say anything. "Did they say it went okay?"

"Yes," she said. "It went great."

"Was Faith Frank angry with you?" he persisted.

"Cory," said Greer, "I'm here of my own free will, okay? Don't worry."

Over the next day and a half, back at his own house, he watched YouTube clips of the panels and speeches at the summit, and tracked down various Loci hashtags and mentions, some of which were nasty, accusing the foundation of taking "blood money" from ShraderCapital, but most of which were enthusiastic. "What great energy at the Centauri Center," someone wrote. "Amazing event," someone else wrote, and there were more details about how dynamic the speakers were and how responsive the audience was.

He watched the video of Faith Frank's keynote. She was unequivocally sexy at sixty-eight. He liked her boots; they had a hint of kink about them. Her speech was intense and serious and witty and rapturously received, and he understood why Greer would be so into her. Women sometimes liked to be dazzled by other women; he thought that if he were a woman, he would be into Faith Frank too.

Then he watched the others, all female: the astronaut, the naval commander, the hip-hop artist, the poet whose collection about poverty in America had just won an important prize. Some of the speakers were earnest and well-meaning; others, like the poet, were thrilling. Plus, there was an impressive multimedia aspect: enormous wraparound screens showing the speakers out and about in their real lives, and excellent acoustics when a girls' choir from the South Side of Chicago sang. Emmett Shrader had spent a lot of money on this, and Greer had missed it all. He felt terrible about it, despite her reassurances.

One morning his mother rose up from her bed and came into the kitchen, where Greer and Cory sat with his aunt Maria. "What's going on, Mom?" he asked warily. "What do you need?"

"I feel the spirit of Alby," she announced. "Gênio Dois. He is here. He wants me to shed my skin." She held out her arms and showed them the marks where she had been pulling and scratching at her skin. Later, online, Cory would read about psychotic breaks in the context of mourning. Now he just stared at his mother and couldn't think of anything to say to her.

She needed supervision; that was what the aunts and uncles decided. They did what they could, calling her employers and telling them she couldn't make it to work. But they had their own lives and families, and none of them could stay on in Macopee much longer. Even Greer felt she finally had to get back to work, and Cory said of course she had to go.

"What about you?" she asked him the next time they were alone.

"I think I'm going to stick around."

"Really? Can you do that?"

"What do you mean? It's what I have to do."

"Okay," she said unsurely.

"What?" he finally said. "What's the matter?"

"It's just that I'm concerned about you, Cory. It shouldn't all fall on you like this."

"But it does, Greer."

"I think you're an amazing son," she said, but this didn't seem at all like a compliment to him.

"Right, I'm amazing," he said tightly. "I'm incredibly amazing. And now I have to stay."

.   .   .

Alby's room called to Cory with the strange ferocity of sound waves coming from deep inside a cave. He had ignored the room until now, but then once the relatives were gone and he had officially moved back into the house and called to quit his job at Armitage & Rist, shocking his employers (his immediate supervisor had said, "You're really giving all of this up? No one does that"), he was pulled toward the room his brother had inhabited.

And then, once he went inside, he couldn't stay away. Cory sat for a long time on the blue rug, with his old bobblehead basketball player figurines above him on the shelf, nodding vigorously at the slightest footfall, and with Alby's action figures scattered all around. One had an arm raised; one was kicking nothing; one had its torso twisted all the way around into an impossible stance; all of them were frozen into their last, permanent positions.

Cory had also taken out Alby's school papers and drawings and notebooks, and was obsessively reading everything, as if there might be clues to be found there and decoded, which would prove, somehow, that his little brother was actually still alive in some until-now-undisclosed location elsewhere in the world. This was the fantasy Cory had constructed; it relieved him to linger in it.

Alby's handwriting was large and erratic, and his teacher had constantly circled words in red pen, admonishing him, "Try to be neater, Alberte." But the content of Alby's work was sophisticated, occasionally even long-winded. In his class essays he expounded on dinosaurs and Incans and the Big Bang, using statistics to back up his work, but still he digressed. "Try to stay on topic, Alberte," wrote that same teacher, and Cory wanted to punch her in the nose.

Then there were the notebooks. At first he didn't understand what they were, or what purpose they served. There were three of them in a pile, with that familiar black-and-white egg-drop pattern common to school notebooks everywhere. When Cory opened the first one it appeared to be a kind of homemade spreadsheet. In his brother's enormous and childlike but highly controlled handwriting were cryptic stats and notes:

AUG. 6

10 AM

TEMPERATURE: 76 DEGREES

15 MINS OBSERVATION

MOTION: SOME

DISTANCE: 4 CENTIMITERS

VELOSITY: (4 CM DIVIDED BY 15 = .27)

AUG. 7

RAIN!! NO OBSERVATION

STAYED INSIDE WITH PLAYSTATION INSTED

AUG. 8

10 AM

TEMPERATURE: 82 DEGREES

15 MINS OBSERVATION

MOTION: NONE

DISTANCE: NONE

VELOSITY: NONE

NOTES: DOES TEMPERATURE AFFECT DISTANCE AND VE-
LOCITY? CHANNEL 22 NEWS SAYS THERES A HEAT WAVE
COMING THIS WEEKEND, SUPPOSABLY! THEY ARE OF-
TEN 100% WRONG. WE WILL SEE WHAT HAPPENS.

And then, on the weekend, there were further statistics, with the notation, "WAVED FRONT LEFT ARM. DISTRESS? CANT BE SURE."

Front left arm. Cory didn't know what he had meant.

And then he did. He was seized by comprehension and immediately horrified, like someone who has driven hours from his home and then suddenly remembers he's left a pot on the stove. Cory shot up into a standing position. Frantic, he looked around the room. No one had been in here since Alby died except for one of the aunts, who had straightened up a little. In the corner on the floor by the window was a box. He crouched down and opened it; inside was a little empty bowl and a few pieces of old, dried-out meat. This was Alby's pet turtle Slowy's home—Slowy, who had been entirely forgotten, and was now missing.

Now Cory knew what Alby had been doing in the driveway that morning, why he was so low to the ground and why his mother hadn't seen him. "Oh my God," he said, and he dropped the notebook and ran downstairs, pushing through the front door without a coat on, peering hard at the ground all along the strip of brown lawn to the side of the driveway.

The turtle was there in the grass, easily camouflaged. It had been there this whole time, but no one had thought to look. No one had remembered it even existed except for Cory, who picked it up now and cradled it against his cheek, saying, "Slowy. Slowy."

The shell felt dry and cold; the turtle was dead, he thought, and that was fitting, that was appropriate. Slowy and Alby were like Romeo and Juliet, and should have been buried in the same casket. A boy and his turtle, packed together for all eternity.

As Cory stood with the flat bottom of the turtle pressed to his face, he felt a rumble from inside the shell that was like the vibration underfoot when a subway train approaches. The turtle was waking up from its hibernation, or perhaps its deep grief. It reached out a pale, mosaic-textured arm and lightly raked Cory's cheek, as if waking him from his own long and fitful sleep.

The next day he contacted his father in Lisbon at the relatives' carpet store, telling him in a loud and bursting voice that Alby's death hadn't been Benedita's fault after all. "See, he was lying on the ground studying Slowy," Cory said, and though he was sure his father would say, "I am so glad to hear this. I'll be on the next plane home," Duarte simply said that he needed to stay in Portugal for now, and that he would be in touch when he could.

Over the weeks that followed, his father was only in occasional touch. Cory took scrupulous care of Slowy, making sure his box was clean and that he had ample water and food, and taking him out on the carpet in Alby's room, beside the bed where Cory now slept at night, because there was actually some consolation to be found in lying on superhero sheets in a bed that his grown body filled from stern to bow. In the mornings he made breakfast for himself and his mother; he suspected if he didn't feed her, she wouldn't eat at all. He made sure she took the medications she'd been prescribed; he checked her arms for scratches; he did the grocery shopping at the Big Y; he drove her to see Lisa Henry, the social worker she'd been assigned; he kept her company; he played the Portuguese card game Bisca with her at the kitchen table and usually let her win.

One evening when they were playing cards the phone rang and a voice said, "Hello, this is Elaine Newman. Is Benedita there?"

"I'm sorry, she can't come to the phone," Cory said, for his mother never wanted to talk on the phone anymore.

"Are you her husband?"

"I'm her son."

"Ah. You have such a deep voice. Your mother cleans house

for me," the woman explained. "I teach at Amherst College. My family and I were in Antwerp during my sabbatical year and now we're back. I told your mother I'd be in touch when I returned. I hope," she said with a worried little laugh, "she held Thursday mornings for me, like she said she would. I should warn her, though: the place is a *mess*."

It really was. Cory arrived at the house that Thursday at nine a.m. After all, they did need the money. The Filipina housecleaner Jae would have been shocked to see Mr. Cory in pink rubber gloves, scrubbing a toilet, he who had never learned how to clean up after himself at all. He spent a lot of time savagely working on the Newmans' toilet and the mineral stains in their tub and the grove of dust beneath their enormous four-poster bed, whose nightstands held two different kinds of books. Professor Newman's side had a thick hardcover on it called *Van Eyck and the Netherlandish Aesthetic*. Her husband's side had a paperback mystery with raised letters and a bloody knife on the cover, called *The Mice Will Play*. People's marriages were like two-person religious cults, impossible to understand. By the time Cory had finished the entire house, and collected the cash that had been left for him on the Caesarstone counter beside the Sub-Zero, whose surface he had carefully wiped down with Weiman stainless-steel cleaner, he felt flushed with industry.

"You take after your mom," said Professor Newman with admiration when she called that night.

The job was his now, every Thursday morning, and he took surprising pride in the simple act of cleaning up, something he had never really thought to do before, because it had been done for him by his mother his whole life, and then, briefly, by Jae. Once in a while, when Greer had come over during high school or later on during college vacations, she'd automatically picked up the gym socks that Cory had left around, or his sports drink empties. He'd had a lifetime of being catered to and cleaned up after by women, but he only now realized this.

Sometimes when he was vacuuming Professor Newman's Persian rugs or ripping an old ratty Princeton T-shirt into strips to use for dusting, he thought about Jae Matapang, and felt unaccountably sorry that he had barely spoken to her in Manila, she who had touched all his intimate things, who had braved his filth. Once he had tried to have an extended conversation with her, but it had been extremely awkward. As she bent over the toilet in the shared bathroom, scrubbing away the pinkish-brown halo left by the urine and shit of all of them plus the vomit that had flown out of McBride one night after they all stayed out too late doing shots with clients at the Long Bar at the Raffles Makati, Cory approached her and said, "Uh, Jae?"

She looked up at him, startled, lifting the dripping loop of a scrub brush. "Yes, Mr. Cory. What is it?" Jae was tiny and game-hen bony in the grayish windbreaker that she wore all the time, her hair pulled back with a net like someone working a fast-food fryer.

He flushed. "Oh, I was just seeing if everything is good."

She gazed up at him. Finally she said, "No. Some things are not good. Some things are evil. Some people. The terrorists in Mindanao."

She had taken his question literally, having never heard the colloquial question about whether everything was "good." He just nodded in awkward acknowledgment, then she swiveled her focus back to her task, plunging the brush again into the toilet in this apartment that Cory and Loffler and McBride kept like this in part because they were so busy, and in part because they could.

At home each day now in the house where he'd grown up,

Cory learned to clean up the place the same way he did for Elaine Newman. He cooked dinner for his mother every night too. Not only had he never cleaned up after himself before; he had also never cooked a real, full dinner in his life either, unless it was a box of Ronzoni spaghetti and a jar of Ragú. Every day he began to look through his mother's Portuguese-language recipe cards, which at first were as incomprehensible as Alby's "scientific" notes. Soon he'd cracked this code as well. "OL" was *óleo*, "oil"; "UP" was *um pouco*, "a little"; and on and on. Cory was pleased with his code-breaking abilities, and the food came out surprisingly tasty. He was now a housecleaner, companion, and cook. He was bringing in a small salary, the house was in good shape, and there was decent food to eat. His mother might never really recover, but she ate and she lived.

Sometimes Cory's aunt and uncle came to visit from Fall River, and occasionally they dragged his cousin Sab along. The cousins had disliked each other ever since their teenaged fissure over porn. Sab was still known in the family as a hopeless case, but also a bad influence. The little kids were kept away from him. The situation was delicate; whenever family gatherings were held at Aunt Maria and Uncle Joe's house, Sab was usually on the premises, and the other parents took notice. "Leave Cousin Sab alone," was the repeated refrain to the little cousins. Or, "Cousin Sab is tired." Or, "Cousin Sab's room is off-limits." By nineteen, Sab and his friends had been reputed to be using and selling cocaine and Xanax. His parents, anguished, kicked him out, then took him back in again, and there he lurked.

Home on winter break from Princeton each year, Cory had seen Sab looking more and more broken; the only mitigating factor was that he no longer seemed mean, just ruined, barely filling out his shirt collars, his head bopping forward to an internal beat, a wavy smile always in half play. "Hey, Cousin Cory,"

Sab said whenever the families were together. "Give me a hug, college man."

"What's up, Sab," Cory would say wearily, putting his arms around his Ichabod Crane–looking first cousin.

"Not much, not much. Getting into the Christmas spirit, you know what I'm sayin'?"

But now, once again back at the Pereira household in Fall River for Sunday dinner, two months after Alby's death, hoping the visit would somehow force a little bit of life into his depressed and dazed mother, Cory deposited her into the blobby arms of a recliner in the den, with the aunts nearby and a couple of little cousins running around. Then he climbed the stairs to the second floor and banged on the door that he hadn't approached in years.

"S'open!" Sab called, and Cory entered the fetid room where his cousin sprawled on a heavy carved teak bed, smoking a green bong. Sab held up a finger, let the smoke roll from his mouth, and then said, "I am truly surprised to see you here. You must be desperate for friends, living at home and all."

"Something like that."

"That whole time you were away at your Ivy League college, did you feel better than all of us in the family? Be honest."

"All of you? No, just you."

Sab tipped his head up and laughed; he was uncharacteristically friendly in response to Cory's visit to his room. "You got me there, and I deserved it. Sit down already."

Cory sat in an armchair and took a hit from the bong; the column of old water burbled like a Roman fountain. Soon the room wasn't as grotty, and his cousin not as awful. Cory was feeling fairly relaxed when Sab pulled out a tiny glassine envelope from his dresser and said, "And now, the main attraction. Better than *Beaverama*."

It was heroin—"*snorting* heroin, see, like *drinking* chocolate," Sab explained. "Designed to be snorted and never injected. A mellow feel," he went on like a sommelier. "What do you say? Want a bump?"

Cory, stoned, said, "Okay."

"Well, this is a big day in Fall River." Sab chopped a little brown powder onto glass. "Cory the Great snorts H with his fucked-up loser cousin."

"Cory the Great, that's a good one."

"Well, you'll feel great in a minute anyway," said Sab, handing him the square of glass and a short piece of plastic straw. Cory remembered drinking Strawberry Quik with Sab through this same kind of straw. Circus Straws, the name on the box had read; he didn't know why he remembered this, but the memory arrived in an image of tremendous sadness and regret: a box of straws that bore a picture of an elephant trapped behind bars in a car of a circus train, and two boys sitting together with pink milk mustaches.

Now the powder went into his nostril as easily as if it were coke, which had sometimes been in evidence at parties at Princeton, where so many people had money. There was an MSG taste in Cory's throat from the heroin—part fish and part brine, chemical and fake but intriguing. Yet almost immediately his brain was seasoned with a vigorous and lacerating flurry of poison salt that seemed to stream from the holes of some hidden shaker. He seized forward and vomited a straight column of amber onto his cousin's carpet.

"Oh my God, I'm sorry, Sab," he said, clapping a hand to his mouth, and then he vomited some more through the spaces between his fingers. At first he felt only this sick feeling, nothing more, and it seemed as if the drug wasn't going to work on him. In his grief he must have been drug-resistant, like one of the newer forms of bacteria caused by overuse of hand sanitizer. But then he thought that that was a strange thought to be having right now, so maybe the heroin was starting to work after all. Cory lifted his head a little, and the room buckled and sank as if the whole house had been built on a sand pit. Cory sank down with it, falling on his side onto the shag carpet, bracing himself with one arm.

He stayed there with his eyes shut for a long time, until he heard a reedy-voiced version of Sab distantly saying to him, "You can open them now." He licked his lips and took a moment to try to remember what those words meant. What was he supposed to open? Presents?

No, not presents, eyes.

Open your eyes, Cory. So he did.

Incredibly, the world had been cleansed, rinsed off, made softer and ineffably better. Sab was smiling gently from what appeared to be a patch of sunlight on the bed, and Cory smiled up at him, two beneficent cousins finally reunited in the love they had once felt when they used to kick a soccer ball around the street, and look at porn with their teeny tiny Q-tip boners, imagining the way the world would one day take shape for them both.

They should drink glasses of Strawberry Quik together again now, he thought. They should ride a circus train throughout the land, their arms thrown around the neck of the sweet lumbering elephant that patiently looked out from behind the bars. Cory remembered that Alby was still dead, but he also knew that he didn't have to wrestle with that thought every hour of every day.

Right now was one of those times when Alby's death simply wasn't relevant. He hummed to himself as liquid pleasures rolled across him from a chemical tidal pool. He wanted to tell Sab how relieved he felt, but he had entirely lost the ability to talk, and his tongue was just a wet fish lying in his mouth. So instead of talking, Cory closed his eyes again and was grateful for quiet and immobility.

The two cousins stayed that way for hours, barricading themselves in the bedroom and ignoring the bangs on the door of family members who called to them, "The lamb is on the table! The Sunday lamb!" and then, "The lamb is getting cold!" and then finally, "Cory, your mom wants to leave right now."

By the time he made it downstairs the sky was dark, the little-kid cousins had all fallen asleep and been carried out to the cars in their fathers' arms, and his mother was dozing in the same easy chair she'd been placed in that morning. Aunt Maria was scraping lamb bones into the garbage and loading the dishwasher, and Uncle Joe was already in bed for the night.

"What were you boys doing up there? You missed my entire meal," Aunt Maria said, looking them over with a suspicious eye. "Were you *drinking*?" she asked.

"Sorry, Mama," Sab said, though of course neither of them smelled of alcohol.

"Drinking will get you nowhere. You'll turn into a bum."

"I know. It won't happen again."

Outside under the street lamp Cory helped his mother into the car. Through a miracle, driving twenty-five miles per hour in the breakdown lane and forcing himself to stay awake and alert, he safely got them home, although it took a long time.

The next afternoon, having slept for thirteen hours, Cory awakened to a cracking headache that seemed at the cerebral-hemorrhage level, and then he remembered the dirtlike powder that his cousin had chopped on a piece of glass and handed him. The headache was the least he might have expected as an after-effect, never having snorted heroin in his life. There was a text from Sab, who said, "u want to hang later? More bumps in store for us." As if they were friends now and could return to their early days back in Fall River without any mention of the intervening schism. Cory ignored the message. But when Greer called he made the mistake of picking up.

She was in one of those outstandingly articulate moods she'd been in sometimes lately when she called from New York. She would usually spend the beginning of the conversation asking him how he was doing, using the hushed and joyless voice that people used when speaking to someone who had experienced a terrible loss. But he didn't want to talk about that with her anymore; he had other concerns these days: namely, taking care of his mother and the house, and also taking care of Elaine Newman's house. Treating it all with the seriousness with which he had treated a client's presentation during his brief career at Armitage & Rist.

Then, when Cory wasn't particularly responsive, Greer would tell him about herself and her own life, which was what she was doing on the phone now, as if everything were normal between them. "Faith gave a special sermon at All Souls. You know, the Unitarian church on the Upper East Side," she was saying. "It was all about sexism in everyday life. She can speak to anyone about anything. A reporter from the *New York Times* came; she's doing a profile. She said this is a great moment for this kind of piece. What with *Fem Fatale*, and those newer websites, and Opus still being so visible, and now, amazingly, us. Loci. 'The place where women come together to talk about what matters,' is how she put it. I don't know if that's accurate, but I guess now we'd better make it accurate."

"Uh-huh."

"That's all?"

"I don't know what you want me to say, Greer."

"You sound peculiar; are you okay?"

"I'm tired."

"Me too, actually. Very tired. I'm working a lot," she went on. "Even though the first summit's over, it now starts all over again for the second one. Listen," she said after a moment. "I have some news." When he didn't say anything, she said, "Do you even want to hear it?"

"Of course I do," he said, but having been questioned, he thought: *Do* I want to hear it? He realized that he was exhausted at the prospect of hearing it. He was already pre-exhausted by whatever it was she was going to say.

"You know that multimedia event we're going to do?"

"No."

"The one about girls and safe schools around the world."

"Yeah." He remembered nothing of such an event, but suddenly he saw girls in burqas and saris and kilts and rags, swinging satchels, riding shaky thin bicycles, heading down sunbaked dirt roads toward distant, low school buildings. The image was so vivid that he wondered if it was the product of a few last misguided opiate-addled neurons firing into the weeds.

"We're actually going to need to hire a consultant," Greer said. "I know that's your area of expertise, and I can tell you more about it if you're interested." They were both silent, him taking this in and her letting him take it in. He didn't say anything, so she quietly said, "What do you think?"

"No. Thanks, but no."

"Are you sure? You answered so quickly."

"Sorry. There's no way I could do something like that."

"But why not? You've been home for a couple of months now, Cory. Maybe it's time to start thinking about your life again. Even just a little. Would that be the worst thing? It wouldn't take away from your mother."

"This is my life."

"Well, yes, a temporary version."

"I don't differentiate," said Cory, his voice tight. "It's all temporary, obviously. Everything is. My brother *died*, Greer, my dad left, my mom collapsed. That's the order of things. The world doesn't need my consulting skills, believe me."

"You don't know that."

"There are plenty of people who can take my job at Armitage and do it just as well or much, much better. I'm sure they already have. I was a fake in a suit and tie in Asia, that's all. It's easy to take a recent college graduate and say, 'Okay, come be a consultant,' and I'm sure there's real merit to that. But at some point that recent college graduate is going to need to figure out the world a little, beyond consulting. The noncorporate parts. The human parts. The corners, you know?"

"So that's what you're doing now when you stay at your mom's house all day cooking and sitting in Alby's room? You're figuring out the world and all of its corners?"

"Yeah," he said. "Exactly."

"Well, I thought I was supposed to be figuring out the world alongside you," she said, her voice shaking a little.

"You were," he said. "And you will be. And I'll be doing it with you too," he added quickly.

The call ended in mutual unpleasantness, and Cory staggered up and fed his mother, and then fed Slowy. He let the turtle sit on Alby's carpet for a while, until finally it opened its eyes and blinked twice, like a coma patient trying to send a message, saying: *I'm still here.*

How was it, Cory kept thinking, that when a person died they were no longer anywhere? You could search the entire world and never find them. It was one thing for a body to stop working and be carted away under a sheet; it was another thing for the sense of that person to evaporate. The textural and indisputable sense, as strong but as hard to pinpoint as a gas. Cory opened one of his brother's notebooks and turned to a clean page, then began to write:

DATE: MONDAY, MAY 23

CONDITIONS: UNBEARABLE SADNESS EXACERBATED BY FOOLISH HEROIN USE. [HEROIN SHAKEN NOT STIRRED, AKA INHALED NOT INJECTED, BECAUSE I AM NOT ACTUALLY A SELF-DESTRUCTIVE ASSHOLE, DESPITE MY LINGERING, NONSTOP SADNESS.]

OBSERVATION: ALBY IS NOWHERE TO BE FOUND. NOWHERE. NOT HERE, NOT ANYWHERE. YOU AREN'T HERE, ARE YOU, BRO? IN YOUR OLD POWER RANGERS SWEATSHIRT? NO, YOU'RE NOT. SOMEHOW, THIS IS NOT AN ELABORATE PRANK, EVEN THOUGH IT TOTALLY FEELS LIKE IT.

TIME SPENT THINKING ABOUT THIS TODAY: 45 MINUTES.

AMOUNT THAT UNBEARABLE SADNESS WAS LESSENED BY DIRECT THOUGHTS OF ALBY: 0.0000%

Every day for five days, Cory wrote his observations in the journal, but he soon became aware that nothing was changing for him, there were no glimmers of improvement, so by the time the weekend arrived he left the journal on the desk and sat down on the bed and turned on the PlayStation. All the video games that Alby had loved were in a shoe box beside the bed, and he went rifling through them.

If Cory couldn't be with Alby, then at least he could feel what it had meant to *be* Alby. He sat cross-legged on the small bed, playing game after game that Alby had played. He played Peep

Peep and Growth Spurt and Mixed-Up Kids and all the other games; mostly they were loud and clownish and pulled you right in so that you felt yourself leaving this world and entering that other, differently lit one. Some of them were mystical, ambient worlds, like Calyx, a game for adults that Alby had loved.

While Benedita slept or wandered around whispering or picking at herself, Cory played. "Go, go, go!" he quietly called to the screen as his little car roared along the Möbius strip of a cartoon track, and he felt himself galvanized by the colors and the music, and then, when he'd had enough, he calmed down by playing an hour of Calyx.

He snorted heroin once more with Sab, but shortly after that second time, he understood from his own wretched response, and the days of recovery afterward, even longer than last time, that that was enough, and that any more than that, he would be taken up by it; he would be taken. Instead, he let himself be taken by Alby's video games and notebooks, that whole compact and abandoned world.

Greer made another trip to Macopee before a Loci event in Cambridge. Though the distance between New York and Macopee wasn't too much greater than the distance between Ryland and Princeton, the trips were less frequent, and it was only Greer visiting him, never the other way around. Whenever she came to see him, the rhythm in the house was thrown off. His mother seemed agitated with Greer around, maybe even self-conscious about appearing unwell in front of her. She retreated to her room and didn't eat.

And though Greer kept trying to get him to come down to New York—he'd sworn to her he would—he didn't want to leave his mother for the weekend, even with one of the aunts, who didn't know everything that had to be done. So Greer came there, and it wasn't great. This weekend, Loci would be cosponsoring a mini-summit about sexuality and the law at the Kennedy School of Government at Harvard. She drove up in a rental car a day early, and she came into Cory's house and looked around. The Pintos' place was clean and orderly again—he'd gotten good at that—but she didn't even comment, and it actually hurt his feelings a little.

His mother drowsed in her chair; eggs were lightly knocking together in a pot of water on the stove, emitting that distinct hard-boiled smell. Everything was under control here, but Greer just said quietly, "Cory, what's going on?"

She looked as if she might cry, and he was slightly offended by that. What was so terrible here that could almost bring her to tears? What was she seeing? He'd been trying so hard to manage every aspect of his mother's life, and Greer had come in and basically held a mirror up to everything, which wasn't something he'd asked her to do. How could he not take care of his mother? How could he go back to Manila to be a consultant when in fact the one who needed his consulting skills was right here, in a housedress with a repeating pineapple pattern, agitated and confused and unwell?

How could he return to being interested in his "relationship" with Greer? Relationships were a luxury designed for people whose lives were not in crisis.

For some reason Greer didn't understand any of this; it was so unlike the way she had always understood everything about Cory since they were teenagers and lay together in her upstairs room, their bodies being revealed to each other for the first time like monuments undraped at a public ceremony. He had shown himself to her, his slightly crooked penis and his heart fat with longing, and then, indisputably, the love he'd been storing up. His toes like fingers. His desire to do something useful with himself someday, to spread money around the globe because he hadn't had much money growing up, and because he'd learned in his economics classes about how everything was connected through intricate systems. And Greer had shown him all that was hers as well: the small, warm body, and the muted self that, these days, was being replaced by something less constrained. She was less timid; Faith Frank had brought her out more than he ever could.

But he had the distinct feeling that she didn't understand him anymore, which was news, because for years they had always taken each other's understanding for granted. "What do you mean, what's going on?" he asked.

"We had a life," she said. "Not living together, I know that, but we told each other things, and we were in it together. Come on, why do I have to say all this? You know what I'm talking about. You've basically removed yourself from me."

He just looked at her. "This doesn't only go one way, Greer."

"You think I've been distant too?" she said. "I always call you and text you. I want to hear everything."

"Yes, you're very responsible."

"What do you want, Cory? Am I supposed to move up here with you too? Maybe I am," she said frantically. "Maybe that's the only way I can show you what I feel."

"No," he said. "This isn't about obligation, Greer."

"But you don't go to me for comfort anymore. You don't go to me for anything. Not even distraction. Our lives are just totally separate. You're not even trying! I know you're upset, I know you feel shattered. But when I try to get you to come down to New York to see me and be alone with me someplace where we can really talk and be together, you say you can't."

"Right. Because I can't."

"I have an apartment now, Cory. I have big spoons. I just don't have you there." He didn't say anything, and so she kept talking, making it worse. "I know your mother needs protection and care, of course she does, and you have to see that she gets it. But I know you can get other people to help with that, at least sometimes. It's not the sum total of who you are. I haven't heard you talk about anything else in so long. You seem completely uninterested in the outside world."

"In your world, you mean," he said, and this was a little mean and he knew it. But it was true. Her world had become abstract to him; she had stayed firmly in it, planted in it. No, he didn't think she should move here. She shouldn't give up her job with Loci and Faith Frank and come up here to live with him. Though really, he thought for a second, if she had done that, then finally they would be living together. They could live in Greer's bedroom; her parents would leave them alone. They could live there and his mother could heal and he could heal, and they would have some version of a life. But Greer couldn't do that, and he would never, ever ask her to, because she would have to give up so much. This time of life was meant to be about adding on to yourself, not taking away. It was all backward now, and he didn't know how to stop the backward motion from continuing, accelerating.

"All right, fine, my world," she said. "But also your own world. The one you had."

"I don't have it anymore."

"You could have a little of it," she pressed. "Just once in a while. You deserve it. You're a person, and you still have to live. Why won't you come down to New York for the weekend? You haven't even seen my apartment in Brooklyn, not once. And I sound spoiled saying this, and I hate that. I'm sorry, but I had this whole thing in my mind. We'd get Thai takeout at this place I go to. We'd sit in my bed. We'd walk in Prospect Park. You said you would leave your mother with your aunt Maria just for one night. One night. And then you always cancel."

"The logistics are complicated."

"I know they are, but I feel like being involved with me is this gigantic burden that you feel like you have to carry out. More of a burden than taking care of your mother. You have to *want* to do it. I can't make you want it. That's the thing about a relationship. Whoever is more aloof always gets to set the terms."

"So now I'm aloof."

"Well, yes, kind of." He didn't say a word, but just sat there, taking this. "Cory," Greer tried, "it's okay to still care about things. But you don't seem to believe that. How long are you going to stay in this state where you're totally removed from everything? How many months are you going to keep doing this?"

"Fourteen."

"What?"

"I made up a number. I'm trying to show you how completely ridiculous this line of thinking is. How can I put a limit on it, Greer? I'm needed here."

"Aren't you needed elsewhere?"

"I'm not irreplaceable elsewhere."

"You had a plan, and it made sense. Doing consulting for now, saving money, then doing your app. You were so excited about it."

"I had to adapt," he said. "I'm starting to think that you're the one who can't."

"Can we please go somewhere and discuss this?" Greer asked, agitated.

So they left his mother alone for an hour and went to Pie Land, the pizza place where once, before they were in love or even tolerated each other, he used to stand and play Ms. Pac-Man while Greer sat stealthily watching him. He would see her in his peripheral vision, and would play better and harder and longer, as if for her, his rival at school.

Now, on a weeknight in summer, the grown versions of themselves entered this same place, which was empty, apparently doing more takeout business than dine-in. There was even a Pie Land app for the phone.

"Help you?" said the counter person.

"Kristin, hey," said Greer. It was Kristin Vells, who lived on their street, and who'd been on their school bus year after year. Kristin who had been in the bottom reading group, the Koalas. She now wore a red Pie Land smock, and was as affectless as ever as she rang up their slices and their sodas. "You living at home?" Greer asked her.

"Yeah. It's not too bad." Kristin's eyes passed across the two of them, and she said to Cory, "You're living at home too, right? I've seen you." As if to warn him: Don't think you're so much better than me, the way you two brains always thought you were.

"Yeah," he said. He was no better or worse than Kristin Vells. Now Cory noticed that the Ms. Pac-Man machine was gone. Everyone had their own games at home these days and didn't need to play in public. Over recent years, since the start of the large-scale retraction into the self, Cory had come to understand that feeling, and he actually wished he was at home right now too, playing another one of Alby's video games.

He and Greer sat at a table and she held her dripping slice away from her as she ate, saying, "I can't get anything on my outfit. I have so few clothes with me."

"Greer," he said. "Look at me." Her eyes did a worried sweep up from plate to face. "I don't know what our lives are going to be like," Cory said, improvising. "Because who would have expected this would happen to Alby?"

"No one," she said, her voice small.

"But it did, yeah it did, and then this other thing happened to my mom, and now this other thing has happened to me."

"What thing?"

"Falling from grace with you." His voice ached with strain. "Things are different for me now."

"I know."

"But different in various ways."

"Like what else?"

"I don't know. Things that don't seem like me. For instance, I snorted heroin," he said.

There was a dreadful suspension of time and a quick sequence of facial expressions he'd never seen on Greer before, and then she said, "You have got to be kidding me."

"You know, this is a moment when you being all shocked isn't going to do either of us any good."

"Well, I'm sorry. Do you want me to be fake?"

"Fake would be good. Fake would actually be excellent. What I'm trying to tell you is that I'm basically in a state that is not like any state I have ever been in. And you can say to me, oh, I ought to get a job as your *consultant* for some upcoming high-profile event in San Francisco, but that would mean that you don't understand where I am right now. Where my mind has taken me since this happened."

"I loved Alby too, Cory. I think about him all the time, and I just fall apart." Her voice was winding up and tightening. "I can picture him sitting with me, reading *Encyclopedia Brown*. I can picture him there, and I get so upset that I don't know what to do."

"I get that, but it's not what I'm trying to say. I let myself be a consultant-in-training for a while, like we agreed I would, and now it's over, sooner than it was supposed to be, and instead I'm here. And you, you're out there working for this good place, working for someone who's this shining example. You write moving speeches that matter, and you're doing great. Stay with it, Greer. See it through."

"So what will you do now?" she finally asked, her voice formal and unfamiliar.

"Oh, I guess I'll do what I'm doing. Live here and take care of my mom and clean a professor's house—and another house that my mom used to clean—and hang out with the turtle and be present."

"Cory, listen to how you're talking. You don't even sound like yourself."

It was too much for her, this *otherness* he was demonstrating. She couldn't tolerate it, and she would never say that. She would never say to him, "Enough already, Cory," but instead she would just keep trying, as if he were an extremely complicated school project. Right away he remembered the condensation project at the long-ago science fair, with all those ice cubes and funnels and water balloons, and his mother standing in front of it, speaking in her broken English. He didn't want to be Greer's project, the dreary object of all her hard work. It had never been hard work before.

From behind the counter, listening to everything, Kristin slid a whole pale pie into the oven for a take-out order, pushing the flat wooden paddle forward like someone making an aggressive serve in an obscure sport. Rain popped lightly against the plate-glass window, and the sky darkened in this town that Cory had lived in for so long and never imagined he would live in again.

"I can't talk about this anymore," said Greer. "I'll drop you off at home and say goodbye to my parents, and then I have to get to Boston. Faith is meeting us in Cambridge at the bar of the Charles for a brainstorming thing, and tomorrow is the event."

"Then you should definitely get going. The rain."

Together they dutifully looked out at the rain, which was quickly getting heavier. He imagined her in her little red compact rental car, her jaw set as she drove with wipers mewing, heading toward Boston and a good hotel and women's rights and a solid future and Faith Frank, who waited there like someone who could provide relief, which he could no longer do.

They both dropped some money on the table for Kristin, neither of them wanting to cede the task of tipping to the other. Because of that, it turned out the amount they left her was far too great, which was either an insulting gesture or a magnanimous one, depending on how you looked at it.

SEVEN

Very early each workday morning in the large, ivy-wrapped house in the suburb of Scarsdale, New York, Zee could hear the Vitamix TurboBlend 4500 roar as her mother, the Hon. Wendy Eisenstat, made vaguely newsprint-colored smoothies from blueberries and kiwis and protein powder and stevia and ice. "Dick, flaxseed or no?" Zee heard, and then the Hon. Richard Eisenstat called out his preference on this particular day. Then both judges went for a run through the local landscaped lanes of this expensive town, side by side like twin steeds, before leaving for their jobs at the Westchester County Supreme Court. Though Zee had an open invitation to run with them, the thought of it was terrible: running with her parents in the town where she'd grown up, living with them once again like an oversized child, while working at a job she hated. Running, yet getting nowhere.

Sometimes Zee and the other paralegals at Schenck, DeVillers, an enormous law firm in the financial district of New York City, were asked to stay very late. Up and down the corridor, lawyers sat in their individual offices, hunched over laptops or phones or black plastic bento boxes. But in an improvised area at the far end of the hall was a little gypsy encampment, where the paralegals all recognized one another as part of the same loosely delineated tribe, yet were also separate, weary, and guarded, in possession of complicated backstories that moderately absorbed Zee and served as one of the only ways she could keep herself at all interested in her job.

Across from her in the paralegals' cluster was the heavy woman who had worked in a morgue, and who on breaks told stories about that job, and they all gathered around to listen. Also among them was the long-fingered, long-wristed man; recently Zee had discreetly Googled "abnormally long fingers" and the first hit she got was the medical term *arachnodactyly*. Fingers like a spider. He definitely had that.

And surely the other paralegals thought of Zee as just another kind of singular workplace character—in this case, the androgynous, sexually appealing gay woman. In the underheated office at Schenck, DeVillers on this very cold night in winter, she wore a peacoat and watch cap, which gave her the appearance of a member of a boy band who was trying to go incognito.

"I wonder who decided to turn the heat way down," Zee said to the young bearded slam poet with whom she shared her corner of the hallway. "Schenck or DeVillers."

"DeVillers, for sure," he said.

"I'm thinking Schenck. There's a kind of *Schenckian* coldness to this place."

He laughed; they often tried to amuse each other in this way, because it helped to pass the time. Then there was silence for a long stretch, as all the paralegals typed with cold fingers on cold keys. If you had your eyes closed and suddenly came upon the sound of all that typing, you might not know what it was, for it almost had a rusticated, babbling-brook quality to it, the way so many elements of technology did, as if to trick people into be-lieving that they hadn't actually given up everything they'd ever loved about the natural world in exchange for the meager glow of a backlit screen.

Though Zee disliked working there, at least it was a relief not to have a job where she had to dress like a robot monkey woman, but instead could wear a slightly neater version of her usual clothes. Throughout her life, intermittently fearing her parents' eventual deaths, the only positive aspect about that inevitability was that finally there would be no one on earth who would say to her, "Would it kill you to wear a skirt?"

In the skirts she had worn over time, for them, the plaid kilt and the Indian-print cotton, the slit leg and the ruffly peasant midthigh, the transgressive crotch-high micromini and the long dark sedate one she called First Violinist with the Boston Sym-phony Orchestra, she had felt nearly deranged with falseness, as though the clothes would at any moment fall away from her in an act of gender deciduousness, leaving her naked and exposed.

Once, home at her parents' house during the long winter break in college, Zee had sent a series of postcards to Greer up in Massachusetts, with the caption "Would it kill you to wear a skirt?" (Greer, of course, actually liked wearing skirts, and wore them all the time, even when it wasn't required. Also, Cory had said Greer looked very hot in them.)

On the first postcard, Zee drew a woman wearing a skirt and tripping over the hem, causing her to fall off the edge of a cliff.

The second postcard showed a woman lying in a pool of blood, the fabric of her skirt patterned in sharp little knives.

And the last postcard showed another woman wearing a skirt and collapsing in a heap. Beside an arrow pointing to the skirt was the caption "Stella McCartney's Most Unpopular Design, the Poison-Lined Mini."

It wasn't that Zee imagined herself to be male; she just dis-liked some of the trappings of femaleness. At her bat mitzvah, under duress, she had worn a green minidress with enormous white wildflowers on it, and a pair of airless tights, and all she had wanted to do the whole day was swap the dress for jeans, or at the very least pull off her tights and run around bare-legged. They encased her legs in such a way that Zee knew she could not go through life in tights, the way her mother did; though in her mother's case she really *could* have gone bare-legged, given all that robe. No one would ever have noticed.

At the law firm, Zee herself was noticed; one person who noticed her was a first-year associate, a toned and thin-lipped recent graduate of Georgetown Law who was of no real interest to Zee, though she did smell intriguingly like fresh-cut grass. But Zee didn't want to get involved with anyone now. It would have been too hard to do that while living in Scarsdale. "I'm not in the closet," she'd explained to Greer when they first met at Ryland, but she wasn't comfortable introducing anyone to her parents. And anyway, she wasn't sure she would want that person to see her posters of the Spice Girls and the endangered baby chinchillas.

Animal rights, and then being a vegetarian, had started on a class trip to a petting zoo. Zee had squatted among the baby chicks with down floating in the air around her like pollen. The chick sounds were soft yet insistent and seemed to have more in common with insect life than animal life. But when Zee held a little quivering packet of chick between her palms, she was suddenly goony with love.

The next day she checked an oversized book of animal pho-tos out of the Scarsdale Public Library, and late that night, sitting in bed with the book open in her lap, Zee began to look at color pictures of baby chicks and otters and fauns. There among the most darling photos in the world appeared one that was incongruous and startling and absolutely terrible: a photo of a baby seal in a trap, its mouth open in pure-form pain. The seal's eyes made a direct appeal to Zee Eisenstat, who found herself first shocked and crying, and then churning at the injustice. These animals were *life*, she thought, her mouth going tight; they were life, and more than that they were *souls*, and because of that, she had to do something.

When Zee's parents were out playing tennis with another two-judge couple, Zee sat at her desktop computer posting on an animal rights message board under the embarrassing handle Me&myanimalpals. Soon she received several responses. DANNYSGRANDMA wrote back to Me&myanimalpals with advice on how to get started "in the animal rights community." Vikingfan22 wrote to ask if by any chance she lived in the Twin Cities, because, if so, maybe they could meet for "a couple of cold ones." No one knew she was an eleven-year-old girl, and her anonymity gave her courage. She was a baby chick but not a baby chick. Like everyone else on those message boards, she was impelled by the sense of something tender being destroyed.

Later on, Zee's MySpace page was thickly spread with adamant statements about animal rights and shocking photos of animal cruelty, as well as a few shots of puppies and kittens frolicking (*other* people's puppies and kittens; her mother was allergic), in order to even things out. She constantly posted pictures, and in high school she spent a few Saturdays standing in a parking lot picketing outside a local fur store. But by then she had also branched out broadly into the world of humans and how they kept one another down.

All kinds of social justice movements stirred her and she found herself a dervish of activity online and in the world. At college, handing out leaflets against the war in Iraq, she'd try hard to imagine herself in Karbala, instead of inert Ryland. She went in the direction of what drew her, and as a result her grades were poor, just as they'd been in high school. Her math SAT score had been so low, and the essay she had to write apparently so unreadable, that her guidance counselor had stared at the printout from the Educational Testing Service for a long time, tapping his pen and frowning, before thinking of how possibly to advise her about college choices.

Though Zee knew she would always be political, and would eventually become one of those feisty old women, those *coots*, protesting whatever futuristic cause needed her voice—pollution caused by jet-pack fuel emissions; equality for the robot population—sometimes you were not a political being but merely a sexual one. In this version of herself she regarded the hot first-year associate at Schenck, DeVillers and decided against pursuing her, or letting herself be pursued. Zee was in a moment of flux, as she thought of it. This was her life now, but it wasn't really her life. There had to be something else ahead, something better and more engaging, like what Greer had, working at Loci and living on her own in Brooklyn and being committed to Cory.

Zee's erratic work hours sometimes allowed her to sleep late, and when she woke up it was just her in the big house. Sometimes, if she wasn't needed at Schenck, DeVillers until later in the day, she even watched afternoon talk shows, but these depressed her. "I think," she'd said to Greer on the phone recently, "daytime talk shows are a plot to keep women dumb and passive. Whenever I watch one of them, I feel my brain matter disintegrating. Today the topic was 'My Son Is a Gang Member.'"

"So don't watch it."

"But it was so interesting!"

"Well, there you go."

"I need something to do with myself. Something compelling," Zee said. "My whole time growing up, while you were reading all those books by Jane Eyre—"

"Jane Austen!"

"Yes, that's what I meant. While you were doing that, I was out protesting."

"You could go out protesting now," said Greer.

"I'd love to. I'm just too tired when I get home. My job has weird hours." Zee sighed. "I wish I worked with you at the foundation. It would be like going to work and being political all in one. I even like saying it: 'the foundation.'"

"Well, it's not all that great," said Greer. "You know that I'm basically an assistant."

"I doubt it," said Zee. "Anyway, it's a lot better than what I'm doing."

Greer had originally tried to get her a job at Loci; she'd given Faith the letter Zee wrote, but it hadn't done any good. "No worries," Zee had said to Greer, which was an expression she and Greer both hated, so it was spoken by her ironically. Young, thin, uninteresting-looking women standing behind the counter in boutiques singsonged this phrase in response to just about anything: "Nuclear holocaust?" "*No worries!*" The expression was absurd, because everyone knew that everyone had legitimate worries all the time. How could you not have worries, particularly if you were a recent college graduate entering the world at this fragile moment? The US economy had been saved from falling into a hell pit, but by the end of 2010 it was still precarious.

Being needed was something that Zee wanted too. Being needed or loved; one of these or both. Preferably both! They weren't the same, but they occupied related territory. Love would happen to her too, or maybe it wouldn't. Maybe her life would never settle, would never gel, either professionally or in terms of love. Still: *no worries!*

The letter Zee had written to Faith Frank and given to Greer in a bar in Brooklyn had begun:

Dear Ms. Frank,
I am sending this to you courtesy of the hand-delivery service of Ms. Greer Kadetsky, who is my great friend from college. In Greer, you could not have a better, smarter, or more quietly diligent person working for you. She is super-focused and organized and well-read. Me, I'm different.

Then Zee had gone on to write a little bit about herself, moving quickly through the highlights of her political involvement, talking about how energized she was about various feminist issues and gay rights, including marriage equality, which was going to be the next *Roe v. Wade.* The letter was short, and she ended by telling Faith that as the child of two judges—"not kidding!" she wrote—she had grown up watching her parents interpret the law, while she herself was detained following an animal rights demonstration outside Van Metre Furs in sixth grade.

It had been clear to Zee, early on, that her parents, being judges, tended to judge everything in their midst. That might have included all the children in the family, but the Eisenstat boys were spared some of the scrutiny because their mother had gotten it into her head early on that boys could not be tamed, so there was no point in even trying. The Hon. Wendy Eisenstat and the Hon. Richard Eisenstat let Alex and Harry have the run of the neighborhood until long past the hour when most kids had gone off to math tutors or Torah study or bassoon lessons or lacrosse.

Alex and Harry, a year and a half apart in age, neither of them a good student or nimble with the Hebrew alphabet or particularly musical or athletic, liked to ride their skateboards up and down the smooth, wide surface of Heather Lane, where the Eisenstats lived in a $3.5 million Tudor with a pool and a greenhouse and a lawn that went on and on until it became indistinguishable from that of the Tudor next door.

The Eisenstats' judgment—mostly Judge Wendy's—fell on Zee, although she wasn't Zee yet, not in the beginning. She was still Franny then, Franny Eisenstat, because when her parents fell in love, up in New Haven when both of them were at Yale Law, Richard Eisenstat had said to Wendy Niederman, who sat beside him in Procedure, "One thing you should know about me is that I am a J. D. Salinger fanatic."

"J. D., as in 'Juris Doctor' Salinger?" she said.

"You're funny."

"I try."

"Ask me any Salinger trivia," he said. "Anything about the Glass family, even about the most obscure members of the family, the ones no one's heard of, like Walt and Waker."

To which Wendy had crowed, "Walt and Waker Glass! I can't believe you know who they are. I actually love Salinger too." Not long after that, when they were spending all their days and nights with each other, essentially living together already without calling it that, Richard had gone into a used-book store in New Haven and extravagantly bought Wendy a jacketed, only slightly foxed first edition of *Franny and Zooey*. So it wasn't really much of a surprise when, after having two boys who were not named for anyone in particular, her parents recalled the sentimentality of that early date—the moment when Richard had pressed the gift-wrapped book into Wendy's hands, and she had taken off the wrapping paper and seen the white cover with the very recognizable font, and then touched it emotionally against her chest, because this man knew what she liked. They recalled this moment, after their daughter's birth, and so they named the small sack of pink and floral-smelling skin Franny. For a while it was a good name for her, a perfect name.

But when Franny Eisenstat grew older, the name felt to her frilly and inessential, and she had no connection to it. That pink sack of Franny no longer existed. She was now someone who wanted absolute control over her image—and wanted to be seen as angular, confusing, an exciting human puzzle. At her bat mitzvah, she felt shame at being ensconced in the green dress for which her mother had taken her shopping at Saks, under pressure. All the other women at the bat mitzvah seemed comfortable in the dress-up clothes of regular womanhood. Women like Linda Mariani, Judge Wendy's blond and busty law clerk, who often staggered into the Eisenstat house on heels, carrying an armload of files piled so high that they covered her face. At the synagogue Linda's dress was canary-yellow and it pulled taut across her chest, straining the stretchy material.

"Congratulations, Franny," said Linda that day, and during the obligatory hug it almost seemed as if the pressure made Linda release a very female perfume, the way a sofa cushion, when sat on, lets out air.

After the ceremony, the adults went into one side of a long ballroom, and the kids went into the other, and an accordion door closed between the two. There was a karaoke machine on the kids' side, and everyone wanted a turn. Because they were thirteen and it was 2001, gay jokes were the height of hilarity, and everyone tried to turn all the karaoke songs into puns or double entendres about being gay. There on the orange-and-gold, floating-trumpet-patterned carpeting, two girls began to sing a song by some ancient brother-sister duo from the 1970s called

Donny and Marie, with new lyrics, holding microphones that had been in stands from some already-forgotten bat or bar mitzvah or wedding from the previous weekend.

One girl sang, "*I'm a little bit homo . . .*"

And the other one sang, "*And I'm a little bit les-bi-an.*"

Then they pretended to French kiss, one girl dipping the other girl back. It was meant to be both disgusting and hilarious, but much later, back at home on Heather Lane, when the Eisenstat family sat in the living room opening the last of the presents—all the Lucite picture frames, and the gift cards from Barnes & Noble and Candles N' Things that would soon get lost and never cashed, and all the checks in variants of eighteen dollars, because eighteen corresponded to the lucky number *chai*, Hebrew for "life"—Franny rose from the whitecaps of wrapping paper, shuffling through it all, ankle-deep, and went upstairs to her own room, where she lay in bed and thought about those two girls from her class singing that hideous old song.

But what she held on to, what stayed, as specific as something that could be placed inside one of the picture frames she'd been given, was the image of the two girls kissing. Other than that, the whole day had been a festival of falseness, from the recitation of her Torah portion, which she'd performed terribly, for she had never been a good student, to the Truth or Dare game that she and all her friends eventually played in one of the other banquet halls, during which Franny had ended up French-kissing Lyle Hapner, whose claim to fame was his impression of the president of the United States getting laughing gas at the dentist. Lyle had a strange-looking mouth that seemed in danger of swallowing her, the way a snake might swallow a mouse. She felt small with him, and as if she wasn't inhabiting her full self.

That was it: why did she have to go through life feeling half-

full? She wondered if some people got to feel *fully* full, or whether
it was everyone's fate to feel as if the state of being human was one
in which the self was like a bag of something wonderful that had
already been half-eaten.

But lying in the dark at night in the splendor of her house, the
much-loved youngest child of two highly accomplished judges,
she began her mission toward fullness. Which maybe was the
same as realness. Again, there weren't words for this, not yet.
Words would come later, and lots of them. Words spoken to
other women, in beds or leaning against a wall in an alley, in a
new voice that shocked her—shocked her that the strong feelings she had always felt meant *this*. That those feelings = being
gay. Who would have thought? Everyone but her, apparently.

The mission started at thirteen, and was revisited at sixteen,
when Franny managed to make her way into the city to the East
Village, to a women's bar called Ben-Her. Her parents thought
she was with two friends from school that day seeing *Wicked*.
Franny had worked out something convincing to say about
the Broadway show. If anyone asked her about it, she would
tell them, "I particularly loved the song 'For Good.' It's really
haunting."

But while her friends went in a cluster to the Gershwin The-
atre, she headed down to the bar she had read about on *Fem
Fatale*, in an article titled "Where the Girls Are: A Roundup of
the U.S.'s Best Lesbian Watering Holes." The words themselves
were disorienting—"lesbian watering holes" suggestive of female anatomy—and as with the time that her friends had sung
that song after her bat mitzvah, she felt herself called to attention
and yearning, like an alien who has received a message from its
home planet.

So there she was at Ben-Her, underage and underprepared for

what she would find. In the heat of a spring night, jammed into a narrow storefront that in its last incarnation had been a Polish pierogi joint, the women in their tank tops and other thin warm-weather clothes stood talking face-to-face, chest-to-chest, everyone as close and intimate as it got without kissing. Franny wore a pocket T and cutoffs and Doc Martens; she looked like a hot butch Girl Scout or hot femme Boy Scout, take your pick. Her blond hair was cut medium-short and blunt, in a fashion that to her was mild but distinctly sexual, subconsciously designed to draw in women who looked like this, as well as others who looked more feminine. She liked those women too, was excited by their femininity but also by what struck her as their more secret, encrypted desire for women. The bar smelled both woodsy and spiced. Zee took out a fake ID that belonged to a friend's older sister, and showed it to a bartender in a retro bowling shirt, a small tattoo of Betty and Veronica stamped onto her neck. "What can I get you, cutie?" asked the bartender, and Franny shivered in happiness at being spoken to this way.

"A beer," she said, not knowing you were supposed to request a particular brand. But the bartender found her one, cementing Franny Eisenstat's lifelong love of beers, in particular Heineken, which she would always picture being held in that curved hand. Franny perched on a wobbling stool in the corner and drank her beer while watching the anthropological scene all around her. The music was from her parents' twenties, Eurythmics' old classic "Sweet Dreams," played loud in that shoe box of writhing women, and she leaned her head back against the wall and just watched. Soon she became aware that someone was observing her, and she flushed in self-consciousness, ducking away and then looking back. The self-consciousness shattered into confusion as the person was revealed to be her mother's big blond law clerk, Linda Mariani, who kept staring and finally pushed toward her through a wall of women.

"Franny?" she shouted. "Franny Eisenstat? You're *here*?"

Linda took Franny by the hand and led her outside to the stoop beside the bar. Both of them were sweating; Linda was soaked through her silk shirt, her face glazed with melting makeup. She was forty years old and a lesbian, and she asked Franny, "Have you ever been here before?"

"No."

"I didn't think so. I've never seen you here. Does your mother know?"

"No." Franny said this with emphasis. "You've been here before?"

Linda laughed. "Oh sure. Listen," she said, "you shouldn't be at a bar. You're too young."

"I can make my own decisions." Even speaking with such a swagger, Franny felt ashamed. She was trying on a whole new self here, and the experience was getting strange.

"Don't be cocky. You'll get hurt." Linda wiped at her own face with a tissue, and Franny saw that it came away smeared with flesh-colored makeup. Suddenly she had an uneasy image of Linda Mariani having sex, her makeup coming off on a pillow.

On another night, a visit to Ben-Her led to Franny's first sexual adventure, which was with a woman whose power was simply in the moment and not in the world. She had power because Franny was attracted to her. Alana was eighteen, with an overbite and the kind of hair that had submitted to one too many flat irons. She worked in retail, she said, and though she was an ordinary-looking person and not particularly articulate, when she took Franny back to her older sister's studio apartment in a tenement building around the corner from the bar, simply that Alana was female and desired Franny was enough to make the encoun-

ter monumental. The sixth-floor walk-up apartment was decorated with knickknacks and bamboo furniture. The shelves held
no books, only stuffed animals wearing tiny T-shirts with sayings
on them. A raccoon wore one that said I'M WITH STUPID, and the
tiny stuffed zebra beside it wore one that said STUPID. Franny,
raised in a large, tasteful house filled with original art and books—
and in fact personally named after someone in a book—could not
help but feel snobbish.

But when Alana said, "Lie down," in a voice that Franny
would later come to understand had been almost suffocated with
sexual arousal, Franny obeyed. Above her, Alana crossed her
arms and lifted off her own shirt, revealing small, slightly pes-
simistic breasts. Then she removed Franny's shirt and skinny
jeans, saying to her, not unkindly, "Is this your first time?"

"Yep," Franny said, trying to sound cheerful and game, but
her voice came out surprisingly untried.

"Okay. Well, then, let me just say this. The point is for it
to feel good, right? There is no other point whatsoever. You
don't have to try and figure out what it means, or whether we're
going to be in a relationship, because I'll tell you right now
we're not."

"Got it," said Franny, and then before she knew what was
happening, Alana dove down upon her, her mouth between her
legs—*yikes*, a woman's mouth between her legs, licking her there
with knowledge and patience and need. The strong sensation
was instantaneous, like the moment when a mask with anesthe-
sia is put over your face, or in this case a mask with reverse an-
esthesia, in which you feel more and not less. She easily went
under.

Franny never saw Alana again, but she did go back to Ben-
Her three more times before her parents discovered where she
had been going during those trips into the city. One night senior

year, she took Metro-North home from Manhattan as usual, and walked into the house on Heather Lane to find her mother waiting in the kitchen in a peach-colored bathrobe, though she might just as easily have been in her black judicial robe. Judge Wendy Eisenstat looked at her with serene confidence and said, "You haven't been seeing Broadway shows. That was a lie about crying at the end of *Phantom of the Opera*. Let's get that clear. I know you've been going to a women's bar, using a fake ID, which is illegal."

"How?" Franny asked in a light wail.

"Linda Mariani has been stealing office supplies from my chambers. Nothing big, mostly a lot of Hewlett-Packard inkjet cartridges, but we had to let her go because they add up. And as security escorted her out, she turned to me in front of everyone, mind you, in front of *everyone*, and said, 'By the way, Judge, your daughter is gay. Ask her where she goes on all those trips into the city.'"

So all was revealed, and Franny and the judge both became teary. "I wish I hadn't found out from my law clerk," her mother said. Finally it was decided that Franny should see a therapist in order to "sort everything out." After their conversation was over, Franny's father, who had been hiding in the den, gently approached her. "Your mother's manner is kind of absolute," he said. "If it's any consolation," he added with a small laugh, "she's that way on the bench, too. But just know we both believe in you and love you a lot. You'll do fine." He gave her a hug.

A few days later, Franny agreed to see Dr. Marjorie Albrecht, who had a therapy practice in the basement of her nearby Larchmont home. Dr. Albrecht was a former member of the Tri-State Modern Dance Troupe who was now working as a psychotherapist. She was a willowy, sun-damaged woman who wore leotards at all times, and who, even when she was listening to you intently, might do a casual arm-stretch over her head. Most of her clients were teenage girls—girls with eating disorders; girls with anger issues; girls who cut themselves shallowly but meaningfully in order to feel better. Girls who hated their mothers or fathers; girls who were disappearing into a morass of self-hate and hair in the face; girls with bad-news boyfriends. Dr. Albrecht also had a good number of patients with sexual identity issues.

Franny was at first defiant at having to go see her, but soon she came to like the early-evening sessions. Her mother would drop her off at the curb and drive to Starbucks and read a brief while Franny went in and sat and talked with the therapist, who at some point would suggest that they could "make some movement" while they discussed whatever was on Franny's mind.

"I really loathe being called Franny," she confided one day as they swept around the basement studio with its gleaming wooden floors and its mirror and barre. Somewhere overhead came the footfalls of the family Albrecht.

"So change it," said the therapist, leaping diagonally across the room and landing like a cat.

"I can't. I was named for *Franny and Zooey*, a book my parents love. It would hurt them too much."

"Oh, they'll live."

"Maybe I could be Zooey," she said shyly, and Dr. Albrecht grabbed her hand and they twirled. So Zooey it was, for a week. The name proved too . . . *zooey*, too animalistic, and ultimately too ugly. With Dr. Albrecht, she discovered that she didn't dislike being female, she just disliked the metonymy of this lightweight female name standing in for all womankind. If you heard that someone was named Franny, she thought, you might assume some things about her—such as that she was totally feminine and perhaps prone to blushing—and you might be wrong. It was while dancing around that room the next time that she decided to collapse *Zooey* into *Zee*.

It was amazing that her name had come from those sessions with Dr. Albrecht, but more amazing still that a betrayal would come from them too. This would take years to discover. Off at Ryland College, where Zee had gone after being such a middling student in high school, she was in the library getting a book for her psychology class, when she accidentally came upon a volume with its author's name stamped in large gold letters on the spine. MARJORIE ALBRECHT, PhD, she read, shocked. "Whoa," Zee said aloud in the stacks. The book had a long boring psychological title.

She opened it and began to read. Each chapter was a different case study. Chapter 3 was called "A Girl Named Kew: Lesbianism as Mask and Mirror."

"*Whoa*," she said again.

"Kew" was raised by a workaholic mother who put her profession before parenting, and who likely struggled with her own gender issues, and a father who was removed and gentle and passive, hardly providing the template for a young girl's future passions and fantasies, but instead staying obstinately weak and distant.

Is it any wonder that this young girl came to my consulting room so confused about her sexuality, and so reluctant to accept her femaleness, that she actually announced she was going to change her name to one that, like the garb she chose to wear, sadly bore no traces of femininity?

My heart ached for this very young patient who could not let herself enjoy the wonders of her own female self or embrace the love of men. It seemed to me that she had entered treatment too late, and that she would have no choice but to lead a "gay" lifestyle, unconsciously denying herself that which had been denied her and which she craved with a hunger she could never even feel.

We did a great deal of movement together, "Kew" and I, and in the furious motions she made I could sometimes see the real heterosexual self that wanted to be seen but sadly did not know how.

By the time Zee had finished reading, she was crying out quietly in injustice and insult. And when the light in the narrow aisle between metal bookshelves suddenly clicked off with a soft little catch like a release of breath, Zee was relieved. She thought she might pass out in the musty dark. Never had she felt as misrepresented, and yet she still couldn't shake it off, and had to wonder if any or all of what Marjorie Albrecht had written was true. If Zee's need to occupy the place she had essentially created—a zone where a person could have a name like "Zee" or "Kew" and wear a tuxedo shirt and yet not consider herself a cross-dresser or in any way be doing a weak imitation of men, but merely be finding for herself the most natural and graceful way to exist in the world—was in fact a result of something having gone psychologically wrong. She didn't tell anyone about the book except for Greer, nor did she return it to the shelf. Instead she casually checked it out of the library and brought it to the dorm, and in front of Greer, despite fire regulations, she took a cigarette lighter and calmly set the book ablaze.

"We used to dance together," Zee said softly, remembering the lovely feeling of flying across that room. "That's why I'm a good dancer. But I can't believe she wrote this."

"I can't either. You don't deserve this, Zee. No one does."

At one point, when the flame swelled the cover, it even made a tiny sound like a human voice crying out from somewhere far away, though soon it was drowned out by the sound of the fire alarm clanging through the halls of Woolley. Dr. Albrecht hadn't been trying to be cruel; she believed what she had written. And maybe Zee, to her own horror, believed it a little bit too.

She was used to thinking that you could be as queer as you wanted these days if you lived in the right geographical area. But though the book had burned and become unrecognizable, causing Zee to pay the Metzger Library a lost-book fine of sixty-five dollars, and though she had hooked up with a couple of gasping women in college, she felt part of a sometimes unworkable struggle. She had already been betrayed by two different older women in her life: Linda Mariani, that *cunt*; and of course Dr. Albrecht, who had seemed so warm and trustable as they danced around the room.

Zee distracted herself from the incident with the book by joining the school's terrible improv troupe, and sleeping with one of the other members, Heidi Klausen, who was fair-haired and European and refined. She had told Zee about the Swiss cookies called *Schwabenbrötli* that she used to bake when growing up in Zurich, and she said that she and Zee would bake them together sometime. So one day Zee came to her off-campus apartment and said, "Teach me to make those *Schwaben*-whatever cookies," and Heidi had agreed. They'd fed each other warm cookies on Heidi's futon. Zee didn't understand what drove her, a few days later, to hook up with her former RA, the confident Shelly Bray. Of course Heidi found out about it, because Shelly Bray could not keep it to herself, and Heidi became furious, yelling at Zee in the middle of the quad, "*Fock* you, Eisenstat, I made myself vulnerable to you in all ways. I even showed you how to bake *Schwabenbrötli!*" In reply, Zee said, nastily, "Right, your *Nazi* cookies," but Heidi was Swiss, not German, and anyway she had done nothing wrong.

Zee went through women, or they went through her. "I'm a slut," she once said easily to Greer as she headed across campus for a late-night meeting with a girl she'd met in an anthropology seminar. She had never been in love, but only temporarily infatuated. There had been bursts of physical pleasure, ephemeral shooting stars.

Her good friend Dog watched her longingly throughout college as she went about her all-female business. He watched all women longingly, she'd noticed, but he had a particular soft spot for Zee. He was always hanging around her room, flopped on the bed. He was extremely good-looking, objectively, though he had a beard that was just shy of Amish. Why didn't anyone tell men that women didn't like that look? They could leave them anonymous notes saying, "Friends don't let friends wear beards without mustaches."

Dog was one of the kindest people Zee had ever met, and he listened to all her stories about her hookups, nodding and taking it in and being very understanding and contemplative—he himself had had many hookups with women since he'd been at Ryland, but he never liked to talk about himself, and instead always ceded the floor to Zee—but then at the end of her filibuster he said, "So will you give me a shot?"

"A shot? No."

"Is it because I'm a ginger?" he asked with a puckish smile.

"Dog, seriously? I've just been sitting here talking about being gay, and you want me to give you a shot?"

"We could just do *some* things," he said shyly, long-lashed, looking down.

"No," she said. "Sorry."

But then one Friday night, after the Heidi debacle had taken place and Zee was worn out, and Greer was off visiting Cory at Princeton, and Chloe was at a party, it got really late, and Dog was lying on top of the covers on her bed half-asleep, so Zee, feeling affectionate and bored, lay down beside him. He put an arm around her, delighted.

"See, that's not so bad," he said.

She thought that they would just sleep, maybe, if it was possible to fall asleep under these conditions, but he said to her, "Would you mind?" and took her hand and held it for a second in his own much larger one, and then, when she didn't object, he took it and placed it on his chest, at the place where the bramble of hair crept over the top of his T-shirt. She felt his heart, and didn't pull away. And then, finally, he put her hand on the hardest, hottest crotch in the world. A big, hot boulder. She practically leaped away.

"Sorry," he said. "I ache for you. I walk around campus like this all the time. It's almost a disability. I should get extra time on tests."

She returned her hand there out of friendship, but didn't look, imagining that beneath his pants he had a nest of hair as red and mohairlike as his beard. He was the nicest guy in the world, and she thought this as she moved her hand awkwardly, like the mechanical claw in one of those crane games at arcades. He was much too excited now, and she was much too unexcited. It was a mistake to have done anything with him, and she knew this right away.

"You can't sleep here, you know," she said to him after he had an orgasm on high volume, and they lay together with his chest heaving in recovery.

"Why? We could talk all night. You could tell me more things. I'd like that."

"I don't want to talk all night, Dog. You are the greatest, you really are. But I am only attracted to girls. It's the way God made me," she added uncertainly, though since her bat mitzvah she had pretty much left God in the dust.

Finally he loped off down the hall and went back upstairs to the room he shared with Kelvin, while Zee lay in bed and felt confused and even a little ashamed. Over time Dog got involved with all kinds of other girls on campus, and his friendship with Zee stayed as strong as it had ever been, and neither of them ever referred to what had happened. Once in a while Zee wondered if she had even dreamed it. Women were it for her, but even so, she knew she had problems with them; something difficult often happened between her and them, but she didn't know what, or why.

After college, she had thought it would be great to work with Greer at Faith Frank's foundation, but apparently that couldn't happen. She felt rootless and lost at Schenck, DeVillers, her first job after graduation. By winter she knew she had to get out and go someplace where she felt needed. Then, one late night at the law firm, the arachnodactyly guy, whose name was Ronnie, mentioned to Zee that his sister worked for Teach and Reach, the nonprofit that trained recent college graduates and then placed them in jobs in public and charter high schools around the country. The training session for the current batch of teachers had taken place over the summer—a whirlwind six weeks—though now it was the middle of the school year and everyone was in place. But there had been a few dropouts recently, Ronnie explained, and the organization was worried about what to do and getting frantic. Did Zee want his sister's email?

It was startling how easy it was to be hired by Teach and Reach. "I'll be honest. We are looking for enthusiasm as much as anything else," the woman on the phone told her. So that was how Zee found herself relocating to Chicago in late winter. "I hate not being in the same city as you," she'd said to Greer, though really the two friends hadn't seen each other as often as they would have liked. Zee had stayed over in Brooklyn once in a while, but their schedules didn't often overlap. Zee didn't spend too much time thinking about why there were openings for teachers now, and why she was so easily welcomed in. She was too desperate to get out of her paralegal job. Instead she allowed herself to feel flattered by the job offer, even though in retrospect there was no reason to feel that way.

Training was accelerated from its usual six weeks down to two and a half. "We believe you to be a fast learner," said a guy named Tim, who was in charge of the trainees.

"Would you please write that in a note and send it to my parents?" Zee said. "They would be very amused."

In Chicago Zee lived in a six-flat on which her parents grudgingly paid the rent, because Teach and Reach salaries were laughably low. "You'd need to live on a barge in China in order to be able to afford working there," Judge Wendy said.

"And yet the commute would be impossible, Judge."

"Franny, you can joke all you want."

"Zee."

"All right, *Zee*. But I have to tell you point-blank that I wish you wouldn't take this job," said her mother, who had steadfastly disapproved of her move, despite understanding that the job was worthwhile, even noble.

Zee began teaching history at one of the Learning Octagon™ charter schools after the two-and-a-half-week lightning round of prep in their training center. The Teach and Reach teacher Zee was replacing had quit very dramatically in the middle of a school day, throwing up her hands and asking, "Where's the learning? And where's the octagon?" Then there was a substitute for a while, but he hadn't been trained in the method-ology, and all seven schools in the Learning Octagon™ network (it was awkward that there were seven, not eight, but one build-ing had had a lead paint issue and had been indefinitely shut down only days before the start of the term) were contracted now with Teach and Reach. So Zee started at the facility on the South Side, armed with a formal teaching plan.

She walked into her first-period ninth-grade class, which she imagined would be a scene of chaos, but instead the students seemed to have been given a sleeping potion; at 8:20 in the morning they were half-lying across their desks in the drafty third-floor classroom. Most of them were African-American, and several were Hispanic, and a couple were white. None of them looked happy to see her, or happy to be there, or even happy to be awake; she didn't blame them at all. She remem-bered feeling this way herself in high school and was immedi-ately sympathetic. So at the very least they would have a sympathetic teacher.

"Good morning," she said as she unnecessarily straightened the few belongings on her desk and sat on the unforgivingly squeaking green chair behind it. No one replied. "Well, maybe it's not such a good morning," she said. "Maybe this morning sucks."

"No shit," some boy said. There was vague laughter, and some mild surprise that Zee joined in the laughter too, though she hadn't found his comment funny. When in Rome, she'd thought, followed by: I really don't know what I'm doing here.

"You will feel uncertain sometimes in the classroom, maybe a lot of the time in the beginning," Tim had told her. "That's totally normal." She thought of this now as she looked out over the class. "I'm Ms. Eisenstat, and I'll be your teacher tonight," Zee impulsively said. "May I tell you about our specials?"

They looked at her with unimpressed faces.

"What do you mean, *tonight?*" a girl asked.

"And what do you mean, *specials?*" asked another girl in the back.

Zee was mortified at her own joke; what was she thinking—they did not go to pretentious restaurants, or probably to restaurants at all. Most of them received free lunches. She realized that any kind of bonding she might do with them wouldn't be around her pathetic attempts to amuse them or to seem starkly different from their previous teacher, who had abandoned them. She wanted them to need her, or at least tolerate her. She didn't want them to overwhelm her and make her feel that she too had to leave her job in the middle of the year, in the middle of the *day*.

Being in the world as an adult meant that you didn't just quit. Things couldn't necessarily be "gotten out of." Sophomore year at Ryland, Zee had initially had a roommate, Claudia, who smelled of B.O. and had no comprehension of the importance of good hygiene. Judge Richard Eisenstat had made a telephone call to the dean after Zee had been curtly told by the dean's secretary that she had to suck it up; there was absolutely no way she could switch dorm rooms. Somehow, though, when the judge called, a new room was found: a single. Things could be gotten out of—apparently many things, most things. But she didn't want to get out of this thing. These students, she decided, needed her. She looked out over their unreadable faces and got started with that day's prepared lesson on the Second World War. Almost immediately the classroom became a place of indifference, with occasional spurts of anarchy. Some days, no one listened. She found herself begging them to listen, trying to bribe them. A couple of kids were outright menacing, including a large girl who said in an incongruously babyish voice, "I'm going to fuck you up," in response to a request to put down her pencil at the end of an exam, before immediately crying and apologizing. Always there were trips to the principal, and sometimes visits from Big Dave in Security, who made things worse, escalating whatever in-room squall was taking place.

Greer called and said, "Quit! Quit!" but Zee, almost in tears, said, "I can't do that to them. I won't." Most days weren't about fear, they were about unbelievable frustration, even rage—her own. But she also felt nearly ill with sympathy over what her kids didn't have, didn't know, and couldn't do. One boy had the worst breath, and finally he shyly revealed that he didn't have a toothbrush or toothpaste, and had no money to buy them; so she bought them for him. At Zee's request, Greer sent cases of her parents' protein bars, and Zee went out and bought packs of thick socks and gloves, always gloves. There was a sense that nothing did anything, that she was just another clueless person armed with supplies, throwing them into a volcano.

And then one morning that spring, when Zee was waiting for the train, a text came from Greer, saying, "Are you available? It's an emergency." Soon they were on the phone, and Greer in a guttural explosion told her the most terrible news: Cory's little brother had been run over by his mother's car and killed. You didn't have to have met a child to know that his death was the worst thing you'd ever heard. At age twenty-two, Zee could imagine the death from the point of view of the child and the parent and the sibling, all at the same time. Greer was sobbing, and Zee wished she had something to say to her, some way to soothe her. But they were in different cities and lives now, so the best Zee could do over the next few weeks was text her frequently, saying, "How are you doing?" despite already knowing the answer.

At lunchtime each day, after a rough or maddening morning, Zee sat alone in the teachers' lounge, mostly listening to tales of other classroom experiences—small tragedies or tense near-misses, or else anecdotes about bureaucratic stagnation, and un-related references to weekend activities such as online dating or bowling.

She sometimes took special note of the guidance counselor, Noelle Williams, because she had been particularly unfriendly from the first day. She never spoke to Zee at lunch, but sat in a small group of administrators, daintily eating a cup of yogurt, her plastic spoon knocking against the bottom and sides, her posture freakishly straight. When she was done eating, she put her trash into a neat little bundle, her hands practically compact-ing it. She never left traces of herself behind. Noelle Williams was twenty-nine years old, her hair cut close to her head, reveal-ing her skull's perfect, pleasing shape. Her delicate ears sprouted many tiny rings, and her outfits were immaculate, never creased. Zee had always felt stylish, in her own way, but Noelle's perfec-tion was a reproach.

One day at noon, Zee nervily planted herself on the sagging couch beside the guidance counselor, whose lack of interest in getting to know Zee was obvious, though this in itself made Zee want to win her over. What had Zee done to piss Noelle Wil-liams off? Zee asked her, "How long have you been working in Chicago?"

The woman looked at her directly, appraisingly. "Three years," she said. "I was here at the inception of this school."

"Oh great."

"And before that I was getting my master's. And then work-ing in a school out in the suburbs."

"That must have been pretty different from this place."

"Yes," said Noelle, and she didn't smile with bitter irony, or add any details to show that while working here was unmanage-able, they were both in it together, and the only way to try to manage it was to be ironic. She wasn't being ironic, nor was she welcoming.

"I'm just getting my feet wet," Zee went on. "Any tips about the teaching? It's hard to sustain anything in there."

"Do I have any tips about how you should teach your classes?" asked Noelle. "First of all, I'm not a teacher. But also, I imagine that you were given all the tips you need, were you not?"

Were you not? Zee almost mimicked her words back to her. What a cunt, she thought. "Well, I was given a crash course in teaching history," Zee said, "but teaching actual high school students is something else entirely. And teaching these kids—it's just barely happening. Too many crises, and too much tuning out. I get pretty despondent."

"I understand." Noelle didn't say anything more.

There was a moment of cool silence, during which Zee ate the sandwich she had sloppily made that morning in her tiny kitchen. Now the innards were falling out of the soft and floppy thing, a spill of dissonant ingredients that should never have been put together: apple slices, and a few whole baby carrots on their way out of this world, and a stiff Elizabethan ruffle of kale, all of it vaguely pasted together by a spackle of miso and a squirt of low-fat mayo from a squeeze bottle purchased at the bodega around the corner on the first lonely night she had moved to this city, knowing no one.

Noelle watched as vegetables tumbled onto Zee's lap, and was that actually a *smile*? A slightly unpleasant smile as she saw Zee get slimed by her own lunch? Zee dabbed at her shirt with a rough brown paper towel from the dispenser, leaving an oblong of oil behind, and when she looked up to say something else to Noelle, she saw that the door of the faculty lounge was pneumatically closing, and Noelle was already on her way to deal with some new problem.

It might have gone on like this for quite a while, the guidance counselor being rude and unfriendly, and Zee continuing to try to win her over, and perhaps one day Noelle would've said to her, "Zee, what are you doing? Why don't you stop? Can't you see I just don't like you?"

But instead one afternoon, a month into the job, Zee's student Shara Pick said, "Miss Eisenstat?"

Zee was at the whiteboard creating a timeline that stretched from 1939 to 1945. A few people seemed very interested; one student in particular, Derek Johnson, knew everything about the war already and was contributing a lot to the discussion. "Yes?" Zee said.

"Can I go to the bathroom?" Shara asked, and then she stood up and wobbled in front of her desk. She had to go, and she had to go now. She was a bumblebee-shaped white girl, and wherever she went a cloud of chaos accompanied her. Crumpled sheets of paper, pens that leaked, little plastic microbeads from some unknown source. She was generally ignored in the class, seen as trashy and pitiable, and she didn't seem to fit in anywhere. During lunch she sat alone, staring into the middle distance as she ate a bag of Doritos and called it a meal. Zee had been informed by the assistant principal that Shara was considered "at risk." Her parents were meth addicts in and out of recovery, and she and her sisters had recently moved in with their kind but half-blind grandmother.

The year before, the parents had both shown up for curriculum night, high out of their minds. "It's a mess," Zee had been told, and she had kept an eye out for Shara, who always wore a coat to class that had one of those Eskimo hoods that reminded Zee of the cover of the old Paul Simon album that her parents had listened to during her childhood. Shara dozed frequently, which worried Zee, who was on the lookout for signs of drug use in this vulnerable girl. But whenever there was an in-class essay Shara would hunch down over her desk with her elbows and tongue out in a posture of deep, touchingly childlike concentration, and would turn out something that was surprisingly impassioned. Maybe there was a hidden interest there, a hidden possibility.

"Sure, go," Zee said, and she stayed at the whiteboard, writing up a list of factors that had led to war. She wrote and wrote so much in a tiny hand that the board appeared covered in wire mesh, though only some students were taking any of it down in their notebooks. Others were gazing out at her in comprehension or incomprehension or daydream, and a boy in front named Anthony was doodling extravagantly in his notebook, the detail work of skulls and devils impressive, if evidence of an extreme interest in Satanism that should probably be reported to the administration.

A girl in the last row was doing her acrylic nails on top of her notebook, the strong smell wafting up toward the front of the room. The smell spread, the felt pen that Zee dragged across the board uttered its occasionally shrill report, and the teenagers in the room shifted and settled and resettled. Someone howled like a wolf, at length, for laughs. The afternoon had a low-blood-sugar quality, with only thirteen minutes left until class ended. Zee would have had them write in their journals for a few minutes, and maybe let one of them play a song on the phone, which tended to focus the entire room. But then an awareness came over her, as strongly as the smell, that Shara hadn't returned from the bathroom. Zee sent Taylor Clayton out to check on her, and while Taylor tended to be a hesitant girl, only moments later she banged back into the room, knocking against the door frame and saying, "Something's wrong with Shara!"

Shara was curled up on the floor of her stall in the bathroom, and somehow Zee and Anthony, who'd been pressed into service, got her down to the nurse's office. "It hurts so bad," Shara was crying, and she held her stomach and rocked back and forth.

The nurse, as it happened, was showing a drug film to another class, and only her aide sat at the desk in the small green room, putting tongue depressors into a jar one by one, *thud thud, thud,* and looking terrified when Shara was half-carried and half-dragged in and was then laid down on the bed.

"I'll get Jean," the nurse's aide said as she ran from the room, scattering tongue depressors.

"Tell him to leave too," Shara said, gesturing toward Anthony.

The boy ran out, relieved, and then Zee sat beside Shara, rubbing her arms and saying whatever she could think of. "It's probably appendicitis," she said, talking rapidly and idly. "My brother had that once. He screamed all night. But when they took it out he felt better, and you will too. Did you know that the appendix serves absolutely no function?" she added, because she couldn't think of what else to say, and she wanted to distract Shara from her pain.

"No," wept the girl.

"Well, it's true."

Then she became aware of someone hovering, and there above them was Noelle Williams. "What's going on, Shara?" the guidance counselor asked in her calm voice.

"I'm *sick.*"

"I think it's appendicitis," Zee put in.

"And you know that from where, your training at Harvard Medical School?" said Noelle.

"Well—"

"Or was that a unit at Teach and Reach?"

Zee simmered but said nothing. It wasn't appropriate; this girl was suffering. Noelle crouched down and opened Shara's coat, which was something that Zee hadn't thought to do. The guidance counselor gently unzipped it and parted the two halves, revealing Shara Pick's full abdomen, astonishingly round beneath her sweater. With the coat off it was impossible to miss.

"May I raise your sweater?" Noelle asked, and Shara nodded. The skin of her abdomen was stretched and shining, the navel asserting itself like a pencil eraser, and below that was a bisecting dark stripe of skin, something called *linea nigra*, Zee would learn later when she sat at her computer and looked up every single thing, every single moment, locked in studiousness the way Greer would have been if she'd been there for this.

But armed with no knowledge yet, only instinct, in that moment in the nurse's office Zee and the guidance counselor looked at each other, alarmed, across Shara Pick, and then Noelle said to Shara in a soft voice, "Sweet pea, did you know you were going to have a baby?"

"I thought, yeah, maybe I was."

"Well, you are, and Miss Eisenhower and I are going to help you."

Zee didn't correct her. Everything happened so fast from that moment on. 911 was called; Shara made deep sounds in her throat, and she braced her legs and arched her back.

"I'll look up what to do," said Noelle, and while Zee encouraged Shara not to push, to keep her legs together, to wait, Noelle sat at the nurse's desk—the nurse, Jean, why wasn't she back yet? On the old gum-colored Dell desktop computer Noelle punched in a password, and then *success*. She Googled the sparest and most economical collection of words she could think of. She was an excellent Googler, it would turn out.

Now, swiftly, Noelle located an online visual guide to delivering a baby in emergency circumstances with no training and no equipment. "Okay, I've got instructions here," she said. In a quiet and controlled voice, Noelle read, "'What should I do to help someone in labor?'"

Somehow they managed to hold Shara off, to keep her from delivering a baby into their unschooled hands. Finally Jean returned, followed immediately by the EMS team, a man and a woman, both young and competent, who raced in and took over. "Push, Shara," they told her after they had assessed the situation.

And then the head emerged, the *face* emerged; and once that explicit sense of humanness appeared, it was as if everything else stopped. As soon as there was a face, everyone marveled. Same as a death. Everyone *knew* death existed, Zee thought; most people had known since childhood. The newspapers were filled with the tiny print of paid death notices and real obituaries, and sometimes one of Zee's parents looked up from the paper while they drank their breakfast smoothies before heading to the courthouse, and mildly said to the other something like, "Oh, did you see that Carl Sagan died?"

Zee thought of Cory Pinto's little brother—gone. She thought of the faces of everyone she knew, trembling in the gelatin of their own temporariness. We're overwhelmed by faces, Zee knew, the ones that leave and the ones that come, and she was overwhelmed by this one now.

Suddenly Zee realized that something thick was wrapped around the baby's neck. It was the umbilical cord, looking like the bicycle cable with which Zee had tied up her Schwinn all over the Ryland campus. She watched the paramedics carefully get it off. It was as if they were unlocking that bicycle chain in the rain, working the slippery thing, with its intimations of something complex beneath the surface, out from among the spokes. The baby's head was sprung.

"There we go, Shara," said the male paramedic tenderly.

"One more, Shara," echoed Jean the nurse.

"You can do it," said Zee.

And then Noelle said, "You're doing great!"

Shara pushed heroically, and eventually there was a sound like a boot pressing into mud as the baby's shoulders rushed out, late for an important meeting, and the human face was revealed to be attached to a human body, genitals swollen and full and declaring: *girl*.

Though they did not like each other, they were both in desperate, shaky need of decompression, so Noelle Williams and Zee Eisenstat found themselves sitting together for a very early dinner in a nearby restaurant after the workday, which ended for both of them immediately after Shara's grandmother arrived and everything was revealed to be stable, at least medically. Zee tried to go to the hospital with her frightened student, but Jean the nurse said no, she would go instead. There was nothing more for Zee and Noelle to do.

Noelle chose a small soul-food restaurant called Miss Marie's with wood paneling and an excellent soundtrack featuring Smokey Robinson and the Miracles. A tin bowl of pickled green tomatoes was placed on the table, and Zee sliced one hard, feeling the give of the skin, knowing that even though her knife was dull, she could cut this. She had nearly delivered a baby today, after all. The baby of a baby.

Poor Shara Pick, she thought. Poor Baby Girl Pick. There was nothing she could do for her students but buy toothbrushes and tube socks and assist at a delivery, and feel a constant sadness or anger or fear. "What's going to happen?" she asked. "Her family is such a mess."

"Oh, I know. It's as sad as it gets," said Noelle. "Her parents came to school once and they could barely stand up. I don't know what they're like now. The social worker is heading over to the hospital tonight, and we'll follow up tomorrow, but it's all very bleak."

"Will she be allowed to come back to school?"

"Sure, there are various options. But I have no idea what she's going to do. We have a program for mothers, but honestly it all kills me. Why did no one see that that girl was pregnant? Oh, that was a rhetorical question. It's a question that will be put to the entire faculty and staff when we meet next. And I'm going to suggest we have an emergency meeting, because none of us noticed it. We can't just say, 'She was carrying small,' though clearly she was. That baby was like a hand puppet. And yet the EMS team said she was fine. Small but fine. Her lungs sounded good."

"I feel terrible that I missed it. But I couldn't see anything. Shara wore a parka to class every day," said Zee.

"That in itself was a warning sign."

"I didn't know that."

"Of course you didn't."

At which point Zee wondered how much shit she was meant to take from the guidance counselor. Why did Noelle dislike her with such ferocity, even after everything they had done together today, and the raw drama of it?

"What did I ever do to you, Noelle?" she asked.

The waitress appeared then, cutting off the confrontation, so they ordered dully from the menu. Chicken for Noelle, a vegetable medley for Zee. When you were a vegetarian your restaurant meals were heavy on medleys.

Then Noelle looked up at her with an expression that was surprisingly not hostile. "Zee," she said. "It's not you. Well, it is you. It's your trusting nature. Your idealism."

"I wasn't under the impression that those were bad qualities." Zee swirled the beer in her glass, and suddenly had a surge of desire to be drinking beers with Greer instead of with this unfriendly woman. Everyone said Chicago was such a great city. "The Art Institute," they exclaimed. "The nightlife. The music. The *lake.*"

But Zee had seen very little and done very little, because it was hard to love a city when you were entirely alone in it. Or at least hard for Zee. Maybe she could convince Greer to come visit some weekend. Together they could go down to the edge of the shining lake and throw stones and talk about what was painful in their lives, and what was hopeful. But the unfriendly woman here had a command over Zee. It wasn't deserved, but it was real. Noelle, she noted, had a sexy throat.

"They aren't bad qualities, in a vacuum," Noelle conceded. "But when my kids get used, I consider those qualities less than helpful."

"Your kids?" said Zee. "They're not my kids now too?"

"You think of your students as your kids?"

"Why shouldn't I? You know something, I deserve some slack from you," Zee said. "I'm new, I'm muddling through, and I just went through a *thing* today. I joined Teach and Reach to do some good. I really did. And if that's not happening, well, I don't know what else to do. But ever since I came to this school you've hated me."

"You think this is about you?" Noelle said. "You are just a cog in the Teach and Reach wheel, so please don't inflate your position. I know we've had a rough day, and we had it together, but if I hated you I would not be sitting with you right now. I would be far away from you."

"Oh, so you're saying you like me? That's puzzling. It sure doesn't come off as liking."

"You're going to have to work harder if you want me to like you. But it sounds a little more possible than your other goal," said Noelle. "Saving the students in the Learning Octagon network."

"They need all the help they can get."

"Not from you, sweet pea." This was almost murmured, the same endearment Noelle had used with Shara during the delivery, and she had meant it tenderly then, but now she meant it sharply, lovelessly.

"Then from who? Who else can help an octagon made up of only seven schools, where everyone starts off with nothing? I acknowledge my privilege. I grew up in Scarsdale, New York. But why should my class background disqualify me? Does my experience have to be the same as my students'?"

"My mother is a solidly middle-class office manager for an allergist here in Chicago," said Noelle. "She raised my sister and me all by herself—my father died of a heart attack when I was five—but we had everything we needed, just like you. Music lessons, orthodontia, lots of books on the shelves, and a life of consistency. That is my mother's strong suit. I am not saying that anyone's experience has to be the same as the students'."

"So what are you saying?"

Noelle leaned closer across the table; from this sudden proximity, Zee was given a different view. She didn't simply have to be intimidated by her or admire her physically. As for the possibility of being betrayed, this had nothing to do with the older women in Zee's past, Linda Mariani and Dr. Marjorie Albrecht, who had both shockingly betrayed her, or even Faith Frank, who hadn't betrayed her but had simply had no interest in hiring her, despite Zee's heartfelt letter. Noelle Williams had given her no expectations at all. Zee didn't have to be hurt by her. She could stand up to her if she chose.

"We were told," said Noelle, "that a dedicated team of teachers would sweep in on their dedicated horses, and they would save our schools. But in fact what's happened is that a team of completely unprepared teachers, right out of college themselves and with virtually no training except for a crash course that is far shorter than the course you'd need to take in order to become an air-conditioning repair person, have been sent into our schools. And we're told to be grateful. We're told that this is good enough, and that we should be respectful of the notion that people like you are willing to accept a low-paying job in order to do something worthwhile. When in fact, no, it is not good enough, at least not to me. Some of my colleagues feel differently from me. They approve of Teach and Reach, and think it's an admirable enterprise that's worthy of our support. But since Teach and Reach came, it's worth pointing out that things are no different.

"Now, I am comforted by our president. A black man. And brilliant and kind. I just love him to pieces. But nothing is going to change the baked-in bad stuff all that fast. And in various ways, Teach and Reach is just making everything worse. It can't take any criticism, and therefore it will never change. And all it keeps doing is trying to squeeze our schools to fit into some corporate-driven shape. Veteran teachers are being laid off, but Teach and Reach keeps going. It degrades the profession of teaching. And of course this program is targeting black and brown communities. It would never fly in a white school. And you know what's going to happen? There are forces out there that are lying in wait, taking their time, knowing they will have their moment. You and some of the others, you're not bad people, I know that, but you're not skilled and you're not prepared, and you're only doing these jobs for a little while. You're not here for the duration; no one even thinks you are. You're here postcollege to try and do something good, and once you've had that experience, you're going to turn around and do something else. Probably something less good but more financially rewarding. I don't blame you, Zee. I'd do it too if I were you. But we need people who are here for the long run. Because things are going to get so much worse, and then what will happen?"

"So you're saying I should quit now?"

Noelle looked at her steadily. "Is that really what you think? No, of course I'm not saying that. You shouldn't do that to these kids, not in the middle of the year; not like some people. They crave stability. You stay, and you finish the year, and you do your best, and then you decide. Look, I'm sure you're a fine person, and I'm sure you're a person who is trying hard to . . . what do you say to yourself, 'get involved'? I know that feeling; I have had it myself. But sometimes the way to get involved is to just live your life and be yourself with all your values intact. And by just being you, it'll happen. Maybe not in big ways, but it'll happen."

"I saw it differently," Zee said quietly. Noelle nodded. "In any event, it happened really fast. I was living with my parents and working as a paralegal. I really hated it. My best friend works for Faith Frank. She has a women's foundation, and I thought maybe I could work there too. But that didn't happen. I had to get out of the law firm, not to mention my parents' house. But Judge Wendy Eisenstat made it very clear that whatever I did, I needed to make a living wage."

"Who?"

"My mother."

"You call her Judge Wendy Eisenstat?"

"Yes. Or Judge Wendy. It drives her crazy. She prefers Mom. But honestly, she's had such a judicial presence my entire life. When she shows up in my dreams, sometimes she's wearing robes. My dad too. He's the other Judge Eisenstat, but he's more low-key."

Noelle smiled; was it the first smile? At least it was the first unambivalent one. "So I guess," she said, "your name isn't Eisenhower."

"No."

"And yet you didn't correct me."

"I wouldn't do that. It might make you self-conscious."

"Do you correct your students when they say something wrong?" asked Noelle.

"Yes. Teach and Reach tells us we're supposed to."

"Do you always do what everyone tells you?"

"If they ask nicely."

"Well, I'll have to learn to ask you to do things nicely then," said Noelle. "Note to self."

Zee paused, trying to figure out this turn. "That would be a good idea. You might even see some results," she finally said. "Better than test scores. 'No *Woman* Left Behind.'"

There was an open playfulness between them now; they'd gone from friction to childbirth to an angry soliloquy to this new, uncertain stage. I am so confused! Zee thought, looking at Noelle's small, ornamented ear. "Is your mother very maternal?" Zee suddenly wanted to know.

"Medium. She's more like the steward of a ship. A nice ship, though. Yours?"

"She's been good at what she does. I can't complain. Seeing Shara today, I was thinking that she's just entering that whole parade, isn't she?"

"What parade?"

"Oh, a mother begetting a tiny potential mother. She wasn't even sure she was going to have a baby," said Zee. She poked around at her plate. "I can't even imagine," she added.

"What, having a baby?"

"Right, yeah. My body, all of this equipment that I possess; I've never spent a lot of time thinking of it as reproductive. I had a movement therapist when I was a teenager who apparently thought I was denying my womanhood. But I wasn't! I never have. I like being a girl. I just want to be the one who says what that means. My idea of hell would be to suddenly give birth without knowing it was going to happen."

"That's anyone's idea of hell."

Suddenly, urgently, Zee asked, "Will we definitely find out what happens to Shara and her baby? Can we go see her? And if she doesn't come back to school, is this going to be the last we'll hear?"

"I'll make sure we hear, and that we find a way to help her if we can. I will try not to let her slip through the cracks."

"She's a mess, but she likes history. She's good with dates," said Zee. Maybe this was an exaggeration, but she wanted to say it. Someone had to stand up for Shara Pick, to declare her worthwhile as more than the carrier of a baby that she might soon turn over to someone else's arms, and as more than a collection of uncontrollable parts. "She must have been so scared," said Zee. The body did not always do what you asked it to. It had its own ideas, its own trajectory. Even now, she thought that her own body was like a tuning fork that was responding to Noelle's very particular pitch.

"*You* look scared."

Zee looked up. "It was very scary. Very shocking."

"I don't mean that. I mean now," Noelle said in a constricted, nearly formal voice. "Because of me."

"Okay," Zee admitted. "You can be a little scary."

"Is that all I am to you? A scary person?"

Zee took her time, trying to make sure she was understanding what was happening, the new voice Noelle was using, and what it meant. There was a familiar feeling here; Noelle had to be aware of it too. Think, think, Zee thought, wondering if she had missed an interpretation. Nothing else occurred to her. Crisis usually abated to reveal calm, but this one was revealing another, different kind of crisis. "No," Zee said. "Not only."

"Then what else?" This was said as a direct challenge.

All Zee would say was, "This is weird."

"You don't like it?"

"I don't know what it is."

"Are you sure you don't?"

"Okay, I guess I do," said Zee.

"Is it okay, then?" asked Noelle, and Zee nodded.

Neither of them knew what to say next. They went back to the business of eating dinner, and they drank their cold beers and shared a banana pudding for dessert, both spoons dipping into the same beige mass, reminding Zee of watching Noelle in the faculty lounge eating a cup of yogurt, which made that little galloping-hooves-on-plastic *knock knock* sound. It was the sound of a self-contained woman eating the international symbol of female food: yogurt. Women with their calcium needs. You could go so many places in the world and find women eating yogurt.

"Want to get the check?" asked Noelle. She waved an arm around for the waitress. She was a little drunk, Zee realized, and she felt worried that perhaps Noelle's low-level drunkenness was the cause of her apparent interest in Zee. Maybe Noelle had been tricked into flirting only by virtue of the beer, and later she would be horrified with herself, because after all maybe she was a guidance counselor at a charter school who was as straight as the day is long.

"You're tipsy," Zee said. "That's why you're being this way? Three beers?"

"No," Noelle said. "I deliberately had that third beer *because* I was starting to be this way."

"'This way.'"

"Attracted to you."

"Oh."

Noelle drew a finger down the side of the beer glass, bisecting the condensation. Why was it that the words *attracted to you* were like lightning? It *slayed* Zee that Noelle Williams, the imperious guidance counselor, an older, African-American woman with an impossibly elegant bearing, was attracted to *her*.

"Okay then," said Zee, and they both laughed.

And how strange, too, that laughter would characterize so much of what they did from that night on, even if some of it was the laughter of helplessness in the face of what was unfixable. There were other bad things that happened at the school: a boy beaten so severely on his way home that his eye popped from its socket; another Teach and Reach faculty member giving up the ship; a broken boiler that rendered the school uninhabitable for two days.

But on the night after Shara's baby was born, they walked from the restaurant out into the suddenly blowing snow—spring snow, because this was Chicago—onto a quiet street, and got on the train, which took them mostly in silence and fluorescence toward Zee's six-flat, because it was closer than Noelle's place, which was a good forty-minute ride, and in forty minutes the spell might well have been broken. Thank God the place was clean, Zee thought as she threw on the lights.

"Studenty," Noelle declared, and Zee saw the room as Noelle saw it: The sofa that was covered with a generic Indian-print fabric. The small framed flyer on the wall advertising a college speech in the chapel several years earlier, given by Faith Frank. The clementines in a blue bowl. The photo of Zee and another woman, clearly her good friend, in graduation gowns. The new life that Zee Eisenstat was trying to settle into here in Chicago.

"Yeah, I can't help it," Zee said. "I was a student for so long that it's the only way I know how to be."

"I remember all this," said Noelle, who then decisively brought Zee toward her by the shoulders, which was as much a relief as it was a thrill. They kissed for a long, leisurely time. When they lay down on the narrow mattress that Zee had purchased at a garage sale upon moving here, and had carried on her own back like a Sherpa the seven blocks home, she couldn't help but think a little bit about power: who had it right now, the older woman or the younger one. Power was hard to understand sometimes. You could not quantify it or calibrate it. You could barely see it, even when you were looking straight at it.

"That's what everyone was talking about at the first Loci summit," Greer had said recently on the phone when the subject came up. "The meaning and uses of power."

"The summit you missed, because of Cory's brother."

"Yeah. But everyone who was there—the rest of our team— said that it was clear that it's a topic we're going to return to, because no one can get enough of it. It excites everyone. Power! Even the word is powerful."

"Right," said Zee. "It has the word *pow* in it. Like in a comic book."

To live in a world of female power—mutual power—felt like a desirable dream to Zee. Having power meant that the world was like a pasture with the gate left open, and that there was nothing stopping you, and you could run and run.

Noelle looked formidable with or without her clothes, though of course without them she was more vulnerable to Zee's impressions of her. Their hands were on each other—on Zee with her curated boyish look and Noelle with her carefully feminine look that was slightly tempered by the nearly shaved head and prominent hipbones and the careful comportment, giving her the quality of one of those artist's mannequins. The arms and legs could be rearranged any way you liked, link by link, and this was what sex was too, when power was fluid. You could rearrange the other person, and they could rearrange you.

Now the snow fell steadily, and after a long, expressive round of new-person sex, the two women finally settled themselves in for the night. Power had been there a moment ago, but now it wasn't. How strange that Zee had just been thinking about it, and suddenly it was irrelevant. The day had been impossibly long and difficult, and all that she needed to do now was collapse.

"Sweet pea," Noelle called her before they slept, in a third and entirely different use of that term of endearment.

PART THREE

I Get To Decide

EIGHT

The red awning above the storefront read QI GONG TUI-NA RELAXING INVIGORATING UNFORGETTABLE MASSAGE, words that did not register as interesting to most New Yorkers passing this street corner in the west 90s on a mild night in the fall of 2014. But Faith Frank knew their significance, and once a week after work she had the car and driver take her there, for she just loved a good Chinese massage. She felt, simply, that these bracing, almost disconcertingly vigorous massages helped her marshal her thoughts and make good decisions and stay calm and dispense advice to all the people who came to her for it.

She had discovered this one day, two years earlier, when she'd had a bad stiff neck, and in desperation on the way home from work she'd asked her driver, Morris—her contract with Loci had included the use of a driver and car—to stop there. As Faith lay on a table in this dim establishment with her face in a cushioned cradle, and a small woman working an elbow into the base of Faith's spine, ideas began to jump out of her as if sprung from captivity. So now here she was again on this night, with another stiff neck. She'd been all checked out by her internist and found to be in good health, but the body still needed fine-tuning at this age. As Faith approached the staircase to enter the establishment, her cell phone softly pulsed against her breast like a companion heart, and she reached into her coat.

LINCOLN, read the display. "Oh hey, honey," she said, invigorated in the way that she always felt when he called.

"Hey, Mom." The voice of her son, Lincoln Frank-Landau, had been cautious since childhood, as if he was afraid to expect too much from life. "You're in the middle of something?" he asked. The answer was always yes, not that she always told him that.

"Well, I'm about to be. Getting a Chinese massage in a minute."

"Your neck is tight again?" he said. "Mom, you should slow down. All that travel is bad for you."

"Oh, my schedule's not so bad."

"I actually don't believe you. I saw on your website calendar that you have that Hollywood event coming up. And I saw who was going to be there. Jesus!"

"No, Jesus is not going to be there, Lincoln. We couldn't afford him."

"Well, it's still a far cry from what you used to have at Loci in the beginning. Female sea captains."

Faith laughed. "Well, ShraderCapital told us we needed to go high-profile. Everything is about branding, they say, which of course is a despicable thing, because it really means everything is about corporations. But here we are, in the America of today. So now, yes, we have the female action star of *Gravitus 2: The Awakening*. And did you read about the feminist psychic who's been hired to entertain between talks?"

"No."

"Oh, it's such bullshit," Faith said. "I imagine her standing before a huge group of women, closing her eyes, and saying in this really spooky voice, '*One . . . day . . . you . . . will . . . stop . . . menstruating.*'"

Lincoln laughed easily. "Plus complimentary manicures, right? And all that foodie type of food. I saw a picture on Instagram recently. What were you serving?" he asked. "It was really exotic. Maybe pelican butter?"

Faith laughed too, and said, "Something like that." But the subject of the excesses of the foundation, four years in, was actually depressing to her. Over the past two years in particular, the foundation had been relentlessly urged in this direction by an increasingly vocal presence at ShraderCapital. "I keep telling Emmett that rich women attending conferences with massages and wonderful food doesn't get at anything," she said to Lincoln. "That it doesn't grapple with structural issues like parental leave, child care, equal pay. It doesn't put hands on levers. And yet, as he kindly reminded me, we have to grow. And they've been generous."

As she talked, she began to mount the stairs in the narrow, dark hallway. Distantly, a thin Chinese version of Muzak could be heard. "They've agreed to some things that they have no interest in," she went on. "Though fewer and fewer over time. But I think I told you about the rescue mission we funded recently. One of those special projects we sometimes do. I had to fight for this one, they're getting so infrequent."

"Ecuador, right?"

"Yes. The young women who were saved from trafficking. A hundred of them. And then they were hooked up with female mentors."

"Don't say 'hooked up,' Mom. It sounds like you mean something else."

"Good point," said Faith. "But you get the idea. We connected them with women who taught them a trade. So sure, we may have a psychic, and mani-pedis, and fancy lunches with pelican butter, but we also have missions like this one. So maybe it evens out."

"Maybe," he said.

"Actually," Faith said, "one of the rescued young women is flying in for that LA event. And I'm supposed to introduce her."

"Is it essential that you do it? Your neck? Your exhaustion?"

"Lincoln, I love you with all my heart, but please don't tell me what to do. I try not to tell you what to do." There was a churlish silence, and she wanted to break it fast, so she said, "So how's the tax code?"

"Still kicking."

"And still shockingly unfair?"

"Depends on your bracket," he said.

This last part was a kind of vaudeville routine that they had been amusing only themselves with over the years since he'd become a tax lawyer. Lincoln was thirty-eight now and lived in Denver. Unmarried, dedicated, he resembled his father, Gerry Landau, an immigration advocate to whom Faith had been married only for several years, until his shocking death at exactly the age Lincoln was now. Gerry had been a pale, mild man who looked hamsterish with his aviator glasses off. With them on, he looked more himself: thoughtful, brainy, distracted. She'd liked him right away. The first time he took Faith anywhere in his car, an old yellow Dodge Dart, he'd had to clear so many papers and books and a bag of bagels off the passenger seat in order for her to sit down that it was comical.

"When you went to antiwar meetings," she asked Gerry, "did you speak up a lot?"

"Are you kidding?" he said. "Those guys wouldn't let me get a word in. And when I did speak, they interrupted."

"Same," she said.

Lincoln, now, looked like Gerry then, but much squarer in style, and with less hair. Already her son's hair had fled his head, as if pushed away by the complexities of the tax code. She still hoped he would fall in love, her reserved and mild son. As a boy, Lincoln had always been resourceful and independent. But after Gerry's sudden heart attack and death, Lincoln drew into himself and wouldn't discuss it, preferring to act as though it hadn't happened. Faith ached for Lincoln much more than for herself. She knew she would never marry again, would never give him another father. She was a loving, busy mother, distracted by her demanding work at *Bloomer*, and her political activity, and all the interviews she was asked to give back then. She rarely cooked, except for the occasional steak.

Once, when he was ten, Lincoln had screamed at her, "Why can't you be like other mothers?"

"What do you mean?" she asked.

"Why do I have to have Mrs. Smith?"

"I'm sorry, I don't know what you—"

"Why do I have to have Sara Lee?" he asked, a little hysterical now.

She'd said, "What? Who *are* those women?" But then immediately she realized. "Oh, Lincoln, I'm who I am," she'd said. "I'm who you got, and I try to be the best I can."

"Try harder!" he yelled.

She tried harder. But as he grew, they were so different. Lincoln was serious, steadfast, methodical, and liked things to be a certain way and a certain way only. Having a prominent feminist as a mother had made him neither wildly political himself nor a misogynist. Once, when he was a teenager and some reporter had asked him if he was a feminist, he'd said, "Well, obviously," offended at the question. But that was the extent of it. He was conventional, reserved, yet their love was mutual, established, sometimes distracted, and never in doubt.

She missed his young, vulnerable, ownable self. You never knew when you were lifting your child for the last time; it might seem like just a regular time, when it was taking place, but later, looking back, it would turn out to have been the last. Lincoln's increasing lack of neediness was hard for Faith sometimes, but it was also something of a relief to think that he was all right on his own. In this way, they were actually alike.

"Now tell me what's going on with you," she said to him.

"Another time. Go have your massage, Mom."

She watched the phone go dark, then held it in her hand for a few more seconds. It was the closest she could get, these days, to holding Lincoln himself.

Faith pushed through the glass door of the massage place and entered the anteroom where young Chinese women sat on a sofa, waiting for their appointments and walk-ins. One of the women stood and nodded, and Faith nodded back. "You want thirty, sixty, or ninety minute?" the woman asked, and Faith said, "Sixty." Then with no further comment she was led down a long unlit hall; from inside the curtained cubicles came the sounds of flesh being battered by hands.

The masseuse, whose name was Sue, started on her through the towel, working along the spine and shoulders and neck, oh the neck, all of which were desperate for attention. The long strokes down the length of the back, punctuated by occasional sharp pokes, dropped Faith stupefied into a hole, as if the face cradle were a tunnel and she was going down inside it, to the place where everything waited that had come before.

. . .

They were twins, having shared a uterus, and then, later on, a bedroom. That bedroom, on West Eighth Street in Bensonhurst, Brooklyn, wasn't much bigger than the uterus had been, relative to their growing bodies, and so a red gingham curtain hung from a rod dividing the two halves, providing what passed for privacy in that household. At night, though, lying in their separate curtained compartments, neither of them really wanted privacy. They just wanted to talk. They were born six minutes apart in the winter of 1943, wartime, Faith first and then Philip, and their differences were obvious to everyone. She was the student, the serious one, beautiful but remote; he was more popular and sunny and accessible. She worked harder, and he slid by on slapdash charm and athletics.

At night, through the curtain, Faith and Philip asked each other advice about dating. "Well, the first thing I would say is don't date Owen Lansky," Philip said. "He will definitely want to go all the way."

She was touched by his protectiveness, and he was proved right about Owen Lansky, who was extremely pushy and had a head of oiled hair that, if you were locked in an embrace with him, would leave your face shining wet.

They often talked so late into the night that their mother sometimes appeared in the doorway in her robe and said, "You two! Go to bed!"

"We're just talking, Mom," said Philip. "We have a lot to say."

"What do I need to do to get you to sleep?" she asked. "Do I have to hit you over the head with a frying pan?"

"Save your frying pan for breakfast," Faith said. "Good night, Mom!" As soon as their mother left, Faith and Philip returned to their fevered and intimate conversation.

It wasn't just brother and sister who were close. The entire Frank family made up a kind of four-person team. They had boisterous dinners, and they played charades; all four of them were crack players. When guests came over for the evening, they were asked, "Do you want to play charades?" and if the answer was no, they were rarely invited back.

Throughout the twins' childhood, their overworked housewife mother, Sylvia, and tolerant, easily amused tailor father, Martin, were encouraging to both of them. They were made to feel as if what they did, the path they were on, their whole way of being in the world, was good enough. Their childhood was happy, and the transition into adulthood was meant to be happy too. But one night their parents said they needed to have a "family discussion."

"Let's all sit in the living room," said Martin. Sylvia sat beside him. It was unusual to see her just sitting there, not fussing around or pulling something out of the oven.

Philip pointed to Faith. "She did it, not me. It was all her. I had nothing to do with it." Faith rolled her eyes.

"Here's the situation," said Martin. "You know you're not the only ones in this house who stay up late talking. We do too. And one conversation we've been having late at night is about your education. We're both so proud of you. But as your parents, we worry."

"What are you getting at?" Faith asked. She had a sense, almost immediately, that this was about her.

"Every day there are terrible stories in the newspaper," said Sylvia.

"We used to live in a safe country," said Martin. "But just last week in the paper I read about a man who hurt a girl on a college campus. She was walking back to her dormitory late at night. We don't want you to find yourself in a situation like that, Faith. I don't think we could bear it."

"I'll walk places with friends at college," said Faith. "Twos and threes, I promise."

"It's not just that," said Sylvia. Then she looked at Martin, both of them unbearably uneasy.

"Sex," Martin finally said, looking down. "There's that to think about, honey."

Oh, don't worry, Faith thought. I'll definitely do *that* in twos.

"There will be pressures on you," said her father. "You've been very sheltered up until now, and I'm afraid you don't know what college men might want and expect."

For more than a year, Faith had been quietly thinking about going away to college to study a subject like sociology or political science or anthropology. She had mentioned college once in a while, and neither of her parents had given her a sense that they wouldn't let her leave home and go away to school. Though they had been surprisingly vague about the subject, she had somehow trusted that when the time came, it would all work out.

"Please don't do this to me," she said. For she wanted exactly what her parents feared. She saw herself studying, but then putting down the book to embrace a man who would embrace her back. "I'm a good student," she tried, her voice catching.

"Yes you are, and we want to protect you. We want you to live at home," said her father. "There are excellent schools in the city."

"What about Philip?" Faith asked.

"Philip will go away to school," her father said easily. Faith glanced at her brother, who looked away. "It will be good for him. Look," he went on, "you're different people, and you need different things."

Faith stood up, as if somehow towering over her sitting parents would help her cause. "I don't want to live at home," she said. She turned to her brother. "Tell them you agree with me," she said to him.

"I don't know, Faith," he said. "I think I should just stay out of it."

That night in bed, Faith cried so hard that Philip pushed aside the curtain with a screech along the rod and appeared in her side of the room in the street-lamp light. He wasn't just her brother now; he was a male going off into the world. "Look, our folks are great," he said. "We couldn't have asked for a happier family. They're kind of old-fashioned, but maybe they're not totally wrong. You'll get a good education. We both will."

They were never particularly close after that. When he went off to the University of Minnesota, he wrote her letters describing the different clubs he had joined, and, as an afterthought, the classes he was taking. "This girl I'm dating, Sydelle, she helps me study," he said. "She's a smart one. Not as smart as you, though," he felt he needed to add.

Later on, even into middle age and after, they still spoke every year on their shared birthday, though Philip was always the one to call her, never the other way around. Faith just didn't ever feel compelled to pick up the phone and speak to him. He had gone away to college but had never become very intellectual. He'd once proudly told her that the last book he'd read was called *Chicken Soup for the Realtor's Soul*. They had nothing in common anymore except a birthday.

Faith, forced to live at home when she went to school, became a sociology major at Brooklyn College, and she loved her classes, especially the ones where everyone got to talk. She found herself accepting offers of dates from boys she met at school, though always her mother or father stayed up and made sure she got home by her Cinderella curfew. It was maddening to see one of them waiting up in the living room, yawning like crazy and looking her over when she walked in, as if to check for external signs of an intact virginity. And once, when she stayed too late at a party, her father actually showed up at the house in Flatbush. He waited for her outside under a street lamp in his coat with the collar of his striped pajamas showing underneath. She was aghast to see him, and walked home beside him wordlessly.

In fact Faith held on to her virginity, not wanting something furtive and lurid to happen at a party or in the backseat of a Chevrolet. Sometimes Faith and a girl from her Logic of Inquiry class named Annie Silvestri went out for drinks at a bar near the school, and sat smoking Lucky Strikes and looking good. Within minutes they always received the attention of a table of guys, and there was a power to be found in that, and a power in walking away from it.

But also, the whole idea of sex—of wanting it, wanting intimacy, wanting experiences away from your parents—soon shifted. The world was changing, her parents had said, and it kept changing further. The day President Kennedy was assassinated, Faith and her friend Annie clung together and wept into each other's wet neck. For months it was all they could think or talk about, and throughout that time, Faith spoke more in class, wrote her college exams with a harder, more furious pen. She wanted something; sex was still part of it, but not only. Finally Faith graduated, and though her parents assumed she would get a job and keep living at home until she found someone to marry, in the spring of 1965 she sat them down in the living room—it was gratifying to be the one with news this time—and announced that she and Annie were going off to Las Vegas together. They had decided on their destination almost arbitrarily—they both wanted experience, and Vegas seemed so different from Brooklyn.

"Absolutely not," said her father. "We forbid it. We will cut off your funds. I'm serious, Faith."

"All right, if that's what you feel you need to do," Faith said tightly.

Her parents didn't go through with the threat, but she made sure never to ask them for any money. With savings from different part-time jobs over the years, Faith and Annie traveled on the 20th Century Limited to Chicago that summer, and from there they took a Greyhound bus to Las Vegas, where they were both immediately hired as cocktail waitresses at the Swann Hotel and Casino. Every night the cocktail waitresses walked the floor with their arms upraised, balancing trays, their hair swirled in matching Nefertiti beehives, smiling vaguely at all and none.

Faith Frank at twenty-two was tall and long-waisted but also small-boned. Her face had its own contradictions, the forehead high and the nose unusually strong, nearly beakish, but in all that strength was a great beauty and an unmissable intelligence and sympathy. She had large gray eyes and a cascade of long, dark, curling hair, though the styles of 1965 dictated that female hair often be kept aloft, and that it be sprayed generously and indiscriminately to hold it there. "We should buy stock in Aqua Net," Annie said once as they got ready for an evening, in the room they shared in the unofficial cocktail waitresses' barracks, on a side street off the Strip.

As if making up for lost time, Faith got involved with a black-jack dealer at Monty's. When she finally went to bed with him she was disappointed, for he sprawled upon her sluggishly, his energy so low that she thought: This is sex? *This?* as she lay beneath him like someone pinned by an overturned car. At work, there was the opposite problem. Faith found herself slapping off men; they didn't really bother her so much as lightly disgust her. Because how could men who behaved like this think that women would ever like them? How could men like this even hold their heads up? Yet they did.

One night at the casino, making the usual perambulation with her tray amid the bing-bonging and the clash of glass and the drifting web of smoke, Faith saw a smartly put-together man and woman sitting at one of the blackjack tables. They looked older than Faith but younger than almost everyone who came in there. The woman sat very close to him, whispering in his ear. He was a slender man with close-cut black hair and dark eyes. She kept whispering to him, and he nodded but seemed detached. Eventually the woman went to the powder room and the man took that opportunity to glance up at Faith. "I probably should pack it in now," he said. "I'm down by a lot. But it's hard to just walk away."

"You should. The odds are against you," she said. This was the kind of remark she was expressly forbidden to make, and he regarded her with surprise. "I mean, I'm here every night," Faith went on. "Basically, there should be a sign up that says 'Abandon All Hope, Ye Who Enter Here.'"

The dealer, a rigid man in a Stetson, regarded Faith with suspicion. "What's she saying to you?" he asked the man.

"She is quoting literature," he said, and then he turned back to Faith. "So what do you think I should do?" he asked.

"I've already told you."

He smiled. "I imagine you're full of opinions on a lot of subjects."

"You don't think I'm just another girl bringing you your Scotch?"

"No," he said. "And you don't think I'm just another low-level executive in the field of cookies and crackers, here in Vegas for some relaxation?"

"Cookies and crackers are important," Faith said. "Especially if you're a starving person."

He smiled. "Well, if *you're* ever starving," he said, "come to me and I'll feed you." At that moment, the woman he was with materialized. He smiled with regret at Faith, then turned away from her, his hand on the small of this woman's back. Why do they call it the *small* of a back? Faith suddenly wondered. What a strange word.

Faith spent six months in Las Vegas, getting involved for a while with a trumpet player at the Sands named Harry Bell, who invited her to come see any show she wanted. During the seduction period, he invited her into the main nightclub at the Sands when no one was there; in the chilly, enormous room he took her up onto the stage, and she said, "Won't we get in trouble?" but he said, "Nah." Faith stood on the dark stage in this place where all the top acts had stood, and she looked out into the darkness, imagining what it might be like to have people sitting in seats looking up at you with absorption, listening hard. But she wasn't talented, she couldn't sing or perform in any way, and so that would never happen.

"You look good up there," Harry said, watching her, but Faith quickly slipped from the stage.

In the days that followed she would sit at a table in the crowded club and wait for him, and then they would head to his apartment and go to bed together as the sky got pink above the clusters of neon. One morning, when she was in bed with Harry in his hotel room, he tapped Faith lightly on the nose and said, "You've got a big honker, don't you. But you're so sexy, you can carry it."

She said nothing. It hurt her, not because it was untrue—she did have a strong nose, and it did look pretty good on her. It hurt her because she had been lying relaxed with him, similar to the way her childhood dog Lucky would sometimes lie in deep sleep on her back, paws up and dipped at the wrist. Her dog, lying like that, was happy in her doggish openness. Which, Faith thought, was all she herself really wanted when she went to bed with someone. To lie exposed and free and unself-conscious.

Yet her nose was too big, and a man had pointed it out. In bed, no less. She would never forget it.

But what she would mostly never forget from those six months in Las Vegas was what happened there to her friend and roommate Annie Silvestri. Annie had been dating Hokey Briggs, a comedian who opened for Bobby Darin, and one night when both women were home in the barracks and had just turned out the lights to go to sleep, Faith heard crying coming from the next bed.

"Annie, what is it?"

Annie switched on the small lamp and sat up. Somberly she confessed, "I skipped a period, Faith. I don't know what I'm going to do."

The next day, Hokey Briggs tensely drove the two women around from doctor to doctor, in search of someone who would perform an abortion. But it was hard to find anyone, and the one doctor who agreed wanted way too much money. Finally Annie got a name from a friend of a friend. She begged Faith to go with her, and though Faith was afraid, she said she would. At the given hour, the two women climbed into an unwashed blue Ford Galaxie that idled in front of the barracks.

Once they were in the car, an older woman in a head scarf and sunglasses told them, "Get down," and then started to blindfold them both.

"No one said you were going to do this," Annie protested as the cloth went around her face.

"Do you want to meet the doctor or not? Come on, hold still."

They were driven around for a long time, and finally they were brusquely taken out of the car and helped into the back door of a building, where the blindfolds were removed. Annie was told to follow a nurse—or someone posing as one—into a treatment room.

"Can my friend come with me?" Annie asked.

"Sorry, honey," said the nurse.

Faith was actually relieved, because she was afraid of what she might see in there. She stayed in the waiting room for a long time; at one point, crying came from deep in the office. Eventually the nurse appeared and said, "Get her home and put her to bed. Take care, dear," she added to Annie.

The serious bleeding began in the middle of the night, accompanied by strong, stuttering cramps. In the barracks, the cocktail waitresses gathered around Annie (the rest of them thought it was just a very heavy period) but no one really knew what to do. Finally, after everyone else had gone back to sleep, Faith decided Annie had to go to the hospital. Near dawn, she walk-carried Annie into the landlord's borrowed car, and they made their way there. In the ER, one nurse in particular gave Annie the leper treatment. "You're going to ruin my very nice floor, *Mrs.* Silvestri," she said sarcastically.

"Is there something I can take for the cramps?" Annie asked, gasping.

"You'll have to ask Doctor for that," she said. "It's not my department." And then, leaning closer, the nurse added, "I could have you thrown in the slammer, did you know that? I could call the police right this minute, you little harlot." Then another nurse came into the room, and the first nurse straightened up and fussed innocently with paperwork.

Two days later, having been transfused three times, Annie was sent home with a box of off-brand sanitary pads—"Fotex"— and a warning from an extremely young male gynecologist about "not giving it up so easily. Though of course," he'd added, "it's a little late in the day for that, wouldn't you say?"

That night, back in the barracks, Annie said to Faith, "I was thinking that he's right."

"Who?"

"The doctor. It is late in the day. Late to be here."

"What are you saying? I don't understand."

"Let's go home, Faith," said Annie. "Please. It's time."

What made you become the person you are today?" interviewers sometimes wanted to know over the years, asking the question as if they were the very first person to have asked it. "Was it a single thing? Was there an aha moment?"

"Well, no, there wasn't one in particular," Faith always said. But she thought that maybe there had been a series of moments, and that this was the way it was for most people: the small realizations leading you first toward an important understanding and then toward doing something about it. Along the way, too, there would be people you would meet who would affect you and turn you ever so slightly in a different direction. Suddenly you knew what you were working for, and you didn't feel as if you were wasting your time.

Faith was living in Manhattan in 1966, sharing the tiniest of apartments with Annie on Morton Street in Greenwich Village. She and Annie were like two audience members who had arrived in the middle of a show; so much was already going on. The political protests were loud and urgent, although they had been sealed away from all that, trapped in a time tunnel when they worked in the casino, and now they had to catch up. The two women stayed roommates through different temp jobs, and through voter registration in Harlem and volunteer jobs at an antiwar organization that operated out of a storefront on Sullivan Street, where Faith typed the weekly mimeographed newsletter, *A Peace of Our Mind*. She attended meetings and lectures and teach-ins. The war dominated conversations, and everything was punctuated by the best music she'd ever heard. Various friends crammed into the apartment on weekends, and the place was filled with marijuana smoke. "Mary Jane, I love you so," a boy sang as he sprawled across the shag rug of her living room. Faith was often high on grass on weekends, but never during the week, because it interfered with political strategizing, as she and Annie called it when they sat together at their tiny kitchen table and discussed how best to organize. It wasn't that Faith had become political in some sort of moment of epiphany; it was more that the world had moved and she had moved too.

While this was happening, the high hair of the first half of the decade precipitously came down. Faith intentionally dropped a full can of Aqua Net hairspray into the bathroom garbage pail, where it began to hiss and unload its pressurized contents. For years her hair was full and floaty. By 1968 she and Annie Silvestri, still roommates, wore jeans and Indian-print shirts instead of the modified stewardess dresses they'd been wearing for so long.

At the antiwar meetings Faith attended, at first she had mostly sat and listened. Some of the men who spoke were unusually articulate. Faith, when she spoke, was perceived as smart and articulate too, but the men felt free to cut in and interrupt her.

She tried to talk about abortion reform, but they weren't interested. "You can't compare it with Vietnam, where people are actually dying," someone said one night, cutting her off.

"Women are dying here," said Faith, and people started shouting at her.

Another woman cried out, in Faith's defense, "Let her talk!" but Faith was shut down anyway, and finally she stopped trying.

As Faith was walking out of the meeting, the woman who had yelled out on her behalf came over and said, "Doesn't this make you so furious sometimes?"

"It does! I'm Faith, by the way."

"Well, hello, Faith, I'm Evelyn. Listen, I'm getting together this weekend with some women, and we drink hard and let loose, and you will definitely get your say. You should come."

So Faith went with Evelyn Pangborn to a long dark apartment in upper Manhattan, where a group of women sat around drinking and smoking, and when they weren't being dead serious and full of rage, they were also very witty. They argued and plotted; a few of them said they were part of a group that was planning to disrupt the Miss America pageant in the fall. Several of them had already been arrested for acts of civil disobedience. Some were part of ad hoc radical groups that had splintered off from the antiwar groups. A black woman said, "I can't tell you how often I go to a meeting and get treated with condescension and hostility." There was a young suburban mother at the meeting who complained that her husband was indifferent to her exhaustion.

"I just feel that motherhood has me right where it wants me," this woman said. "And then I hate myself for feeling so cold and angry and unmaternal."

"Oh, I hate myself for feeling a thousand different ways," said someone else. "I am a temple of self-hatred."

"Why are we so hard on ourselves?" asked someone with great plaintiveness. Faith thought, it's not that I'm so hard on myself exactly, it's that I've learned to adopt the views of men as if they were my own. When Harry the trumpeter back in Vegas had told Faith that her nose was big, she'd taken in that opinion. When men filled a room with their voices and insisted to her that abortion was a middle-class, second-tier concern, she'd tried to defend her point, but had been overrun.

Faith began telling the women about accompanying her friend for an abortion in Las Vegas. "We had to wear blindfolds, and we drove around and around. And when she almost bled to death, one of the nurses treated her like a criminal. I think that as long as we keep our blindfolds on, you know, literally and figuratively, then we're really—to use a word that's relevant here—in trouble."

"We can't have men making our decisions anymore," some-one else said. "What I do with my body, and how I choose to spend my time—all of it is my decision. I get to decide."

"That sounds like song lyrics," said the woman whose apart-ment this was. "I . . . get . . . to . . . de-cide."

"I . . . get . . . to . . . de-cide," they all jokingly sang along with her, this diverse group of women with frizzed-out hair and slo-ganed T-shirts, or secretarial suits, or soft and durable housewife-wear, or expensive designer trappings. Faith thought that she didn't have to like them all, but she also recognized that they were in it together—"it" being the way it was for them. For women. The way it had been for centuries. The stuck place. She sang along with them, her voice coming out in a loud quaver. But it didn't matter that you quavered; it only mattered that you made yourself heard.

Afterward, out on the street heading for the train, the young mother said to Faith, "You're a very good speaker! Very passionate in a quiet, appealing way. We all liked listening to you. You're sort of hypnotic. Has anyone ever told you that?"

"No," said Faith with a laugh. "I promise you, no one ever has. Nor will they ever again." It was a compliment that both pleased and affected her, and suddenly she flickered on the image of herself standing onstage at the nightclub at the Sands. Standing still on that dark stage, imagining she was appearing in front of an enormous audience.

The woman was named Shirley Pepper, and she said that before her baby was born she had worked at *Life* magazine, and that she hoped to return to work as soon as she could get decent child care. "That's another critical issue in this goddamn country," said Shirley. "No access to cheap, good child care." Later, Shirley Pepper, by then back in publishing, was the one to come up with the idea for *Bloomer* magazine. "There are things we can do that *Ms.* isn't going to be interested in," she said. "We can be a little rougher around the edges." There had been small publications for women circulating for some time; there was a desire for more of this. The women's movement had by then fully taken off, and Faith had gotten involved. Back in August of 1970 she had marched in an enormous crowd down Fifth Avenue. The three demands that day had been for free abortion on demand, 24-hour childcare, and equal opportunity in employment and education. Later, she couldn't remember what was written on the sign she carried. One of those three things? All of them? She had felt the outrage, the thrill. It was in the air that day, and of course then it was everywhere. There was talk of misogyny. Patriarchy. The myth of the vaginal orgasm.

Shirley had gotten to know many women activists over the years, and she brought in some of them to help start the magazine. She indefatigably rounded up investors—an arduous and painstaking task—with the help of her willing husband, who

worked for IBM. Faith was brought in to be part of the magazine because of her calmly pleasing speaking style, as well as her
ability to listen and her willingness to work. But probably also
because of that indescribable thing about Faith—how you didn't
really know her, but you just wanted to be around her.

The early days of *Bloomer* included wild-eyed all-nighters at
the Houston Street offices, reached by the ominously slow and
constantly breaking elevator, which had been inspected many
times over by one Milton Santiago, who had signed off on its
functionality again and again in the same familiar, slanted hand.
"Milton Santiago, you are a disgrace to the elevator inspection
industry," the women said. "Milton Santiago, if you were *Millie*
Santiago, this shit would get done!" They laughed and worked
in the open space with the tall, dusty windows, secure in their
mission, as well as in the inevitability of their plans and ideas.
Frustration and rage at the injustice that women experienced all
over America and the world lived side by side with bake-sale
optimism about everything that could be done to wipe it out.

"I'll be your Sherpa," Faith had once told a cluster of other
editors and young assistants as she led them down five flights of
stairs in darkness after a late-night closing, the elevator once
again predictably broken. "Come on, everyone!" she called,
flicking open a Zippo lighter. That night the flame gave the
women's faces in those close quarters the stuttering light-and-
dark appearance of people in a Flemish painting, all eye-gleam
and contrapuntal shadow and rose cheek and curved hand—if,
in fact, the Flemish artists had ever painted groups of women
together without men.

They followed her, laughing and stumbling a little, holding
on to one another in the narrow stairwell, someone's hand on
someone else's shoulder or hip, all that jutting female convexity
contained in a single, steeply pitched corridor. They planned fu-

ture issues as they descended the stairs, feeling certain that their enterprise would last as long as the earth itself. The women were flushed with happiness, made greater because it was a communal flush. At the bottom there were easy hugs among friends in the way that women did, and that men wouldn't do for at least another twenty-five years.

And soon they were all petitioning, going to Washington and to panel discussions and raucous events, making bang-on-a-can-loud noise. "Bra-burning," journalists wrote about the women's movement, though bra-burning wasn't actually a thing. In retrospect, Faith thought that some of what had happened during this time looked a little absurd, but she was reminded by older activists that the vanguard had to be extreme so that the more moderate people could take up the cause and be accepted. Faith was often exhausted in those years, falling asleep in someone else's lap in the hallway of a municipal building. She had a soft shoulder bag made out of different pieces of patchwork fabric, and she took it with her everywhere. At first it contained leaflets, cigarettes, chocolate, policy papers, phone numbers, though later on it also held baby bottles and loose diaper pins.

But before all of that had happened—before *Bloomer*, before Faith Frank became Faith Frank—still on the very first night, after the evening in the apartment in upper Manhattan full of women who had something to say, Faith excitedly returned to her own apartment in the Village. Annie Silvestri, who had remained her roommate over all these years, was rolling up her hair with orange juice cans and getting ready for bed, but Faith was in an excited mood and wanted to talk about what had happened that evening.

"I told them about your abortion," she said.

Annie turned around. "What? You did?"

"Well, I didn't use your name or say who you were, of course.

But I told them about it to make a point. We need to make a point. A lot of points."

"Oh for God's sake, Faith, I don't *want* to make a point," Annie said.

"I understand, but there are other women out there who've been through the same experience. We need to talk about it."

"'We'?"

"Yes, we. Women are already doing this. I want to help them. Everybody's been there for civil rights and stopping the war. For years everyone has been out there. We need to be out there like that for legal abortion. Why don't you want to be part of it so that other women don't have to go through what you did? I don't understand."

"That's the difference between us," Annie said. "I've been through enough, and I don't feel the need to figure it out or talk about it. It happened to me, Faith, not to you. It happened to me, and it was really horrible, and I have spent a lot of time trying to separate myself from that night when I hemorrhaged and was treated like dirt. You can say we need abortion reform, and you want to be part of it, and good for you, but I never want to talk about that experience ever again, and I am not kidding you. So if you're going to keep being my roommate, if we're going to keep living here together, that's one of the ground rules."

They shared the apartment for a few more months, though their friendship had changed. Neither of them talked about the change, and when they were both home at the same time they came together for a shared meal, often a quick TV dinner, but the conversation kept to new boundaries. Faith was propelled almost exclusively by political work, and Annie, who had begun dating a law student, was quietly reading up on everything he was studying, at first so they could have something to talk about, but then because it interested her too. She found she had a pre-ternatural skill for reading and comprehending legal language.

Annie married the law student, who got an academic position teaching undergraduates at Purdue. "We're going to the Midwest, can you believe it?" Annie said. There were a few postcards back and forth in the beginning, and then silence, and nothing was heard of her again for a very long time. Faith continued to go to antiwar rallies, but now she became increasingly involved with abortion reform, attending smaller meetings—all women, everyone talking, but not at once. Along with the others, Faith was lifted onto the lightest but strongest breeze; she wondered if it was her own consciousness, or something entirely different. Whatever it was, it pulled her along.

I n the early months of *Bloomer*, after advertising had been tentatively secured for a few small, modest issues and there had been a flurry of initial press about the magazine, Faith and two other women went out to find advertisers for future issues. "If we don't sell more ad space," said Shirley, "we're going to go under permanently in about a minute. We are an underdog. I think we're going to really have to push ourselves here."

One morning in the summer of 1973, during a meeting at Nabisco, Faith, Shirley Pepper, and Evelyn Pangborn sat in a conference room with three men, pushing for an ad buy, giving their usual spiel. It didn't go particularly well—it rarely did—for it was hard to convey why a massive corporation ought to advertise in this number-two magazine for women's libbers that was likely to fail soon and become just a quirk, a footnote from this rolling time.

The men at Nabisco said they would "see," and that they

would "think about it." Finally one of them stood and said, "Thank you, ladies, we will put our noggins together and reach a decision." They were more courteous than some—really, more courteous than most.

On the way out of the meeting, one of the men looked at Faith and said, "Wait. I know you."

"Sorry?"

He pulled her aside and she looked at him; he'd been coiled in a corner the whole time in his chair, a businessman in his mid-thirties, lean, tailored, sideburned, dark and attractive. Something about him registered in her now, but it was still unclear to her what it was.

"Didn't we meet a long time ago?" he asked quietly. "In Las Vegas? At the Swann?"

She stared at him, shocked, and then it returned to her. He'd been the man who'd come to the casino one night with a woman, the man who had flirted with Faith and told her about how he worked in the field of . . . cookies and crackers, that was what he'd said.

"How did you possibly remember me?" Faith asked him. "It's been, what, seven or eight years. It's sort of insane that you re-member."

"I'm good that way. You warned me that the house would always win. I think you saved me from ruin, so thank you."

"You're welcome. But also, I look totally different now. No uniform. And . . . my hair."

"Right, it was sort of vertical back then, I think. Do I look different to you?"

She looked him over for an extended and pleasurable mo-ment. He was much more stylish than his colleagues, less aggres-sively corporate, and leaner and younger. His dark hair was longer than it had been back in '65, of course. He wore an expensive suit now that was cut well, and, she saw, no wedding ring. He smelled interesting, acidic.

It would turn out that he was right, he was good that way; he remembered everything from every moment. But the catch was that he remembered it only if he was paying attention, which he didn't always do.

"Can we explore the question of that ad space a little more?" he asked. "I'm not sure any of my colleagues were convinced by your pitch. To tell you the truth, I'm pretty sure they weren't."

"You mean just me? Or me and the others?"

"Just you. One-on-one might accomplish more."

Of course, there was strong flirtation here again, as there had been in the casino; it wasn't hidden, but was out in the open like his acidic fragrance, and didn't supersede the truth of what he was saying. Faith and Shirley and Evelyn hadn't been very successful selling ads so far; from here they were going off to talk to the people at Clairol, but it was obvious that their standard pitch wasn't working very well.

"I think it requires a longer conversation," he said. "Dinner with me tonight? While it's still fresh in our minds?"

"Fresh in our minds," she repeated pointlessly. He wanted to sleep with her, and she would have been ridiculously ignorant if she didn't know it.

She wasn't going to sleep with the Nabisco executive, though his face was worth contemplation for some reason, and she could imagine the underlayer of his body beneath his clothing. It wasn't just that she could imagine it; as soon as she imagined it, she realized that what mattered was that she was imagining it. But she couldn't sleep with him. Let him think she might. That was a business transaction. She studied his face and then finally said, "Sure."

"Why does he want to discuss it further with you?" Shirley

asked irritably as they stood hanging from straps on the IRT going back downtown.

"I'll draw you a diagram, Shirley," murmured Evelyn.

"I'm not going to sleep with him, for God's sake," said Faith. She didn't tell them that she'd met him a long time ago, and that, freakishly, he had remembered that they'd met; and that, perhaps almost as freakishly, she had come to remember it too. "But sure, fine, I'll have dinner with him, why not? I'll make him listen to the magazine's objectives."

"Maybe he's a stealth women's libber," said Shirley, "and he wants to help us strategize. And if Faith can spin a magic web across his vision that enchants him and seals the deal, then that's fine."

"Oh yes. I am full of enchantment," Faith said mildly.

"You are, actually," said Evelyn. "You're one of those people who other people enjoy. It's a talent."

When Faith arrived at the Cookery that night at seven, he was already waiting at a table deep in the back. Because there was candlelight in this Greenwich Village club and not fluorescence, he appeared softer to her than in the boardroom at Nabisco. He wore a Nehru jacket now, and his dark hair looked silky. "I'm glad you came," he said as they drank the red sangria he'd ordered before she arrived. Though she thought there was a slight chauvinistic tinge to this, he probably wouldn't have seen it that way. They knocked their glasses together, each with a small paper umbrella in it. She drank hers quickly, even though sweet alcoholic drinks generally made her feel thick-brained and a little slow. Tonight, though, the wine was just a loosening agent.

Emmett Shrader lifted the umbrella from his drink, shook it off, and wordlessly dropped it into his jacket pocket. She was going to say to him, "Do you have a paper umbrella collection at home?" but didn't, because that would have sounded flirtatious, and she wanted to be serious here. When he asked her to tell him her "whole story," she did, talking about Brooklyn and her parents' overprotectiveness and her need to get out of there, and he listened in a way that no man had listened to her in her life.

"Go on," he kept saying. He said he was interested in all of it, and she took him at his word, telling him how she had gotten passionate about women's rights. She was prepared for some sort of sparring, because this was what it was often like with men. But what Emmett said was, "I think what you and the other women are doing is essential." The words were an intoxicant. "But may I add," he went on, "and please stop me if this is unwarranted—I wish you could dominate a little more. *Make* us buy ad space. Force us."

"That wouldn't work," Faith said.

"Why not?"

"Because when a man speaks that way, people say he has authority. When a woman does, everyone resents her and thinks she's their mother. Or their nagging wife."

"Ah. I see what you mean," he said. "Okay, so just be urgent. I'm in advertising, so I know a little bit of what I'm talking about. And also, if I can say one more thing? You ought to be the main person doing the talking; you more than the others. You've got something."

"Well, thank you," she said, uncomfortable but pleased. Then, "What about you? What's your story?"

"Oh. My story. Let's see," Emmett said. "I've resigned myself to working at Nabisco, and it can be all right. But mostly there aren't too many surprises, and that's a shame, because I like surprises. You're a surprise," he added.

He took her hand then, which was shocking but not; she had expected it, and here it was. He stroked it once, then twice, with his thumb. This was a business dinner, mostly but not entirely. She had planned for the proposition moment and now it was occurring, but she was no longer resolute about turning him down. Sexual desire hadn't weakened her or made her think with her body. It hadn't weakened her at all, but instead it had changed her thinking. She felt a strangeness wash over her, the carbonation of arousal. This feeling was always a little sickening at first, before it settled in.

"Go to bed with me," he said. "I'd like that more than anything."

"More than buying ad space."

"Yes." He kept stroking her hand, and she didn't move. "We can go to your apartment," he said. "I know you live nearby. I looked you up in the phone book."

She glanced down toward the candlelight, her face growing warm, itself a candle. "I guess that's your commanding voice," she said. "And I'm just supposed to fall into line?"

"Faith, I'm not commanding. I want you to want it too."

So then they were in her apartment, a small box of a studio on West Thirteenth Street, in which she had lived alone since Annie Silvestri decamped to the Midwest. As Emmett folded his clothes on the chair, Faith thought of how he was the first businessman she had ever slept with.

Emmett wore beautiful, formal shoes with little holes in them, she saw as he untied them and began to place them against the wall beside her rose suede boots. "They look like a Nabisco cracker," she said.

"What?"

"Your shoes. The pattern of little holes on top."

He looked. "You're right." Then he smiled. "The Social Tea

biscuit. One of our classic items. By the way, I like your boots," he said.

He straightened his shoes out neatly; his shiny dark shoes and her soft, pastel boots were in such contrast that this in itself was somehow exciting. His underwear, she saw, looked as crisp as a sail. His body was gorgeous, almost reptilian but not quite. He wasn't entirely warm-blooded, but she didn't care at the moment. He was absurdly attractive to her with his dark longish hair and that citric scent that somehow made him manlier than anyone she had known since her father. But of course he was nothing like her father.

In bed Emmett smiled lazily, opening his arms and enclosing her. "Come here," he said, as if she weren't already right there. But he wanted her even closer, wanted to be inside her at once, an idea that she thought she understood in that moment, because she not only wanted him inside her, she wanted to be inside him in some way too. Maybe even to *be* him. She wanted to inhabit his confidence, his style, the way he walked through the world, which was so different from the way she did.

Do this, do that, they said to each other in the imperative ways that people spoke during sex, forgetting manners. He hoisted her on top of him and looked up at her with an expression that was foggy with excitement but topped with worship. "Oh my God," he said as she was held there above him like a hovering angel. Faith realized that she actually didn't mind being seen that way: a vision. They paused in the mutual moment, and his eyes almost rolled up into his head, then he regained himself, as if remembering what was happening, and then he pushed into her so deeply that she felt as if she might be cleaved in two. Yet he did no damage.

When he came, he groaned extravagantly and then said, "Oh, Faith," and lost all his crispness, all his clean edges. Afterward he quieted down and renewed himself, and then he turned his attention solely to her. Her orgasms, three of them in a row like gunfire, were thrilling to them both, and he quietly said to her, "That was my favorite part."

They lay in bed recovering from the trauma of exhilaration. Then, finally, he reached onto the night table and drew his watch back from the surface, clicking the silver clasp into place on his long wrist. "Well. Time to go," he said.

"Where? It must be two in the morning." Faith looked around for the peachy, illuminated face of the Timex clock.

"Home."

There was a long, dreadful silence, and then she said, "You're married." Another silence, just as dreadful, and Faith prepared to say something angry. But she wasn't angry, just sad in a grave way, for she understood that, despite the absence of a wedding ring, she'd already intuited that he was married, and so she'd deliberately not asked him this question before going to bed with him. Had she known the answer for certain, she wouldn't have been able to do it.

She had possibly even met his wife, she realized, back in the casino years earlier. She recalled Emmett's hand on the small of a woman's back. The proprietary way they were with each other. But even more than that, she also knew he was the father of a child—at least one. That was what had subconsciously registered in the Cookery tonight when Emmett lifted the little paper umbrella from his drink, then shook off the spatters and dropped it into his jacket pocket.

Who else does that but a father who plans to bring it home to give to his child—probably a daughter—as a gift? Faith couldn't be furious at Emmett, because she had known it all and had ignored her own knowledge.

She sat up in her bed and watched as he dressed himself, as he turned each shirt button into its little slit with exactness even in the dark room. At one point he looked up from the buttoning. "You know, I didn't lie to you," he pointed out. "Had you asked, I would've told you."

"I suppose."

"My wife and I aren't close that way. That's not what we're like. You and I could have something completely different. Something spectacular, based on tonight. I mean, what we did together, what we felt—I wasn't making it up. We could have more of that. We could *be* that."

"I don't do that," Faith said, cold now. "At least not knowingly. Not to my sisters."

"Sisters?" he asked, confused. "What are you talking about? Oh. Like all women are sisters, you mean; a women's lib thing. Believe me, my wife is not your sister."

"But you get my point. I don't betray other women."

"You mean you're moral."

"Something like that," she said.

"Duly noted. I'll call you tomorrow."

"Please don't."

"About the ads only," Emmett said. "Let me talk to the people in the office, and I think with a little persuading we can buy some space in your magazine."

"Sure," she said flatly.

He did call her the next morning; she was still at home when the call came. "Look, I need to tell you something," Emmett said, and his voice seemed calm but strained, different. "My wife knows about you." Faith just listened, shocked. "She confronted me when I got home last night, and she said, 'Don't lie to me,' and I really couldn't. She wanted me to tell her your name, to tell her everything, and so I did."

"God, Emmett, why did you do that?" Faith said.

"She's right here and she wants to talk to you," he continued. "Can I put her on?"

"Are you insane?"

"No," he said, and he sounded sad then, or maybe it was just the distortion of the connection, but for some reason Faith hung on, and then there was the sound of the phone being handed over, and a woman came on the line.

"Faith Frank, this is Madeline Shrader," she said, her voice soft and bland. Faith didn't say anything. "I wanted to say that my husband is not yours for the taking. You may think he is, because he acts that way. But you have to remember that he stood beside me during our wedding ceremony and promised to love and honor me as long as we both shall live. And you know what, Faith Frank? I am not dead yet."

Faith couldn't take another second of this, and she quietly hung up. She pictured Emmett with his wife. She saw the triad of husband, wife, and child—a little girl who was perhaps five years old, and who sat fiddling contentedly with something in her hand: a paper umbrella that had been in her daddy's drink.

Faith hated herself ferociously, and then remembered the way the women had spoken to one another at that first women's gathering. Why are we so hard on ourselves? they'd asked one another.

Sometimes, she thought now, being hard on yourself was appropriate.

"There isn't going to be any ad money from Nabisco," she told Shirley Pepper at work on Monday, after climbing the stairs because the elevator was broken yet again. She was out of breath, and leaned against a wall.

"Oh no? Why is that?" Shirley asked. She looked up from where she sat clacking away at an IBM typewriter that was as heavy as a tractor.

"It's complicated," said Faith.

"All right," Shirley said evenly. "Look, it's not a tragedy, Faith. Anyway, I think we have a lead with Dr. Scholl's. We'll live to fight another day."

The magazine got some attention and lasted, in some modest version or another, for over thirty more years. In the first years of *Bloomer* the three earliest members of the editorial staff went on occasional talk shows and spoke earnestly and passionately, and did what they had to do. The talk-show hosts were often louts in wide, silvery ties who made jokes at the women's expense about hairy, angry feminists no one would ever want to date. Shirley, Faith, and Evelyn never laughed along with them, but kept appearing on the shows to say what they felt was important, even if they were ridiculed.

At some point, Faith separated from the pack. She was so much better at speaking than the others. It wasn't that she was an ideas person—that was never the case, exactly—and it wasn't even that she was much more articulate, but it was something else. People had to want to hear you. They had to want to be around you, even when you were saying things that they didn't really want to hear. This quality was on display in 1975, when Faith appeared on a late-night talk show opposite the novelist Holt Rayburn, who had become very famous with his Vietnam novel *Cloud Cover*. Rayburn, in a jacket with wide lapels and a paisley tie, his mutton-chop sideburns fencing in a face that always looked like it was itching for a fight, was smoking incessantly, and the set of the TV show had its own low-hanging cloud cover.

"The thing about women," he began, and the host, Benedict Loring, leaned in.

"Yes, yes?" said Loring. "The thing about women? Oh, I love sentences that begin this way, don't you?" He made a lascivious face, and the audience laughed and clapped.

"The thing about women," Holt Rayburn repeated, "is that they want you to do all kinds of things for them—'Open this jar, I'm helpless. Go to bed with me, I'm incredibly horny. Pay for dinner, I'm saving my money for a rainy day'—but then they go out there on TV and they've suddenly turned into these angry women's libbers who say, 'We want to do things for ourselves.' I mean, give me a break. You can't have it both ways, ladies. Either you're little girls who need us to take care of you, or you're steamrolling bitches who can do everything on your own. And if that's the case, the second version, then fine, go to bed with one another like some of you are already doing, because clearly you don't need men. And while you're at it, try to have babies without us too. And pay the rent. Let me know how it works out for you."

The audience reaction was *huge*. More laughter, more clapping, and then everyone calmed down, immediately understanding that Faith was the one to pay attention to now. Faith, who sat across from him. How would she react to this? She was a women's libber who had been brought onto the show solely to occupy that role. What would she say or do? Faith sat still, her hands in her lap. She realized that she looked like a joyless schoolteacher, and this irritated her. But there was no good way to look when the men in your midst began talking this way about women. You could look prim, or you could look angry, or else you could laugh along with them, which was the worst of all.

She decided to bypass Holt Rayburn entirely. He was an ass, a well-paid ass of the literary variety. Men like him romped through the world, and it wouldn't be possible to take away his sense of freedom or security. She ignored him now and looked right at the camera, which confused both him and the host. One of the cameramen waved to her, mouthing, *"Look at the men, look at the men,"* but she ignored him too.

"I think men are afraid that if women are doctors and lawyers and the openers of jars," Faith said, "then the men will have to do so-called women's work, and God knows that scares them out of their minds. There's nothing we can't do, but there's a lot that they're afraid to do."

The audience was with her now. The same people who had been clapping for Holt Rayburn were clapping for her. "Like throw a children's birthday party," she said. "Oh, or give birth." Whooping ensued. "We've always found ways to get things done when men weren't there to help. We're resourceful and determined and patient." Now she turned back to Holt Rayburn, who had let the cigarette between his fingers burn down to an ignored, fragile column of ash. "You, Holt, did mention one legitimate problem. But I think I've figured out what to do about it." Faith smiled her beautiful, calm, and sunny smile, and then she crossed her long legs in their baby-blue suede boots and said, "I have decided that from this day forward, I will never buy food in jars again."

That sound bite would be replayed for decades, until finally it was hardly ever played again. A few years after the show Holt Rayburn, drunk after a book party in the Hamptons and with several DUIs on his record, struck a woman on a dark road, and as a result she had to have a leg amputated. He served a couple of years in jail, and by the time he got out he had written a novel about it, *New Fish*, which became a bestseller, though a more modest one than *Cloud Cover*, but by then he was weary and sallow-faced. He died of a stroke that year, a small, sweating man who seemed confused by why things were becoming different in the world, different for women and different for him.

Being a good and appealing public speaker elevated Faith Frank and made her not just speak more but do more. Faith went to marches for the Equal Rights Amendment. She hung around after meetings, long into the night, to talk to many women. When abortion clinics were targeted, she was one of the people who tried to work with judges to make sure people were safe. Partly she did all of this because of Holt Rayburn and the image of the hard-to-open jar.

Faith was comfortable around all kinds of women, including lesbians, some of whom she got to know pretty well. One of the most vocal of them, Suki Brock, had kissed Faith once during a rally, and Faith had just smiled, touched her arm, and told her she was flattered.

"Listen, if you ever swing that way, Faith," Suki said, "swing over to me first, okay?"

Faith had said, "Sure thing," which was code for no. She didn't want to be kissed by Suki, or any other woman, even the ones who proudly called themselves separatists. Faith had seen a photo of two women farmers, looking like a kind of single-sex *American Gothic*, one of them wearing overalls and no shirt. Her breasts poked out like parentheses from either side of the overall top. Women these days had begun moving to farms and communes and collectives. Was it a utopia? Living with anyone had its challenges, Faith knew. There was no perfect way to live.

Faith traveled easily among radical women, among housewives, among students, wanting to learn, as she said. "What do you stand for?" a very young interviewer from a student newspaper once asked her.

"I stand for women," Faith said, but while early on this was a good enough answer, later it sometimes wouldn't be.

Back then, being this person, this Faith Frank person who elicited strong and perhaps not entirely explicable feelings in many people, she became who she had been meant to be. After her appearance on the talk show opposite Holt Rayburn, Faith rose up, becoming more famous than the magazine of which she was one of several editors. Her books became bestsellers; her TV appearances attracted many viewers. Over time, she deliberately kept herself from thinking too often about Emmett Shrader, though of course she followed the narrative of his rise: how he had begun as a low-level executive at Nabisco but then, using the money of his wife, heiress Madeline Shrader, née Tratt, she of the Tratt metals fortune, he had started his own venture capital firm, ShraderCapital. Everyone knew how *that* had gone, the phenomenon it was, the billionaire he became.

But everyone also talked about his unsavoriness, perhaps no worse than anyone else's at that level, but more disturbing because of his liberal leanings; they spoke of some of the surprising connections he made and shady projects he invested in, one involving a gun-cleaning company touted by the NRA, another a baby food manufacturer that sold its products to the developing world at sharply upticked prices. But all of it appeared to be counterbalanced by good. Business conducted at that level was something that Faith couldn't even begin to comprehend.

The *Roe v. Wade* decision in '73 had created an antichoice siren call that needed to be responded to and battled, and Faith was committed to it. Three years later, Anne McCauley from Indiana, rising up out of nowhere, it seemed, won a Senate seat based on her outspokenness against abortion. "We will fight *Roe* every day. We will dismantle it bit by bit over time," she said into microphones, her voice even and reasonable, her posture uncommonly good.

Whenever Faith saw Senator McCauley on television, she thought of how easy it would be to tell the truth publicly about her, to simply release a statement to the press saying that eleven years before Senator McCauley became such a strong and vocal opponent of legal abortion, she had in fact undergone an illegal one herself in Las Vegas. That would probably have put a slamming halt to her antichoice influence and political rise. Faith was furious with Annie for what she'd already done, which in practical terms affected the lives of the poorest women more than anyone else, denying them help. She didn't know what had caused the shift, especially since you might think that Annie's experience with her illegal abortion could have caused her to see the urgent need for legal abortions. But you never knew what went on inside someone else; how, over time, a thought could become an obsession, and a new shell could form and harden around it. Faith had read that Annie was religious. Had she found religion as a way to manage her thoughts about the abortion? Or maybe it was something else entirely. If Faith could see her now, she would say, "Annie, *really*?"

Decades later, the team at Loci repeatedly tried to get Senator McCauley to come speak at a summit. The first time they tried, Faith had said nothing, tensely waiting to see what would happen, what Annie would do. The senator's office predictably said she would be unable to come. That was probably for the best. Because even if Faith had gotten her alone in a room and said, "Annie, *really*?" Annie would certainly have replied, "Yes, Faith, *really*."

They both believed what they believed; their convictions filled them fully. But just as Annie would never reveal her own history publicly, Faith wouldn't reveal it either. It wasn't her information to give. It was private. *I get to decide*, the women had sung at that gathering. Despite everything, Faith never told anyone.

Faith became aware, fairly early on, of her skill at bringing out certain qualities in other women. They wanted to be in her midst, and they wanted more from themselves. She realized that girls and young women actually loved her in ways that were

similar to how Lincoln did. They could seem a little lost, or perhaps in need of inspiration. Perhaps the most important thing
she gave them, she realized, was permission.

"Tell me what you want from life, Olive," she'd said to a shy
girl, a high school intern at *Bloomer.*

Olive Mitchell looked at her gratefully, as if she'd waited sixteen years to be asked that question. "Aerospace engineering,"
she said breathlessly.

"Excellent. Well, then, pursue that with your whole self. I
suspect it's tough to break into that field, right?" The girl nodded. "So you'll need to be entirely tenacious and unimpeachable,
which I know you already are. I believe you can do it," she added.

It had been years since Faith had thought of Olive, but she
knew that she had gone on to study aerospace engineering, for
she'd written Faith a letter of extreme, nearly poetic thanks,
with a photo of her standing in a research lab, smiling with un-
alloyed happiness. That was so long ago. It was hard to keep
track of the young women Faith had met, so many of them shining and shot through with promise.

Young women came and went through Faith Frank's door
wherever she lived and whatever she did. Inevitably some of
them were close at hand, and she wasn't often severely lonely.
Sometimes, over the years, she experienced a very particular
desire for the company of a man, and when that happened Faith
would arrange to meet up with Will Kelly, a Democratic strategist
she'd met at a function in the late 1980s. Handsome, hangdog,
bushy-mustached, never married, he had a kind of policy-wonk/
beachcomber mix to him that she found seductive. Though he
lived in Austin, Texas, Will would fly up to be with Faith; they
would have dinner and a night of companionable, somewhat
aerobic sex and good conversation. Then it might not happen

again for months, and this was fine. Being alone was something that Faith had perfected over the years. When you were alone you didn't have to worry about every little detail on your body, whether your legs were like prickly pears or whether after a cocktail party you were Brie-breathed. Unlike many people she knew, she often preferred her own company.

When *Bloomer* folded in 2010, it was a blow of all kinds. For months Faith felt down, unneeded, and then suddenly that billionaire ghost from her past, Emmett Shrader, telephoned, or anyway his assistant did, and Faith agreed to come to his office for a lunchtime meeting. When she arrived, a table had been set in his enormous British men's club of an office with the startling views.

Emmett stood and walked toward her as she entered. She'd seen various photos of him over the years, had watched his hair change from dark to silver. A few times she'd Googled him. From the doorway she saw that he still had no fat on him, but remained lean in the way that a billionaire with a trainer and a butler and a health-conscious cook can do. But when he came closer, Faith became aware of a different feeling. A nostalgia for Emmett's lost younger self, coupled with a nostalgia for her own lost younger self. Together the two nostalgias combined to create something that was immediately emotional and even very slightly sexual in nature. Standing there, she had the general sensation of want, though she couldn't immediately determine what it was she wanted.

Did she want him, or did she want younger him, and along with that, younger her? Did she just want to be young again, period? She recalled the night they had spent in bed, and then its unhappy, crashing postlude. His face was still strong, and a word came to mind, a word associated with power, *craggy*, though God forbid a female public figure should become craggy. They'd mock her on Twitter, say she'd let herself go and she should put a bag over her head. His body was still tight and impressive, encased in the beautiful clothes of the very wealthy male, the tie hanging like an icicle. Sexual attraction was not an island; it was part of an archipelago that included trappings and context. He was in the context of his ridiculously massive office, and of the years he had lived since they'd seen each other last, racking up his victories like a big-game hunter.

"Faith," he said, and his voice was soft, his eyes almost wet. He took her hand, but then let go and put both arms around her. The hug was surprising, so different from the air kisses or the double air kisses that were ubiquitous on the island of Manhattan. The hug was genuine, and it was a relief. "I am so glad to see you," Emmett said when they released and pulled back and looked at each other. Then he sat her down on a brown leather couch the size of a buffalo, and he sat across from her. She listened as he spun the tale of a women's foundation that he wanted his firm to underwrite and that he wanted her to run. "We will hold summits, lectures, huge gatherings around a chosen topic, and invite the public. We won't solicit outside funding," he said. "We'll charge for tickets, but beyond that all the costs will be ours."

"Slow down," Faith finally said when he had spoken uninterrupted for several minutes. In the background, men and women dressed in white prepared the lunch table. "First of all, I want to say I'm very flattered."

"Don't say that," he said. "People say that when they're about to say no to something."

"Well, before I came in here today, I asked around and tried to get some more context," Faith said. "You've been stellar in so many ways, Emmett, and yet you've also been known to take the moral shortcut."

"Look, Faith, my firm is involved with many projects," he said. "I haven't been sainted, that's true. We try a lot of things, and not everything works. But we're doing very well, and if you look at our donation history, I think you'll be reassured. We give a lot to women's causes."

They looked at each other in silence for a hair-raising amount of time. She wanted to unnerve him, even as she was sitting there. "You care about women's lives?" she finally asked.

"I think you know the answer to that."

"Remember John Hinckley?" she said. "The guy who shot Ronald Reagan? He said he did it to impress Jodie Foster."

"You think I'm offering you this to impress you?"

"Maybe."

"Even if that were the case, which it's not, let me assure you that this foundation will involve the maiming of no presidents," said Emmett. He rubbed his eyes, as if she was exhausting him, and probably she was. Maybe he was wishing he'd never called her in, for she was being such a pain in the ass. But she had to see this through. "Look," he said, "I only want to do something good."

"Something that involves women."

"Well, yes."

Then, her voice quieter, she added, "Something that involves me."

Faith was overexcited at the thought of having access to the kind of money and resources that Emmett was offering. She'd never had any of it before, and she'd never thought to want it. She could hardly imagine what it would be like. Back at *Bloomer*, they'd had to fight with Cormer Publishing to pay writers even a small amount, or to get two-ply toilet paper in the restroom.

She wondered if, in accepting the offer, she would be selling out. Shirley Pepper was long dead from coronary artery disease;

she couldn't ask her. Bonnie Dempster, ever since *Bloomer* folded, had been making a very unpredictable living working for a small, all-women home-decluttering company called, embarrassingly, Stuffragettes. After the meeting in Emmett's office— she told him she'd have to think about it—Faith called her to get her opinion, and it was Bonnie who said to Faith, "Well, you do tend to be a little gullible, Faith. It's great that you're not cynical, but I would be careful. Also, is this something you'd actually love to do? I mean, is it good enough?"

Faith called Emmett the next morning and said, "You know, I'm not sure we'd really be making a difference. It would be a kind of high-end lecture bureau, and that is not something I've had experience with. Or wanted to." He was quiet. "How would we connect with women?" she asked. "How would we change people's lives?"

"I'm telling you, we would. *You* would."

"Thank you," she said after a long moment. "But I'm going to have to say no."

He seemed shocked, and the call quickly ended. Faith went for a long walk in Riverside Park, trudging along, thinking of what she had just turned down. It was hollow to her, what he was offering. What more would she need? What would make it good enough? An hour later she got into a cab and returned to his office without an appointment. He was there, and when she was shown in to his office again, she said, "There would have to be another component."

"Tell me," Emmett said.

"Every day I hear stories about the plight of women all over the world. I would like to think that in addition to providing speakers, we could also get out there and do something. If we find an emergency situation where we feel we could be of some immediate help, I'd like to have funds made available to take action, so that women could see relief right away." She looked at him. "Are you already dismissing this?"

"Of course not."

"We could be, say, eighty percent about speakers and summits, but twenty percent about what we could call, I don't know, 'special projects.'"

"Deal," he said.

Over time, both arms of Loci, those uneven arms, had been highly productive. Women were forever *summiting*, endlessly climbing with ropes around the waist, wielding pitons. The summits were about ambitious topics, such as, recently, leadership—leadership being something that everyone now wanted, as if the world could be made up entirely of leaders and no followers, the way children might crave an all-fireman, all-ballerina society. And there had been a good number of those special projects over the years. Loci had paid the salary to employ a community health worker in a rural village in Namibia, and had paid for the defense of a woman on trial for the murder of her husband, who had abused and terrorized her for a decade.

But by 2014, over four years in now, it had become precipitously harder to get any of the ideas for the special projects that Loci presented past the people upstairs. These projects, you could tell, were a nuisance to them, a money pit. It wasn't just that ShraderCapital had become stingier since the start of Loci; it had, but there was also outside resistance to some of the work. "Africa doesn't need your help," someone wrote in an influential online magazine, and it kept getting reposted elsewhere, replicating endlessly.

Faith was used to being criticized, and to being hated. There had always been some of that back in the height of the *Bloomer* years. But on Twitter at the inception of Loci, people wrote #bloodmoney and #FaithlessFrank. And then soon the concern became less about Faith's collaboration with Emmett Shrader than it was about the foundation itself.

But by now it was clear not only that Loci hadn't kept up with all the galloping changes in feminism, but that the way it presented itself was also a reason for vilification. Loci was doing good business, and naturally people were writing things on Twitter like #whiteladyfeminism and #richladies, and the hashtag that for some reason irritated Faith most, #fingersandwichfeminism.

She understood their complaints, she really did. There was so much waste with these events and receptions at which they were now supposed to seduce other corporations and big donors. People complained, with justification, that they shouldn't have to give money to a foundation that was backed by a billionaire. And Loci was never supposed to have had to seek outside funding; ShraderCapital had been covering all costs. But that had changed, inexplicably; Emmett had gotten pressure from within.

So Loci at this moment in time was an uneasy hybrid. She'd adapted to the twenty-first century to a degree, but what she knew how to do best she had learned back in the beginning. The beginning had been the profound place for her, the pit, the root.

Despite the hazing on Twitter and elsewhere, the summits were doing so well, and the people upstairs had been weighing in more frequently and conducting studies and focus groups. Because of their input, the foundation had been encouraged to go celebrity-heavy; Lincoln had noticed, and so had most people. A shallowness had crept in. Too much of what happened at these events was just frivolous, Faith knew. That had rarely been the case in the beginning.

Some of the team seemed demoralized. Months earlier, like a doctor on grand rounds, Faith had gone around to check in on them, and soon realized morale was dangerously low. When she got to the cubicle of Greer Kadetsky, who'd been at Loci since nearly the start, to her surprise she found Greer with her head down on the surface of her desk, lightly asleep at eleven in the morning. Greer was usually focused and sharp, though lately that was less true. Lately, she could be seen whispering with the others, dissatisfied by the memos that came down from upstairs. Faith had been trying to pretend that the changes at Loci were not close to reaching a point of no return, but she couldn't keep it up, and she knew she shouldn't keep it up either.

"Good morning, sleepyhead," Faith said softly, remembering that this was the way she had awakened Lincoln for school when he slept through his alarm—there had been cloaked irritation in her words then, as there was now—and Greer was mortified.

"Faith, I'm so sorry." She sat up quickly and reached up as if to smooth out her face.

"Sleeping on the job. That's not typical. Is it really so bad here now?" Faith asked. "Maybe it is," she added. Then, "Grab some coffee and come talk to me in my office, Greer."

Sitting on the white couch, and squinting in a band of sunlight, Greer said, "I didn't really have that much going on this morning. At least, not that much that needed my immediate attention. That's the way it's gotten for me. It just feels so corporate lately. There's so much attention to money, now that we're supposed to solicit funds. I thought ShraderCapital was paying for everything. I miss the way it used to be," Greer said bluntly. "When it was smaller. I miss writing speeches for those lunch talks."

"You did a great job with them. I'm sorry they got phased out. Not my decision."

"And I also miss the way those women used to come into the

office. And I sat with them with my little tape recorder and I got to know them, and I saw what it was we were doing. I saw it; it was right in front of me. Someone's life."

"As you know, I agree with everything you're saying."

"I'm not sure we're doing anything, Faith," Greer said. "I like to think we are," she added quickly. "It's hard to know how much we ever did, quantifiably. We don't have a product. And I know that from a money standpoint we're a huge success now—and when we started, we weren't. But I feel like we're in a rut. Or anyway, I am."

All Faith had to do was poke at it a little bit, and Greer told her everything she felt; she'd always been this way, and it was no different now, though now she spoke less haltingly. Like the others—at least the ones who had been there since the beginning—Greer Kadetsky disliked the glitter of the foundation, the fact that she never directly got to help anyone. Greer still did a lot of writing—strong writing, Faith thought—but it was all for the newsletter or the annual report, which certainly added to that corporate feel she described.

"And when was the last time we did a special project?" Greer persisted. "They energized everybody here, because we could see something happening in real time. Where's our money going, exactly? I know that Emmett funded the foundation so it could be big. So it could be different from your experience at *Bloomer*. But my understanding of being big is that it means you have an impact, isn't that right? You can tell me to stop talking, Faith, but I just think sometimes there's a self-satisfaction about the whole thing. Not from you. Not from us. But from the events themselves. It doesn't feel so good to me these days. Maybe it will change, but I don't know. So I fell asleep. Sorry," she added.

"I know," said Faith. "I really do know." And because she

couldn't think of anything else to say yet, she put a hand on Greer Kadetsky's shoulder and said, "Let me work on it."

"Turn over, miss," said a voice, and Faith, marinating deep in her memories, made a grunting sound, returning from all of that to the present moment. She had to take a second to remember what that present moment was. The smell of baby oil struck her first. Then the all-string version of "You Don't Bring Me Flowers." Then the awareness that her face was mashed against a vinyl cradle whose towel had slipped off. The massage had placed her in a stupor.

She obediently rolled onto her back, one breast briefly flapping out from the protection of the towel. She opened her eyes and found herself staring, much too close, into the face of her masseuse. It was startling to really take in how young the woman was. She was almost a girl. Maybe she was a girl. Maybe this was child labor. Jesus Christ. Immediately Faith felt all her muscles contract, and the woozy dream state calcified. "May I ask your age?" Faith asked calmly.

The woman looked down. "I am not a girl," she said. "I am mom of two. Boy and girl. Keep young by working hard." She laughed dully, as though she had been asked this question many times before.

"Do you like working here?" Faith persisted, but the woman didn't answer.

This was a question that now preoccupied her. The day after Greer Kadetsky had fallen asleep at work and then expressed her work frustrations, Faith had called a meeting in the conference room, which turned into an hours-long session, like a kind of consciousness-raising group from the past. They had all sat around the table and she listened as one by one they told her why they had originally come to Loci, and why it felt different there now. They told her about their worries that the summits were elitist, that there was a kind of feel-good feminism in the air. "I recognize that feminism can't only be 'feel-bad,'" said one of the newer hires, a very bright IT person, a trans woman named Kara. "But there's too much of an emphasis on how everything feels, one way or another, and less on what it does." This was the refrain, said in various ways.

Someone else said that she missed the special projects, and everyone chimed in. Yes, the special projects, which brought immediate results. In a way, Faith knew, another special project might remind them all of what they were doing there. Afterward, Faith had gone upstairs to see Emmett. She couldn't tell him how unhappy everyone was downstairs—that seemed risky. "If they're so unhappy, let's end it," she worried someone at ShraderCapital might say. Instead, she told him she had a good idea for a special project. "It's been a while, Emmett," she said lightly but she hoped strongly. Then she described for him the project she had in mind. Again and again at work over the years there had been bulletins disseminated about human trafficking, an issue around which she felt helpless. Loci had brought in speakers before, but now it felt like it was time to do something more.

Iffat Khan, who was now a researcher on the team and no longer Faith's assistant, had shown Faith some material on a situation in the Cotopaxi province in Ecuador, where young women—in many cases girls—were being lured from home and brought to Guayaquil to become prostitutes. It definitely qualified as an emergency. "If we can save a number of them, it would shine a light on the larger situation," she said. "Maybe other corporate entities and charities would get involved. It could be an ongoing rescue mission." Shrader looked gloomy and unconvinced, so Faith told him the rest of her idea. "I was thinking that after the rescue we could connect these young women with mentors. Older women who would teach them useful skills. How to read, first of all, if that's needed. And computer literacy. Along with a trade. Textiles, maybe. They could learn to knit, and eventually form . . . a textile co-op. A women's textile co-op." Faith was excited by her own idea, polishing those last three words individually as she said them, but Emmett just kept looking at her, unconvinced. "And then we could bring one of the young women over here to speak about it," Faith said. "What do you think?"

"What, we would fly her here?"

"Sure, why not?"

Emmett paused, slightly more engaged, and bobbed his head from side to side, considering. He promised to bring it up to the relevant people upstairs, and in June of 2014, a memo came to Faith from upstairs telling her that they were actually going to do it. She was very excited. Mentorship was still a very popular concept right now, everyone was talking about it, and the idea was surprisingly well-received. Someone at ShraderCapital had found a local contact in Quito. Alejandra Sosa was described as a dynamic leader involved with human rights issues in the developing world; her résumé was peppered with acronyms, the names of NGOs with which she'd consulted. All those capital letters, when looked at on one sheet of paper, had the effect of a firewall, or a code that could only be broken by someone much smarter than you.

A hasty Skype session was arranged. Members of the Shrader-Capital and Loci teams in New York sat around a rock slab of a conference table up on 27 facing the projected image of a group of women in a modest Quito office. "Faith Frank!" said Alejandra Sosa. "This is an honor of honors. You have been very

important to me as a woman." Sosa was forty years old and confident, sexy. Faith liked her at once. They exchanged easy conversation about their shared mission. Alejandra Sosa knew of
some skilled older women who could be hired to work with the
hundred young women and girls after they had been rescued and
relocated. To become their mentors. ShraderCapital would fund
it, and the agency that Alejandra Sosa oversaw in Quito would
take care of distributing money and making arrangements. She
was very reassuring, and at the end she said, "It is gratifying to
work with you, Faith Frank. You are a force for good."

Faith had said to Emmett and his team, "I liked her tremen-
dously, but we need to vet her, of course. You hear about the
scamming that goes on in aid work when there isn't oversight. I
don't want to get caught up in any of that."

"Of course, do what you need to do," said the COO, and in
the background one of the assistants piped up, "No worries."
The researchers down on 26 found that Sosa had a record of
achieving results. The secretary of the executive board of UNI-
CEF had written her a fulsome, nearly weepy recommendation
letter. Then, a couple of weeks later, word came that the modest
rescue mission had gone well, and that one hundred traumatized
young women had been paired with older women. The young
ones were offered transitional housing in an apartment building
in Quito, where they would recover from their ordeal and learn
a trade, through which they could make a living and start a new
life. Before the end of the year, as Faith had proposed, one of the
rescued young women would be brought here to be introduced
onstage and say a few words after the keynote at the mentorship
summit coming up soon in LA.

Faith had already begun working on the keynote, but now,
deep into October, lying on this table naked under a towel,
having her body indelicately pushed and pulled, she thought:

I should turn the keynote over to Greer Kadetsky. Let her not only write it but also deliver it. Greer was forward-looking, smart, and passionate. She had the ability to listen well and draw people out; they connected with her and trusted her. Look at those wonderful lunchtime speeches she had written. Plus, Greer was on the verge of becoming her own person, and this would help push her further. She would get to write two speeches, one for the young woman from Ecuador, and one for herself. In her own speech, she would finally be speaking as Greer Kadetsky.

Faith understood that Greer had hit that plateau that comes several years into a new position. She needed proof that her work mattered, not just a nebulous hope that it did. Otherwise, she would continue to feel discouraged, and also she would be in danger of leaving.

What if they all leave? Faith thought. Of course there would always be someone else who would come; people left now and again. Helen Brand had left last month to be a national reporter for the *Washington Post*. No one was ever irreplaceable, and yet she always felt a pang, like a kind of brief grief, when someone left, followed by a slight start—almost an increase in respiration rate—when someone new arrived.

Give it to Greer, she told herself. Faith recalled one specific conversation with Greer Kadetsky, way back in the earliest days. Greer had called her up, crying, and had told her that there had been a tragedy in her personal life and she couldn't make it to the very first summit, which they'd all been working toward around the clock. A child had been killed, Faith remembered; Greer's boyfriend's brother? But it was so long ago that she couldn't recall the details. She just remembered Greer's voice on the phone, saying, "Faith?" and then the tears, and how she, Faith, had immediately gone into soothing mode. As soon as she got off the phone with Greer, she was on another call, scrambling, yelling a little to find someone to take up the slack. That was what it was like, running a foundation. You soothed and you scrambled and sometimes you yelled.

And then one day, sometime later, Faith had overheard Greer speaking to someone in a pleading voice on her cell phone. Faith had come over to her, concerned, and asked if she was all right. Greer looked up, nodding, but she didn't look all right. That afternoon Greer had come to Faith's office door—this was no surprise; all the young women eventually showed up at Faith's door—and she came in and planted herself on the couch and told Faith everything. She and the high school boyfriend had had a rough breakup. "I don't know what to do," Greer had said. "We've been together for so long, and it wasn't supposed to end, ever." Then she'd begun to cry in the sort of loose, phlegmy way that distantly reminded Faith of when Lincoln had been a little boy with croup.

Faith had listened, and while she hadn't offered any prescriptions, she'd told Greer that she was welcome to come in and talk whenever she liked. "I mean it," she'd said, and she did mean it, because Greer was one of the good ones. She had come far; she was sterling, loyal, smart, modest—exactly the right person to have hired and promoted. But now Greer was flagging, and needed to be reminded of why she was here at Loci, four years in. Give her this, Faith thought.

Plus, Lincoln was right: Faith was tired and overworked. She was seventy-one years old, and though some people said that seventy was the new forty, it wasn't. This massage today was desperately needed. She wished she could stay on this table for six thousand minutes, with this compact woman pounding her back and placing a line of hot, clicking stones up and down her spine and massaging her neck with baby oil until it was just a loose string gently connected to a head that felt as light as a balloon. Faith was sick to death of the pace she'd been keeping, and she couldn't bear to go speak at another Loci summit so soon, not the kind of summits that these had become.

No more psychics. No more pelican butter.

Let Greer do this one. It would be a symbiotic touch.

All of this was what Faith thought about as her masseuse went to the other end of the table and began to rub her feet.

Sue pressed a particular place under the big toe, and Faith startled, then composed a list with two items on it:

1) Arrange meeting with Greer to discuss LA. Be sure
   to find out if Greer speaks Spanish, which would be
   a help.
2) Encourage Greer Kadetsky generally. She still needs
   encouragement. They all do.

Faith vaguely recalled their first meeting, back at Greer's college campus. Greer had been so bright and filled with feeling, but beyond that she had also been upset with her parents. Of course Faith had been reminded of being upset with her own parents at that age. Both sets of parents had held their daughters back, even as they loved them. Faith had been touched, seeing this in Greer, and who knew why you were impelled to do anything you did, but Faith gave Greer Kadetsky her business card, the way she sometimes still gave it out to young women, smiling at them in a way that she hoped would have significance. And apparently it did, for Greer was still here all these years later.

And Faith, indisputably an old woman now, still thought about her own mother and father with a tenderhearted bunching-up of feeling, despite their unfairness toward her over half a century earlier. They hadn't known better; they were of their time. She could still almost cry now recalling their gentleness, and all the games of charades they'd played, and how she and Philip had run around the Bensonhurst apartment after a bath, squealing and smelling good, finally being caught up in a towel held out by their mother like a toreador. They had left their wet footprints everywhere, though they dried fast and left no trace.

Her parents had held her back, maddeningly, but just for a while. Her brother hadn't taken her side, and she'd held it against him at first, and then after she'd stopped holding it against him, life had taken over—her life, which was so different from his; and finally it was as if they'd barely ever been siblings, let alone twins. Lying on the table, she tried to make a note to be the one to call him on their birthday in a few months, and not the other way around. Get a jump on the day and be the one to call him, asking him if he and Sydelle were planning to come east soon. "I'd really like it if you did," she would say. "And we can even play charades. So start practicing."

Suddenly the hands working on her body began to chop, moving with vehemence up and down over these old bones that had been everywhere, and maybe were starting to slow down.

"Done!" cried Sue the masseuse, and she slapped Faith's legs with her two forceful hands, the sound ringing out as if in triumph.

NINE

The afternoon of the speech at the mentorship summit in LA was dipped in heat, despite the fact that it was early December. LA was heat and smog and noise, but none of that was felt or talked about inside the cultural center, which was its own self-contained ecosystem. Heat and smog and noise had been replaced by a subtle veil of scent and an ineffable sensation of cool. Also, the event was lacking long, wearying lines, because all the bathrooms, including men's rooms, had been opened up. Women powered easily through. "Have I died and gone to heaven?" one woman asked another at the hand dryers, which seemed to whirr more pleasingly than usual.

Drinks and canapés were circulating in the lobby; slender Bellinis and gemological tuna tartare slicked with yuzu gelée. There was a discreet manicure station here, where women sat with fingers spread; here and there, other women openly nursed infants and no one looked askance. The feminist psychic held sway in a corner. The women here were wealthy and progressive, believed in equality, gave money to left or center-left candidates, and bought tickets to events like this one to see the roster of speakers, including the female film actors and directors. The audience was well-dressed; it was a sea of soft pastel and the occasional basic black, because even though this was California, New York roots ran deep. Clavicles were exposed, understated jewelry on display, and the conversation took place in voices of concern, interrupted by a couple of familiar shrieks that you might hear in a restaurant when there's a large group of women at a table. Everyone here knew that shriek, which signaled the happiness of women spending time together.

Greer Kadetsky and Lupe Izurieta stood together watching the scene. They had flown there from New York, the morning after Lupe had arrived from Ecuador. Lupe, pretty, early twenties, in a yellow dress, was exhausted from the long trip and overwhelmed by the number of people in attendance. Greer said, "Do you want something to eat?" pleased to be able to use the high school Spanish that she had studied back in Macopee, and took her over to one of the runway-long buffet tables, but the food must have looked so strange to this young woman from Ecuador—it looked strange to Greer too. High-end, fussy food.

"No," said Lupe in the world's softest voice, which reminded Greer of her own voice back at the beginning of everything. It wasn't that she was loud now, but she was different.

A tech guy found them and said, "It's time to get you both miked. We're starting in fifteen." Backstage in the greenroom before the talk, the tech guy brought out some equipment and said, "Who wants to go first?"

Greer tried to explain to Lupe what would happen. Before she could finish what she was saying, the tech guy had reached a hand inside the collar of Lupe's dress to clip on a microphone, which made her tense and gasp. "It's okay," Greer said, though she knew it wasn't, for Lupe, but he had moved too fast. Then his hand withdrew, and Lupe breathed out in relief. She was the most frightened person Greer had ever met, and she had sat in silence throughout the flight from New York to LA. Presumably she'd also sat that way during the very long flight from Quito to New York, her first airplane trip ever.

"Are you okay?" Greer asked her now.

"I am well," Lupe said, but she didn't look well.

Greer didn't feel very well herself. She hadn't wanted to give this speech at all. When Faith had offered it to her in October, she'd thought she was kidding. "Come into my office," Faith had said. Greer had entered the white space and taken in the walls that had been breaded bit by bit with photos of girls and women.

"Greer," said Faith. "It's your time." Faith told her that she wanted her to travel to LA to appear onstage with one of the young women from Ecuador, in order to introduce her, and write her speech for her, and then also write and deliver the keynote mentorship speech herself.

"I can't do that," Greer said, shocked.

"Why not?"

"I don't give speeches. I write them for other people. Or I used to, anyway. Short ones."

"Anyone who ever gave a speech," said Faith, "was once someone who didn't. You're what now, twenty-five?"

"Twenty-six."

"Well. It's definitely time."

Greer wondered why Faith was giving her this gig. She remembered something Faith had said to the team once, early on: "Men give women the power that they themselves don't want." She'd meant power to run the home, to deal with the children and their friends and teachers, to make all decisions about the domestic realm. So maybe Faith, like one of those men, was giving Greer something she didn't particularly want. Maybe Faith had no interest in giving this speech, and so that was why she was giving it to Greer—passing the power on to her in order to get rid of it. Greer saw, at that moment, Faith glance toward her minimalist desk clock, like a therapist nearing the end of the hour. Greer had overstayed her welcome. Why hadn't she just said yes?

"Okay, great, it's a deal," Greer said with forced liveliness. "Shoot me now," she added, putting her finger to the side of her head and trying to laugh.

The bad moment had fled. All you ever had to do to make a bad moment flee was acquiesce. This was true everywhere in life, even though so much of Loci's focus was supposedly on *not* acquiescing. She stood to leave, and Faith looked up at her and said, "It'll be a good thing, I promise."

The dozen or so times Greer had come into that office over the years, unrelated to work, had been because Faith had seen that something was wrong and had called her in; or else because Greer had felt welcome. Faith had encouraged her to come in and talk whenever she wanted. After originally telling Faith about her Cory problems, Greer had returned to her office months later, after a weekend up in Macopee during which Cory had broken up with her. "I love you and I'll always love you," he'd said stiffly, like someone in a school play, "and I really don't want to hurt you. But I just can't do this anymore."

Faith comforted her in the aftermath and told her that the best thing you could do in a hard moment in your life was work. "Work can help," she'd said. "Especially when you're suffering. Keep writing those speeches for those women, Greer; keep imagining their lives, what they go through. You'll find yourself going outside yourself and into them. It'll provide perspective. And any time you want to talk to me, let me know."

That was three and a half years earlier. Over time, in their broken-up state, Greer and Cory spoke far less frequently, and now she was only in touch with him on the occasions when she went home to visit her parents in Macopee. As each year since their breakup passed and they moved farther away from each other, she was able to see, objectively, that Cory had turned into a tall, skinny grown man who lived in his mother's house with a plastic-covered sofa and video games and a turtle. The sensation she experienced each time she saw him there—him!—living like this and turning into this new and different person, was as strong as a flare-up of a chronic illness.

Since the breakup, Greer had had occasional relationships and hookups that were mostly decent, and once or twice excruciating. She sometimes met someone for after-work drinks at the kind of bar where everyone was young and worked for progressive startups, or for culture websites with names like Topsoil. By age twenty-six Greer had finally developed a lasting look. The blue streak in her hair had been rinsed away a few years earlier, replaced by highlights, but her eager, sometimes sexy nerdiness remained, and it had become fully stylish. Chunky eyeglasses were in. She wore those glasses, and often a short skirt and bright tights and little black boots, whether to show up at work or attend a Loci event or go out for drinks in a cluster at night.

Sometimes the drinking people gathered on the Skillet, a former lighthouse/party boat moored on the Hudson, downtown. The surface shifted beneath her feet as she drank and shouted and flirted. Since becoming single, Greer had forced herself to get good at flirting. The men she met all seemed to say they were "several years out of Wesleyan." Their beds were never made, or else made poorly, when she climbed into them. No one yet had the time or inclination to take care of themselves, and it was unclear when that would ever begin.

Two months before the LA summit, on board the Skillet, Ben

Prochnauer from the office had opened himself to Greer like some kind of obstinate flower. They stood close together, the way he had once stood with Marcella Boxman—she who was long gone from Loci, on to be a Social Innovation Fellow at Cambridge—and he spoke urgently to her.

"So. Do you ever think of me that way?" he asked.

"'That way'?" Greer stood back and looked at him. They had been working together for so long. In the early years he had flirted with her, but it had seemed like little more than a reflex. Now, with no warning, he was genuinely hitting on her. His face had the glinting optimism of a found coin. Greer slept with him that night on the futon in his studio apartment in Fort Greene. The surprise hookup was the sort of event that the two people in question suspect they will look back on one day with vague, sentimental affection, overlooking the sadness that had gotten them there.

When it was time for her to go onstage that day in LA, Greer walked out, miked and lightly quivering, her vision darting around in the darkness as if she were a goldfish who'd been poured into a new bowl, while outside the bowl loomed a thousand invisible women. Nearby on the stage stood the sign-language interpreter, patiently waiting. The room stayed quiet, with just the occasional obligatory and somehow recognizably female cough, followed by scrabbling in a purse for a lozenge, which was unwrapped in a quick sequence of rustles.

"Please forgive me if I seem a bit freaked out at the moment," Greer began. "Most of the speeches I give are in my head." There was warm laughter. "I wouldn't be here," she said, "if it weren't for Faith Frank." Applause. "She is the best, and she wanted me to come in her place. I know you'd rather hear her speak, but you've got me. So! Faith Frank hired me, originally, based on nothing. She took me in and she taught me things, and more than that she gave me permission. I think that's what the people who change our lives always do. They give us permission to be the person we secretly really long to be but maybe don't feel we're allowed to be.

"Many of you here in this room—can we actually call this a room? It's more like a landmass—probably had someone like that, didn't you?" There was affirmative murmuring. "Someone who gave you permission. Someone who saw you and heard you. Heard your voice. We're all really lucky to have had that."

Then Greer introduced Lupe, speaking of her hardship and bravery, and how proud Loci was to have helped her and the rest of the young women. "Now, starting over after a traumatic time," Greer said, "she's been connected with her own mentor. A woman in her country who is teaching her everything she knows."

Lupe appeared onstage and took her place beside Greer. She took out a little folded piece of paper on which was the Spanish version of the words that Greer had written for her. Lupe smoothed down the page and giggled in her lovely way; the crowd, in response, was warm and understanding.

Finally, Lupe began to read aloud, slowly and carefully. Then Greer read the same words in English. "I speak today for myself and the others who were there in Ecuador when we had the bad experience. We left our homes, and it was not what they said it would be. We were afraid. They wouldn't let us leave." Back and forth they went, conveying the emotional story about how Lupe had been living a bleak life that did not seem like it would ever get better. Lupe looked so frightened and upset as she recalled what had happened to her that Greer felt that way too, just as she had felt when she wrote those lunchtime speeches. She reached out instinctively and took Lupe's hand, holding it as Faith had once held hers. In her high school Spanish she whispered to Lupe to take her time, to not worry about a thing. The audience would wait. They weren't going anywhere. So Lupe took her time, and finally, together, going back and forth, she and Greer got to the part about how she and everyone else had been rescued, and taken away from the neighborhood in Guayaquil where they had all been forced to live. And then, once she was resettled, how an older woman had come to see her and invited her to learn some new skills. Lupe had agreed to go; together they went to a building where there were computers, and people who taught English. "I am learning," Lupe said in English, and the audience clapped. There was also a room in the building filled with sample equipment to make textiles. Lupe was shown how to use a hand loom, and also how to knit. Her mentor had sat with her in the corner by the window and showed her some different stitches. "I have gotten good at this. Later," said Lupe, "we want to form a women's textile co-op." Her short statement was done; Lupe had gotten through it. Greer put her arms around her, and the applause began.

Later, Greer would find out that a few different women had been holding up their iPhones to record the speech. If the twenty-first century taught you anything, it was that your words belonged to everyone, even if they actually didn't. It wasn't that the moment had been that special, but for the people in the room it was. "You had to be there," women would probably say to one another, after showing the clip to friends. An earnest moment between two women onstage at a feminist summit was not much of a big deal. It didn't go viral, unlike the speech given later that same day by the female action star. The women at the summit had all stood at the beginning and end of that one, celebrating the Australian heroine from *Gravitus 2: The Awakening*, which had become so huge. In a now stupidly famous scene in the movie, her character, Lake Stratton, had said to a gang of corporate supervillains and their henchmen after being mocked by them for being female, "It's true: I may not be in possession of balls." Beat. "*So I borrowed a couple.*" And just then two enormous wrecking balls swung through the window of the skyscraper office where the standoff was taking place, instantly killing the villains.

What mattered about that movie was not its content, which was puerile. It seemed that in order for a female to have a huge cultural moment, it helped if she had a not overtly feminine name and was a hot, front-loaded, violent wench. What mattered, really, was that the movie had taken in $335 million, and maybe in the future, movie studios would develop more films with female stars.

Greer's moment onstage with Lupe wasn't like that. It was smaller, and fleeting, but the applause went on for a very long time. Afterward, out in the lobby, a cluster of women surrounded the two of them, encircling them with enthusiasm and questions. "I loved what you had to say about how there are people who give us permission," one woman said to Greer. "I know what you mean, because I had exactly that experience."

Across the way, a middle-aged woman approached Lupe and pulled something from a bag. "This is for you," the woman said, and she pressed upon Lupe a lump of white wool and a pair of needles, to which was attached the beginnings of some sweater or blanket. "I'm a knitter too," said the woman in a too-loud voice, as though that would help Lupe understand. "But I'd like you to have it."

Lupe took the needles and wool, but Greer didn't know what happened next, for she was carried off on one wave of women, while Lupe was carried off on another.

One woman said to Greer, "My person wasn't a teacher, she was a neighbor. Mrs. Palmieri. I took care of her cat sometimes when she went away. She would invite me in when she was home, and we'd talk about cooking. She gave me a lot of advice."

"Mine," said another woman, "was actually my grandfather. An amazing person. He was a tail gunner in the Korean War."

After the event was over, Greer said to Lupe, "You were so wonderful. They really loved you." The young woman looked shyly away; was she pleased or just self-conscious? It was hard to tell. Greer remembered something that Faith had said during her speech in the Ryland Chapel. She had told them that if they said what they believed, then not everyone would like them, or love them. "If it's any consolation at all," Faith had said, "*I* love you."

Could that have been true? Yes, Greer thought, it probably had been, because right now she felt a kind of love for Lupe Izurieta. And Greer knew Lupe as little as Faith had known everyone in that chapel.

After the building had cleared, Greer and Lupe went back to their rooms in the hotel, which were connected by a door that they didn't open at first. Greer lay down on the king-sized bed and Skyped with Ben back in New York. He had slept over twice in the last week; their relationship had no propulsion, but it felt physically relieving, his body pleasurably heavy on her like a weighted blanket, his hands and mouth resourceful and in motion. "I think they liked it," she said to him now. He came close to the screen, the camera giving him a fisheye-lens convexity that made her think about Skyping with Cory over the years: at Princeton, with his messy room behind him, and in the Philippines in the middle of the night, while afternoon blazed in America. Ben's face on-screen was still not entirely familiar, though they had slept together a number of times.

"Great job," Ben said. "I watched the live feed with Faith and a couple of people from upstairs," he said. "We all thought you were great. And it was very emotional, that moment with the girl."

A text appeared from Faith a little later.

NAILED IT! THANK YOU AGAIN.
YOU ARE THE BEST.
   Xx
   FF

A little while later Greer quietly knocked on the door that separated her room from Lupe's. She used her high school Spanish to ask whether Lupe wanted to get an Uber with her and go into LA for dinner. There was a long pause, and maybe Lupe's response was one of dread; maybe she would've preferred to be alone tonight. "Or we could stay in," Greer quickly added. Then the bolt was slid, the door opened, and the two of them stood looking at each other. "But I mean we should celebrate," she said. "You were amazing out there." Lupe had done something today that she had never done in her life: gone onstage and spoken before an audience.

Lupe nodded, unsmiling.

"Is it okay if I come in?"

"Okay." Greer entered the room, which looked barely occupied. A little orange suitcase was splayed open on a table, revealing the small collection of clothes and belongings that had made the trip here from so far away. Greer wanted to tell her to occupy more space, to drape her modest things around the room, to ask for more, and in so doing to become more. But you couldn't make someone be that way, especially after a lifetime of poverty and then a year of trauma. The world had failed her. Now it was turning. Don't be dispirited, Greer wanted to say, but that would have been demanding, not listening.

They ordered dinner from the menu; that was an ordeal. Who knew what Lupe thought she was getting? Then, when it arrived, they ate it while watching a pay-TV movie about the hostile colonization of the Andromeda Galaxy—a plot so removed from both of their real lives that it was an equalizer, neither more nor less comprehensible to either of them.

Greer sensed, at some point, that maybe she was staying too long. Lupe looked sleepy. Would she actually be able to sleep tonight in this strange bed? What did she think of all this? If Greer had been asked, she would have sat in the desk chair and waited for Lupe to fall asleep. She was suddenly so protective of her. They'd been onstage together, and now, somehow, she was hers.

The next morning the two of them flew back to New York together. On the plane, as she had done during the flight to LA, Lupe sat very still and obviously afraid. During a period of turbulence, Greer saw that she was crossing herself repeatedly. On the floor at Lupe's feet was her purse, and protruding from the top was a froth of white wool and two copper needles, the spontaneous gift from that woman in the crowd. Knitting was supposed to calm you down. Greer gestured toward the wool, but Lupe shook her head and just stared miserably at the seat in front of her for most of the trip. She went home to Ecuador a day later.

Greer spent the weekend at Ben's place, where she lay with him on his opened futon, idly playing around on her laptop while he idly played around on his. Sometimes one of them would slam his or her laptop shut, and the other one would follow, the laptops making a decisive sound like two car doors closing, a big part of foreplay these days. On Sunday morning, Ben slept while Greer went through the emails that had collected overnight. As she sifted through them she saw one from Kim Russo, who used to work for the COO at ShraderCapital until she'd left a few months earlier to work for a solar energy company.

> Hi Greer,
> I really wanted to talk to you, in confidence. Any chance we can meet? Kind of important. Thanks—
> Kim Russo

Greer wanted to ask Ben what he thought this was about, but then her instinct was that she shouldn't. She didn't say anything to anyone. The two women met before work the next day in a coffee shop in downtown Brooklyn. At ShraderCapital Kim had dressed in the conservative uniform of the corporate woman, but since she had been at her new job, her clothes were relaxed. But Kim herself was tense; she shook her head at the giant laminated menu as it landed on the table and ordered only black coffee, which she drank in a hard draft.

"Look," Kim said. "We don't know each other well. But you always seemed like you really cared about what you did. It made me wish I worked on twenty-six instead of twenty-seven."

"It's a good place," Greer said mildly, waiting.

"But ShraderCapital was a natural path for me after Wharton. They were very flattering when they hired me." Kim looked down and swirled her cup. "I saw your speech. Someone sent it to me. You were good."

"Thank you."

"I need to say something."

"Okay."

Kim centered the coffee cup between her hands and made sure that Greer was paying attention. "The mentor program in Ecuador is bullshit," Kim said.

Greer waited a second out of politeness, then she said, "I appreciate your opinion. I know there's legitimate criticism of doing things like this overseas. I know it can seem like privileged meddling. But it isn't bullshit. It gives these women a chance."

"That's not what I meant. I meant it's bullshit, as in it doesn't exist."

Greer just looked at her. "Okay, that's just not true," she finally said. The coffee shop hummed and rang with its weekday morning noises. Menus were slapped down, and the glass door kept swinging open. All around them, other, more ordinary conversations over coffee were taking place. There were men with wet, slicked-back shower hair and jackets and ties; women fragrant and blown-out and optimistic and all business; moms with strollers blocking the fire exit.

"It is true," Kim said.

"I highly doubt it."

Kim said, "We can go around and around, but I have to get to work, and I really think you want to know what I have to say. They sent you out onstage in LA with that girl. They sent you there, and they knew it wasn't true. In my world, that's unacceptable."

Greer couldn't take in what Kim was saying, because it didn't make any sense and she didn't know what to do with it. It was as if a dog had brought her a present from the wild: a dead bird, bloodied and grotesque and still warm, which was then deposited at her feet.

"How do you know this?" Greer finally asked.

"I was in on the meetings upstairs, months ago, when they were planning everything."

"But it's ridiculous," said Greer, hearing her own voice fade a little, as if going out of frequency.

"Maybe, but it's true. It really bothered me a lot the way they handled it at the time, but when I left ShraderCapital I stopped thinking about it. Then yesterday I saw the video of you in LA. They let you go out there, Greer, and they trotted that girl out too. They didn't care that it wasn't true."

"Exactly what isn't true?" Greer managed to say. "The whole thing?"

"The rescue was real. The security group apparently went in and saved those girls."

"Well, good. That's a relief."

"But the mentor part never happened. They just pretended it did."

"But why would they do that?"

"There was a fuckup," Kim said. "Their contact in Ecuador."

"Alejandra Sosa."

"No, not her. The next one. I thought you knew."

"Next one? She's the only one we hired. Faith had her looked into. Scrupulously."

Kim shook her head. "She was good. I agree that she would have done the job. But there was a change. The COO's wife knew a woman in the region who she liked; she wanted her to take over the day-to-day operations. So she asked her husband, and he asked Shrader, and Shrader said sure, whatever. So Alejandra Sosa was sidelined, and I'm guessing now that no one told Faith. Anyway, the new person was a disaster. She never found mentors. The building that we'd rented just sat empty. Squatters have been living in it. The COO's wife was mortified when we found out, and everyone just wanted the whole thing to go away, because it stinks. No one wanted to talk about it."

"Can't this person be sued?"

"It's much too late for that. But that's really not the issue. I don't think you understand. As you know, we had all these brochures printed up, soliciting donations to keep the mentor program ongoing. The donations were coming in, and maybe they still are. And once ShraderCapital found out the truth, they didn't shut the fund down and make a public statement and give everyone back their money. They decided that that would be terrible PR. So they just allowed it to keep going, which is, as you can imagine, illegal. And of course Loci's name is all over the brochure."

Greer closed her eyes; it was all she could think to do. She thought of Faith, and Emmett, and a bank account filling with money, and a news story, and all of them on trial for fraud. The mind could go wild on just a moment's notice. Greer felt pressure in her chest, and a medical term swam up to her: *unstable angina*. I'm only twenty-six, Greer thought, though right now that age didn't even sound particularly young.

"But let me ask you something," said Greer. "Lupe Izurieta, who came to LA with me and appeared onstage. What about her? She agreed to read that statement in Spanish about her mentor, who taught her all those skills. Computers. Knitting."

"Right, she agreed," said Kim. "Someone wrote it for her."

"I wrote it," said Greer, shocked. "Faith asked me to."

She thought of how frightened Lupe had been, and she had assumed it was because of having to speak about her trauma publicly. But maybe it was because she'd had to stand up there reading a lie that she'd been told to read. Greer looked at Kim to find some hint of craziness, an image of a disgruntled former employee who wanted to punish the company where she used to work. But Kim was just looking back at her with an unbroken gaze, waiting for her to respond, and then Greer remembered something else. She thought of Lupe on the airplane with the puddle of white wool and the knitting needles sticking out of her bag, untouched. She'd thought, on the plane, that Lupe would want to knit during the flight so she would be less afraid.

Maybe the knitting had remained untouched because she didn't actually know how to knit. Maybe her mentor wasn't a knitter at all, because she wasn't real.

When Greer went into Faith's office half an hour later and flatly asked if they could speak in private, Faith's face took on the particular expression that Greer had seen at different times over the years: empathy and attentiveness. Faith said, "I'm heading out for an appointment at the hair salon. Why don't you meet me there at twelve."

"Okay."

"But don't spread it around. The thing I hate most about going there, above and beyond the obscene amount of money, is the amount of time I have to give over to it. If I added up all the time I've spent in such places, I could probably have traveled the world. Done something much more significant than sitting in a chair being passive and wearing a plastic cape like a superhero of nothing. Anyway, we'll have time to talk. I'm taping a segment for *Screengrab* later, so I have to look decent."

Greer found Faith behind the privacy screen reserved for VIPs in the very back of the Jeremy Ingersoll Salon on Madison Avenue, a long deep room that was filled with flowers; the flowers crowded the place and gave it a strong perfume that fought with the formaldehyde in the Brazilian Blowout formula to create a tropical breeze that somehow, at least for Greer, also invoked death and decomposition. Greer waited nervously while the stylist finished with the foils. They glimmered and dotted Faith's scalp like gum wrappers. The stylist set the timer and left the two women alone.

"So," said Faith, smiling but serious. "We apparently have exactly thirty minutes together. Talk to me, Greer." It was unnerving how different Faith looked in her cape and with her shining head, the scalp hooked up not with electrodes but with a conduit to youth and beauty. Faith seemed to notice the way Greer was taking in her appearance, and she added, "Oh, I know, I look strange. But if you saw how I really look when I go too long between appointments, you'd think it was stranger. Or maybe you've already seen it."

"No, I haven't."

"Well, I have to come here so often that it's kind of like a crack addiction, and Jeremy Ingersoll is my dealer. If I didn't do all this, then I would be very gray, and I'm just not wild about how that looks on me. And I have to feel okay looking in the mirror."

"Of course."

"It isn't cheap, vanity. And it gets more expensive all the time. When I started going gray, I worried that if I let it go, I would look like a sorceress. And that was not what I wanted. I wanted to look like myself, that's all. You'll know what I'm talking about someday. Not for a long time, but you'll know."

She looked directly at Greer in the mirror, and Greer thought about how she had so often craved moments of personal conversation with Faith over the years. Here was another one, and Greer was about to kill it by telling her what Kim Russo had said. She wished, suddenly, that instead of repeating that information, she could say something new from her own life, her own love life. She wished she could blurt out something vulnerable and real.

"So what's going on with you?" Faith asked easily.

Greer looked at her hands, then back at Faith in the mirror. "Here it is. Apparently there's no mentor program in Ecuador," she said. She paused, letting Faith take this in. "There was never a mentor program," Greer went on, "but we said there was, and we took people's money, and we're still taking it. And I went onstage in LA and gushed about mentors and wrote a thing for Lupe to read, but none of it was true. I've been told this by a source, Kim Russo from upstairs, and I believe it."

Faith gaped at her. "You're certain?"

"Yes."

"What about the rescue?" Faith asked, agitated.

"That was real."

"Thank God for that. But really, no mentor program?"

Greer shook her head. She explained what had happened, and why it appeared to be true. Faith didn't say anything at first, but just sat there with her mouth grimly tight, and finally she said, "*Shit.*"

"I know."

"I can't believe ShraderCapital. I mean, I can," Faith said. "They often cut corners. But this one is its own pay grade." Greer felt a chemical swoon of relief. Her anxiety shifted, became something almost a little exciting. Faith hadn't known. Greer hadn't thought there was any way she had known, but still. And more than that, Faith was angry, and Greer was angry along with her. The two of them stewed together, betrayed by the people upstairs. "I've been called gullible, you know," said Faith. "It's a reasonable criticism. To think I could be in business with these people, and that it would never be a problem."

They sat in the shared gloom of their intimacy. But then Faith reached out to brace herself against the counter and swiveled her chair so that she was facing Greer directly, no longer looking at her in the mirror. And then she said, "But I guess I don't understand what you thought you were going to accomplish, rushing in here and telling me this news."

Greer blinked, suddenly flooded and undefended, confused. Her face, naturally, heated up. "Well," she said stiffly, "I thought I was just telling you the truth."

"Fine. So here we are surrounded by the truth."

"You sound like you're angry with me," Greer said. "Don't be angry with me, Faith. It isn't my fault." Faith didn't say anything, but just kept looking at her. "I assume we'll want to do something now," Greer said after a moment.

"There's no next move here, Greer."

"Yes there is. There could be."

"Such as?"

"We could break with ShraderCapital," she tried, though she hadn't thought ahead and was just riffing now. And as she riffed, she was still distracted by the idea that Faith was angry with her. That made no sense. She needed to calm Faith down now, because they had both been wronged, and Faith needed to understand that. Suddenly Greer imagined herself and Faith with two hobo sticks, two bindles, leaving Loci and heading out onto a dark road.

"Break with them. Yes, but that's shortsighted," Faith said. "Where else am I going to get money to spread the word about the plight of women everywhere? Do you want to give me millions of dollars, Greer?"

"No—"

"And it's not like we could join up with anyone else." Faith's voice was picking up speed now. "I've been doing this kind of thing since the year of the flood. I have my ways, and I have my limitations, as everyone will tell you. There are other, newer foundations that have a far more progressive agenda. And I admire them. They are connecting with what's happening right this minute. If you go to most campuses now, you'd better be thoughtful about gender pronouns. I've tried to incorporate as much as I can to stay on top of what's happening out there. And to stay relevant too. But most places just don't have the money we do, so they scrounge around. They're always fighting for equality, doing it the way they're doing it, and I'm doing it the way I'm doing it." She took a breath. "You take what you can get. Doing good and taking money don't go together well. I have known this for all of my adult life. The wheels always need grease."

This was a kind of speech, Greer realized, and once she understood that, it made sense, and she felt that she didn't have to say much except to ask the occasional question, to rebut the occasional point. "But you just accept it?" Greer asked finally.

"No, I do not 'just accept it.' I try to keep an eye on what I can, while being fully aware that I can't keep my eye on everything. The fraudulence of the mentor program in Ecuador disgusts me. And it makes me very angry. But mostly, you know what? Mostly it depresses me. And it reminds me of what you have to do if you're trying to get something done in the world and your cause is women. Because look, if four years ago I'd said no, Emmett, I refuse to touch your money, you know where I'd be right now? Sitting at home learning ikebana."

"I'm sorry, what's ikebana?"

"The Japanese art of flower arranging. That is where I'd be. I would not get to introduce thousands of people to the plight of the Yazidi women of Iraq. I would not be bringing in women who were denied abortions after being raped by their fathers. God, listen to me: I don't even know why I always put in that detail—the fathers. It should be enough just to say women who were denied abortions. That's the point. It's their bodies, their lives, despite what the senator from Indiana will tell you.

"I know the things people say about our foundation. That our tickets cost too much, and that we mostly get wealthy white people to come hear our lectures. 'Rich white ladies,' they say, which is insulting. You know we're always trying to bring in more diverse audiences and bring down costs. But I've had to adjust my expectations about what we do, and I've also had to perform the song and dance that they've been demanding upstairs. The celebrity speakers. The fancy food, which my son makes fun of. And the feminist psychic, Ms. Andromeda, with her ridiculous predictions.

"But in order to get a women's foundation to really take off, Greer—because even the phrase 'women's foundation' makes most people tune out—sometimes you have to throw in a psychic."

"So what's the alternative to leaving?" Greer asked. "We just go back to work and act like this didn't happen?"

Greer thought of Faith in the Ryland Chapel, up at the pulpit, with her dark, curling head of hair and her tall sexy gray boots, and the encouragement that she gave to everyone in that room. And then the special encouragement that she gave afterward to Greer. Faith had helped her and taken an interest in her, and had put her to work, and for a long time the work had felt like it mattered. Once, a year earlier, Beverly Cox, the shoe factory worker who had spoken up about the wage inequality and harassment she and her fellow female employees had endured, had come hurrying up to Greer on a street in midtown in winter and said, "Wait, I know you. You helped me write my first speech." She turned to the other people she was with, all of them visiting from upstate and bundled in thick winter coats, and said, "You remember I told you about her?" Her friends nodded. "I never thought I could speak in front of people," Beverly said to Greer. "I never thought anyone would want to listen. But you did," and she'd hugged her, and her friends had taken photos with their phones. "For posterity," Beverly said, and she gave Greer a handout about a union event she was speaking at up in Oneonta the following week.

Faith had brought Greer toward all of this. Her connection to these women had done something for both her and them. She thought of Lupe, but not with sentimentality, only with pain, and she knew that if they were to see each other on the street, Lupe would not be happy to see her. Perhaps Lupe would say something in Spanish, something that was well beyond Greer's comprehension.

But they would never see each other on the street. There was no street. Lupe was back in Ecuador. What was she doing? What would happen to her? Maybe she was still adrift, lost. Where was she living? What was she actually doing with her days? She would never be part of a women's textile co-op; that much Greer knew.

Now Faith appeared like some foil-headed Martian, talking calmly about staying on at the foundation under the aegis of ShraderCapital, which had had no problem pretending it was overseeing a nonexistent charity on another continent. "Maybe it's not moral to keep working for ShraderCapital," Greer said, actually lifting her chin slightly higher.

"You really think this is just about them?" said Faith. "Don't you think I've had to make compromises before? My whole working life has been about compromise. Even back at *Bloomer.* I didn't have access to real money until Loci, so I'd never seen it on a big scale. But it happens. All the people who work for good causes will tell you this. For every dollar that's donated to women's health in the developing world, for instance, ten cents is pocketed by some corrupt person, and another ten cents no one has any idea what happens to it. Everyone knows, when they start out, that the donation is really only eighty cents. But everyone calls it a dollar because it's what's done."

"And that's acceptable to you?"

Faith took a second. "I always weigh it," she said. "Like with Ecuador. I'm ashamed of what happened. But those young women are free and presumably out of danger. I have to weigh that too, don't I? That's what it's about, this life. The weighing."

Greer hadn't known this about Faith, and she hadn't known that Faith was considered gullible. Because despite working for her, she had never asked Faith much about herself. She hadn't thought she was allowed; she hadn't thought it was her place. She hadn't plaintively asked her, "What's it about, this life?" To which Faith would've answered, "The weighing."

"I still sort of can't believe you're okay with staying at Loci, given what they did upstairs," said Greer.

"Well, I'm seventy-one years old and I take Fosamax for bone density—or lack of it—and I have a stiff neck half the time despite my addiction to cheap Chinese massages, or maybe because of it. I may need to scale back, but I'm not going to start over. The reason I asked you to give that speech is that I was exhausted. I need to be protective of myself, not run around like I used to do when I was your age." Quickly, Faith added, "But that's not the only reason I asked you. You deserved it. You needed something big. Something real, that would remind you of why you wanted to work here to begin with." She paused. "And you came through." Greer felt a familiar prickle of gratification that could arise so easily in the presence of Faith Frank. "But I am genuinely sorry you went up onstage in LA, now that I know the circumstances," Faith said.

"You say you can't go anywhere new, but there might be a better situation," said Greer.

Faith tipped her head down slightly, and her scalp was revealed in a series of crazy, broken pink lightning bolts. The foils made the faintest sound, like tinsel. "No," she said. "I told you, there isn't. And even if there is, I'm not going to start looking. It's my choice," she added. "And *I get to decide.*" She said this with equal emphasis on each word, as if reciting a line from something, but Greer had no idea what.

"Well, I have to believe in what I'm doing," Greer said.

"And I hope you'll keep believing. Now that you've told me what you've learned, you can help me keep a tighter leash on them upstairs. I could use a partner in that." Faith paused, looking at her fully. "Will you be that?"

Greer had the unrelated thought that if there were a fire in this salon right now, Faith Frank would have to run out into the street with all the other women, and everyone would see her looking like this, and they would all be so confused. Faith Frank, famous, glamorous feminist, is apparently as gray-haired and fragile and bony as anyone, and as mortal, and as compromised.

Faith's assistant Deena Mayhew appeared then, coming around the bend into the screened-off area. "Here you are," she said. "You almost done?"

Faith, suddenly cool and regular, as if she and Greer had been discussing nothing of consequence, squinted at the timer. "I can't read that without my reading glasses, sadly. Greer, can you?"

"Seventeen minutes," Greer said dully.

"Okay, good," said Deena. "Then we get you back to the office, Faith, and Bonnie preps you for the taping."

Right, Greer remembered, Faith was going on *Screengrab* later.

"There are several talking points from the pre-interview," said

Deena. "And it's such great exposure at this moment, because of the mentor program." She smiled at Greer and added, "I'm still hearing such good things about LA."

Greer looked across at Faith. "You're talking about Ecuador later on *Screengrab*?"

"Possibly. Among other topics."

"I brought the bullet points if you want to have a look," said Deena. Then, again to Greer, "Sorry, but can I just borrow her for a minute? Tight quarters! Give us a few, then we'll all head back to the office."

Greer stepped to the side, allowing Deena to move closer to Faith, and together the two of them looked over a file, Faith squinting and murmuring, and Deena gesturing with animation. Greer stayed back, leaning against the counter where combs hung in a bottle of blue water, suspended and preserved like specimens. She imagined picking up the heavy jar with both hands and hurling it at the wall.

When it was time for Faith to get rinsed and shampooed and dried, Greer stood stiffly while Deena spoke into her phone, letting the voice-recognition function spit out its errors that would need to be manually corrected. "Look at this," Deena said to Greer, holding up her phone and showing her a comical mistake. "The phrase I actually said was 'fat shaming,' which was translated as 'Fetch, Amy!'" Finally Faith returned to them, exquisite. Her hair gleamed, her boots made her tall, and the three of them strode out through the Jeremy Ingersoll Salon, past the row of other clients, all rich, all women, though none in need of a VIP screen.

Women, women, women, all of them sitting patiently in their vulnerability and vanity, sitting there as women did. Because even though you might care about the plight of women in the world, you still wanted to look like yourself, as Faith had said.

Out on the street two people walking together immediately recognized her, and Faith smiled at them as she always did. She hadn't changed. Apparently it had always been about the weighing.

The office was buzzy when they returned, and Faith went on ahead while Greer hung back. She couldn't sit down at her desk; she couldn't go into the kitchen and get coffee and chat with people. There was nothing for her to do or say now. She just lurked. Ben, seeing her, came over and said, "Hey, where'd you go? I heard you were meeting with Faith outside the office. Planning a surprise party for me, I guess."

"I don't even know your birthday," she said. This was true. She didn't know his birthday, though they had worked together for more than four years. Surely she had known it at some point; there must have been cupcakes every year, or at least some years. But Ben hadn't resonated in such a way that she needed to know, or thought to know, the day of his birth.

"You seem weird," he said, but she didn't reply. Up ahead, Faith was heading into her office. Greer followed, and behind her she could hear Ben say to one of the new staff, "Is something up? Do you know what's going on?"

Greer sleepwalked to Faith's door and knocked on the frame, though the door was never closed; the office was like a patient's room in a hospital. If you needed access, you could have it. Already there was a cluster of people in the office. Faith, Iffat, Kara, Bonnie, Evelyn, Deena, and a young assistant named Casey, a recent hire. Greer in the doorway, her voice strangled, said, "Faith, can I talk to you?" Faith looked up and nodded and lifted her arm and waved her fingers to bring Greer over. Then everyone politely dispersed, going elsewhere in the large room to continue their conversations about whatever summit or mini-summit or idea for a speaker needed to be discussed.

"You're really going on TV and discussing the mentor program?" she quietly asked Faith at the desk.

"Well, it was in the pre-interview. Mitch Michaelson might ask me about it."

"You could cancel." Greer looked around, making sure no one was listening. They weren't.

"That would be unprofessional," said Faith. "And there are other things I want to talk about and call attention to. It's a good opportunity. We need press; we always do. You know that."

"But it's not just about getting press," Greer said, even more quietly. "Come on, we do the work we do whether we get attention for it or not. We do it for women. You've always made a point of this." Greer paused, picked at something on her sleeve, looked back up. "I didn't understand, in the beginning, what we were doing here," she said. "I just knew I wanted to do it. I gravitated toward working here. Toward working for you," she added, her voice thickening. "But then it wasn't just about you. It was about them. It's still about them." She was shaky, thinking that this sounded like a speech, and she hadn't meant to give a speech, especially one that she hadn't written down. Speeches needed to be crafted, edited, revised; this one wasn't. "And now this place where we work, it isn't for me anymore. So I can't do it."

"What can't you do?"

"Stay at Loci. I can't, Faith. It's not right." Faith still didn't say anything, so Greer said, formally, "Okay, I'm going to go now."

Faith was looking at her, taking her time. Greer thought, I am not going to wait or get her permission to go. I'm just going to go. But she stopped, briefly, picturing her cubicle with all the photos and cartoons she had tacked up above her desk. Over time they had curled and faded. Having quit, she would have to go and untack them one by one now, leaving behind a Morse code of tiny holes for the next person, signifying nothing. Greer had an unexpected image of Cory giving up everything in his life, just walking away from Armitage & Rist and all that had been carefully planned out for him.

Greer saw that everyone in the room was finally paying attention. They had stopped their conversations and were looking up, aware of the change around Faith's desk. Even looking at Faith they could see it beneath the surface of her face, like underground fasciculation from some neurological storm. A storm was gathering. Oh shit, a storm was gathering in Faith Frank.

"Well, all right then," said Faith as everyone watched. "I guess that's it."

"I guess it is."

Greer experienced one of those bile squirts in the back of her throat, and she swallowed it down. It was as if her voice alone had quit her job, her voice had stepped up and made the executive decision and done all the speaking, while the rest of her had simply listened and watched. Was this what it meant to have a voice that wasn't always an inside voice? It came out of you as if through your own personal loudspeaker. She wondered where the reward was for speaking up, where the catharsis was. Right now she just felt sick.

She had only made it to the door when Faith said, "It's actually kind of funny, in a way."

Greer turned around. "What is?"

"You make it sound like you care too much about what you do to stay here. That you care too much about women. About sticking up for them. Yet look at what you did all those years ago. To your best friend. I can't remember her name."

"What are you talking about?" Greer asked, though she didn't really want to know.

"Your friend wanted to work here," Faith said. "She gave you a letter to give me, and one night over drinks you told me about it, and you said that you didn't want her to work here, right? So you never gave me the letter, and you lied to her and told her you did, didn't you? And I suppose you were fine with that."

Fainting was a real possibility, Greer thought. She looked around helplessly; everyone in the room seemed scandalized but distant. No one could help her. Faith wasn't wrong about what Greer had done to Zee; hearing it spoken aloud was terrible, and the act she described was inexcusable. But it was just so unfair, she thought, just so unnecessarily mean of Faith to say it, and yet she also thought that maybe there was always going to have been a moment like this one at the end, at least if Greer was ever going to be able to go off and do something on her own instead of being a perennial extra-credit-doer, a handmaiden, a good girl who thought that what she had for herself was enough. Good girls could go far, but they could rarely go the distance. They could rarely be *great*. Maybe Faith was giving this confrontation to her as a gift. But probably not. Faith's anger had fastened itself on her at last; it had taken a long, long time, but here it was. Maybe Faith had a right to be angry. Greer was leaving her to deal with ShraderCapital on her own; Greer was saying to her: *You* deal with it, I can't. And also, Greer was implicitly criticizing Faith for knowing what she knew and staying.

"What did you do with it, Greer?" Faith asked. "Did you throw that letter out? Did you read it? In any case, you decided not to give it to me, and not to tell the truth. Not a great move, I don't think."

Greer wasn't going to faint. Instead, she ran.

PART FOUR

Outside Voices

TEN

When she first became interested in trauma, Zee Eisenstat had taken a course called Assessing the Nature of Emergency, and as the instructor described various scenarios, Zee filled her notebook with the hard scrawl of disaster. Everything she learned in that course, and much of what she went on to learn later at her job, was about the acute, terrible moments in other people's lives. She was a crisis response counselor in Chicago, and had been working in the field since leaving Teach and Reach three and a half years earlier. First she'd gotten a degree in counseling, but even while she was in school she'd immediately been put to work. The worse the crisis, the more she could focus, somehow; Zee didn't buckle or back away, like some people did at first.

Her work took her around the city. She would quietly appear at the door of people's homes after something shocking had happened: a person had died by suicide; there had been a hostage situation; someone had had a sudden bout of psychosis. She was known to be uncommonly skilled at what she did: light-footed, unobtrusive, deeply useful. Once in a while, weeks or months after a trauma, she would hear from families. "You were like my own personal saint," one man wrote her. "I didn't know who you were, only that you suddenly showed up." Another man wrote to say, "I sell snow tires, and I would like to give you a complimentary set." Zee had become highly valued in the trauma community, and, as she'd proudly told Greer, she had been cited in the *International Journal of Traumatology.* "I know that doesn't sound like a real journal, but it is." That night, Greer had had a vegan cake delivered to Zee's door in Chicago.

In fact Zee had received her certificate in traumatology, having completed several internships in the prosaic trenches of a social-service agency. The birth of her student Shara Pick's baby had been the first trauma she had witnessed; Shara had dropped away, had never returned to school, and was apparently raising her child with her grandmother and her sisters. Repeated calls to her had gone unanswered. But the experience of that trauma still lived sharply in Zee, and she was drawn back to find other such experiences and offer help of some kind. Apparently they were everywhere, different kinds of them, all over the South Side and beyond. You did not subspecialize, at least not in the certificate-granting program in which Zee enrolled, and which the Judges Eisenstat had kindly agreed to pay for. You had to be a generalist when it came to terribleness.

The first case Zee was called in for during her training involved a nail bomb that had been sent in the mail to the New Approach Women's Clinic, and which had detonated in the waiting room, blinding the temp receptionist, Barbara Vang. The late-day crowd had been sitting and waiting for their Pap smears, their very first pelvic exams, their abortions, their pregnancy tests. The package bomb was opened without much interest by the temp, her fingernail slipping under the edge of the Scotch tape that heavily crisscrossed the surface as she set up a phone appointment for a man who had felt a pea-sized lump below his nipple. Would the clinic see him, though he was a guy? Yes, she said, they would. She pulled the tape and her hands opened the paper, and the afternoon waiting-room quiet was shockingly breached. When the crisis response counselors were hauled in, Zee was among them.

Her two leaders were Lourdes and Steve, older but not old, because probably not a lot of people could last into old age in trauma work. Both of them, she noted as they made for themselves and some of the witnesses a little yurt in the alley beside the clinic, possessed a composed and impressive calm.

Lourdes and Steve practiced a kind of listening that involved much more than simply paying attention with tilted head. Over time Zee would learn to do it too, but on that first day, in the ad hoc yurt with the weeping women who had been right there when Barbara Vang opened the package that exploded in her face, Zee just sat shallowly and respectfully listening, watching how her supervisors tried to ease traumatized people into a state in which they could bear to live. "We need to give them the equivalent of swaddling," Lourdes had said. "We never increase their stress. We let them tell us how to treat them."

Since then, there had been many improvised yurts, a whole tent city of trauma stations all over various parts of Chicago. By now Zee was a legitimate expert, and she ran her own trauma team and taught workshops for volunteers. She was doing an additional certificate program in a new post-traumatic stress method that involved guided imagery and special breathing. What made it manageable was that the traumas that filled her daily life were not her own, and so they were removed and at least a little distant.

But then Greer called. "I quit my job," she said in a shaky voice, which was startling in and of itself, because to Greer,

Faith Frank could do no wrong. But then, in tears, Greer went on to say, "It ended badly with Faith. A lot of shit went down."

"Wow. What happened?"

"I'll tell you when I see you. It's complicated." There was a sound of nose-blowing. "For a long time I thought I was doing something real and honest there. And you know it got semi-bullshitty, and that there was less for me to do that I cared about, but still I tried. And she gave me that speech to deliver, and it went so well, Zee, and I was so excited; it was one of those defining moments we've talked about. But it turns out it was something else. ShraderCapital did something wrong, and Faith is okay with looking the other way; business as usual. I even ate her *meat*," she added. "Repeatedly."

"What do you mean, you ate her meat?"

"Forget it, nothing."

"So what will you do now?" Zee asked.

"I have no idea."

"Come to Chicago." Zee couldn't remember offhand what the weekend held; whatever it was, she would try to move things around, to ask one of her colleagues to fill in for her. Her job required so much flexibility, because people's emergencies did not happen according to any particular schedule.

Over the years at work, Zee had gotten her reorientation time down to practically nothing. These days she could answer a phone in the middle of sleep and sound perky. She could drive a car dripping wet from a shower. Sometimes she was awakened at dawn and had to get on the train while the sky was rosy with optimism, in order to head out to the scene of a homicide or suicide, a fire, a moment of unparalleled bleakness or chaos. Other times she drove to her job in the middle of the night, and was so hungry when she left that she would try to find one of those places where cops gathered on breaks, and there she would sit among men and women in uniform, ordering eggs and home fries and butter-soaked toast—hoping this would somehow shore her up after what she'd just seen.

She and Noelle lived in an apartment off Clark Street in Andersonville, which had a pretty significant lesbian population. Noelle had stayed on at the school in the Learning Octagon™ network despite the many problems, and she was now principal, a terrifying figure to some of the students, but still a figure of resplendence to Zee. In Andersonville, a place where she and Noelle could sometimes walk around holding hands, she thought about how furtive she often felt most other places. It was as though she had folded the furtiveness into her entire self.

Over time she had begun to describe herself in a matter-of-fact way as queer instead of gay. Queer felt stronger, queerer, its difference front and center. For Zee, *lesbian* had gone the way of the cassette tape. She'd always said she was political, but looking back on it, she felt it had been an avocation; now her work life was political in some deep and consistent way, she thought, because she entered the homes of struggling people, and saw what their lives were like. The windows and bulletin boards of cafés and stores in this neighborhood were thick with volunteering signage. Zee gave hours to a group that was involved with homeless youth. And they always needed help at the HIV groups, and also a group that was organizing around racial justice. Someone Zee knew always wanted her to come to meetings in a church basement.

Zee did not want to spend her free time in a church basement. At first she pictured the low ceilings and the long tables with bottles of Apple & Eve apple juice. She saw folding chairs, and even heard the scrape of chair foot on linoleum, and the creak as more chairs were opened, and then someone said, "Make room, make room," and the circle widened. But she came to like some of the meetings, and she started to run others. Noelle went sometimes too, though often she said no, exhausted at the end of a workday, feet up, more work to do.

Right now, when Zee got off the phone with Greer, Noelle was on the sofa composing her weekly letter to parents and guardians. "So listen," Zee said. "Greer is coming here tomorrow. She's going to stay with us. I assume that's okay, despite not giving you any warning."

When Greer rang the bell in the early afternoon the next day, having taken an Uber from O'Hare, Zee was ready for her in the way she was always ready at work. She was prepared for the emergency that was happening to her closest friend. She sat Greer down on the couch and put a glass of very cold water in her hand, because hydration was surprisingly helpful, one of her instructors had said, and water was free, and ubiquitous. It couldn't put out anyone's fire, but it could make the person remember: I am part of the real world, a person holding a glass. I haven't lost that ability. Sometimes Zee would watch the person lift the glass and drink, and she was relieved to watch the hand move, the segments of the throat move, to see the way the body participated, even now.

Greer drank gratefully, and when she was done she looked up. "Thanks for pushing me to come here," she said. "I really didn't expect to suddenly be unemployed."

"All right," said Zee. "Talk to me."

So Greer told her a long and convoluted story about young women in Ecuador; about a successful rescue, and a botched post-rescue. But when she was done talking she didn't look any more relieved. She was actually wringing her hands, Zee saw. Always, with clients, Zee looked at the hands; were they in fists, were they in prayer formation, or were they in this kind of desperation?

"And there's something else," said Greer.

"Okay."

Greer took in a ragged breath and then stood up in front of Zee as if about to do a little presentation. "I wasn't going to say this, ever," she said, "but now I guess I am. Now I guess I have to." She closed her eyes, then opened them again. "I never gave Faith the letter."

"What are you talking about? What letter?"

Greer looked down at the floor and her mouth twisted up strangely, in the stroke face of the about-to-cry. "*Your* letter," Greer said, and then she stopped there, as though it would be so obvious what she meant.

"What?"

"Your *letter*," Greer tried again with agitation now, and a little sob. Then she thrust out her hands, as if that would clarify it. "The one you gave me like four years ago to give to Faith, when you wanted a job there too. I still have it. I haven't opened it or anything. But I have it. I never gave it to her."

Zee just kept looking at her. She let the silence expand, trying to work out what this actually meant. "I'm confused," Zee said. "Because you told me you gave it to her, back then, and that she said there were no jobs."

"I know. Zee, I lied to you."

Zee let this moment bloom its shitty little bloom. Whenever she found out something shocking or even disappointing about someone she cared about, she was taken by surprise. She thought about her clients, and how surprised they always were by behaviors in the people they loved, which, from the outside, might not have seemed surprising. A depressed husband took his own life. A grandmother collapsed. A daughter who had been agitated had a psychotic episode. Zee's clients were more than surprised by all of this; they were shocked to the point of trauma.

Today, Greer had come to Chicago in her own kind of shock. She had been an acolyte of Faith's, but had been startled by Faith's betrayal. It hadn't ever been even between Greer and Faith, and never could be.

But maybe it wasn't entirely even between Greer and Zee either. Greer had made it uneven, and now they too needed a correction. What was astonishing was that Greer and Zee, unlike Greer and Faith, had had an actual friendship. It had been real, but look at that, Greer had secretly fucked Zee over anyway.

Zee might actually have had a chance to work for Faith back in the beginning, to help push the foundation forward. It was possible that Faith would've said yes after reading her letter. "I know it was horrible," Greer was saying. "I mean, I'm sure it doesn't make it better to say that you wouldn't even have *liked* working there, but it's true. In the beginning it was good, but then you know it got so impersonal, and I stopped getting to meet the women whose lives we were trying to help. It was like we were just pouring money into a speakers' bureau and that was it. And I literally had the thought, several times: Zee would hate this. In your work you're actually there on the ground. And we're just at arm's length too much of the time. I remind myself of this sometimes, as though it somehow makes it better that I did what I did to you. But I know it doesn't make it better. It was horrible of me," she repeated.

"Yeah, it was," said Zee in a quiet, contained little voice. Maybe Greer was right, and she would have hated it there. But what did it matter? The thing that mattered was that Greer had kept her from being there, which was so peculiar, so hurtful, and made everything between them appear strange and different now. "But why would you do that?" Zee asked. "I was the one to talk to you about her. I was the one who basically led you into everything. You had barely even heard of Faith Frank."

"It was . . . about my parents, I think," Greer said. "About wanting someone to see something in me."

"*I* saw something in you. And Cory did too."

"I know. This was different." Greer looked down; she couldn't even seem to make eye contact with Zee, and maybe that was just as well. They needed a rest from looking so hard at each other. All Zee did all day was look hard at people. Her eyes were tired from all that looking, studying, empathizing with, scrutinizing; all that helping, helping, helping.

Now Greer was ashamed, so let her be ashamed, Zee thought. Greer had actually done a thing to her, a real thing.

Zee had gotten over her disappointment four years earlier and gone on to have a life that Faith would approve of; she was sure of that. Working one-on-one with people, instead of with roomfuls of them. She did emergency work that mattered, often involving issues that concerned women. But as the truth of what Greer had done became familiar information now, Zee felt as if the long affection that she had felt for Greer since college was made thin and wan. She felt exhausted, and was sorry that she'd invited Greer here for the weekend. Were they going to discuss the letter, and what Greer had done to Zee, again and again?

Greer came forward on the couch and took Zee's wrists like a desperate suitor. "Zee," she said. "I'm the worst person, I know I am." Zee stayed furiously silent. "Apparently I never knew that I'm one of those women who hates women, like you always say. I confessed to Faith about your letter back in the beginning. She reacted like it wasn't a big deal! But yesterday when I quit my job, she was hurt and angry, and out of the blue she brought it up in front of everyone. She *busted* me. Said I was a bad friend. A bad feminist. A bad woman. And I guess she's right. I didn't want to share her, I didn't want to let you in. I am the *cuntiest* woman, Zee. I am a *cunt*," Greer said fiercely. "I seriously am."

Zee was still shocked and a little lightheaded, but she also felt tight and ungiving. She was probably supposed to say no, no, Greer, you aren't any of those things. You made a stupid mistake. Women sometimes do really bad things to each other, just like men do, and just like men and women do to each other too. But she didn't know if she felt this way, and anyway she didn't want to comfort Greer; she didn't want to direct her trauma training at her when she could have been directing it all day today at other people who needed it. Zee imagined telling Noelle everything tonight in bed while Greer lay on the opened sleeper sofa in the living room. "You won't believe what Greer confessed to me," she would whisper. And Noelle would of course be furious on her behalf.

"It was a really selfish thing you did," Zee finally said to Greer now. Greer nodded vigorously, relieved. "You could have just told me you weren't comfortable with me working there. You could have said that to me."

"I know."

"And you know that I have a history of being betrayed by women, right?" said Zee. "Starting with that law clerk of my mom's who outed me, remember?"

"Yes," Greer said in a trembling little voice.

"And now you've done it too."

Greer looked so terrible, all shiny and messy and horrified. A good friend would say yes, yes, I forgive you, and the two women could embrace in the way that women did. Women, who could be so easy with each other. Women, who were physical and loved each other, even when they were not lovers and never would be. There had always been an agreement, unsaid but binding, that the two friends would look out for each other. On the stupid reality TV show that Zee and Noelle sometimes watched—the one where the rich women from different gated communities spent a year living together in a Conestoga wagon—whenever the women weren't fighting and clawing at one another, they said to one another, "I've got your back." Even *those* women, those ludicrous women pumped with collagen and money, had one another's backs, but Greer didn't have hers.

Zee moved away to the far end of the couch, experiencing her own small trauma. "When Faith showed more interest in you in the ladies' room, I felt a pang," Zee said. "I did! Because I'd been this little activist before college, and you were basically home reading books and having sex with your boyfriend. Which is fine; it's just different. But I wanted to help you. You'd had this bad experience at that frat party. And you were shy. But the meek shall inherit the earth, right? For someone who was always so shy, Greer, and who couldn't ask for what she needed, in fact you've asked for everything you needed. You basically went in and got what you wanted, and made yourself *known*. You raised your hand that night in the Ryland Chapel. You raised it faster than me, and you got your question answered. And then you called Faith on the phone, and finally got a job with her. And you even gave her a frying pan. That took chutzpah. And, of course, you kept my letter from her. These are not classic shy-person actions, Greer, I'm just saying. They're something else. Sneaky, maybe." Coldly, Zee added, "You really know how to act in the face of power. I've never put that together before, but it's true." She stopped and looked straight at Greer. "You know, I didn't need to work at your foundation," she said. "I found what I like to do. You went to work for Faith Frank, the role model, the feminist, and I didn't. But you know what? I think there are two kinds of feminists. The famous ones, and everyone else. Everyone else, all the people who just quietly go and do what they're supposed to do, and don't get a lot of credit for it, and don't have someone out there every day telling them they're doing an awesome job.

"I don't have a mentor, Greer, and I've never had one. But I've had different women in my life who I like to be around, and who seem to like me. I don't need their approval. I don't need their permission. Maybe I should've had a little more of this; it might have helped. But I didn't, and well, okay, fine, you're right, I'm sure I would've hated it there, and I don't think I would have stayed very long. But I would've liked the chance to find out."

"I'm so sorry," said Greer.

"You want to know how often I think about the fact that I didn't get to work for Faith Frank? Almost never."

"Really?" Greer seemed impossibly grateful to hear this.

"Yes."

"Will you forgive me?" Greer asked.

"I need time," Zee said.

ELEVEN

She wasn't sure why she decided to call home late that night while waiting for the plane in Chicago. But it was just too lonely to sit there in O'Hare with CNN blabbing overhead, waiting another long hour for the flight. Her mother answered. "Are you all right?" Laurel said after the flat swap of hellos.

"Why are you asking?"

"Something in your voice."

"Actually, not really," Greer said. "I'm in the airport in Chicago. I was supposed to stay over with Zee but I'm not. I'm flying to New York tonight, but then I don't know what I'm going to do." Her voice split.

"Come home," her mother said.

The Macopee Public Library was quiet, and though a library was supposed to be quiet, this one had the feel of a failing restaurant that would soon go out of business. It was dim there in the light of day, and a high school girl drowsed at the checkout desk, her services not really needed. But in the back was a room called the Emmanuel Gilland Children's Room—whoever Emmanuel Gilland had been. It was the place where Greer had found *A Wrinkle in Time* as a girl, and had sat at a blond-wood table absorbed in its fully realized world. Scattered nearby were a couple of vinyl beanbag chairs leaking synthetic beans. On this day when Greer, lost and uprooted, entered the room behind her mother, who was in full clown regalia—the nose and wig and dotted outfit and size 90 shoes—she could hear sounds of children and parents who were already there waiting for the show.

Greer had been in breath-holding mode; her mother had asked her there today because the show happened to be right in town. And Greer, who didn't even understand why she'd said okay when her mother told her to come home for a few days of recovery—home to the place that had been such a lousy home much of the time—had also said okay, agreeing to sit and watch Laurel perform as a library clown. But she felt uneasy about it, worrying that her mother would look failed.

The children arrayed themselves on the carpet and Greer sat in the corner on one of the beanbag chairs, which held her insecurely. In the dancing-mote light from the tall windows, Laurel jumped into place before her audience and said, "Good afternoon, ladies and germs." Greer looked away as quickly as she could, letting the cornball joke roll past in the air, just another tumbling dust mote. But amazingly, there was laughter.

"You said *germs*, clown!" cried a boy no older than four. "Didn't you mean *gentlemen*?"

"That's what I said!" cried Laurel. "Ladies and germs!"

"YOU SAID IT AGAIN!" the boy screamed, and now others piped in too, all of them shouting at Greer's clown mother, who wore an innocent expression, and who was rising to the occasion in a way that was unfamiliar to Greer.

But it wasn't just that Laurel was apparently a good performer. After the show ended—a well-paced hour that used water squirts and expanding wands and deliberately ham-handed juggling and even a pratfall on the carpet, and then, finally, a "reading" from a wordless picture book called *The Farmer and the Clown*— the children stayed to meet the library clown. Greer watched as her mother took a boy and girl on her lap at the same time.

"I would like to be a clown when I grow up," said the girl.

"I would too," said the boy dreamily, throwing his head back and closing his eyes. "I'll be called . . . Clowny the Clown."

How was it, really, that Greer had never known that children liked her mother's act? That they looked up to the library clown, and that she meant something to them? Greer felt only remorse now; it choked and overtook her.

"Mom, you were great," she said when they got back into the car on the street outside. "I had no idea what your act was like."

"Well, now you do," her mother said cautiously, putting the key in the ignition and starting the car. "No harm, no foul."

"No, but really, it was excellent," Greer said. Plaintively, in the gray afternoon, she asked, "Why didn't I know that?"

"What, that I could juggle? Or use a squirt bottle?"

"No, not that." And then, feeling brutally sorry for herself, she asked, "How come you never did your act for me when I was little?"

Her mother turned off the engine. Her nose and wig and outfit were stuffed in a bag on the backseat; only the collar re- mained, half in view under the top of her coat. "I didn't think you'd like it," she finally said. "You were quiet but so serious." She stopped.

"Go on," Greer said.

"Dad and I always felt we should stand back and let you do what you did. And that was even more true when you got together with Cory." His name was shocking spoken here without warning. "I used to think of you as twin rocket ships," Laurel said. "Remember that?"

Greer did. She didn't want to talk about Cory with her mother. So she said, "Why didn't you and Dad ever find something you really wanted to do? Something you could throw yourselves into?"

Laurel got quiet, her mouth a little wavy. "Some people never do. I don't really know why." She looked away. "We never had an easy time. We both had a way of retreating. Though we did do some things. And we did have you. That's not nothing." Then her expression changed, and she asked, "What happened down in New York, darling?"

In the passenger seat beside her mother Greer choked out the story about the fake mentor program in Ecuador, and about Loci, and Faith. "I had to leave. I couldn't stay. I don't know; was I being too pure? When I told her I was leaving, she just turned on me, Mom, I couldn't believe it. It was humiliating. I was so destroyed."

"No you weren't. And you're *not*. But that must have been very upsetting; I can see that."

"She was upset too. We both were." Greer shook her head. "What am I supposed to do now?" Greer asked. "Mom, I've quit my job."

Her mother looked at her. "Do you have to know what to do immediately?"

"Well, no."

"Don't you have some money saved up?" Laurel asked, and Greer nodded. "Then take a little time. Go slowly."

"But I hate that," Greer said.

"What? Going slowly? Why, what's the rush?"

"I don't know," said Greer. "It's not the way I'm built."

"What, you're afraid that if you go slow you're going to become like Dad and me?"

"I didn't say that."

"I know you didn't. But you'll never be us; that's not going to happen. And you don't always have to feel the compulsion to keep striving toward something for the sake of striving. No one will think less of you. There are no grades anymore, Greer. Sometimes I think you forget that. There are never going to be grades for the rest of your life, so you just have to do what you want to do. Forget about how it looks. Think about what it *is*."

Greer nodded again. "And take a little time doing *what* now? I don't have anything."

"That's just it," said Laurel. "Who knows? You don't have to know yet. Can't you just wait and see?"

They were silent for a while, and then Greer blurted out, "But it isn't just what happened down in New York. It's also Zee. I betrayed her."

"What?"

"I don't know why I did what I did. And I don't know how to undo it." At that point she began to sob.

Laurel fiddled with the sticking lock on the glove compartment, got it open, and pulled out a flattened packet of tissues. "Take one," she said. Greer blew her nose endlessly, until it was probably as red as a clown's. "You will work on this," said Laurel. "You work so hard on everything."

They drove home from the library in a state of quiet recovery, and as they pulled up in front of the house and Laurel leaned down over the backseat to get her bag, Greer saw Cory through the car window. He was letting himself out of the front door of his house. She had known she would see him while she was here; it was just a matter of when.

The sight of him always shocked her and broke her down a little each time she visited: that he was right there, but not connected to her anymore. That they were growing older separately, now in their mid-twenties, this period of peak hope, which wouldn't last that long. He had been changing physically, gradually; the longer the time passed between visits, the more obvious it became. He was still handsome but entirely grown, and he looked to her now like a young suburban dad. Skinny as always, neatly and plainly dressed in a down vest and jeans. It was startling how Cory had fully inhabited the life he led here and didn't look anymore like someone pretending.

Her mother got out of the car, waved to him, and then went inside. Greer went over to him and they hugged in that only upper-body way they'd done since the breakup. His hair was slightly longer than she remembered. That's new, she wanted to say, but maybe it wasn't new; maybe his hair had been long for some time.

"You want to go somewhere?" she thought to ask, and he looked hesitant but then said okay, just for a little while, he had to be somewhere; and so they walked to Pie Land. Kristin Vells no longer worked there, or at least wasn't working there now. Over pizza and plastic cups of soda Cory asked her, "So what's the deal with your being here? Traveling for work?"

"No."

He looked more closely at her, tilting his head the way he used to do on Skype. "You okay?"

"Not really. I quit my job."

"Oh, wow," he said. "You want to say more?"

"No. Thanks, though." It would have been such a relief to tell him, a relief to feel the information passing from her to him, planted in his brain, where he would think about it too. "Tell me what's going on with you," she said.

"Deflection. You do it so deftly."

"I try."

"Okay," Cory said. "Some things are new with me. I've been working at Valley Tek, the computer store in Northampton."

"Do you like it there?"

"I do, yeah. And I'm still cleaning houses."

"Ah."

"You'd be amazed at how filthy people are. I mean, *amazed*. They shed their skin, and the floor of everyone's house is basically like the floor of a forest. Flakes. Droppings. I know, that's a lovely image. But it's interesting. And Valley Tek is interesting too. Every day is sort of like, what particular weird problem will someone bring in today? And some of us get together after work and play video games." Then he added, self-consciously, "I've actually been writing a game myself. A guy at work was encouraging me to do it so we could develop it together. He's a programmer."

"Really? What is it?"

He took a second. "It's called SoulFinder. Sort of a corny name, but I'm not great with names. What it is, is you try to find the person you've lost. But I can't describe it well. It's not ready for human consumption yet. I don't know if it ever will be, but I like to think it will."

"I hope it will. How's your mom?" she asked finally, needing to find something to say. "What's going on with her?"

"She's okay," he said. "I mean, she takes her medication when she's supposed to, which is really good. For a while there she wasn't compliant, and that was hard. But it's kind of calm in the house these days, actually."

"You think you're here for the long run?" Greer asked lightly.

"If this isn't the long run, I don't know what is."

Greer knew that it was. Your twenties were a time when you still felt young, but the groundwork was being laid in a serious way, crisscrossing beneath the surface. It was being laid even while you slept. What you did, where you lived, who you loved, all of it was like pieces of track being put down in the middle of the night by stealth workers. Until a few days earlier, Greer had had a crowded life that she believed in and was frustrated by. Cory in his twenties was someone who had come to the rescue of his broken mother and stayed.

"If you ever get down to the city," she said casually when they stood to go, "you could stay with me in Brooklyn. I have a sleeper sofa."

"Thanks," he said. "That's nice of you. I might get there."

"Okay. I'll see you when you do," she said. She wanted to say to him: Once we were twin rocket ships.

They walked back to their street and stood in the neutral zone between their houses. "How's Slowy?" Greer suddenly asked.

"Oh, he's good. Well, I mean, I don't really *know* if he's good. There's no way to know. But anyway, he's basically the same."

A few days later, on her last night there, when Greer and her parents found themselves in the kitchen at the same time, getting ready for dinner—they had eaten together each night, her parents seeming to understand that Greer wouldn't want to eat alone now—her father said, "You saw Cory? Anything new with him?"

"He works at the computer store in Northampton," Greer said. "And he's inventing a computer game or something. But mostly, you know, he still lives here with his mother. He even still cleans a couple of the houses she used to clean. So, I guess that's what he's up to. Not that much."

"Greer," said Laurel, "what are we supposed to do, shake our heads and say that he's accomplished nothing?"

"No. Of course not." But she burned at being called out now.

"It seems to me," said her mother, "and this is really outside my sphere of knowledge, since I'm not the one who's been working at a feminist foundation. But here's this person who gave up his plans when his family fell apart. He moves back in with his mother and takes care of her. Oh, and he cleans his own house, and the ones she used to clean. I don't know. But I feel like Cory is kind of a big feminist, right?"

TWELVE

When Faith Frank emailed Emmett Shrader to invite him to her apartment, he thought about replying with a joke about how it had been forty-one years since he'd last been to her place, and that he thought she'd never ask. But somehow he knew from the terseness, even coldness, of her email that there was something wrong. She had to speak to him, and she wanted to do it out of the office. Even more peculiarly, this was to be arranged without the help of Connie and Deena, the usual gatekeepers. Though people always came to Emmett and never the other way around, he immediately agreed.

Here he was now, on a Sunday evening, in Faith's large, butter-colored living room on Riverside Drive—a slightly faded place, he noted. The Hudson River glowed dark under the moon out the large window. There were vases placed around the room, and the occasional forgotten teacup. She didn't even offer him a drink. This was serious.

He sat in an easy chair, and she sat across from him and said with formality, "I am furious with you."

He looked hard at her. "You want to tell me why?"

"No, I want you to figure it out."

He tried. Various scenarios passed before him in a loop of footage, none seeming accurate.

"Lupe Izurieta," Faith finally said. "Ring any bells?"

"What?"

"Lupe Izurieta," she repeated, unhelpfully.

"What are you talking about?" Emmett sat there in such confusion that he thought this might be what it was like to have a stroke. *Loo-pay-a-zoo-ree-ate-er*, he thought, turning the syllables over and over, but they made no sense.

"From Ecuador."

Then the syllables re-formed themselves correctly, and he understood what she had said: *Lupe Izurieta*. Right, oh right. The girl they had brought over to speak in LA. One of the one hundred girls they had paid a lot of money to rescue.

"Oh," he said.

"So the mentor program really doesn't exist?"

He paused, thrown, trying to be careful. "It was supposed to have existed," he tried. "We had every intention. Does that count for anything?"

"What happened?" she said. "Just tell me."

"You won't believe me, Faith. But when it got discussed upstairs, a lot got said. I'm ashamed to say this, but I wasn't entirely paying attention at the time."

People had always described Emmett Shrader's attention span as pealike, flealike. Let them say that, he'd always thought; he didn't care. But still he had to find a way to manage his boredom, and that could be difficult. Sometimes, in meetings with clients or with his board of directors, he found himself falling, as if off a cliff, down onto the shoals of boredom. He did whatever he could to avoid this. That might involve playing a dropping-bricks game on a phone that he discreetly held out of sight in his lap, or else noodling around with the wire widgets that sat on his broad black chunk of a desk for no other reason than that the interior decorator had bought them for him from a young artist in Barcelona "who works in wire," she'd said excitedly.

He had barely noticed the widgets until he found himself idle in a meeting, and there they were, waiting to be toyed with. He could've kissed the interior decorator for having given him something to do with his hands at that moment. He remembered her as smelling candied, and having an excellent bosom. He loved the way women, clothed, had *a* bosom, a single entity, but when unclothed, it cleaved into two discrete parts, two breasts, like the way you could separate an orange into halves by hooking your thumbs into it.

When Emmett tired of the games on the phone and of the sculptural widgets, he didn't know what to do with himself. He often let his thoughts take him far afield; he imagined sex with his decorator, or what Chef Brian might prepare for dinner that night, hoping it wasn't halibut in parchment, because these days far too many things came in parchment, and unwrapping that virtuous little package was basically the opposite of being a child on Christmas morning.

Now he tried to remember the sequence of meetings about Ecuador that had ended in failure and then deceit. First Faith had come up with the idea of doing a special project that concerned sex trafficking there. Of course he wanted to please her, so he'd immediately turned it over to two associates. A contact in Quito had been secured and hired, and a two-pronged plan had been put in place. First there would be a rescue of one hundred girls who had been forced to work as prostitutes in Guayaquil. A local, fearless security team had been engaged for the job. And next, once the girls were rescued, they would be matched with older women who would serve as mentors and teach them a trade. Women learning from women, an admirable project.

"It'll look great," someone at ShraderCapital said. "We should be doing more things like this."

It was all put in place and ready to go. But during a second or third meeting, when all the outstanding details were supposed to be worked out, Emmett was only half-listening. That was the meeting at which Doug Paulson, the COO, said he had something he needed to bring up. "I hate to insert this at the zero hour," he said, "but when Brit and I took the kids to the Galápagos she met this woman, Trina Delgado, who organizes on behalf of charities in South America. Brit thinks she is the real deal. And when I told her about what we've been doing in Ecuador, she suggested it would be great if we could bring Trina in."

"What do you mean, bring her in?" asked Monica Vendler, the lone woman at this high level at ShraderCapital.

"Well, I'm wondering if it's too late to sideline the person Faith hired. It would mean a lot to my wife to be able to work with Trina."

"If you think she's good," said Greg Stupack.

"I don't know about this," Monica said.

"Brit really likes this woman," Doug repeated. "I thought helping other women was a central part of Loci's mission."

So the first woman had been swapped out for the second one, and everything proceeded. But when the rescue mission was days away, a meeting was suddenly called. Doug Paulson, slightly red-faced now, haltingly explained that Trina Delgado, to whom they had already paid an exorbitant and nonrefundable fee, turned out not to have been good with "follow-through." The story quickly tumbled out of him. "She acts like she's doing everything she can, but I think she's a fucking grifter," he finally said. "Brit feels horrible, and so do I." Trina had never hired mentors, but had taken ShraderCapital's money. Nothing was in place, absolutely nothing.

"Why am I not surprised?" asked Monica acidly. "So if we don't have mentors, are we still going ahead with the rescue?"

"It's a good outfit," said Greg. "Highly rated. Plus, we pre-paid."

"What were they supposed to teach these girls, anyway?" asked Kim Russo, the COO's pretty, blond, broad-shouldered young assistant.

"All kinds of things," said one of the other assistants. "English. Computer skills. Also, a trade. Knitting. Weaving."

This last remark propelled a side conversation that incorporated an even worse word, *weavings*. God, *weavings*! There was nothing duller to Emmett Shrader than textiles and fabrics. The thought of entering a fabric store or a crafts store made him delirious with horror.

"You know, we could keep the first part of the mission but forget about the second. The follow-up," said Greg.

"And what about the donations we've been receiving for the mentor program?" Monica asked. "We sent out a ton of brochures, and Faith's people handed them out at the last summit. We're getting a surprising number of donations, and the money is just sitting there. It's too late to return any of it. We'd look incompetent."

"Well, we can't do anything else with it, can we?" asked her assistant. "It's a restricted gift."

"We could put it to very good, similar use," said Doug, "the next time Faith wants to do one of her special projects. We'll channel these funds over there. It's not like they'd be used for personal gain. I mean, my God, no one is making a penny out of any of this. The whole thing, our whole support of Loci, is only charitable."

"Yes, we're saints," said Monica.

"What is your point?"

"That it's also rehabilitative," she said. "You know very well. It cleans up our act. It hoses us down."

Greg folded his arms and said, "I must ask that everything that's being discussed in here today behaves the way a housefly does."

"What do you mean?" Monica said, annoyed.

"That it never leaves the room."

There was mild, self-conscious laughter, and then they had a brief vote and decided they would go ahead with the plans, even in the absence of mentors. Carry out the rescue. Later on, invite one of the Ecuadorian girls to LA, as they were going to do. Continue to accept donations that arrived, earmarking them for next time, and later quietly close the fund and say the program had been a success, but now it was over because they had reached their goal.

"What about Faith and all of them downstairs?" asked Kim. "What will you tell them?"

Shrader sat fiddling with the wire sculptures, and then he realized that the whole room was looking at him, waiting. Very reluctantly he let the wire/silver/magnet things drop from his hands in a little waterfall of clicking parts. "I'm going to leave that up to all of you," he said.

So the rescue mission had taken place under cover of darkness, and had been a success. The rest of it, the mentor part, was "still not on track," but anyway the girls were free, and that was what mattered most. No one at ShraderCapital knew what had happened to them since then, though. Emmett Shrader, with his pealike, flealike attention, never followed up on any of this after that meeting, or apprised Faith of the situation—and really, she was out of the loop, since apparently no one had told her in the first place that her contact had been replaced with Paulson's wife's contact.

By now the mission was months in the past, and mostly it had been forgotten. Donations were still coming in, but luckily not too many. After a while everyone had gotten very relaxed about it, and in the run-up to the LA event someone was tasked with inviting one of the rescued girls. The travel agent arranged everything, and Greer Kadetsky introduced the girl at the summit and wrote her speech, and gave an excellent speech herself, and everything was perfectly fine and unremarkable until a couple of days later, according to Faith, when Greer apparently heard from some unnamed person who told her that there had been no mentor program after all.

"Tell me who it was," Emmett said, but Faith refused.

He thought about the early days of the foundation—how exuberant he had been. It was like being young again. It was like having sex with Faith all over again, though without the sex. It was like some kind of full-mind, full-body fuck. That was what it was like when your entire self was engaged. That was what it was like to pay attention.

When Faith had first signed on with him, he had sent Connie Peshel down to the skeletal space that was then the twenty-sixth floor, to find something suitable for her. "Windows for Ms. Frank everywhere," he had instructed Connie.

"I can't punch through walls, Mr. Shrader," she had complained. What a sourpuss. She had been with him since he had founded the firm back in the seventies. His wife, Madeline, had liked her, and everyone said it was because Connie Peshel was so frankly ugly: a thick neck that could have had bolts in it, and a face dappled with what once, a million years earlier, had been teenage acne, onto which for some reason she spread a layer of foundation the color of candy circus peanuts.

But Madeline hadn't been particularly relieved that Connie was homely. She didn't even care if Emmett wanted to screw his secretary or not. She had known that he had slept with various different women while they were married. It was the way he was built, and it was part of their unspoken deal. But the deal also tacitly stated that he could screw them only if he didn't respect and admire them, and that he could not screw them if he did. The equation was simple. This way, there was never any real threat to the marriage, because while Emmett Shrader liked sex with all kinds of women, he wasn't one of those men who would throw over his whole life for someone intellectually uninteresting.

Madeline had called all the shots from early on, because she was rich and he was poor. The money that had started Shrader-Capital all came from her family. Marrying into the New York Tratt fortune when you were the son of a milkman from Chicago had had its severe stresses. At all Tratt family functions, he was iced out. No one wanted to talk to him or look at him then. Together in the earliest days of their marriage, attempting to show his supposed indifference to her wealth, Emmett worked at a dull job at Nabisco, and Madeline volunteered with charities. They were a bored young couple who occasionally toured Europe, and went out to Vegas to gamble. Only later, when Abby was born, was there a flicker of life in the household. Madeline was a good mother, natural and lively, but because she had been raised with nannies she reflexively hired one for Abby, so her days were still unfilled.

And Emmett was often unfaithful. This was nothing special; many of the men he knew had frequent dalliances; it recharged their batteries, that was all. But when Emmett returned home on a warm night in 1973 after that single, stupendous sexual encounter with Faith Frank, a young so-called feminist at that new women's magazine that was trying to get Nabisco to buy ad space, he knew this was different. He was so excited and disturbed by what had transpired that he had sat in the darkness in the living room of the Bronxville house, talking quietly to himself, trying to figure out his next move. The sex with Faith had been snappingly dynamic, revelatory. He had ached for it throughout their dinner at the Cookery and during the cab ride to her little apartment; and then in her bed the ache was furiously resolved, the tip of his long penis touching the depths of her, as momentous to him as if it were fingertip meeting fingertip in *The Creation of Adam* on the ceiling of the Sistine Chapel. It wasn't just sex, it was connection. To be attached by all nerve endings to this person of substance and sympathy. She was independent, which somehow made him want to be dependent on her.

But then she had said that thing to him, "You're married," summarily killing the possibility of his ever seeing her again. So after he left that night he went home and sat in his chair in the dark living room, thinking of Faith's glorious body, the look and feel and taste and smell of her—Cherchez, she'd said her perfume was called—but it was more than that. Her perfume was mixed with saline, which was mixed with something ineffably specific to Faith. He pictured her brain packing her beautiful head, rendering her inquisitive and sharp and exquisitely attractive.

He had told her he would call her the next day about the Nabisco ad buy, but he also planned to beg her to see him again. "You *have* to see me," he would say when he called. He would plead with her, tell her that he and his wife led separate lives and that his wife wouldn't really care, even though there was no world in which that was true.

Madeline had heard him come in, and she silently entered the living room in her satin dressing gown and took a look at him sitting there in this fraught, stimulated, shattered state, and she *knew*. How did she possibly know? But somehow she did.

"Who is she?" Madeline asked.

"Oh," was all he said, deflating.

"For God's sake, Emmett, just tell me. It's better that I know."

Because he was a bad liar, and because he was still inside the circle of strong feeling that Faith had created, he said, "A woman I met at the office."

"Tell me her name."

"Faith Frank."

"She works at Nabisco?"

"No. She wanted us to buy ad space in her magazine."

"You mean she's a lady editor?"

"Yes."

"*Redbook? McCall's? Ladies' Home Journal?*"

"*Bloomer.*"

"I don't know what that is."

"Women's lib," he explained weakly. "You know."

His wife was silent, staring at him. "I imagine she's more beautiful than I am," she began. "But is she more interesting than me? And is she smarter?"

"Madeline, don't do this."

"Just tell me, Emmett."

He looked down at his clasped hands. "Yes."

"Which? More interesting, or smarter?"

"Both."

His wife took this in. She had asked, and now she had to absorb the answer, though it was cruel in a way he hadn't meant. "She's someone who's going places?" she wanted to know.

"I get that sense, yes."

"I see."

When he had first met Madeline, he had thought her sexy and witty and bright, but he had realized a few months into their marriage that she possessed a limited repertoire of commentary, and that when held up to scrutiny, the things she said weren't really all that witty. She had no passions, and her intellect was limited. He was bored with her by now and she knew it, and it was a bad, tight-quartered situation for them both. "I'm very sorry," Emmett told her. "I don't know what's wrong with me. I wanted her. I wanted something that was . . . exciting to all parts of me. I know it's rotten. But, Madeline, I feel very held back in my life. The fucking biscuit people. There is no one to talk to there, to spar with."

"So that's what you did with her? You *sparred*?"

"In a sense of the word."

"I don't think that sense of the word is in *Webster's Dictionary*." Then Madeline was quiet, thinking hard, trying to find an equitable solution that would save their marriage. Finally she said, "All right. Here's what I've decided. I want you never to see her again."

"You're in luck. She wants that too, actually."

"But you were planning to convince her otherwise, weren't you? To *make* her see you. And you're very convincing. You're bored, Emmett. As long as you're bored, it's a danger to me and to us. Tell me, what would make you un-bored? Work?"

"I work. I work on Oreos and Lorna Doones and Chicken in a Biskit."

"I mean work you loved," she said. "Where the stakes were high."

"I can't even imagine that."

"Work that excited you, and challenged you as much as some sexy, interesting woman does, and which involved people you could spar with in the office. Deals you could make. Big ones that you could live or die by. How does that sound? Exciting enough for you?"

He looked at his wife mildly, noncommittal. "What are you saying?"

The following week, Madeline released a massive sum of Tratt family money into an account in his name, a gesture that ran contrary to the agreement they'd drawn up before they married, at the insistence of her stuffed-shirt parents. It was as though it was hostage money, ransom money. With it he founded ShraderCapital in 1974. There was no question of not using his own name; he needed "Shrader" to be all over this thing, and not discreetly. It was a way to prove himself to her parents, and to her, and to everyone. Much later on, venture capital firms and hedge funds bore names that were very sword and sheath, very castle keep. The Mansard Fund. Bastion Equity. Split Oak Trust. The goal was to make the firm or the fund sound like a fortress that could resist all invading armies. Eventually these places had proliferated to such a degree that no evocative-sounding words were even *left*. It was sort of like the way writers had long been pillaging all the good phrases from Shakespeare plays for the titles of their novels, so the only phrases still available meant nothing. Soon, Emmett thought, people would be writing novels called *Enter, Guard.*

From the start, Emmett, a fast, impatient learner with a freakish memory, surrounded himself with wise finance men to advise him. Soon ShraderCapital did shockingly well, and over time Emmett made a fortune that was exponentially far greater than Madeline's family's. "I can eat the Tratts for breakfast, lunch, and dinner," he'd often say to his wife, to whom he would forever be grateful. She was pleased, having realized that she sort of hated her parents too. They were very pretentious people. Her father sometimes wore a monocle.

But before then, there was another thing. The morning after that night of reckoning in the dark living room, when Madeline had provisionally agreed to give Emmett enough money to start his own firm, she'd also said to him, "I'd like you to get her on the phone now. This Faith Frank person."

"What?"

They were at the dining table in the middle of breakfast when she brought this up. The housekeeper was serving grapefruit halves, and Abby was saying to her parents, "Why is it called *grape*fruit when it doesn't taste anything like grapes?"

"I want to talk to her," Madeline said.

So he had been forced to go into the den and dial Faith's number and put his wife on, and sit there, humiliated, while Madeline said something to Faith about how Emmett wasn't hers for the taking. "He stood beside me during our wedding ceremony," Madeline hissed, and Emmett thought back to their wedding, and how uncomfortable he'd felt that day, standing there in a boxy suit. Luckily, Faith hung up on Madeline right away, but it had to have been humiliating for her as well. For a long time, Emmett would feel guilty for having allowed Madeline to put Faith through that. It was a weird moment, a perverse one, in which one woman had wanted to prove her dominance over the other one, in front of him, and he had let her. He'd been so weak, and it shamed him.

Madeline went straight upstairs to the bedroom after the call, and didn't return to the breakfast table, but Emmett did. Abby was sitting all alone, poking at her food. Emmett suddenly remembered something, and he went and grabbed his jacket, which he'd left last night on a chair by the door. He felt inside the pockets, and then he presented the little paper umbrella to his daughter, saying, "For you."

"Oh, I love it, Daddy," she said. "It's so tiny. And my doll Veronica Rose will love it too."

Sometimes, though not very often, it was possible for him to make a girl happy.

Emmett Shrader didn't speak to Faith Frank again in any meaningful way for nearly forty years. He became a large figure in business who appeared on the cover of *Fortune*, and she became an approachable, sympathetic heroine to women. Once every decade or so they accidentally found themselves in the same enormous, high-ceilinged room, attending the same black-tie event. But invariably he was in that room with Madeline, who over time took on the look of a figurehead on a ship, her hair swirled as if carved of wood, her gowns regal, hiding the now-thick body he had once desired, when it was far less thick.

Fairly regularly, Emmett slept with women who were not his wife, but as he grew older this was more for the physical exercise than anything else, as though his cock needed an aerobic workout, as well as his heart, oh, his heart. But never were the women he slept with all that interesting to him; that was the condition that Madeline had set, and he would honor it forever. Never were they anything like Faith.

Madeline, as she aged and they grew apart, became ironically more interesting herself, and certainly more compassionate. Her interestingness sprang from that compassion, and she gave large sums of money to progressive causes, which often involved women's rights. She sat on the boards of museums but also on the boards of women's clinics in the Bronx and Oklahoma. Even when Emmett wasn't in attendance, she overlapped with Faith here and there, and the two women once found themselves uncomfortably sitting only three seats away from each other at a dinner devoted to maternal care in Africa. Neither of them said a word to the other. The images projected on-screen, of girls with agonized faces, girls suffering the indignity of fistula— what a horrible word—blocked out any long-ago image of young Faith Frank, and how Emmett had slept with her, and had begun to love her starting that night.

But then, in the year 2010, Madeline Tratt Shrader, a dynamic and plump major philanthropist, age seventy, asked Emmett's assistant Connie to schedule a dinner for her and Mr. Shrader at the Gilded Quail, a restaurant in Chelsea that had the ambience of a private railroad car from the nineteenth century. A waiter came bearing plates dotted with examples of molecular gastronomy: horseradish "air," sous-vide trout with a "root infusion," a shot glass filled with three layers of intensely flavored soups that went from icy-cold to hot as you threw back your head and drank. Then the waiter retreated with such solemnity that it was as if he had seen a ghost: perhaps the gilded quail itself, in hologram form, eyes glowing gold.

In the dark and narrow space Emmett looked at his wife across the landscape of a thousand years, in awe of the life they had had, their daughter, Abby, grown now and in finance on the West Coast and the mother of two surfboarding sons who said *dude* a lot. A cold conch shell with a virtually unreachable pink glazed interior was what the Shrader marriage was now.

Madeline lifted a fork of gently and purposefully wilted lettuce, studiously chewed it, then said, "Emmett, I have to tell you something."

"All right."

"I've fallen in love."

His first instinct was to smile as if it was a joke, but of course it wasn't, and then he felt the self-consciousness that the evening called for—his wife's having made a formal appointment to see him, and see him alone. They had not had dinner alone by themselves in months, nor shared a bedroom in a decade.

"With who?" he asked, incredulous, too loud. One of the waiters thought he was being summoned and stepped forward, then realized his error and quickly retreated.

"Marty Santangelo."

"Who?"

"Our contractor. And we want to be together."

Emmett sank back against the cushion of the antiquity that served as a dining chair. He took *umbrage*. He felt wounded in some way that he couldn't name, despite the aspic chill of their marriage. Maybe it was because Madeline had made everything possible for him in the beginning. Maybe it was because they had been going along like this for so very long that any change— even a potentially welcome one—would have to be initially disturbing when you found out about it.

Emmett Shrader did not like change unless he initiated it, and he was often initiating it, though in small ways. He knew that people described him behind his back as having ADD, and once, as an elevator closed, he heard someone say, "Give that man some Adderall!" followed by peals of group laughter. Maybe the assessment was accurate, but he was shocked at the idea that Madeline should want change, and sitting in the Gilded Quail with his marriage ending, and having eaten only the second course out of *eight* courses—six more to get through with his future ex-wife!—he wanted to cry into his fist.

Madeline moved out soon after that night. In the first days of his sudden, late-life singledom, Emmett was as wildly alone as he'd ever felt, reaching for the Viagra and fucking women all over the city, in their apartments and townhouses, and in his apartment, where the walls were glass and the views were so ostentatious that the women always said "Oh!" and he had to impatiently wait for the moment of wonder to end, and in a suite at the Carlyle Hotel, and then in a *ryokan* in Kyoto, and once in the private compartment of an Emirates flight to Qatar.

Once he contracted chlamydia from a pretty young finance blogger, but it was easily treated by azithromycin. Often he tasked Connie with buying Hermès scarves for women afterward, and occasionally even those Birkin bags that women often craved so deeply and weirdly that it seemed like a Darwinian urge.

And then one morning in that same strange and exhaustingly active year, Emmett saw a very small mention in the *New York Times* that "*Bloomer* magazine, which had its moment back in the heyday of the women's movement but never entirely caught on, yet valiantly kept publishing," was closing. There were quotes from two of the founding editors at the magazine, and one of them was Faith Frank. Her name on the page seemed to him set in boldface.

"We got a lot done," she was quoted saying. Shrader's throat and chest felt thick as he remembered Faith Frank and their one night. But it wasn't just sex he remembered. He also remembered how much he had wanted her in his life. There are some people who have such a strong effect on you, even if you've spent very little time with them, that they become *embossed* inside you, and any hint of them, any casual mention, creates a sudden stir in you.

Because Madeline had put a lot of their money into women's causes, Shrader had been regarded over time as sympathetic, an advocate for women. Sometimes he felt guilty that he was getting away with it, while actually holding no deep convictions in this arena. But then he thought that by now he did have such convictions; they'd become real. Whichever was true, he had never been allowed to spend any more time with that unequivocally authentic advocate for women, Faith.

Now the rule about never seeing her was finally lifted, like a curse in a fairy tale. Madeline had her new life with the contractor. It was the middle of the night when he turned on his bedside lamp and asked his butler to get his assistant on the phone at home in Flushing. Connie Peshel answered the phone in a frightened voice. "Mr. Shrader? Is everything all right?"

"I'm fine, Connie. I want you to call Faith Frank tomorrow."

"Who? The feminist? That one?"

"Yes, that one. Find her contact information and make an appointment for her to come in. Tell her I have a business proposition."

Faith had come without asking for any details. She had sat right across from him in his office, and she was still elegant and impeccable and super-smart up close, and Emmett desired this much older version of her all over again, but with a new, churning feeling that reminded him he was no longer that dark-haired young Nabisco exec in a Nehru jacket, and that she had changed too. In her bed in 1973 he had swept his face up and down and to some extent into her body and along the planes of her face with an urgency that must have contained the subconscious knowledge that what they were doing would never happen again. He had eaten her like she was his last meal. They were all over each other; he smelled like Cherchez, she smelled like lime. They were both raw and messed up by the end of it. He, at least, was left besotted.

Since that long-ago night, Faith had gone out and lived and had an enormous career, just the way he had done, both of them making inroads, digging in, having an effect on many other lives. Now after all these decades of digging they were back together. How amazing life was, with all its surprise endings. Not that this was an ending. Maybe it was a beginning. He didn't know how this would work, what would happen. He just knew he wanted her near him every day.

"Why am I here, Emmett?" she asked him the afternoon she came to his office. "Is this our second date?"

He roared in pleasure. "Yes," he said. "If you would like."

"Well, usually the man takes less than four decades to call the woman again, or vice versa. I think it's a little late for us."

"Are you sure? I could bring you a corsage and a Whitman's Sampler. Remember those? Each chocolate was labeled. 'Molasses chew.' 'Cherry cordial.' 'Cashew cluster.' You look great, Faith. I like your style. You're rocking a sort of elegant European stateswoman thing here."

"I'm not sure that's a compliment, coming from you."

"It is."

"Well, then, thank you, Emmett; you look excellent too." She crossed and recrossed her long, booted legs, and said, "So let's move past the fact that once upon a time, you and I had a moment."

"A moment of great feeling. Which ended in true sadness. Star-crossed, wouldn't you say?"

Faith smiled. "I would. And maybe now you can tell me why I'm here."

He laid it all out for her, and he brought in two young associates to show her the prospectus he'd had drawn up for the women's foundation that he wanted her to run. "Primarily it will function as a platform for the most vibrant speakers on women's issues," he said.

She had immediate misgivings. "I don't know that I should be in business with a high-flying company like yours, no offense. How would it look?" she asked.

"It would look shrewd," he said. "Everyone will be jealous of how you don't have to beg for scraps all the time, the way you did back at your little magazine. Cormer Publishing were cheapskates. I looked into their numbers and none of their magazines do well. I mean, *Figurine Collector. Empty Nester.* Who needs these magazines? Give me a break."

She had said no, but then she'd come back with a counterbid involving funding some special projects, and they'd agreed. For a while, Loci had mostly done what it was meant to do, but in recent years, others at ShraderCapital had pressured Faith to change the feel of the foundation, to make it sexy, as someone said. They could charge more that way, and get a lot more press. That singer Opus—who had now become a movie star too— was coming to their big bash soon. He knew that Faith hated the reliance on celebrities, and the manicures, and the psychic they hired, but what could she do?

At a recent summit, that psychic, Ms. Andromeda, had announced that she saw a woman president in the future. The crowd erupted. But then the psychic, studying her cards or chart or crystal ball or whatever it was she used, apparently said, "I see . . . Indiana."

"Oh shit," said someone else. They were all glumly quiet, imagining a moment in the future in which Senator Anne Mc-Cauley, who gave the appearance of a kind, well-spoken grandmother, had won the presidential election and women were forced to undergo back-alley abortions again, and doctors were thrown in jail, and scores of teenage girls delivered babies against their will into this heartless new world.

The operating budget had appalled his CFO when Emmett first announced his elaborate plan to underwrite a women's foundation. But damn if it hadn't worked. It was good for disenfranchised women, on whose lives a spotlight was shined, and look at the donations that now poured in. It was good for Shrader-

Capital and its image, which was constantly in need of repair, and it was personally good for Emmett, who got to see Faith every single workday, after not seeing her for so very long and missing her with a strange and persistent melancholy.

There were days, over these four years, when she came up to his office at around five p.m.—or he came to her office—and he luxuriated in having her there across from him. She'd take off her boots and rub her feet, and she would sit there quietly talking, radiating intelligence. She told him about her day, and he told her about his. They drank a good Malbec and were enveloped by long, happy silences. Once in a while they talked about their respective children, Lincoln and Abby, one serious and consistent, and exceptional to his mother because he was *hers*; the other one stormy and highly successful. Still he thought of Abby as his little girl, and he remembered the exact feeling of her undiluted, Electral love for him: a girl on a father's lap, all crinoline and hot bottom.

Sometimes, as he and Faith sat together, he said a few words about some woman or other who he'd slept with recently, and how she'd provided a physical outlet, which was worth a lot these days as he entered the terrifying arena of old age, and Viagra was as important as sunscreen. Faith listened well, not judging, and she sometimes told him a few shreds of detail from her own life, but mostly she was private. They talked about the people they'd known in common in the old days. He unloaded all his rage and frustration.

And they always laughed a lot. Faith had the greatest laugh. And the greatest throat. She was the whole package, he thought. But now, sitting in her living room, having lost her respect and incited her anger and contempt because of the stupid botched Ecuador mentor project—that was a torment.

"I find it hard to believe that you allowed us to step deep into lies just because you didn't pay attention during a meeting," she said. "You know it's more than that. Attention is a smokescreen. You have the ability to be attentive; I've seen it. You're attentive toward me."

"I should have listened better in that meeting, and I shouldn't have let them switch out that woman you liked, and I should have shut down the fund and announced the whole thing publicly. Punish me, Faith. Just don't ice me out."

Faith tightened her mouth, and for the briefest moment she looked like every woman in the world who was angry at a man.

"I'm going to tell you what I've decided to do," Faith said, "and I don't want you to say anything. I just want you to listen."

He nodded, folding his hands in his lap in an exaggeration of listening. This was *super*-listening, the kind done by higher beings, and he tried to imitate it now.

"I'm not going to make a stink," Faith said. "That would imperil the foundation and stop us from doing anything ever again. And while I detest the moral vacuum that apparently exists upstairs at ShraderCapital, I can't just quietly quit my job, because where else would I go? I'll continue to take your money, Emmett, but I won't approve of it. I'll take it and I'll use it, and I will watch it closely, because I don't really have much choice.

"We were all put on this earth to row the boats we were meant to row," she said. "I work for women. That's what I do. And I am going to keep doing it. I have no idea if this Ecuador story will ever leak out of the building. If it does, it will be an embarrassment, and perhaps it will shut us down. But the bottom line is that I'm not going anywhere."

"Good." His relief almost sprang from his forehead. "I don't know what I would've done if you'd said you were quitting."

"Oh, you'd be fine. You're the one percent of the one percent."

"I was very bored until you came here, Faith," Emmett said.

"Someone once called me a 'privileged narcissist' in an op-ed in the *Wall Street Journal*. I guess it's true sometimes." He thought, but didn't say, that people like him needed someone to remind them not to be privileged narcissists. They needed someone like Faith to do that.

Emmett impulsively took Faith's hand, and for a few seconds she didn't pull away. Then she shifted, and their hands unlinked. "All right then," she said. "It's getting late." She stood up, so he stood up too.

"No one else knows about this but Greer Kadetsky?" he asked. "And whoever told her this?"

"I'm not certain." They sat silently for a moment.

"Well, Greer won't say anything, right?" he asked.

Faith shook her head. "I very much doubt it. But she's already quit. It was an unpleasant moment. She's someone I like, and someone I brought along."

"Yes, in that way you do. Showing an interest in them."

"Showing an interest is only one part," she said. "You also take them under your wing, if that's what they seem to want. But then there's another part, which is that eventually you let them go. Fling! You fling them away. Because otherwise they think that they can't manage on their own. Sometimes you fling them too hard. You have to be careful." She stopped. "Anyway, you should try showing an interest too. In the ones upstairs."

"I will," he said, full of feeling; he suddenly thought of two kids, a boy and a girl, both just out of college, who had been hired at the same time at ShraderCapital. They were snappingly smart and eager, with different, distinctive talents. But both were promising.

"It really takes very little," said Faith, "and they are very, very grateful. They try to show their gratitude. There's the proof," she added, nodding toward something in her sight line.

Emmett turned to look. On the floor, at the foot of the sofa, was a large, open box that contained various items, some still half-wrapped in festive paper, others unwrapped and opened. "What's all this?" he asked.

"Thank-you gifts and sentimental objects and private jokes. Personal connections."

"From who?"

"Oh, from everyone. People I've known over the years. Even people I've met only once. Sometimes they arrive in the mail, and sometimes they're handed to me at summits and speeches. Always it's someone who says I've helped them in some capacity, and if it comes in the mail there's a note attached, and sometimes I have no idea who the person is—the name on the note doesn't even sound familiar, or it vaguely rings a bell—though the note makes it seem as if we had some kind of important encounter. And I guess we did, because it was significant to them. These things have been sitting here for far too long, gathering dust. This is only one box of several. The tip of the iceberg. Deena is going to help me go through them this week. Objects have a different meaning to me now at seventy-one. I can't collect more things. It has to be a time of winnowing."

Emmett bent and slid the box closer and peered inside, fishing around, looking. Here on top was one of those lacy little pillows that women liked, a sachet. He held it to his nose but it gave off no scent anymore.

Here was a key chain with a little boot on it, probably meant to symbolize the sexy suede boots that Faith famously wore.

Here were three different jars: one empty; one with some ancient black jam in it, and perhaps some botulism spores; and one containing jelly beans. The one with jelly beans had a note attached that read:

Faith,
I know you must get a lot of jars, am I right, because of
your famous jar line? I'm sure you can open THIS one! (In
fact, I'm sure you can do anything.)
xxx Wendy Sadler

And here was a T-shirt with a picture of a lobster, and here was
a copy of an old, stupid-looking children's book called *The Brad-
ford Twins' Summer Surprise*. On the cover, a poorly drawn boy and
girl flew a kite. He opened it and saw that it was inscribed:

Dear Faith,
This book was my favorite when I was a little girl, and I
wanted you to have it.
Love,
Denise Manguso (from that dinner in Chicago!)

"So how was that dinner in Chicago?" he asked.
"What are you talking about?"
"The inscription. Who is Denise Manguso?"
"I have no idea."
Emmett kept pawing through the box. Here was a bracelet
made of hemp and bead. Here was a toy plastic spaceship with
the name NASA on the side, and a note with it:

Dear Faith,
I work here at NASA now as deputy director for
engineering, and if you ever come down to DC, I'd love
to show you around. I wouldn't be here, if not for you.
Fondly,
Olive (Mitchell)

Here was a box of homemade fudge. Emmett opened it and saw that it now had a teeth-cracking, long-ago-baked, igneous surface of sugar and nut, entirely calcified.

"What year is this from, Faith?"

"How would I know?"

"Then what decade?"

Here was a peacock feather tied with a ribbon, and here a beautiful pen engraved with the strange words THE PEN IS MIGHTIER THAN THE PENIS.

And here, equally strangely, was a frying pan, never used, a label still on it. What did it represent? Another private joke, he assumed, which Faith might or might not remember, even though the gift-giver had had the impulse to go out and purchase it and give it, for it was a sign of love. All of these women had needed a connection with Faith. She was plasma to them. Maybe it was a mommy thing, he thought, but maybe it was also: I want to be you. There were so many of these women, just so many. But there was only one Faith.

"It must be a burden to you to be the most important person to people who aren't all that important to you," he said.

"I'm not sure I agree with your interpretation. I get a lot from them too, remember."

"What do you get?" he asked. "I'm curious."

"Well, they keep me in the world," she said, and that was all she wanted to say.

He wondered who Faith Frank opened up to. She had her friends, those old women from the old days, including Bonnie, the lesbian with the frizzy hair, and Evelyn, the society lady in her suits the colors of Pez. They were intimates of Faith's, he knew; they'd all been photographed together back in a completely different time. Emmett had a sudden memory of a picture of Faith and the others sprawled around an office. The place looked hectic, messy, busy. But the thing he recalled most was how happy Faith looked among those women, how relaxed and content.

Suddenly Emmett wondered why Faith hadn't found a man to be with her all these years, after having been widowed so young. Why did a strong woman need to be her own shield? Or maybe that was just the way Faith wanted it, because men were a distraction, or too high-maintenance. Or maybe having a man in her life was just one thing too many. He and Faith might have loved each other, he thought now when it was much, much too late.

"I've done everything wrong!" he said, not able to keep this to himself.

"What?" Faith looked alarmed at the outburst.

"I could have loved you," he said. "I could have done that, Faith. We could have complemented each other. We both live these oversized, sort of ridiculous lives. The sex would've been a release, and a revelation. And all the conversations afterward. I would've made you scrambled eggs in the middle of the night. I make good middle-of-the-night scrambled eggs; I bet you didn't know that. But I screwed everything up, and now you think I'm awful."

She stood facing him, still clearly shocked but recovering, one hand lightly massaging her neck for a moment. All she said, finally, was, "I don't think that."

It was getting late, and he would need to go home soon. His car and driver were waiting, and later he and Faith would lie in their separate beds, in which there was plenty of room for another person if they so chose, which tonight they wouldn't. They were older and they had to carefully mete out intimacy. Emmett slid the box back to where it had been; this box that had held the gifts that Faith had been given by the people in her life she'd known or met and had affected as she went through—the people she could sometimes barely keep track of—but it didn't matter if she couldn't keep track, because she felt tenderly toward them all, and they knew it.

Emmett tried to picture what kind of gift he might give Faith to show her how he felt. He couldn't imagine what he could possibly give her—what would have meaning and resonance. But then he realized he did know, for he'd already done it. He'd given her a foundation.

THIRTEEN

Cory Pinto came up with the idea for his video game not in one burst, but over a number of years. He didn't even know he'd been imagining a video game all that time; he just thought of himself as someone who played a lot of actual video games while intermittently thinking heavily and obsessively about losing his brother. But a combination of playing and obsessing eventually made him see what had been inside him. So the story for the game, when it revealed itself, arrived nearly fully formed.

For a long time he'd been periodically preoccupied by the idea that when someone you loved died, you could spend the rest of your life searching the world for that person and yet you would never, ever find him or her, no matter how many obscure places you went to, no matter how many caves you slipped into, or curtains you parted, or houses you entered. The dead person truly no longer existed, and while as a matter of science this fact seemed so simple, it was unaccountably hard to accept it when the person was someone you loved.

But the thing was, after someone you loved died, the people

you still *could* see—a.k.a., the living—might occasionally almost seem to be the person you longed for. There would be a startle of similarity, a flash of familiar head-shape or squirt of laughter, and you would whip around so hard, only to find a person who was not in fact the right person at all. And then you had to wonder: why did *this* kid in front of you, this stranger whose laugh was so unsubtle, whose expression was coarse, get to be alive while your little brother didn't?

And yet, maybe if you really did search hard enough and far enough, you could eventually find the person you were looking for. Maybe, maybe, Alby was still somewhere in the world, over three years after his death. Maybe the secret truth about death is that dead people are whisked away from their current lives and forced to live somewhere else far away—a process similar to reincarnation but taking place not in the future but now. A sort of mortality-based witness protection program. And if you found them they would look the same as they always had. If only you knew where to find them. If only you knew where to look.

This was the premise of Cory's game. He himself felt childlike in his inability to accept Alby's death. Of course, in all the important ways, he did accept it, because he wasn't mentally fragile like his mother; and he was able to socialize and have a drink and a conversation about subjects other than death, and he was able to actually interact well with customers and other employees at Valley Tek in crunchy Northampton, twenty-five minutes from Macopee. The store was a seemingly mellow but demanding place. Customers' attachment to their computers was primal and urgent. They rushed in carrying their laptops like people at the vet cradling injured or sick animals.

"How can I help you?" Cory would gently ask.

"It just crashed! Right in the middle of an unbelievably important project."

"Have you backed everything up?"

"Well, no, not recently." Then, defensively, "I couldn't have known it would crash."

"Let's have a look." Cory would go into the workshop in the back with this pliant and willing machine that had no say in the matter. What ailed it in the end was that it was a machine. You could bring it to life a few times, or even many times, but eventually you knew that the customer would have to abandon and replace it, and you would be the one to help facilitate that.

It was through the store that Cory became familiar with the online gaming community, which of course wasn't really one community, but an astoundingly large and amorphous aggregate of people in separate homes and different time zones around the world who enjoyed playing video games day and night. Sometimes a few people from work played Dota 2 as a team from their separate homes. And after work once a week the employees at the store gathered at the nearby apartment of burly Logan Berryman, thirty years old, who in addition to being the head tech person at Valley Tek and a programmer was part of the not-insignificant contra dance community that had sprung up around the Pioneer Valley.

Logan and his girlfriend Jen lived on the upper floor of a house on Fruit Street with their fiddles, their cat, and canisters of bee pollen that stood in gleaming granularity on the kitchen counter. Relaxing there in the evening, the Valley Tek crew—Logan, Halley Beatty, Peter Wong, and now Cory—drank beer and with bared teeth popped edamame beans from their hairy little pods, and then they all played Counter-Strike for a couple of happy hours.

Logan and Jen's actual, physical world, the progressive world of Northampton, Massachusetts, home of Smith College, consisted of college professors and psychiatrists and various lesbian couples, as well as coffee shops and mixed-breed dogs wearing bandannas, and kids who looked like runaways, though half of them were the children of professors and psychiatrists—lost teenagers who slunk back into their book-filled homes at night in time for bed. It was a world that was sexually enlightened and supposedly egalitarian. In Logan and Jen's apartment as the sun set, the women and men played lustily and freely. It was like an equal-opportunity dream, whereas Cory knew the online world of gaming was studded with full-throated hate. Women were harassed and threatened constantly in that world, a miniaturized version of the real world. Cory had seen the illiterate screeds that trolls had written on message boards, like "I'D LIKE TO CHOP OFF YOU'RE HEAD AND YOU'RE TWAT." As Greer had once said to Cory long ago, after she'd met Faith Frank and turned her attention to feminism, "I tell myself that the language of chopping off body parts is code for: *I don't know what to do about this rage I feel.*"

He imagined being here in this apartment with Greer beside him; there would be the stirring sensation of just knowing that these other people thought of them as a couple. He had the sudden, related thought that if Greer were part of a couple down in New York, dating or hooking up at length or however else she described it to herself, maybe the guy had wooed her with stories of combating misogyny. That would be a good way to get through to Greer. The idea flickered inside Cory briefly, then went away. He had no way to get through to her now, nor she to him. The more you were not with a person, the more your lives diverged. Cory could barely understand how people who hadn't known each other early on in life could ever form a couple. The older you got, the more you developed specific peculiarities. A woman would have to be willing to absorb his circumstances. He was a grown man, after all, who lived with his mother.

Whenever anyone asked Cory about his living arrangements, he didn't say, "I live with my mom," a sentence that might have a Norman Bates–y quality to it. He said, instead, "I live at home." In the year 2014, as the economy had mostly recovered, living at home didn't necessarily mean one thing or another.

He couldn't stay out too late tonight because he had to go home and cook dinner for his mother and settle her in before bed, not that he was going to announce why he had to leave. Maybe they would think he had somewhere to go, a woman to meet. He was a handsome man; he knew that about himself. But in fact the last woman he'd been involved with had been much earlier. Of all people, it had been Kristin Vells. Kristin had been just someone he was aware of on Woburn Road for so long that he had ceased thinking of her as a real person. She was simply someone to whom he and Greer had always felt superior. She had hazily occupied the role of Dumb Girl Who Lives on Our Street. But then when Greer fell out of Cory's life, and Kristin was living at home and working at Pie Land, Cory would go to the pizza place sometimes in the late afternoon as the day sank into a violet-gray funk.

When he walked in, he would sit and have a slice, and if Kristin was there they would engage in a monosyllabic conversation that might or might not finally flower into the polysyllabic. This went on for a while. One day he was there at closing time, and he and Kristin left together, walking back up the street with bodies close, which was interesting in its newness. Kristin Vells had a well-formed body, and the fragrance of dough rose up from it like a sweet breeze from an open window.

"You want to come over?" he boldly asked this woman who had once been three reading groups below him. The beauty of adulthood was that reading groups did not matter! Or at least they did not insure against anything. You could be in the top reading group of everyone in the world, the alpha Puma among Pumas, and still it would not protect you from your brother dying, or your father leaving, or the person you loved no longer being in your life.

Kristin went with Cory into his house for the first time ever, though they had lived on that same block for such a long time. He remembered the day that Greer had first come here, nearly two decades earlier. Walking into someone's house was like entering their body. You saw what they were made of, and what they had been stewing in all this time.

His mother was sitting in front of the TV when he appeared with Kristin. "Ma, you need anything?" he asked her, and she looked up from the recliner that she often sat in during the day.

"I'm fine, Cory," she said, but she squinted uneasily at Kristin. "Who is this girl?"

"Kristin from down the block," Kristin offered. "The Vellses?"

"With the garden gnomes?"

"That's us. But actually they're gone. Someone stole them a while back."

Cory took Kristin upstairs to his room and shut the door. Being there with her, he was forced to compare her with Greer. Here was a replacement woman, a far less interesting model but a woman too, fragrant and female, someone who knew what life was like here in Macopee and wouldn't question why Cory chose "to live this way." Plus, she had a plush mouth, the lower lip bisected into two little cushions. They smoked a joint, which was the only way to manage this moment. Weed had become more of a condiment in his life not long after his brief adventures in heroin with Cousin Sab. Smoking a joint took the edge off, whereas snorting heroin had taken the *side* off, as if in a tornado, and was to be avoided forever.

So Cory and Kristin smoked silently together, and then he

looked up and saw her suddenly perched above him like a construction crane. He lifted himself slowly toward her, their faces colliding. When her mouth opened, she smelled smoky and rusty, as if there was a taint of blood in there somewhere. While kissing Kristin Vells, Cory realized that sexual arousal came in different strengths, different concentrations, but beyond that the body didn't judge who it was kissing. It had been so long since he had kissed anyone at all.

"You were such a fucking little sissy when you were a kid," Kristin said after the kiss ended and they pulled apart and observed each other. "With your neat little clothes. Did your mom iron your shirts all that time? You always looked so neat. So clean. Like, Mama's boy."

"Yep. And now I iron *her* clothes. Quid pro quo."

"What?"

"Nothing."

He couldn't think of anything more for them to talk about then, so instead of talking he eased himself on top of her, using all the strength and interest he could gather.

They remained entangled for a full month—a month in which they smoked weed and lay in bed for a dazzling number of hours. One day as they lay there, the room was suddenly flooded with light and there was a *bang*, and Cory looked up to see his short mother standing in the doorway. "I'm constipated," Benedita announced.

"Oh, give me a fucking break," said Kristin quietly.

"Cory, can you get me the Dulcolax? I look around and I can't find it."

"Yeah, Ma, hold on a sec," he said.

His mother retreated, shuffling away. She had become a shuffler over the years; by now he was so used to the sound of her purple slippers on the floors of the house that it was almost soothing to him, as if it were a fire snapping in a hearth. But Kristin looked at Cory with proprietary anger, and he absorbed it and was angry right back at her, for she had no dominion over him, and why would she think she did?

"How gross that your mom tells you her personal things like that," she said.

"Yeah, well, she's got no one else to tell it to."

"I live with my mom too, but she tells me jackshit. Which is the way I like it."

Cory shrugged, wanted her gone. Caring for his mother had become part of his job, his way of being. He managed her life, made it no more painful than it had to be. He didn't want Kristin intruding on that part; she was meant to ignore it, not comment on it. But here she was complaining, pointing it out, offering her opinions, and now everything that had been briefly erotic about Kristin Vells—the tiny tattoo of a doghouse on her ankle, and her long, well-cared-for hair and willing mouth—became a source of revulsion. Cory was now uninterested in everything that had to do with this person, because she had overstepped her bounds and also insulted his mother. Or, more than that, insulted his mother and him. What they were to each other. No, she had just insulted *him*.

"Kristin, I gotta get up," he said. When he was around her, he found himself speaking like someone he wasn't. *Gotta. Hafta.*

"So, what, Cory, you're pissed at me because I was grossed out about your mom and her constipation?"

"Something like that."

"Fuck you, Pinto."

"Yeah, well, okay, that's so sweet of you to say."

He stood and found his pants, then his shirt, and had never been so relieved to get dressed. But Kristin wasn't moving. She lay in his bed and just took her time. She smoked a cigarette, she flipped around the dial to see what was on TV, and actually settled on a rerun of *Boy Meets World*, from which he had gotten his name. He had watched this episode, in which Cory quits his school's production of *Hamlet* after finding out he has to wear tights, multiple times when he was young, absorbing how all-American it was, feeling so excited by that aspect. He wished he could trade in the name Cory for Duarte now; he was ready to have that be him, except for the fact that it was his father's name too, and that brought out another set of feelings entirely. Kristin took the remote control and raised the volume. She was planning to watch the whole show, he knew.

You take your time, Kristin, he thought, and he went off to find the Dulcolax. It was exactly where he had visualized it: on a bathroom shelf half-hidden by an ancient, cloudy bottle of something called Jean Naté After Bath Splash. He grabbed the Dulcolax and brought it to his mother.

After Kristin left that day, she and Cory became unspoken enemies. Seeing her on the street as she walked to Pie Land, he would give a grudging wave but she would simply make a guttural sound, like, Are you kidding me? and keep walking. Soon he stopped waving. Now he was not only Greerless, he was also Kristinless.

Eventually, as time kept dissolving, in addition to taking care of his mother and cleaning two of the houses she used to clean, he began to teach himself everything he could about computer repair and game design. Cory was a fast learner, and Valley Tek in Northampton had hired him and trained him, and he soon became adept, a natural, learning the weaknesses of the different machines. He was content there with his fellow employees in the safe, minimalist box of the store. At night he went home and cleaned his house and cooked dinner, and then played video games sitting cross-legged on Alby's bed with Slowy nearby. A few months in, Cory began socializing with the gamers at the store. Logan in particular kept an eye out for him and seemed to feel protective of him. He often encouraged him to come up with an idea for a game, which Logan could design. Cory had been trying.

At the end of the evening at Logan and Jen's place, Logan walked him out and said to him on the front porch, "You got something yet?"

"Sort of."

"Okay. I'll take that as a positive response. I'm working on a game myself," Logan said. "I really enjoy constructing systems and game mechanics. But you wouldn't have to worry about that; I'd think it through. Thing is, I found a potential angel investor through some friends. He lives in Newton and he's driving over Wednesday night to discuss it."

"What does he do?"

"Rich oral surgeon. He's a gamer, but he says he has no imagination at all and he wants to get in on this. He likes the idea of indie games as art pieces. He thinks that if he makes his money back, it's a success. I'm meeting him at Hops, the craft beer place on Masonic. You can come pitch him too if you want."

"Oh. Well, I'm not ready for that," said Cory.

"You have until Wednesday. I have a feeling you can get it together by then."

So Cory came home from work and sat down at the table in the living room, with his mother sitting peacefully across from him. In one of Alby's many notebooks he began to write down some readable notes for the game he'd recently been formulating, but which, really, he'd been formulating for much longer. Then on Wednesday night he entered the lacquered wooden hive of Hops in downtown Northampton. It always made him nervous to go to these trendy establishments, because they

reminded him of what he'd once had, even for a little while—
the wealth that had enclosed him at Princeton, and then again in
Manila, before he had given it all up.

William Cronish, DDS, was a thirty-five-year-old, tilted-
chinned oral and maxillofacial surgeon who wanted very much
to look like a nobleman. "I was kind of a Goth when I was a kid,
and I was also obsessed with playing offbeat games. But my dad
and my granddad were dentists, and when it came time to figure
out my life, I allowed myself to get pushed in that direction,
because nothing I was interested in could earn me a living. So
now I have a great practice, but I still think about that other
side of myself. I'd love to be in on the ground floor of some cool
game. I'm not going to make my fortune this way; I already do
very well. But I'm really eager to hear what you've come up
with."

Logan pitched him first. "Witch Hunt," he said slowly, letting each word settle. "It's an RPG. Your avatar is a girl in Salem, 1692. She's just a regular girl. A teenager in a bonnet."

"Does she have to be a girl?" Cronish asked. "Couldn't she be
a villager?"

"A villager might also be a girl," Cory pointed out.

"True," said Logan. "Okay, let me describe how I would
generate environments."

Cronish held up a hand. "You know," he said, "let's stop here.
It seems a little conventional to me. And in fact there have already been a few Salem–related games. And as I told you, I'm
looking for art as much as anything else." The oral surgeon's
gaze shifted to Cory, and he warily asked, "Does your idea seem
to fit the bill a little more?"

Cory didn't want to upstage Logan, who had shown him
such kindness, even if it was of the pitying variety. ("Can't you
help that nice Cory Pinto?" he could imagine Jen asking Logan

plaintively in their kitchen, over a locavore dinner.) "Logan and I are in this together," he began. "The idea was mine and I'll write it, but he's the designer and programmer. I know nothing about any of that."

Logan said, "I can tell you my plans for it. When you listen to what Cory has to say, you might think, whoa, how can that be done given the number of environments we would need to create, but—"

"Wait," said Cronish. "We'll get to that. Maybe." To Cory he said, "But first, just tell me how you see it."

And so Cory began, speaking about his "idea," not in the way that he imagined game designers spoke about their own ideas, but just the way he saw it. "What if you were on a quest to find the person you love, who's died?" Cory said to the two men, his voice low. "And even though you know that the person you love is dead, and that therefore your quest is pointless, you still have to *make* the quest, because you can't believe that person no longer exists. I mean, you believe it intellectually, but you don't really believe it in your heart of hearts. Without even knowing it, you search and search, trying to find the person through dreams, through other people, through an endless cycle of yearning, maybe through drugs, maybe through briefly interesting sex with people you would never have thought to have sex with before. Through whatever means you can find.

"But it doesn't work. It never works. How can it? The person you love is dead. Their body has stopped functioning, their heart has stopped beating, their brain has no more blood flow. There is no way they can still exist. But in the game version, in *our* version, which for the moment I'm calling SoulFinder, you might actually stand a chance of finding them."

He paused here, but again neither man stopped him or asked questions or nodded or expressed any reaction at all, and it was impossible to tell whether he was bombing or succeeding. Cory just kept talking, because there was nothing else to do. "It will be really, really hard, though," he said. "I mean, almost no player can ever achieve it. That will be a part of the appeal. Most people who buy the game won't actually ever experience what they're hoping to experience. But every once in a while a few of them will.

"People will want to know, 'How did you do that? How did you find your person?' But there isn't going to be an easy answer. It's got to be a very . . . emotionally and intuitively minded game. But counterintuitive as well. The people who are able to find their dead will become famous in the gaming world, because everyone will know that it can somehow be done. It's just that you have to try hard enough and long enough to find the person you lost, and eventually you just might be able to transform that longing into skill. Of course, most of the individual games won't even possess the software capability to locate the dead. But some of them will, and if you get one it'll be like holding one of Willy Wonka's Golden Tickets. You won't know it until you test it over months and months of gameplay. But even if you've got one, you still need to do everything right in order to find the dead person."

"What made you come up with this?" asked Cronish, his voice noncommittal.

Cory hadn't planned to get into this, but now he said stiffly, "My little brother died. He was run over by a car and it was the worst thing that ever happened in my family. One thing I've never forgotten since then," Cory said, speaking quickly and not allowing for the moment in which the other person usually said, I'm sorry for your loss, "is that anything can happen at any time. And this isn't a bad philosophy to live by if you're trying to design video games. The whole point of a lot of games, at least the ones that Logan and I have been playing, is surprise, right? The falling boulder. The lightning strike. The ambush. They prepare you for all the real falling boulders and lightning strikes and ambushes that are . . . the decorative flourishes of being alive."

Where were these words coming from? Right away he knew. They were coming from slick Armitage & Rist, and his short stint there. But then there had been a bend in the road. A deep, serious turn, and he had finally emerged in a different form. No consultant now. No partner in a microfinance startup ever.

"When a person dies we say that we lost them," said Cory. "We *lost* Alby. It feels that way to me; like they've got to be somewhere, right? They can't just be nowhere. It doesn't make sense."

Cory reached into his backpack and carefully extracted Alby's notebook, placing it on the table, worrying a little that the surface was damp. "I've made a lot of notes," he said. "You could look at this while we're here, but I can't lend it to you or any-thing, because it belonged to my brother." Cronish began leaf-ing through the pages, as if studying the X-rays of someone's jaw. He was quiet for a long stretch. So much time passed that Logan stood up and went over to the darts corner and began to throw.

Cory joined him, whispering, "Personally, I thought Witch Hunt sounded great. I'd play your game."

"Don't worry about it, man," said Logan, a large man whose entire concentration and energy were now lodged in the pincer formation of his fingers.

At some point Cronish came over to them, Alby's notebook in hand. "I get it," he said to Cory. "My granddad died of a mas-sive stroke when I was nineteen, and it broke my heart. I would do anything to find him, to show him who I've become." His eyes looked bright with excitement.

They sat back down at their booth and discussed it a little more, getting into further detail. Each player would be able to customize a "lost soul." There would be many options for that lost person, not only gender, race, and age, but special add-ons for personality and interests. And there would be a scene, the first time the game was played, in which the player interacts with that beloved person, who at this point in the gameplay has not yet died.

"So basically the game splits into 'before' and 'after' the death," said Cronish. "Is that what you're saying?"

Cory nodded. "We don't show the death scene, because that would become the point, and I don't want it to be the point. Plus, it would make the game really conventional, not to mention gratuitously graphic. The player gets to be immersed in memories, which can be returned to with the Scrapbook function at any time, but mostly the game is about the search for the so-called lost soul. The search will take you all over the world, if that's where you choose to look. Or you can just focus on one geographical region that you have a hunch about. Or even, you know, someone's attic."

"This is a very weird concept," said Cronish. "But also ambitious."

That word, *ambitious*, hadn't been applied to anything Cory had done in a very long time, but it was a word that he used to hear constantly, applied to him and Greer; they'd also often used it to describe themselves.

"The thing is, of course," said Cronish, "and now we finally get to you, Logan—is it actually doable?"

Logan put down his beer glass and said, "Let me describe it in simple terms. We would bring in an environmental artist, or maybe two. I'm confident that we can make a large number of environments out of a comparatively small number of building blocks. I'm really interested in generating systems that teach the computer to make cool things. I think this could be like that. Cory would write a metatext, and it could be adapted for different players. It would include some gnomic messages, but they could be read differently depending on who's doing the reading."

"It sounds like it would have an immersive-theater quality to it," said Cronish. "Which interests me a lot. In fact, would you consider coming down to New York sometime to go to one of those immersive-theater productions? They're doing *The Magic Mountain* on Roosevelt Island, and I heard the production values are excellent."

Immediately Cory remembered Greer's recent invitation. "You could stay with me," she'd said, and he felt a pulse of pleasure at the idea. But maybe he would feel too sad, being at her place in Brooklyn, where he was meant to live and where he'd actually never been over all these years.

Even though there was now apparently going to be an angel investor, it didn't mean Cory would have future "success," a term that had such different meaning depending on context. Were you a success if someone invested in your video game, or only if lots of people actually played it? And exactly how many people needed to play the game for it to be a success? Were you a success to the people who thought video games were a stupid waste of time, or, worse, partly responsible for the death of reading and the collapse of civilization?

It didn't really matter to Cory whether he was a success or not. Yet as his life became absorbed with designing the game, there were other changes too. One night at Logan and Jen's, his coworker Halley Beatty looked at him and smiled in a new way.

"Want to come over later?" she whispered. Halley was uncommonly pale and freckled; there were even freckles on her eyelids, he noticed in bed with her in the farmhouse she rented in Greenfield.

There was no hostility here, as there had been between him and Kristin Vells. No sense of time wasting, a ticking clock in the room getting louder. After Alby died, Cory had reverted to a cavalcade of porn, which he hadn't done with such intensity since he was young. Porn, which always had a familiar feel to it, as gratifying and available and gross as a warm bag of lunch from the drive-up window at Wendy's.

Jerking off secretly in his room, with his mother nearby, as if Cory were a teenager again, he would watch an image on his laptop, all the while knowing and actively thinking: This woman is not into me. This porn star has no interest in me, but probably mild contempt. Not that that stopped him. He'd had few hook-ups in his life. The first ones—Clove Wilberson, then Kristin—had made him dislike himself; the more recent one, Halley, had made him feel limber, more awake, reminding him that this collection of parts he carried around still added up to a young man's body.

One Thursday morning when Cory was about to head out to clean Professor Elaine Newman's house, his mother met him in the kitchen, fully dressed. "Can I come?" she asked.

"What do you mean?"

"Can I come to the professor's house? It's been a long time. Maybe I could help."

Cory didn't want to make a show of his surprise. Though she had stopped picking at her arms and saying that she saw Alby, it had been years since his mother had wanted to go anywhere or do anything, and he hadn't expected there would ever be a sig-nificant change. "Sure," he said. "I've got all the supplies over there." They drove together in silence, and when he let them into the Newman house his mother stood looking around, surveying the rooms. She ran a finger along the surface of the bench in the front hall, and when it came away clean she looked at him with approval.

"Nice," she said. "You use Pledge, not the cheap brand?" He nodded. "Good. It works better." After she revisited the rooms that she had cleaned in her previous life, he took the supply bucket from the hall closet and handed his mother a pair of rubber gloves, and they set to work.

He had not seen Benedita show an interest or make decisions or be fully distracted from her grief in such a long time; he hadn't seen her do anything physical in so long either. But here she was on her hands and knees in Professor Newman's kitchen, cleaning the tile that she used to clean every week. You could say that cleaning someone else's house was a shit job. That it was disgusting to be entangled in someone else's habits and ways, finding nail clippings—finger and toe—and little fluffy hair nests and partly squeezed tubes of cortisone cream or even lube, all of it evidence of a life you really didn't want to think about.

But you could also just say that it was work. And that work was admirable, even if it was hard or unappealing or undersung, or often maddeningly underpaid if you were female, as Greer used to remind him. His mother wasn't above this work. She may not have liked it once, but she was relieved and revived by it now. Throughout the morning she showed him tricks: How to use white vinegar in a number of clever ways. How to fold a fitted sheet so it could go neatly on a shelf in a linen closet. They pushed up the windows of the house and let the air circulate.

"You are very good at this," she remarked.

That was the day that his mother started to become well. He knew it at the time, and he knew it with more confidence later on, looking back. Work was a tonic for everyone, but a special vitamin drink for his mother. At the very least, because she had stopped being able to work after Alby died, work was now a measurement of her recovery. If you could work again, regardless of what kind of work it was, you were getting better.

She wanted to come with him the next time, and the next. Working quietly side by side, dusting Elaine Newman's art history books and cleaning her floors with Bona wood cleaner, the artificial smells all over both of them, Cory watched as his mother climbed up out of a well. He didn't want to rush her; he didn't even ask her each week if she wanted to come with him. But soon she was simply waiting when it was time to go there, wearing the clothes she used to wear for cleaning houses: an old shirt and sweatpants and sneakers.

Cory came to like those trips with her—the peaceful car ride, and then the hours together in the Victorian house, turning on the high-end stereo and playing whatever was closest at hand. The Newmans favored Sondheim. He thought, when he heard the lines *"Isn't it rich / Are we a pair?"* that yes, they *were* a pair, Cory and Benedita Pinto. The child of immigrants was meant to grow up and surpass his parents, but instead he was level with his mother: truly, a pair.

She got better and better, and became scrupulous about taking her medication. One day, when Cory was sitting in the car waiting for his mother to leave the office of her social worker, she came to the door and waved him in. Cory, surprised, went and sat down in the tiny home office of Lisa Henry, the large and patient person who had been taking care of Benedita over the years.

"Your mom and I thought today would be a good time to discuss something with you," Lisa said. "We've been talking lately about what it might be like if she had more independence."

Cory's mother looked up nervously, nodding, and then she was silent. He realized that it was his turn to speak. "Okay," he said. "That's good. Independence is always good. What kind of independence did you mean?"

"Maybe," said his mother, "I could live with Aunt Maria and Uncle Joe."

"Over in Fall River?"

"They have room now, since Sab left."

In a minor miracle, Cory's cousin Sab had straightened himself out through the help of Narcotics Anonymous, and had been working as a sous-chef at the Embers in Deerfield. Those hands that had expertly cut and chopped heroin and cocaine were now involved with a serious chiffonade of basil, and a *brunoise* dice of carrot and celery and onion. Just the idea that Sab knew words like this, French words, was surprising. Sab had his own set of knives that he brought to work, an excellent Wüsthof and a prize Shun, keeping them locked at night in a cabinet at home, as if they were guns. A few months earlier he had married the Embers' pastry chef, an older, divorced woman with two daughters. That era of heroin-dabbling and various-substance-selling had ended with the last vestiges of his adolescence. Like the sickliest of first mustaches, it had been deforested, and Sab had started over.

"Your aunt has been talking with your mom about this for a while," said the social worker. "She knew that your mom had started helping you clean again for her former employer. And that her thoughts are more organized, and the medication is working, and she's being more responsible for her own self-care. Everything seems to be on an upward swing."

"I guess it does," Cory said, lightly stunned. "So if this were to happen," he asked, "what about the house?"

"We could sell it," said Benedita. "It could command a decent price."

He looked sharply at her. "Who taught you that phrase?"

"Your mother called Century 21," the social worker explained.

"Also," Benedita added shyly, "on Thursday nights at ten p.m. I watch *Is There a Buyer in the House?*"

Things were happening all around him, and under him. Sand was churning, moving; Cory remembered the way he had felt when he first snorted heroin with his cousin. The floor had turned soft and dropped, and that was happening again now.

What about me? he thought.

Lisa Henry knew what he was thinking. "Cory," she said, "did you want to come back and see me another time and talk about logistics?"

He looked to his mother. "I don't want to intrude here," he said, but she waved this away. So the following week he returned alone to the office of Lisa Henry, LCSW, where logistics weren't discussed but his own life was. Lisa Henry's voice was so gentle that her tone itself nearly brought him to tears.

"Cory?" she said. "You want to tell me how you're absorbing the news about your mother's plans?"

He was immediately and startlingly angry with her for her softness, her kindness, which made him shaky and suddenly emotional. He didn't know if she was a mother, if she had young children, or if as a therapist she'd just gotten used to talking to everyone this way—speaking to the children her clients once were. A giant of a man, twenty-six years old and sitting in a too-small chair, Cory was nearly wrecked by feeling.

"I'm okay."

"I imagine you're in a kind of overload. You readjusted your whole life after the accident, and now maybe you're thinking you'll have to readjust it all over again."

It wasn't even what she was saying that screwed tight his throat, but that she was taking the time and care to say it, her head tilted in concern. Calling him Cory like that. He heard her voice from a great distance. Cory, she kept saying. Cory? She was like someone calling his name from three backyards away. He felt suddenly nostalgic about his childhood, which lived like its own distant backyard deep inside him. But then he realized, as the therapist kept speaking to him, that what he missed wasn't childhood, or being a child, but being close to a woman. That was what he no longer had.

He recalled the first time he had raked his hand through Greer's hair when they were both seventeen. He had been astonished at its softness. It was like touching some airy, grassy substance. Girls' hair must weigh less than boys' did; there had to be a scientific distinction. Her breasts were supernaturally soft too. Not to mention her skin and mouth. But her softness wasn't only tangible; there was also the softness of her voice. No matter how loud she spoke, he could speak louder. If they arm-wrestled he would always win, but she wasn't weak. Girls weren't weak. They had a softness sometimes, but not all the time. Whatever they had, it was a complement to what he had.

But it had seemed, when Cory broke up with Greer, that she became like a piece of knotted wire. Where were the qualities he had loved in her? He had taken on some of them himself. Because of course everyone was soft and hard. Skeleton and skin. But women claimed for themselves the province of softness, which men cast off. Maybe it was easier to say you liked it in a woman. But really, maybe you wished you had it yourself.

Cory pulled tissue after tissue from a box that had been augmented by an overbox made of gold-painted metal. What a sad item this was, designed to disguise tissues, which Lisa Henry's clients needed all the time. Just being in front of her, they were probably transformed into emotional wrecks. Faced with tenderness, they became *tenderized*, and it made them cry. Cory blew his nose harshly, as if in an attempt to gain control. The goose honk was anything but gentle.

"I suspect you're not used to talking about yourself," she said.

"No, I'm not. It's stopped being a thing for me."

"Why is that?"

He shrugged. "Bad breakup. But it was a long time ago."

She closed her eyes and opened them; instantly he was reminded of Slowy, who often did that. Was Slowy thinking hard in those moments, or was he adrift in reptile space-time?

"I'm not sure time is always a determinant to acceptance," Lisa said. "You still think about this person?"

"Yes. Greer."

"Greer was someone you talked to about yourself, which means about your feelings. And now you've lost that."

"Yeah. That and basically everything else."

The word *lost* made him think of SoulFinder. But he would not find Alby, ever. He had lost Greer in a more ordinary way: a breakup. People rarely spoke of a breakup as tragic; instead, breakups were part of life. But when you and the other person broke up, you could look for them everywhere, and maybe you would physically find them, but even if they were the same person, they were not for you; they were not yours. The evaporation of love was like a kind of death. Lisa Henry obviously understood this. She looked at him with an expression that was so compassionate, it was as though she thought he had been pierced with a thousand arrows.

Time was up. She stood, and then he stood, and they both nodded to each other, and then she opened the door. This one session was enough for him, he realized. Seeing her had been useful, but it was enough. Cory went outside, where the afternoon was fading but seemed as if it had been gently buffed while he was indoors. Boy meets world, he thought, and he headed for his car.

FOURTEEN

Daytime, when you didn't have a job, wasn't just something to rush through, but to spend time in. Greer, unemployed, found patches of sun and little swirls of wind, and a coffee shop in Brooklyn with a good mix of chatter and quiet. She sat in all these places and read books the way she used to when she was a girl, back when there was nothing else she had to do, nowhere else she had to be, and no one looking out for her. She read with "abandon," it would probably be called, though when you read a book you didn't abandon anything; instead, you marshaled it all. After she'd left Loci and left Faith in such a dramatic way, books were still there. She read Jane Austen and she read *Jane Eyre*; the two Janes, which Zee had once confused. She read a contemporary French novel in which all the characters were desperate, and there were no quotation marks, only little dashes, which made Greer feel kind of crazy, but also kind of French.

She sat in the coffee shop taking her time, and she thought about how she'd always wondered who those people were who sat in coffee shops in the middle of the day, and now she knew. Some of them were, like her, the jobless, the lost. She sat there feeling very much unlike herself. She had enough money to last a couple of months, so she didn't need to rush into another job. Loci was over, and more than that so was Faith Frank. Zee was only half-over; they'd had a series of email exchanges recently in which Greer had tried to prostrate herself again, at first seriously, then wittily, and Zee had written back a few short, amused notes, so it seemed that a thaw was starting.

One afternoon when she was home, drowsing on her couch, Cory called.

"Greer," he said. "It's Cory Pinto."

"As opposed to Cory who?"

"You might know another one," he said. "It's possible. So do you remember you told me I could stay with you if I ever came to New York?"

"Sure."

"Feel free to take it back. But I'm coming down to go see a play. Immersive theater. Our investor wants me to go, and he bought me a ticket. I thought I could stay over for two nights, if it's convenient."

Cory drove down from Macopee and showed up Thursday night with a backpack. They hugged awkwardly in her doorway. Right away she ordered takeout from the Thai place, knowing that food would be a distraction from the strangeness. They sat and ate at the small table in Greer's living room. In the low light, with the containers of food open all around them, he told her more about the slow, painstaking creation of the video game, his partnership with his friend from Valley Tek, the environmental artists who had been hired, and the investor who was paying for all of this.

"There's no guarantee it will become anything," Cory said. "It's not mainstream at all, and the market is flooded. But I don't know, is it obnoxious to say I'm a little hopeful?"

"No. I think it's great," she said.

"And as for my mom, I didn't know there could be improvement after such a long time, but there is. I don't think she needs me in the same way."

"That's so great. And what does that mean for you?"

"That's exactly what I asked myself," Cory said. "I'll be okay, Greer, you don't have to worry."

"I'm not worried," she said, but she remembered that she had done nothing but worry about him after Alby died. She had worried so hard that he would lose himself and that she would lose him. But it wasn't that he had lost himself. He was always going to be the person who stayed and helped. She hadn't seen that. "I'm sorry about how I was," she said. "With you."

"Well, I am too. How *I* was, I mean." He smiled. "If there was ever a more generic and vague conversation, I've never heard it."

"It's weird," she said, "the way sometimes you're *in* your life, but other times you're looking back at it like a spectator. It kind of goes back and forth, back and forth."

"And then you die."

She laughed a little. "Yes. And then you die."

"Hey, I watched your speech," he suddenly said.

"You did?" She was shocked, tense; the speech was out there, findable.

"You were good," he said. "It's cool to think of you getting up there in front of everyone."

"Me with my outside voice, not my inside one," she said quickly. Then she added, "Well, that's over, anyway. The whole Loci thing."

What she felt, talking about Loci, above and beyond her anxiety and anger, was a strange and strangled kind of grief. It couldn't be compared with Cory's grief, which would've blown it away, but still it qualified. Her grief wasn't for the job—a job could be recovered from. Maybe she would give other speeches someday, wherever she ended up working, even little speeches in a conference room, to twelve people. And there would probably be other jobs with a do-good tang to them; other offices with desks for Greer to sit at, and a minestrone or *moo shu* smell around the noon hour, and coworkers who had good days and snappish ones. People with coffee on the breath and personal habits that you would learn, as though you were lovers and not just people who worked in the same place.

The grief, being brought up now, as it often was when she thought about having left her job, was about Faith. Faith, who was barely even a fully realized person to Greer. She felt herself well up, and she thought: Here I go.

"The thing about Faith Frank?" she said to Cory. "The thing I keep thinking about? She wasn't my friend, exactly. She was definitely my employer, but that's not the whole description. What was she? I loved what she stood for. I wanted to stand for those things too. And in the end everything fell apart, and she turned on me. Maybe she was right to behave that way. Maybe, even though she's Faith Frank, she's allowed to have a really bad moment too, where she says something not so great to someone else. I just didn't like being the person she said it to. But I'm not one to talk. I did something really bad to Zee." Cory looked at her, surprised. "I did," she went on. "I know, you didn't expect that. It's like people can't help *doing things* to people. I've been working that one through with Zee, slowly. There's movement there. But Faith . . . When I really think about Faith, I get this terrible sensation in my chest, and I feel like I'll never recover."

"You will," said Cory. "And I say that with authority." He yawned right then and, embarrassed, immediately tried to cover it up.

"You're tired," she said.

"No, it's fine. We can keep talking."

Greer went to the closet and pulled out a towel for him. "Here you go," she said. "I'll make up the couch for you."

He took his little kit into the bathroom while she placed sheets on the mattress of the small foldout sofa. This was an era in which sofa beds were frequently opened and unfolded; at this age people were still floating, not entirely landed, still needing places to stay the night sometimes. They were doing what they could, crashing in other places, living extemporaneously. Soon enough, the pace would pick up, the solid matter of life would kick in. Soon enough, sofa beds would stay folded.

Cory came out of the bathroom as Greer was spreading the quilt over the sheets. He wore a different T-shirt, one for bed, and he smelled of some kind of unfamiliar skin lotion or soap; he'd changed his routine, she thought with some unhappiness, as if she should have been alerted to the change. But of course it had been a long time now since they had seen the various products each other used. The private and the mundane, which together became intimacy. Cory went to the opened sofa and lay down on it, his too-tall body needing to be angled in order to fit; she heard the exhausted protest of the springs, and she shut off the light and went to lie down in her own bed across the room.

With the blinds turned, it was sealed-in dark in the apartment, and neither of them had any more thoughts about their missions. Instead they were intensely self-conscious, and each sound that came from somewhere in the room was too much, could make them jump. Neither of them wanted to scare the other, or do the wrong thing, so they lay quietly and respectfully, as if it were nighttime and they were patients in the same hospital ward.

"You okay over there?" she asked.

"I'm fine," said Cory. "Thanks for having me, Space Ka-detsky."

It was so dark that at first she couldn't see him across the room, but could just hear him repositioning his limbs and then yawning again, the hinge of his jaw opening, being held open involuntarily, then closing. He was somewhere over there; that was what she knew. For a little while she didn't see him at all, but then her eyes adjusted, and she did.

FIFTEEN

t was one of those parties where you could never find your coat. Which maybe wasn't the worst thing, because no one wanted to leave and go out into the world, which had changed so stunningly. Even now, years in, no one could get used to it; and conversation at parties still centered around the ways that no one had seen it coming. They just could not believe what had happened to the country. "The big terribleness," said a tall, spindly, and intense woman, director of online marketing at the publishing house throwing this party. She was leaning against a wall in the hallway, beneath a series of Diane Arbus photos, holding court. "The thing that really gets me," she said, "is that the *worst* kind of man, the kind that you would *never* allow yourself to be alone with, because you would know he was a danger to you, was left alone with all of us."

They laughed darkly, this cluster of women and a couple of men, they drank their drinks, and then they were briefly quiet. Indignity after indignity had taken place, constant hammerstrikes against everything they cared about, and they had been marching and organizing and raging, but as a defense they also frequently went into a self-soothing mode, which by now they'd been doing for years. Drinking had become a part of the self-soothing. Celebrating had become essential too, and occasionally even warranted. It seemed, once again, that hopelessness had clarified how valuable the fight had always been. "I assumed there would always be a little progress and then a little slipping, you know? And then a little more progress. But instead the whole *idea* of progress was taken away, and who knew that could happen, right?" said this vociferous woman.

Tonight they were celebrating the fact that Greer Kadetsky's book *Outside Voices* had just spent one full year on the bestseller list. One full year that seemed to put a thumb in the eye of the big terribleness. The book, certainly not the first of its kind, was a lively and positive-leaning manifesto encouraging women not to be afraid to speak up, but the title also played on ideas of women as outsiders.

Greer, age thirty-one now, had been giving talks around the country on her *Outside Voices* tour. She visited women's prisons and corporations and colleges and libraries, and she went to public schools where little girls crammed into gyms, and she told them, "Use your outside voices!" They looked nervously toward their teachers, who stood against the walls. "It's okay," the teachers mouthed, and the little girls screamed and shouted, tentatively at first, then with full throat.

Outside Voices was frequently criticized, of course. It did not speak for all women, Greer was told. Many women, most women, were so, so much farther outside of privilege and access than Greer Kadetsky was now. Still, she heard from women and girls from around the country, who wrote candid, tender, excited notes to Greer on her website and on the *Outside Voices* message board, telling her what the book had meant to them. There was talk of an Outside Voices Foundation, but nothing concrete. The book had encouraged women to stay strong and loud. And certainly staying strong and loud was urgent.

A few years earlier, back at the start of the big terribleness, before she was living with Cory and before Emilia was born, having been freed from Loci, Greer had gone to the Women's March in DC. She'd marched with a group of half a million, and had felt vigorous, chapped-cheeked, elated. Endorphins were sprung into the bloodstream like balloons into the open sky. The high lasted the whole four and a half hours home on a boiling-hot coach bus and for weeks to come, part endorphin rush, part despair. She had been seeing Cory every weekend either in Brooklyn or up in Macopee, where he still lived as he helped his mother sell the house and resettle, and during that time Greer worked at a coffee bar, inhaling steam and foam and cinnamon—"I have cinnamon lung," she'd said to Zee—and all the while at night, in her free time, she worked on her book.

But there were moments now when Greer, falling into a funk of exhaustion or boredom at the prospect of repeating the mantras of her book over and over, wondered whether her book, despite its success, was a little ridiculous. After all, you could use your outside voice and scream your head off, but sometimes it didn't seem as if the screaming was being heard.

Tonight, on this wet, slick and cold night, the publisher, Karen Nordquist, was throwing this party in her showplace of a home, which had a living room with double-height ceilings and a wall of books with a ladder. At some point earlier, Karen had climbed the ladder to give a toast to Greer. Everyone looked nervously up at her as she headed for the top still holding her martini, but she was fearless. And when she stood up there looking down at the room, she said, a little drunkenly, "Wow, I can see the parts in everyone's hair. Very neat." There was laughter. "I can see how much you all care about personal grooming. But more to the point I can see how much you all care about this amazing book, this phenomenon, *Outside Voices*. And so do I. Greer, we love you!"

From down below, Greer said, fatuously, "And I love all of you too." But then she looked around and felt overcome. It wasn't by love, though of course she did love several people in this room—Cory was here, holding Emilia, and there were good friends all around—but this was something else. She was struck by the way everyone was looking toward her with expectation. People wanted one another to *do something*. They wanted someone to say the thing that they could then take into themselves and transform into something else. A word might land in a certain way; or maybe not even a word. Maybe a gesture, or a moment of listening. This platform, Greer's book that tried hard and was encouraging and bracing, was not, she knew, original or brilliant; this platform was definitely imperfect. And Greer wasn't a firebrand. She could never be that.

"I'm going to keep this brief," she said, and she saw some people in the room look relieved. No one ever wanted a writer to go on and on at her own book party. "We're here tonight in this strange time. This long, strange time. Every new thing that shocks us is just that, a shock. But not really a surprise. The success of this book in the middle of this time," Greer said, "has been confusing. But also welcome. Though of course my poor eardrums are suffering. This morning I did a school visit with a group of third-graders, and those girls have pipes. I'm still in pain!" There was laughter. "I've never been loud," said Greer. "You know that by now. Oh, you know everything about me by now." Then she said, "I'm going to read just a tiny amount from the book. An *amuse-bouche*." She picked up the book with its bright cover with the now-recognizable image of the open mouth, and read for exactly one minute and forty seconds, and then she was finished. They all clapped, then they returned to their worried conversations and their drinking. Greer's face was hot, lit, as it always was from public speaking, even now.

Cory came over, Emilia wrapped around his neck, though her eyes looked a little wild. At fifteen months of age she should not have been awake this late, but why not; her mother had been on the bestseller list for one full year. Emilia had stomped around in circles all night, nearly deranged. Earlier, she'd gotten two steps up the ladder before her babysitter snatched her by the collar and hauled her in. Now that babysitter, Kay Chung, who was sixteen and a high school student who lived with her family in Sheepshead Bay, stood on Cory's other side with her hand on Emilia's head. Kay was small and fireplug-fierce, in a bulky Nordic sweater and a little skirt. Greer had hired her on the recommendation of a friend, but Kay turned out to be not only wonderful with the baby, but also wonderful more generally. Kay was, as she described herself without irony or amusement, radical in most of her views, but she warned that that didn't mean they conformed to any one orthodoxy.

"So what are you saying, exactly?" Greer had asked her late on a Saturday night. She and Cory had just returned from a dinner party. They were standing in the front hallway of the brownstone where they now lived, waiting for a car service to come take the babysitter home.

"I'm a skeptical person, I guess," said Kay. Pressed, she tried to describe what she meant. "I want you to know I think *you're* great, Greer. I totally do. My friends and I have all read your book and they're impressed that I sit for you," she said benevolently. "We should all definitely assert ourselves more in the world, that's totally true. But I look at everything that women did and said in recent history, and somehow we still got to a caveman moment. And our responses to it just aren't enough, because the structures are still in place, right?"

She wasn't asking Greer a question, but just wanted to make a point. Kay was always organizing at her school, getting involved in assemblies and mini-marches and what she called "Twitter fires," in which she took a scorched-earth tone and never apologized. She and her friends didn't care about figureheads, she said dismissively, leaders of a cause, like in the past. These figures weren't necessary, and they weren't even real. "We don't need to put people on a pedestal," she said. "Everyone can lead. Everyone can jump in."

She offered these opinions as if they were entirely new; the pleasure and excitement in her voice were stirring. Greer could have said to her, "Yes, I know all about this. Faith said that women said the same thing back in the seventies," but that wouldn't have been kind.

There shouldn't be a hierarchy, Kay explained, because that always led to someone being kept down, and there had been enough of that throughout history, and no one needed it anymore, and it assumed that the white, cisgender, binary view of everything was the correct one, the only one, when in fact it wasn't. We're done with that for good, she said. And anyway, Kay went on in a chatty voice of amazing confidence, it wasn't so much about people as it was about ideas.

Greer didn't know what to say in response to the babysitter's soliloquy except to repeat some of what she had already said in the book, taking a tone of encouragement and rage; "encou-*rage*-ment," she'd called it. Since Kay had been babysitting for Emilia on weekends, Greer had given her every item related to *Outside Voices*: the hardcover, the workbook, the desk calendar, and, Cory said, the snack food. Also, Kay often said,

"If you have anything for me to read . . ." and Greer and Cory gave her books, lots of them, novels and collections of essays, and even some of their old college texts, heavily underlined, plus the book that Greer had borrowed from Professor Malick and forgotten to return. Greer had never made sense of that book, but Kay had said it was very interesting and even really funny to read those outdated ways of thinking.

"Our babysitter is smarter than we are," Greer liked to say to people. "Much. I'm telling you, she's going to go far." But the problem was that the babysitter could not be babied, could not be swaddled and comforted by *Outside Voices*. The small triumph of having a well-meaning feminist rallying cry on the bestseller list did not seem to help this girl, who knew she had a real future but was afraid that everything would be repeatedly smashed to pieces.

Now it was time to leave the publisher's party in Greer's honor, though the party would continue on without her. The older people left and the younger ones stayed. Greer and Cory offered Kay a ride home, but she said no thanks, did they mind if she stayed a little longer? The babysitter had gotten to know a couple of the interns. She quickly kissed the top of Emilia's head, said, "Bye, bunny girl," then returned to the pack of interns, who pulled her in.

"I am so sick of the expression 'outside voices,'" Greer said to Cory in the car heading home.

"You're the one who unleashed it on the world."

She leaned against him, in close quarters because the car seat took up a lot of space. Emilia had already closed her eyes, her sweaty head craned at a bad angle. The car bumped along the quiet streets and headed over the bridge. Almost immediately when they crossed into Brooklyn there was construction. There was always construction. Their brownstone was in Carroll Gardens; they had lived there since the book sale, which was followed immediately by international sales. Cory and Greer had money, suddenly, and it shocked them both and made them both uncomfortable. They had been about to renovate the brownstone when Cory had the idea that they should leave it alone; it was already livable enough, and maybe what they should do with their money instead was give a large monthly stipend to Cory's mother and Greer's parents, who could really use it. And once they did that, it was easy and natural to give away more of their money to people they weren't related to. Neither of them knew how long the money would last; it wouldn't self-replenish forever. Greer had had one bestseller; she wasn't the manager of a hedge fund, and maybe there would never be another bestseller, but at least they had done what they could.

SoulFinder, when it was finally released, had not become a financial success, though it still occupied a small, respected place in the world of indie video games, more of a sleeper than anything else. The people who had played it were passionate about it. Cory's next game was being planned now, and the same investor had already committed. Cory had thought about going into microfinance all these years after he was supposed to, but the process had changed and he wasn't up to speed on any of that, and money was always tricky, and he worried that he might screw it up. He hadn't professionally "landed," and who knew if he would, but it wasn't an emergency that he hadn't. Cory was working, and engaged by work; and he also did a lot around the house, cooking homemade fish fingers for Emilia and vegetarian dishes for Greer, and being in charge of the master schedule. He had it in his mind that he would teach Emilia Portuguese. He had even bought her a DVD of Portuguese children's songs and rhymes. And while the DVD made him think of his mother, up in Fall River now and doing very well, it also made him think of his father, in Lisbon; or maybe he had been thinking of his father to begin with, and that was why he had bought the DVD online. Cory had said that he wanted to go to Portugal at some point to see his father, despite what he had done. To see him and then take the family sightseeing, though the trip would wait until Emilia was old enough to get something out of it.

At home after the party they dropped Emilia into her crib, and she didn't stir. There would be no need tonight for stories, or water, or the motorized light fixture that threw dancing shapes on the ceiling, or more stories, or more water. Greer saw, on her phone, that Zee had texted from Chicago. "I sent you a link," Zee wrote. "Call me. I want to experience your reaction in real time."

So Greer sat in the den and called Zee on the phone; the two of them sat before their separate laptops, and Greer clicked on the link that led to a video, taken on a shaky cell phone. The setting was vaguely tropical. First a balding, thickish man opened the door of a garden apartment. As soon as the door opened, a bucket of wet garbage was flung in his face, and the camera swerved hard to show the garbage thrower, a young woman who began to scream. "You piece of garbage, you deserve a lot worse than this," she shouted, and the man, covered in garbage in the doorway of his own home, seemed shocked at first, and said, "Whoa, whoa, what the fuck," but then within seconds he was laughing and exuberant. "That's right," he said to her, peeling garbage from the side of his face. "Keep throwing it at me, this is assault, keep it coming."

Greer paused the video, froze it in place. "Wait, why am I watching this?" she asked.

"Put it on full-screen," said Zee.

So Greer made the image fill the screen of her laptop, and

then she came close to it so that her face was nearly pressed against his paused face. She studied the blandness, the lazy smile, the wide-spaced eyes, all of it somehow familiar, but still only mildly. When you thought about it, everything seemed familiar. Every story had its antecedents, and every person. The laughing, garbage-covered man and the woman in her fury, captured together on a residential street someplace where the weather was warm. They were familiar at first only in their familiarity, for you already knew this kind of story: the furious woman and the shrugging, indifferent man. Such stories were ancient; Greer had heard them told at Loci and on the road with *Outside Voices*, but she also knew of them from well before that. From reading Greek plays, from growing up as a girl. A critical piece of information was returning from a great and exhausting distance. Greer let it come toward her; she patiently waited for its arrival, observing the frozen face. Then she remembered.

"Tinzler?" she said, her voice made thin with awe.

"Yes."

"Darren Tinzler? *No.* Where did you find this? What is it?"

"Someone sent it to Chloe Shanahan and she sent it to me," said Zee. "Darren Tinzler runs a revenge porn website called BitchYouDeserveThis.com. He publishes footage and photos of women with a link to their Facebook profiles, and he makes them pay a huge fee to take them down. The fees go to some law firm in Chicago that doesn't really exist. And this woman tried to sue but she couldn't because his identity was hidden. And anyway the laws still suck. So she tracked him down, and she went to his door and threw garbage at him while her friend filmed the whole thing. The plan was that they would post it online, thinking that they would shame him, ruin him. But get this: Darren Tinzler retweeted it. He couldn't be shamed or ruined. He just thought it was hilarious."

They were both stoppered into silence, considering all this. Greer and Zee had worn Darren Tinzler's face on their T-shirts thirteen years earlier, had stared at him and his far-apart eyes. He looked similar now, except the face was wider, and the hair was mostly gone, and so was the baseball cap. Their T-shirt campaign had done nothing, and in the ladies' room that night at college, Faith had warned them that if they hounded Darren Tinzler, "sympathy will redound to him," but maybe she hadn't been right. Maybe if they'd stayed with it, Greer thought, he would've eventually been asked to leave school, and he might have had a record that would've chased him for years. Maybe he would have been monitored and watched instead of going unchecked over time, doing whatever he liked.

"It's like we kept trying to use the same rules," Greer said, "and these people kept saying to us, 'Don't you get it? I will not live by your rules.'" She took a breath. "They always get to set the terms. I mean, they just come in and *set* them. They don't ask, they just do it. It's still true. I don't want to keep repeating this forever. I don't want to keep having to live in the buildings they make. And in the circles they draw. I know I'm being overly descriptive, but you get my point."

"You could call your next book *The Circles They Draw.*"

"I don't mean any of this in a bullshit way. I don't mean it to just be words, or clever. I don't know if we'll ever figure out the Outside Voices Foundation, or even what it will be. It definitely can't just be feeling good about ourselves even in adversity."

"I don't know. Foundations? Is that the answer? Look at Loci."

"No, it couldn't be like Loci," said Greer. "That whole money thing. The climate is different now. And you could come help me figure it out."

"Yeah, sure. I'll solve all the problems."

"You have that grassroots experience from Chicago," Greer said. "You're so good at all that. Noelle could find a school here, couldn't she? I know this sounds a little bit like, 'Let's put on a show.' I don't want it to be like that. I'm just saying if this ever turns into something, you could be part of it. And I owe you a job," she said lightly.

"No you don't," Zee said. "You really, really don't." She paused. "And anyway, Greer, I love my work."

"I know you do."

They were both quiet, thinking about Darren Tinzler. A man who degraded and threatened women made you want to do everything possible. Howl and scream; march; give a speech; call Congress around the clock; fall in love with someone decent; show a young woman that all is not lost, despite the evidence; change the way it feels to be a woman walking down a street at night anywhere in the world, or a girl coming out of a KwikStop in Macopee, Massachusetts, in daylight, holding an ice cream. She wouldn't have to worry about her breasts, whether they would ever grow, or grow big enough. She wouldn't have to think anything physical or sexual about herself at all unless she wanted to. She could dress the way she liked. She could feel capable and safe and free, which was what Faith Frank had always wanted for women.

Faith appeared again at moments like this, stamped all of a sudden into a conversation. Walking in the city, Greer would have occasional sightings of an elegant older woman, perhaps flanked by other women, and she would hurry to catch up with her. But then the woman would turn to the side, revealing herself, and not only was it not Faith, it was laughably not Faith. The woman was thirty. Or the woman was black. Or, once, the woman was a man. Or, most often, the woman was someone who vaguely resembled Faith and could have been her stunt double: lovely and accomplished-looking. During the Women's March, everyone buoyed by the sense of being right, Greer was certain that Faith was there somewhere—she wasn't one of the speakers—and that maybe she would see her. Though their relationship had ended in the worst way, the ice would be broken then and there, and everything that had happened between them would no longer matter. Sometimes you had to let go of your convictions, or at least loosen them far more than you ever thought you would. She would call out, "Faith?" and in the middle of the crowd of roaring women, Faith would swivel her head and see her. Their long period of being apart would end. She would be returned to Greer like a lost person in SoulFinder. Although, as Zee once pointed out, in SoulFinder you had to go looking for the person you had lost.

Faith, now, was closer to eighty than seventy. She still worked at the foundation, though three years earlier Emmett Shrader had died of a massive heart attack. His death was itself a significant story, covered widely in the news section of the newspaper and extending into the business section, with profiles and encomiums; but there were also rumors online about the cause of death. He died in bed with a young woman, it was said, having taken a drug for erectile dysfunction. It wasn't that he had been told not to take the drug; he had apparently been told not to have *sex*, not anymore, or at least not the kind of sex that Emmett seemingly liked, which was active, athletic, whole-bodied, heart-quaking.

The foundation was to continue, he'd instructed in his will, though he hadn't paid attention to the details enough to specify at what level, and the people upstairs had decided to reduce Loci's operating budget bit by bit until the foundation essentially became a low-level and modest speakers' forum. It occupied a place in the world similar to the one that *Bloomer* had occupied at the end of its long life.

But still it carried on, and still Faith Frank stayed in charge, with a vastly scaled-down staff and a much smaller office on a lower floor of the Strode Building. Nothing had ever come out publicly about the mentor program. Ben, who was still at Loci, told Greer that Faith often stayed late at work, and because her new office was so much smaller, she'd had to have a few inches shaved off the top and bottom of her suffrage-door desk so that it could still fit. Greer imagined Faith sitting there grimly watching as someone came in with a saw and cut down the door.

Loci no longer held summits, but small gatherings of twenty-five or thirty people or so, the same size as the lunchtime speeches that they used to give as teasers leading up to the summits. Faith wrote very occasional op-eds for the *New York Times* and the *Washington Post,* but had ceased most public speaking. Greer saw pictures of Faith once in a while; more to the point, she sought them out online. It was Faith, despite the deeper lines in the face like a fisherwoman in a woodcut. Faith with the smile, and the intelligence, and always the trademark sexy boots. But Faith in a tighter space, with a lower budget, in wild, uncertain times. Faith still working. Misogyny had stormed the world in an all-out, undisguised raid.

The Senate seat of Anne McCauley, who had retired and whose late-life hobby was canning plums, had been filled by her daughter Lucy McCauley-Gevins, whose views of reproductive rights were even more extreme than her mother's, and who had been given much more support and money. Loci was small; Senator Lucy McCauley-Gevins was getting bigger; *Fem Fatale* had lost its popularity over the past couple of years, but there were other sites to replace it, newer, fresher ones providing sharp commentary, humor, and a receptacle for rage; *Ragtimes*, that sweet little play, was occasionally still performed in community theaters and high schools around the country; and *Outside Voices* showed no sign of falling off the bestseller list.

Also, Opus's old hit "The Strong Ones" was now the song on a famous television commercial, accompanied by the image of a pair of female hands pulling at a sheet of paper towel, which did not rip or disintegrate. Some people defended Opus's decision, said it was good to commodify art, because at least then you could get your message into the shared waters of the culture. Everyone knew that you could never rest, never stop being vigilant, and even though it wasn't always enough anymore just to keep working, still there wasn't the luxury of stopping. Faith sat at her desk in her small office late at night, in lamplight, with papers spread out around her.

For a long time Greer had thought that if she ever did get in touch with Faith, she would give her the latest bulletins from her life. She'd write and say:

Get this, Faith. I ended up marrying my high school boyfriend, who I once cried over in your office. At first I was hesitant to get married; I wasn't sure how I felt about it. But we knew we wanted to have children, so it made sense financially. I knew I loved him, but I don't feel that all love relationships have to culminate in marriage. I was ambivalent at first, but then I came around.

We had a wedding on a hill right near where we both grew up. At the reception, my mother put on a clown show for the kids in attendance. My father stood squinting out over the valley and he seemed really happy for me, but maybe it was only because he had a mild buzz. Also, my friend Zee got married to her longtime partner. We joked about how she was far less ambivalent about getting married than I was. She was raring to get married; it made her so happy. Not just that she and Noelle *could* do it—that it was legal and common and that progress had been made in this huge way—but mostly that they *were* doing it. She loved being involved with every aspect of planning the wedding. The shower. The seating arrangements. The song that would be played for the first dance. She just loved it. Her parents, both judges, presided. Everyone cried.

And Cory and I have a daughter. Emilia, named after Cory's grandmother. My labor was twenty-three hours long, and she emerged looking entirely like Cory, as though I had had nothing to do with it. Only now, later on, am I starting to be carved into the stone.

The main thing about me is that I'm tired a lot. But I'm tired, in part, because my book has had me doing nonstop promotion. The day I sold it, the day I got the call, was so exciting. Sometimes I think about how excited you'd get when something big happened to someone else. How you always said it was good for everyone to see more women doing what they loved. I think you would be excited for me. I've decided you are. But I know you have other things to think about, other people who want your time, which I know you probably have to dole out really, really carefully, preserving yourself. Self-preservation is as important as generosity. (I talk about this a little in my book.) Because if you don't preserve yourself, keep enough for yourself, then of course you have nothing to give.

Did you see that you're mentioned first in the acknowledgments? I wondered if you would see it, and maybe call me, or send me a note and say, "Nailed it!" It's true that without you I would never have written it, and I hope you know that. Despite what happened between us. (Sometimes I think that maybe you regret what you said to me at the end, in your office. I choose to think you regret it, a little.)

But lately, Greer had been wishing she could say something different to Faith.

You made my head crack open in college, she'd tell her. Then, for years, I watched you take whatever you had—your strength, your opinions, your generosity, your influence; and of course your indignation at injustice; all of that—and pour it into other people, usually into women. You never then said to those women: okay, so what you need to do now is pass it on. But that was what often happened: the big, long story of women pouring what they had into one another. A reflex, maybe, or sometimes an obligation; but always a necessity.

At the end of the letter, Greer would say: when I was in your office that last time, and you were so upset with me and called me out on my behavior, even in that bad moment there was a kind of effect. You made it necessary for me to go and apologize to my best friend, to tell her the truth; I don't know why I didn't see that that was what I had to do. I mean, for years I didn't see it.

But as Greer sat and imagined telling Faith all of this, she still didn't know if she ever would. It might be too much information. It might be unwelcome. It might be that she and Faith had always been on a long, leisurely path toward collapse, and finally it had happened. The moment that the older one first encourages the younger one, maybe the older one already knows it might eventually happen. She knows, while the younger one stays unaware and only excited. One person replaces another, Greer thought. That's what happens; that's what we do, over and over.

Who is going to replace me? she thought, shocked at first at the idea, and then finding it kind of funny, and relaxing into it. She saw various women wandering through her house, populating the place like law enforcement with a search warrant, making themselves at home, overturning anything they wanted. She homed in on an older Kay Chung, rifling through Greer's

belongings. Kay wandered around, curious, excited, flipping
through the different books on the shelves, finding ones that Greer
hadn't lent her but which looked good, then eating from Greer's
stash of cashews, swiping a couple of Greer's multivitamins from
the big amber bottle on the kitchen counter, as if they might give
her the energy, power, and stature that she would need, going
forward. Kay went into the den and looked at the soft easy chair
there, the reading lamp angled beside it.

Sit in the chair, Kay, Greer thought. Lean back and close your
eyes. Imagine being me. It's not so great, but imagine it anyway.

At Loci, they had all talked loftily about power, creating
summits around it as though it was a quantifiable thing that
would last forever. But it wouldn't, and you didn't know that
when you were just starting out. Greer thought of Cory sitting
in his brother's bedroom, far from anything having to do with
power, taking Slowy out of his box and placing him nearby on
the blue carpet. Slowy blinking, moving an arm, craning his
head forward. Power eventually slid away, Greer thought. People did what they could, as powerfully as they could, until they
couldn't do it anymore. There wasn't much time. In the end, she
thought, the turtle might outlive them all.

ACKNOWLEDGMENTS

I'm endlessly grateful for the help, encouragement, opinions, and wisdom of my brilliant editor, Sarah McGrath, as well as my tireless publicist, Jynne Martin, and my longtime publisher, Geoffrey Kloske. I also owe so much to Suzanne Gluck, who is simply a perfect agent.

The following people were helpful in ways both big and small, and they have my thanks and admiration: Jennifer Baumgardner; Elly Brinkley; Jenn Daly; Jen Doll; Delia Ephron; Alison Fairbrother, who is uncommonly generous and knows everything about everything; Sheree Fitch; Lisa Fliegel; Jennifer Gilmore; Adam Gopnik; Jesse Green; Jane Hamilton; Katie Hartman; Lydia Hirt; Sarah Jefferies; Danya Kukafka; Julie Klam; Emma Kress; Laura Krum; Sandra Leong; Sara Lytle; Laura Marmor; Joanna McClintick; Claire McGinnis; Lindsay Means; Susan Scarf Merrell, whose instinct and kindness are unparalleled; Ann Packer; Martha Parker; Glory Anne Plata; Katha Pollitt, the brilliant feminist writer whose encouragement and conversations about this book have meant so much to me; Suzzy Roche; Ruth Rosen; Cathleen Schine, who offered her invaluable novelist's eye; Janny Scott; Clio Seraphim; Courtney Sheinmel, for her late-night brainstorms and friendship; Marisa Silver; Peter Smith, a great observer, reader of fiction, and friend; Julie Strauss-Gabel; Courtney Sullivan, who was full of excellent, sage advice, knowledge, and good cheer; Rebecca Traister, for her essential words, on the page and in person; Karla Zimonja.

And finally, as ever, thanks and love to my parents, and to Nancy and Cathy, and to Richard, Gabriel, Devon, and Charlie.